Lulu Taylor

HEIRESSES

arrow books

Published by Arrow Books 2009

8 10 9

First published in Great Britain in 2009 by
Arrow Books
Random House, 20 Vauxhall Bridge Road,
London SW1V 2SA

www.rbooks.co.uk

Addresses for companies within The Random House Group Limited
can be found at:
www.randomhouse.co.uk/offices.htm

The Random House Group Limited Reg. No. 954009

A CIP catalogue record for this book is available
from the British Library

ISBN 9780099524939

Penguin Random House is committed to a sustainable future for
our business, our readers and our planet. This book is made from
Forest Stewardship Council® certified paper.

Typeset by Palimpsest Book Production Limited,
Grangemouth, Stirlingshire

Printed and bound in Great Britain by Clays Ltd, St Ives plc

To Helen Robertson

1

What a day for a bloody funeral, Jemima thought, narrowing her eyes at the sight of the grey drizzle that had been falling all morning from charcoal-coloured clouds. *It's going to bloody well ruin my Philip Treacy hat.*

At the sign for the village, Harry signalled left and drove the Jaguar smoothly down the narrow lane towards the church. They'd driven all the way from Dorset without a word between them. Briefly, after Tara had called to say that Mother was dead, Harry had softened a little towards her. He'd embraced his wife for the first time in months.

'God, Jemmie, I'm so sorry,' he'd said hoarsely. She knew that he was thinking of his own mother, the darling mama who'd died when he was only twelve. He'd never got over it and, what was more, no woman had ever been able to live up to the icon of perfection that gazed down from the portrait in the drawing room.

Harry had eased her into an armchair, brought her

1

a stiff drink and then stayed with her while she sat, white-faced and shocked. She hadn't cried, though. All she could say incredulously was, 'So she's finally gone. I can't believe it . . .'

But the next morning, it seemed that things between them were back to the way they always were, cold and distant and she had a sense of foreboding that open hostilities were not far away.

Jemima glanced over at her husband as he drove. He looked handsome today, and smart in a way she had forgotten he could be when he made an effort. He'd put on his only black suit, the one he always brought out for funerals or when he had to go to London for a business meeting with the family lawyers. It was an ancient suit, made for Harry's father by a Savile Row tailor some time in the fifties, a little musty now but still obviously excellent quality. It was beautifully cut and the rich dark fabric had a fine, velvety finish.

Like so much of what we have, she thought. *Inherited. That's all he cares about – the things passed down to him. I want something new, something fresh in my life. That's the difference between us.*

As they pulled round the small village green, they saw the church. Long black limousines were parked nearby, and the hearse was outside, the coffin laden with flowers. People were milling about in the front, some going into the church, others chatting on the grass verge. It was the great and the good of the county, all of whom had known her mother well, along with some withered old society hostesses who had thrown grand parties in the distant past and knew her mother from their debutante days. Then there were the expensive London cars, sleek and polished, looking like carefully reared pedigrees suddenly let loose in the wild. Jemima knew to whom those belonged: the ones who made their money from her family.

Harry parked the car and then turned to her. 'All right?'

'As much as you'd expect,' Jemima said coolly. 'It is my mother's funeral after all.'

She pulled down the visor and inspected herself in the mirror. Her golden blonde hair, expertly highlighted, was perfectly styled in a demure French twist. Against its shimmering lights, her little black hat and its one curling black feather looked adorable. It went exquisitely with the vintage style, dark grey tweed Vivienne Westwood suit that made the most of her tiny waist and curves. Jemima blinked her large blue-grey eyes at her reflection, making sure her make-up was immaculate and her lashes free of mascara blobs. Then she pulled out her Chanel lipstick and reapplied a slick of bright red while Harry got out and put up the huge black umbrella. He came round to her side and opened the door.

'How thoughtful of you,' Jemima said.

He shrugged at her and held the umbrella close to the car to protect her from the rain.

Nothing will come between Harry and his sodding good manners, she thought. *Not even the fact that he hates my guts. I can't believe he's sorry that the old witch is dead. It's because of her that we're in this mess, after all.*

'Mimi!' Tara came tottering up, looking fabulous in a Dior pencil skirt, pussy-cat bow blouse and black cashmere V-neck, notable for the enormous diamond brooch in the shape of a dragonfly that sparkled on one shoulder. She hugged her sister and then stood back to look at her. 'Darling, I'm so glad you're here. My God, this is all so *tragic*.'

She blinked moist blue eyes at her sister. Unlike Jemima, she was dark haired with the kind of classic cut and restrained low lights suited to a woman with a high-powered professional career that took her into the most prestigious boardrooms in the City.

'Hello, darling.' Jemima kissed her older sister on both cheeks. 'It's certainly a sad day. I think *tragic* might be pushing it, though. When old ladies with weak hearts drop dead after a full and active life spent fucking everyone else over, it's hardly the end of the world.'

'Oh, please, Mimi, not today. Try and think the best of her.' Tara blinked hard again, holding back tears.

Harry stepped forward. 'Hello, Tara, I'm terribly sorry about your mother,' he said gruffly and kissed his sister-in-law. 'I'll leave you two to it and find a place in the church.'

'How are things?' whispered Tara as they watched him go.

Jemima shrugged. 'Oh, the usual. It's like being married to a block of stone. Where's the family?'

'The children are inside with Gerald.' Tara nodded towards the church.

'I bet they don't have the first clue what's going on,' Jemima said.

4

'They do seem a bit subdued. I've tried to explain to them that their grandma is dead but they're too young to really understand what it means.'

'Poor little sausages. I'll go and say hello.'

Tara gave her a grateful look. 'Listen, I must rush. I've ended up organising this whole thing, of course. I need to talk to the vicar. He's wheeled the most ancient old canon you've ever met out of retirement to perform the service. Apparently he knew Mother and Daddy when they were first married, but he can barely stand up. Have you seen Poppy?'

Jemima shook her head.

'Well, watch out. You may need to hold her up. She's almost hysterical, poor love.'

Tara tip-tapped away on her Louboutin heels up the path towards the vicar.

Harry had gone. Jemima waved at some relations and made a quick escape into the church. She went over to her nephew and niece, who were sitting with their father.

'Hello, sweeties.' She kissed Edward and Imogen who looked up at her with timid expressions. They were too young for this sort of thing. She couldn't help but wonder at Tara's sense in bringing them, though she suspected Gerald had more to do with it.

'Jemima.' Gerald nodded at her, his bald head glowing in the light from a ring of ancient light bulbs above. 'A sad day. A very sad day.' He had a sonorous voice with a melodic South African accent. 'We will miss your dear mother.'

'If you say so, Gerald.' She grinned at him. One of

her pleasures in life was pricking the pomposity of her ridiculous brother-in-law. 'I don't know if she'll be missing you over the other side. After all, she couldn't bear you, as I'm sure you know.'

'A funeral is hardly the time for such remembrances,' Gerald said in his snuffly, arrogant way. 'It is fitting that we remember your mother's good qualities.'

'I'll do my best. Let me know if you can think of any.' She heard a muffled sob from the front pew. 'Do excuse me. I think I'm needed elsewhere.'

She swung round on a heel and approached the front pew where a green velvet opera coat, dark plum beret and masses of dark hair glittering with chestnut lights were scrunched up together into a small hillock.

'Poppy?' Jemima ventured.

Her sister looked up, her face ashen and her eyes swollen and red-rimmed. 'Mimi!' She burst into tears again and buried her face in her handkerchief. 'Oh God, Mimi, isn't it terrible? Isn't it awful? I've been in pieces since I heard. I can't believe she's gone. I can't believe we're orphans.'

'Oh, darling.' Jemima slid into the pew beside her younger sister and put her arms around her. 'Mother was going to die some time, you know. We all knew about her heart. And we're hardly orphans in the abandoned little things in rags heading for the orphanage and bowls of gruel way. Tara's well over thirty, I'm nearly there and you're almost twenty-six.'

Poppy sniffed loudly. 'Oh, I knew you wouldn't feel the same way. I knew you wouldn't. You're always so in charge of yourself. But don't you see . . . it's our *mother*. She's dead and gone. It's only natural to cry, to *mourn* her.'

Jemima stared at her sister's waves of dark hair and stroked her velvet shoulder almost absent-mindedly.

Christ, she thought. *I can't muster a tear. I must really have hated the old bitch after all.*

The funeral passed off in the style of so many of the Trevellyan family occasions. It was all done perfectly properly and in absolutely the best taste without a trace of gaudiness or ostentation.

The three sisters stood together in the front pew. Behind them were the dead woman's sons-in-law and grandchildren and then rows of family and distant relatives, the local gentry and smarter friends from London, the women in discreetly expensive black outfits that glistened with ropes of pearls and diamond brooches. Many of Mrs Trevellyan's staff had turned out for the service, though they were mostly at the back and behind the pillars. Jemima spotted Alice, the long-serving, hugely loyal housekeeper, dabbing at her eyes with a hanky. She obviously really cared that the old woman was dead. Then there were the lawyers and directors of the family company, all very sober and respectful, pretending they actually gave a damn.

Jemima glanced back over her shoulder and saw a whole row of crusty old men with white hair or balding heads, wrinkles and rheumy eyes peering through glasses. The directors of Trevellyan, no doubt, not that she could remember ever meeting any of them before.

Among them stood a younger man, distinctively dressed in an exquisitely soft-charcoal suit that Jemima recognised as Prada, and a vibrant purple silk tie. She liked that. Purple had a nice imperial touch to it, and it was a colour of mourning after all.

Who is he? she wondered. He was shorter than Harry but with broad shoulders that promised a lean, muscular physique. He stood out not just because he was significantly younger than the men around him, but because of his dark looks: hair that was almost black, heavy brows over deep brown eyes and an olive skin.

She turned back to the front. No doubt another of those ghastly men, the ones her mother had employed who grovelled and fawned in front of her like she was God. All right, so she had owned Trevellyan and held all of their destinies in her hands – that certainly made her very important but did Jemima have to be constantly reminded of it? *It made the woman bloody unbearable,* she thought.

Jemima could sense a kind of excitement in the church, a nervous anticipation perceptible in everyone from Harry to her mother's staff. *They're all wondering what's going to happen now. What's going to happen to Trevellyan? Well, join the club.*

The order of service was printed on beautiful ivory-cream card tied with a tiny black watered-silk ribbon. Another excellent job by Smythson, noted Jemima. The funeral proceeded exactly as stated: Tara went up to read the lesson in her commanding voice that shook a little only at the end; the vicar gave the address, describing a woman who sounded vaguely like the mother Jemima had known but whose many virtues, 'great love for human kind' and many charitable acts were, frankly, fiction. Then the managing director of Trevellyan, a dusty-looking old man with bad spectacles, got up to declaim the prayers and they all obligingly mumbled the responses. There was another hymn – *God, what a dirge!* thought Jemima, although the people around her seemed to find it very moving, lots of them sniffing loudly into handkerchiefs – and then the service was over and it was time to go to the graveyard for the entombment.

It was outside, when she saw the open tomb where her mother's coffin would be placed alongside her father's, that Jemima felt something for the first time that day. It was horror.

They can't put her in there! she thought, appalled. It looked unbearably dark and cold. Her mother had always slept with the little rose-coloured lamp on in the corner of the bedroom because she hated the dark so much. *But of course – she's dead.*

The finality of it hit her with a sudden and unexpected force. She felt a huge tremor somewhere deep in her chest and swayed for a moment. She put out her hand and clutched at Poppy's coat. The velvet was slippery and treacherous in her grasp and for an instant she was afraid that she would topple forward and fall down. Then Poppy reached out and took her arm and on the other side of her, Tara took the other.

The sisters held tightly to one another as the plain black coffin containing the last remains of their mother was lowered into the deep pit. The vicar intoned the final words of the interment, reminding them all what they had come from and what they would return to.

'Oh my God,' whispered Tara. 'It's over. She's really gone.'

Poppy had stopped crying and was staring downwards with huge green eyes. 'I can't believe we'll never see her again.'

'I know.' Jemima squeezed their hands. 'Lucky us.'

2

The wake was held at Loxton Hall, the family home of the Trevellyans. The long driveway curved downwards to a tree-ringed hollow and sitting cosily in that was the house, a solid and strong Victorian red-brick mansion constructed with the fortune of the first notable Trevellyan. In the mid-nineteenth century, he'd cashed in on the craze for cashmere shawls and the mania for the brand new Paisley pattern, importing shipfuls of exquisite pieces from India. With the fortune he acquired, he built Loxton Hall and founded his company, Trevellyan, a name that became synonymous with luxury.

The broad sweep in front of the house was full of expensive cars. Mourners were greeted at the door by maids bearing trays of champagne, then directed through to the ballroom, a Gothic creation dominated by vast stone fireplaces at either end and an oak-panelled ceiling.

While staff patiently circulated the room with trays

of canapés, the sisters stood apart, surrounded by people offering their deepest sympathy and their sincerest condolences.

'Your dear mother was a wonderful lady,' said one elderly lady in a black dress printed with jaunty daisies. She was wearing a navy blue hat, Jemima noticed, that didn't match her dress. Her irritation at this stranger grew as she listened, or tried to. 'You must be heartbroken, heartbroken,'

'Oh ... yes, yes we are. We're just devastated.' Jemima eyed a passing tray of small smoked-salmon sandwiches and remembered that she'd eaten nothing that day and was ravenous. 'How did you know Mother?'

'She was gracious enough to be a patroness of our society. We are behind the church appeal, you know. The roof badly needs restoration as does the bell and we're trying to raise several hundred thousand pounds. Your mother donated generously, both of her time and money.' The old lady looked hopeful. 'I wondered, Lady Calthorpe, if you were thinking of taking on any of your mother's duties. We would be most delighted to have someone of your position, of your stature, on our committee ...'

'Oh dear. I'm so sorry. How frightfully kind of you to ask but I'm afraid I just don't do things like that.' Jemima giggled. 'It's so funny to think you might want me but really I'd be awful at it. I'm utterly hopeless, everyone knows, far too lazy to be any good to anyone.'

'What a shame.' The old lady was crestfallen and a

little startled by Jemima's levity. She had obviously been hoping to bag a title as her patron. She glanced eagerly over to where Tara was deep in conversation with a distant cousin. 'Perhaps your sister might have more of a mind to help us?'

'I'm afraid you haven't got a hope there either. Tara works all the hours God sends. She literally doesn't have a minute to give to anyone. When she's not working, she's with her children – but she's working all the time, I promise. I'm sure she'd be good for a donation, though, if you ask her. One thing about working all those hours – she has absolutely stacks of cash.'

'Thank you, Lady Calthorpe. And perhaps you might consider a small token to aid the church?'

Got to give the old girl marks for persistence, thought Jemima. 'You're talking to the wrong sister for that, I'm afraid. Ancestral homes need a great deal of upkeep, I've discovered. Now, I'm so sorry, will you excuse me? I've seen someone I simply must talk to.'

Jemima slid gracefully away, careful not to make the mistake of meeting anyone's eyes. She knew that her path was beset by people desperate to talk to her – relatives, neighbours, snooty ladies keen to be seen with a real, live viscountess – but she had only two goals in mind. One was a glass of champagne and the other was the dark Prada-suited man she had seen in church, who was now standing by one of the windows gazing out at the lawn beyond.

She picked up a glass of fizzing liquid with a deft

gesture as she passed one of the maids and came quickly up behind the man.

'Are you admiring our flora or our fauna?' she purred.

The man turned, surprised, and then smiled when he saw she was there, her head cocked on one side, a sweet smile on her face and her eyes wide. 'I wasn't aware there was any fauna out there.'

Jemima looked out of the window and then shrugged. 'Perhaps not. Sometimes the cats sleep on the terrace when the sun has warmed up the stones. We used to see lots of rabbits, munching up the lawn. My father liked to get out his gun and take pot shots at them from the terrace. We used to beg him not to. We would cry buckets over their little furry bodies.'

'It must be strange having such a big garden. It's more like a bloody great field, isn't it?'

'I never knew any different. It's just a sodding hassle to look after, to be honest. Actually, this all looks rather small and poky to me now.' Jemima took a sip of her champagne.

The man laughed. 'Really? You must be joking.'

'No. The house I live in now is twice the size of this. And twice the bloody expense.'

He laughed again. 'I ought to take you home and show you where I'm from. Six of us in a three up, three down. We were considered the posh ones on the street because we had the end house on our terrace and a bigger garden than the rest. By big, I mean about twenty feet long.'

She gazed up at him coquettishly. 'I love your accent. Where is it from? Birmingham?'

'Birmingham? I ought to deck you for that. Can't you tell an honest Liverpool accent when you hear one?'

'No, sorry. I'm not much good on accents further north than Gloucester.'

The man raised his eyebrows at her. 'You should be ashamed to admit that. Ignorance is never something to proud of, as I learned at Cambridge.'

Jemima raised her eyebrows at him. 'Well, well. Feisty, aren't you? You needn't suppose I'm a snob, you know. I can't help my upbringing and I'm very well aware of its limitations. Anyway, you ought to be nice to me. After all, it *is* my mother's funeral.'

'Yes, I couldn't help but notice you during the service.' He bowed his head slightly. 'May I offer my condolences on this sad occasion, Lady Calthorpe, and my sincere apologies for speaking so impulsively.'

'Yes, you may and apology accepted.' Jemima looked carefully at him. Now that she stood next to him, she could see that he had a rather beautiful face. His dark looks made him appear aggressively masculine but close up she was startled by the strong, slightly aquiline nose and the long black lashes hovered over deliciously soft brown eyes. The sensual mouth was just too inviting, especially when it spoke in that attractively direct way. 'So you know who I am.'

'Of course I do. Your social life is not something one can avoid. You seem to have made party-going an art form.'

Jemima laughed. 'It's true, I do like to amuse myself going out. And can I help it if the media seems to take an interest in me? I can't think why anyone is bothered.'

'Let me see – you're stunning, titled and wealthy and you know everybody who's anybody. You're in the newspapers and gossip magazines every week. I think that rich, beautiful young women with the world at their feet have fascinated people since Helen of Troy launched a thousand ships.'

She looked at him from under her long lashes. 'No one's ever compared me to her before. You're quite the smooth talker. What's your name?'

'Ali. Ali Tendulka.'

'Ali. I can see that you've done rather well for yourself and, by the looks of your Prada suit and Patek Philippe watch, you've managed to escape the slums in Liverpool –'

'I wouldn't exactly call Whitworth Road the slums.'

'No doubt you also drive something very fast in silver and have a modern apartment in London with glass walls and a river view. All very commendable.' She smiled at him. 'But why don't I show you a few old bits and pieces we've got here? There's a real Stubbs in the dining room.'

He looked at her with mild surprise. 'Don't you have to mingle?'

'I loathe mingling. Unless I'm with chums, I'm bad at it, very bad. It's much better for everyone if I don't.' Jemima drained her glass and put it down on the window seat. 'Come on, I'm sure we can find some fun away from all this dreariness . . .'

Ali smiled and lifted two more glasses of champagne from a passing tray. 'If you say so.'

'I do.'

She led him through the throng of people, using him like a piece of armour against the those she knew were clamouring to get to her. There was Aunt Daphne and all the Boyle cousins, always so desperate to oil up to the Trevellyans. She spotted Poppy listening to a long speech from the village doctor, who'd known them all since they were babies and was now silver-haired and somewhat doddery. Where was Harry? She looked across the room for his broad back and the mess of fair hair she knew so well. Oh, there he was, deep in conversation with the man from the estate office. No doubt they were talking about land management, or something equally boring. Well, that would keep him occupied for a while longer, at least.

'This way,' she said quietly, steering Ali through the double doors at the far end of the ballroom and out into the hall. She opened the door into another large room. 'The drawing room,' she announced, letting him pass her. Ali handed her one of the champagne glasses. 'Thank you.'

They chinked flutes, their eyes meeting as they sipped from the cool crystal.

Jemima broke the silence. 'After Daddy died, Mother did a little bit of redecorating, so you must excuse her rather Madame de Pompadour style. She was very fond of eau-de-Nil silk and porcelain snuff boxes. Bit too chi-chi for me.'

The drawing room was almost aggressively feminine, with tables draped in taffeta and covered in ornaments, cut glass and silver-framed photographs. The furniture was mostly eighteenth-century antiques with two ormolu cabinets taking pride of place. Somewhat out of place was the modern armchair, a pile of *Country Life* magazines stacked on the floor next to it, that stood beside a startlingly new white lamp. Jemima remembered how her mother had liked the way it directed its strong beam right on to the book or magazine she was reading at the time.

'We didn't use this room much. It's too big really. We girls spent most of our time in the back sitting room. It always felt so cosy.'

'The back sitting room.' Ali raised his eyebrows.

'There or the nursery. We had a television in the nursery, and our nanny would light the fire on cold winter afternoons and let us make toast on it. Have you ever toasted bread over an open fire? It's just delicious.' Jemima smiled. 'I'd like to do that again one day. I can't think why I haven't.'

'Maybe it's because a toaster is just that bit more efficient.' Ali ran his fingers over one of her mother's favourite Meissen shepherdesses.

'Maybe. But where's the romance in that? Come on.' She led him back to the hall and opened the door to the dining room. 'Only used for Sundays and Christmas after Daddy died.' Ali went in and walked slowly around the vast polished oak table. 'It does look impressive when the silver is out and the candles are lit, I must admit. That's the Stubbs there, over the dresser. Known as "the horsey picture" when we were children, but apparently it's one of the finest examples of his work.'

Ali looked round at her, almost frowning. 'You know, when I was a boy, I thought only the Queen lived like this. I didn't imagine that ordinary people could or would.'

'Funny, isn't it?' she replied carelessly. 'Everyone I know does.'

They looked into the library and the study. Then they returned to the hall. Jemima stopped him in a dark corner by a green baize door.

'I won't show you the kitchen, they'll be manic in there at the moment.'

'What about the upstairs rooms? I was hoping for the *full* tour.' Ali leaned in to take her empty glass, stroking the back of her hand as he did so.

Jemima dropped her voice to a husky whisper. 'Actually, there's one more room downstairs I'd like to show you first.'

'Yes? Where?'

'Here,' she purred, and pushed open the door behind him, startling him by thrusting him backwards into the darkness.

'Where are we?' he asked as she entered the room and pushed the door closed behind them.

She tugged the light pull and revealed what was the downstairs loo, a large room wallpapered in red damask and with heavy green velvet curtains closed at the window. The walls were covered in family photographs and old prints and the lavatory itself was built into a vast wooden bench that ran along the length of the far wall, so that it looked like a throne.

'Jesus.' Ali gasped. 'Even the bog is the size of my bedroom.'

'Funny you should say that, darling.' Jemima pulled at the light again, plunging the room back into darkness. She heard the clink of their champagne flutes as Ali put them down. Then the sound of his breath coming closer and harder. She curled her arms up round his neck, pushing him back against the wall. He moaned appreciatively. 'I thought we might get to know each other a little better,' she breathed.

Jemima pressed her mouth up against his, feeling the scrape of stubble against her face. He responded immediately, as hungry for her as she was for him. They kissed fiercely and deeply. He tasted of champagne and the faint mild tang of cigarette smoke.

She felt him bulging against her, a sensation that made her tighten with anticipation and she felt her own rush of arousal. He pressed his hand up to her breasts and she quickly unbuttoned the front of her jacket to allow him access to her. She sighed as he touched the lace on her bra and then slid a cool finger inside to rub a nipple.

She returned to his mouth, attacking his tongue with hers, pushing deeper into him. Excitement bubbled up through her at the pleasure he was giving her as he teased her breasts and also at the illicit nature of their activity. She loved this: the handsome stranger, seduced by her beauty, ravished by her directness and as thrilled as she was by the naughtiness of

20

their situation. She loved the way they were both clothed, reaching only for what they needed of each other, and the sense of urgency and desperation, the animal need that lay beneath their smart clothes and civilised exteriors.

She reached for his groin, pulling his trousers open with a practised flick and releasing his cock, which was iron hard and throbbing with heat.

'I hate to do this,' she murmured, 'but . . .'

From an inner pocket in her skirt, she quickly removed a tiny foil packet and ripped it open with her teeth. In one swift movement, she took the condom out and rolled it swiftly down, sheathing him.

'And here I was, thinking how delightfully unplanned this was,' Ali teased.

'I'm always prepared, darling. I like risks – but not *that* much.' She kissed him again and then gasped as he clasped her round the bottom, picked her up and turned her round so that she was against the wall. Then, as he held her with one arm, he reached down, yanked up her skirt and felt for her panties. There was nothing there.

'You see . . . always prepared . . . Oh God . . .' She sighed and moaned softly as he pushed into her with his fingers, rubbing at her with the pad of his thumb. A moment later he took his hand away and she felt the hard head of his penis pushing against her and then the delightful sensation as he entered her, filling her completely, pushing her back up against the wall as he thrust strongly into her.

She panted as they began to move together, finding

a rhythm that maximised their pleasure. 'Keep doing that . . . Yes, just like that. Oh . . . my . . . *God*.' She pulled in to squeeze him tightly as he reached the peak of his thrust, making him kiss her deeply. He broke away to bite at her neck and shoulders, overcome by the sensations she was giving him.

Their speed increased as he pounded into her and she bumped against the wall, dislodging some family photographs that fell to the floor. She was barely aware of it, knowing only the waves of pleasure that were building up inside her, pushing her towards the brink, and that Ali was going with her . . .

A moment later and they were both gripped by climax, Ali first and Jemima quickly following, propelled over the edge into a spasm of delight by the knowledge that he was coming.

He was still inside her when they heard the voice getting closer.

'Jemima? Jemima, where are you?'

'Oh Christ.' Jemima pushed Ali away and pulled her blouse back together. 'It's my sister.' She began to put her clothes in order as she shouted, 'I'm in the loo, Tara. What is it?'

'I've been looking for you.' Tara came up to the door and called through it. 'We're being summoned to the library. The lawyers want to read Mother's will.'

'All right, all right, I'm coming. Give me five minutes.'

'We'll see you there.'

They heard Tara walk off down the corridor. They looked at each other in the gloom, their eyes now adjusted to the darkness.

'Thanks so much,' Jemima said with a smile. 'That was exactly what I needed. Now, I hate to be rude, but I really must dash.'

Ali had already tidied himself up and was smoothing his hair and reknotting his tie. 'Not at all. I've got to hurry myself.'

'Yes, I meant to ask. Who are you, exactly?'

'Me? No one important.'

'Then why are you here?'

He grinned at her. 'You'll find out, your ladyship. Now, if you'll excuse me. My guess is that we'd better not to be seen leaving together so I'll slip out now. And thank you. It was a pleasure all the sweeter for being so unexpected.'

Then he opened the door and was gone.

Jemima opened the curtains and went to the mirror. Even in the grey daylight that lit the room, she looked flushed and her eyes were bright. She tidied herself up as best she could without her bag of tricks to hand, and smoothed her hair. At least she was a little more presentable. She knew she was considered the beauty of the family. She hadn't been much to look at as a child but she'd grown into her looks. Now, in her late twenties, she was at her peak: a soft pink-and-white complexion, wide-spaced blue-grey eyes above well-defined cheekbones, a straight, narrow nose and lips full enough to guarantee she'd never be tempted by collagen injections. Her blonde hair was just above the shoulder with a long fringe falling prettily down one side. She shook her head a little to make her hair glint in the light.

'Nothing like a good fuck to bring me out of myself,' she murmured. She smiled at her reflection. 'And now we'll find out exactly what kind of revenge Mother has been planning all these years.'

3

Tara Trevellyan ran hastily up the carved wooden staircase and padded along the corridor, oblivious to the fine works of art and family portraits that lined the walls. They were so familiar she never noticed them now.

No one else was about. All the staff were downstairs serving the guests. She went to a door at the far end, paused for a moment to listen at it, and then shook herself.

'Just who do you think is going to be inside?' she whispered to no one. Taking a deep breath, she turned the handle gently, opened the door and silently slipped inside.

The room she now stood in was the grandest bedroom suite in the house, a vast chamber with a flat-fronted window of triple Gothic arches, each one festooned with pink taffeta curtains held back by tassels. A pink cream silk velvet chaise longue rested luxuriously in the niche of the window on the thick white carpet. Against the far wall was a 1930s art deco glass dressing table, covered in cut-glass scent bottles, jewellery cases and silver photograph frames – and, of course, a vast decanter of *Trevellyan's Tea Rose*. A door at the side of the room led into the dressing room and another opposite led into a white and silver art deco bathroom.

Tara knew this room had been her mother's pride and joy. It was strange to be in here without her. Tara could still picture her sitting at the dressing table, powdering her nose with a pink swan's-down duster, wearing her favourite ice-blue silk robe with the mink trimming, or lying in the magnificent four-poster bed supported by twenty soft white pillows while she answered her correspondence and drank sweet tea from her favourite Sèvres teacup.

Now she's gone, Tara reminded herself. *The question is, what has she taken with her, and what has she left behind?*

Of course it was impossible for a dead woman to take anything with her but there was no saying what arrangements she had made before she'd gone. After all, she'd had battalions of tame lawyers prepared to do anything she asked, along with a deep love of meddling with other people's lives.

Remembering that there was not much time before they met for the reading of the will, Tara went swiftly to the dressing table. Four large jewellery boxes sat on the smooth glass surface. *Hell to clean. Poor house-maids, I bet she made their lives a misery. Now ... which one?*

A pink leather Asprey box looked most likely. Or

perhaps it was the splendid enamelled Fabergé case bought by a Trevellyan in the 1920s from a poor Russian princess after the Revolution. The white Cartier box looked less likely but you never knew. Tara decided to start with the smallest, the Lalique glass heart-shaped case. Lifting the lid, she saw that it was almost empty except for a couple of dress rings in amethyst and aquamarine, only semi precious.

Quickly she moved on to the Cartier. It was almost the same as the first – strangely empty except for one or two pieces of little value. Here, it was some Edwardian paste: a parure of jet and marquisite. Worried now, Tara went to the Fabergé. The same again. Where had her mother's jewels gone? Ever since childhood, Tara had seen her mother open her cases and reveal their sparkling treasure – diamonds, emeralds, rubies; exquisitely set in silver, gold and platinum. Jewellery was her mother's weakness and even though her insurers had insisted that the most expensive pieces be kept at the bank, her mother had retained plenty to enjoy.

'What the hell have you done with it all?' she muttered. 'Where is it?'

She turned to her last hope, the Asprey box. The lid would not open. It was locked.

'Shit!' she swore. She caught a glimpse of her reflection in the triple mirror. Her face looked so slender it was almost gaunt but her cheekbones had spots of high colour along them and her blue eyes were anxious. She pulled a hand through her hair and licked her lips. She was used to running on adrenaline – perhaps it was what kept her so thin – but this was different. She could feel her sense of control leaving her.

'Keep it together, Tara,' she muttered to herself. 'Don't let it get to you. There's bound to be a logical explanation.'

She quickly rearranged the dressing table so that it was just as she'd found it and then darted to the door, pausing only for one last look at the room she was leaving. Would she ever stand in it again when it was like this – as though her mother had only just left and would be back in a moment?

Tara shuddered, and then hurried back downstairs.

The gathering in the library looked very Agatha Christie.

'It feels like the murderer is about to be revealed,' muttered Jemima as Tara came in, a little breathless, to take her seat next to her at the front. Someone had thoughtfully put the dining-room chairs in short rows in front of what had been their grandfather's great desk, where Victor Goldblatt, the head of Gold-blatt Mindenhall, now sat importantly, gazing over the documents in front of him.

'Or like someone is about to be expelled,' Tara said softly, slipping on to her chair.

'If history is anything to go by, darling, it won't be you. I'm the one who had to leave three different girls' schools, remember?'

'Answering the call of the wild even then. Were you alone in the loo?' Tara looked over at her sister, who dropped her gaze and smiled. 'Oh Mimi, honestly, of all the times. You are incorrigible. Where's Poppy?'

'God knows.'

'Someone had better find her. We can't start without her.'

'Look, there she is, in the musicians' gallery.' Jemima pointed up to the oak balcony at the far end of the room which had been a favourite place to hide when they were children. Sure enough, Poppy was standing there gazing down upon the gathering, a curious expression on her face as she surveyed them all.

Tara gasped. 'Oh God, she's not going to jump, is she? She's been in a terrible state today.'

'Don't be so melodramatic. Of course she's not. I think she's looking for someone.'

The two sisters exchanged glances.

'Is anyone else . . . expected?' Tara asked meaningfully.

'I don't think so. But you never know who's going to crawl out of the woodwork. After all, it was in all the papers that the funeral was today.' Jemima frowned. 'Let's hope there are no more nasty surprises than whatever is in that will.'

Victor Goldblatt peered up over his gold-rimmed half-moon spectacles and coughed. 'Are we all here? I'd like to proceed.'

'Just a moment,' said Tara, and she beckoned to Poppy. Her sister stared down at her for a moment longer before disappearing to descend the tiny spiral staircase back to the ground floor. She came across the floor to the others, looking almost eerily suited to

29

her surroundings in a long red velvet dress, and sat down. 'Yes, we're ready.'

'Very well. We're here to read the last will and testament of Yolanda Margaret Trevellyan, late of this address. The people gathered today are those who were closest to the deceased, her intimate family and relatives, and those who have an interest in the proceedings.'

Jemima glanced around quickly. The usual suspects were here: her mother's faithful retainers, various of the Trevellyan and Loxton staff, Gerald, Aunt Daphne – *though what she hopes to get out of it, God only knows. Mother thought she was a sponging, useless whinger* – and there at the back, leaning against one of the bookcases that lined the walls, was Harry, his arms folded and a closed expression on his face. Jemima jumped. Standing next to him was Ali Tendulka, last seen pumping into her ecstatically in the downstairs lavatory. She tried to hide her astonishment and the sudden rush of anxiety at seeing her husband and her most recent hook-up side by side. Harry ignored her but Ali caught her eye and grinned. She gave him a look, something between an acknowledgement and a rebuke. What the hell was he doing here? She'd collar him as soon as it was over and find out. Meanwhile, Victor had begun to read in his gruff voice.

'I, Yolanda Margaret Trevellyan, being of sound mind, do hereby commit my last will and testament . . .'

The sisters listened as their fate unfolded. Each had been born to wealth and privilege and to a family name famous across the world. This was their inheritance, the reason why the press had dubbed them 'the Heiresses'. The moment of truth was here.

Tara had been determined to outstrip what she had been born to, and had become independently wealthy in her own right through her extraordinarily successful finance career. Then she had married Gerald, with his South African money, media portfolio and ambitions to be a press tycoon. What more could she want from her mother's will? She needed Loxton like she needed a hole in the head – Gerald had bought an enormous Scottish estate only last year and she was still reeling from this unexpected burden as the old house needed complete renovation and naturally it had all fallen to her – but that didn't stop her wanting it. It would mean everything to her if her mother finally acknowledged her by leaving her the house.

Jemima shifted uneasily as the opening sentences were read out. She felt nervous, knowing that Harry was here. But it was his right, she supposed. After all, he was her husband and Yolanda Trevellyan's son-in-law. He had every reason to be here. But the truth was it made her sick to her bones to think about it. This was his payday. Finally he was going to get his reward for marrying her, for allowing Yolanda to have her way. The old hag had never been so happy as she was on the day Harry and Jemima had announced their engagement and once they were married she loved to remind people of the union as often as she could. 'Do you know my daughter's husband, Lord Calthorpe?' she would ask offhandedly. Or, at some luncheon for the local ladies, she would say casually,

'My daughter, Lady Calthorpe, has a charming home, Herne Castle. Do you know it? Rather magnificent, in its way.' It was all the more galling for Jemima, who found Herne the very opposite of charming. No doubt it was Herne, the never-ending money pit, that had kept Harry with her as long as this.

Well, marrying Harry was the only thing in her life Jemima had done to please her mother and it had worked spectacularly. Now she would see exactly how happy she had made the old woman. And so would Harry.

Poppy twisted her hands nervously in her lap. Her childhood at Loxton had been happy, she had to admit that, and it had bred in her a love of the mad Gothic Victoriana this house was full of. She looked like a Pre-Raphaelite stunner herself, with her thick dark hair that fell into curls when she didn't dry it straight, pale skin, full lips and enormous green eyes. Burne-Jones would have wanted to sketch her as an angel or maiden and she would have captured the heart of Rossetti with her poetic nature and love of art. But despite the priv-ileges and comfort the lucky chance of her birth had brought her, she didn't care for any of it. She had spent her entire adult existence trying to shake off the burden of her inherited money and the life she was expected to lead. She felt as though she was burdened by her wealth, as though it prevented her going out to taste life's adventures. Jemima thought her mad, she knew that. Her sister argued the opposite: that without the struggle to earn daily bread, they were free to do whatever they wanted, to go anywhere and be anything.

But Poppy knew that Jemima was blind to the fact that no matter where she went or what she did, her life was unchanging. She met the same people and did the same things. The same expectations were constantly fulfilled – there were no surprises or challenges. Life inevitably became predictable and taken for granted. Jemima was a bright, clever woman who'd never done anything with her life because she hadn't needed to – and it was money that had done that to her.

Poppy looked across at her oldest sister. Tara, on the other hand, seemed to have the worst of all worlds. She slaved like a donkey, as though penury waited for her around the corner despite her enormous salary and family wealth, not to mention Gerald's money. And when did she find time to enjoy the luxuries this prosperity brought? She had all the toys of the rich: the fabulous London townhouse, the rambling Cotswold farmhouse, a beautiful white bungalow on an island in the Bahamas, the great black SUV and a roaring sleek convertible for herself. She had nannies, assistants, cooks, drivers, housekeepers and gardeners. In the most exclusive shops in London and New York, her personal shoppers were on constant lookout for her favourite designers' new collections. The most unique and exquisite items were sent from all over the world direct to her office, house or the City piedà-terre she used when there wasn't even time to get home for the night, for her to try on. Exclusive and over-priced accessories arrived by taxi at her whim. Her hairdressers, her masseurs, her manicurists and eyebrow threaders, her facialist and dietician, all came to her. The only one who didn't do home visits to Tara was her gynaecologist.

Tara's life passed by in a whirl of meetings, deadlines, hours hunched over her computer, appointments, phone calls, long-haul flights and, occasionally, five minutes to herself or an hour with the children, reading them a story or giving them a bath.

It's like she's on a treadmill and it's killing her but she'll never get off, Poppy thought.

She looked up at the lawyer with frightened eyes and clenched her hands together more tightly.

I'm afraid of what Mummy's will is going to say. But not like the others. They're afraid of what they won't get – and I'm afraid of what I will.

4

'Christ!'

'Holy . . . fuck.'

'This is terrible,' cried Poppy, her cheeks flushed red. She'd always had the cleanest mouth of the three sisters, perhaps as a reaction to Jemima, who'd enjoyed swearing like a trooper since she was about four.

The three of them stood together in the nursery. After the will had been read, this had been the most obvious place for them to retreat to: their private territory away from the rest of the house. With its high bay window looking out over the lawn and up towards the wood, the nursery was the room they'd grown up in. It still housed their old toys – the battered doll's house, the worn teddies and the bookshelf full of their childhood favourites. The great carved rocking horse that had arrived one Christmas from Harrods still pranced in the bay. The old upright piano, where they had bashed out chords and arpeggios and practised exam pieces, stood against the wall, tattered sheet music still propped on the stand.

This had always been their refuge. Tara could usually be found reading a book, lying on the rug in front of the fire, her chin in her hands over whatever it was she was absorbed in. Jemima would often be playing with the doll's house or her collection of vintage Barbie dolls, with their swooping 1960s eye make-up, close-cropped hair and fabulous Jackie O clothes. Poppy was most likely to be playing the piano or sitting at the shabby school desk with her pad and the paint box. Until Nanny came in and told them to clean themselves up, put on the white organza dresses their mother insisted they wear, and come downstairs for the nightly ritual of the family dinner.

Their parents would be waiting for them in the drawing room, in black tie, their mother dripping with jewels. They would converse politely over gin and tonics for the adults and lemonade for the girls, then go into the dining room for a formal, four-course meal, served to them by the butler. Each girl would have to talk about her day and explain what new thing she had learned in the course of it. By the time it was Poppy's turn, she would be white-faced and almost retching with nerves.

It was a routine they all loathed with a vengeance.

'We were the only ones I knew who couldn't wait to get to boarding school,' Jemima would say with a laugh, 'in order to enjoy the relaxed, homely atmosphere.'

Here, in the nursery, was where they were themselves.

Jemima threw herself into the armchair where Nanny used to sit and do her sewing. 'So, the old witch has had her revenge after all.'

Tara went over to the window and stared out, her shoulders stiff with tension. 'I just can't believe it,' she muttered.

'Have I really understood correctly?' marvelled Jemima. 'She's left Poppy the house?'

'All of it,' Poppy said faintly. She was standing by the fireplace, supporting herself with the chimney-piece. 'This whole place. Oh God.'

Tara put her head in her hands. 'Why?'

'Well, it's not as if you or I needed a house, Tara,' said Jemima tartly. 'We've got more than enough already.'

'But Poppy didn't want it!' shouted Tara, turning round, her eyes red. 'And I did!'

There was a pause while the other two stared in surprise at Tara as this revelation sunk in.

'And it's not just the house,' Tara added. 'It's everything in it. Everything. All the furniture, paintings, jewellery, china . . .'

'But you've got more than enough money to buy everything in this house twice over if you wanted it. You don't need any of it.' Poppy's voice was quiet.

'That's not the point.' Tara sat down on the window seat, stretching her slim legs out in front of her. 'Don't you understand? You've no idea what it was like for me, always seeking her approval. Neither of you could understand because she always adored you both. You were naughty, Mimi, but she admired that. She might have seemed disapproving on the outside, but every time you got expelled or ran away or appeared in the papers for being your typical outrageous self, secretly she loved it. You reminded her most of her younger self. And then when you married Harry –'

'The old woman did rather cream her jeans,' agreed Jemima, tucking her legs up underneath her. 'But you were her dream daughter. You were the one who fulfilled her demands. Look at you – head girl, Oxford University, a double first, youngest woman in the boardroom in the City, two gorgeous children . . .'

'Nothing satisfied her,' Tara said softly. She played nervously with her necklace. 'Nothing I ever did was good enough. Perhaps if I'd nearly died, like Poppy, perhaps she would have loved me then.'

Poppy flared up suddenly. 'Don't blame me, Tara! I can't help how Mother and Daddy felt about me. I never wanted to be sick, you know. And I never wanted their love either – not the way they showed it. You know what they were like. Money was everything. They never understood that *I didn't want it*. And I still don't! Do you really think I want Loxton? I'll give it away. I'll give it to you, if you want it, Tara. If it matters to you so much.'

'No, you don't understand. It isn't that I want Loxton. It's that Mother didn't want to give it to me. She didn't want me to have anything. That's what I find so difficult.' Tara turned away again to the window, her shaking shoulders revealing that she was sobbing.

'She wanted to give me Loxton,' Poppy said quietly

as she stood by the piano and ran her fingers silently along the yellowed ivory keys. 'But she didn't want to give me what I really needed: my liberty. Her approval of my choices in life. Respect for my values.'

'Oh dear, dear, dear. This is all frightfully tragic,' drawled Jemima. 'But I think we're rather missing the point. Mother might have singled young Poppy out for a little extra' – Tara snorted at the idea of Loxton and all its contents being simply an extra – 'but she's actually treated all three of us the same.' The other two turned to look at her. 'Don't you see? The most precious thing in her life was Trevellyan. The great family company, the source of all our happiness, the provider of everything. And Trevellyan is what she's given to us ... *all* of us. And that's her biggest joke, because it was the one thing none of us wanted.'

Poppy looked wonderingly at her sister. 'You're right. But if it's so precious, why give it to us? Surely she couldn't trust us with it – she couldn't trust anyone with Trevellyan after Daddy died.'

Jemima shrugged. 'What choice did she have? Who else was there? We are the only ones with the Trevellyan name, after all.'

Tara turned round to face her sisters. Now she was flushed and her eyes sparkled feverishly. 'But the old bitch couldn't leave it at that, could she? Nothing is ever simple in her world. She couldn't leave us the company and be damned! She had to add her condition – her nasty, twisted little sting in the tail.'

'Yes. That did come as rather a surprise, I must admit.' Jemima remembered the murmur of astonishment that had rippled across the room when Victor Goldblatt had added Yolanda's interesting proviso.

'I didn't really understand,' Poppy said helplessly. She went over to Jemima's chair and knelt down next to it, looking up beseechingly. 'I know it's something awful and it had to do with . . . *her*.'

Jemima looked down at her younger sister and stroked her hair gently. 'It's really quite simple, Pops. We've been given Trevellyan, lock, stock and barrel. But there's a catch. If we don't triple sales in exactly one calendar year, then we lose it.'

Tara sniffed as she angrily wiped at her damp cheeks with the back of her hand. 'That's what I don't understand. How can she set us such an impossible task? How can we possibly do it?'

Jemima looked up and stared at her frostily. 'Because if we don't, then Jecca gets it all.'

5

Jemima went down the staircase, as outwardly calm and self-possessed as ever, even if inside she was seething. She saw her husband waiting for her at the bottom of the stairs, leaning against a fine marble-topped cabinet and tinkering idly with the inlaid clock that sat on the top of it. Above him was a full-length, life-sized portrait of Yolanda Trevellyan, dressed in a long, floating gown, the family jewels glittering at her ears, neck, wrists and fingers. She was porcelain pale with the same colouring as Poppy: the green-flecked eyes and dark hair with glitters of chestnut.

Bitch, thought Jemima as she glared at the impossibly perfect painted face. *What a hollow, miserable existence you must have had, to wish this on your daughters.*

Harry looked up as he heard her descend. 'All ready?'

'Ready for what?' snapped Jemima, simply because she was in the mood to be argumentative.

'Ready to come home.'

'What makes you think I'm going back to Herne?'

'Well – aren't you?'

Jemima stood and faced him for a moment and then turned to inspect her reflection in the gilt-edged mirror opposite. 'As it happens, yes. All my things are at Herne. But I'll be packing up immediately to return to London.'

Harry gazed at her impassively for a moment. 'Will you stay the night?'

'I haven't decided. It depends on what time we get back.'

'All right.' He said nothing more but simply waited, watching as she took her hairbrush out of her Mulberry Agyness bag and ran it through her blonde hair.

'I can't think where my bloody hat is,' she said. 'I took it off after we got back from the church and put it down somewhere.' She felt a sudden flash of fear as she remembered what she had done not long after they'd returned from the church. Had she given herself away somehow? She flicked a glance at Harry, who appeared not to have noticed anything.

'It'll turn up,' he said.

'I'm perfectly aware of *that*.' *It's always like this,* she thought with a twinge of sadness, *always speaking in bitter, sharp little nothings to each other.* 'You must be feeling pretty damned pleased.'

'About what?'

Jemima laughed joylessly. 'Oh come on, darling. What? About your nice little legacy from my dear dead mother. She certainly didn't forget you, did she?'

'I'm very grateful to your mother for her bequest. She understood very well what it entails to keep a place like Herne going, and how I need all the help I can get.'

'Whereas I don't, I suppose,' hissed Jemima, turning round to look him in the eye. 'Well, I can tell you here and now that I bloody well do. That place has sucked up hundreds of thousands of pounds of my money. And you may have noticed that I got nothing in that fucking will!'

'Unless I fell asleep and missed something, I believe you inherited a third of the family company.'

Jemima waved a hand angrily. 'That's not an inheritance, it's a fucking *test*. It's a typically cruel practical joke from beyond the grave. A nasty little poke in the ribs from Hell, where I'm quite sure Mother is sizzling away nicely as we speak. I don't want to run the fucking company, I just want the allowance I've always received – and so will you, if you know what's good for you and for Herne. A hundred thousand and a couple of paintings may seem like a tidy lot but you and I both know it won't last long. What about the roof for the east wing? What about the restoration of the Great Hall? What about the million other things that need doing?'

'I know that,' Harry said coldly. 'But it still helps. I'm still grateful for it. And I'll find other ways to deal with the rest. I don't rely solely on you and your money, you know.'

'You could have fooled me, sweetheart.' Jemima spun round on the marble floor to face her reflection again. 'Now let's go home. There's nothing more for us here.'

She marched out of the hall towards the front door without a backward glance, as though it didn't matter a bit that she was leaving her childhood home, perhaps for the last time.

There was no guarantee that she would ever be back.

They drove to Dorset in the same cold silence as they had driven up. Harry put some music on so that their simmering reluctance to speak was not so uncomfortably obvious. Jemima was glad, even if it was classical music.

She leaned her head against the cool window, watched the countryside go by and tried to make sense of everything that had happened that day. She was exhausted by the tumult of emotions and the onslaught of information that was left in the wake of her mother's will reading.

Trevellyan. The great family company. Ever since she was born, the prominence and uniqueness of Trevellyan had been drummed into her. The family and its company was part of the very fabric of Englishness. Sometimes she allowed herself to think heretical thoughts: *all this fuss over a bit of soap and perfume!* But she could never sustain them for long. Reverence for the illustrious brand and all it stood for was too firmly ingrained in her, like childhood nursery rhymes, and she could never escape it.

She knew the family legends like she knew her bible stories. They even had their very own God-like figure:

Samuel Trevellyan, the man who had launched the family into prosperity with his cashmere business. Fate had led Samuel to a barber's shop in Piccadilly one day and it had been a life-changing experience for him, and for his descendants. That day, he met Giuseppe Farnese, a wild, impetuous Italian from Tuscany who didn't just shave and groom his customers. He also offered them the most intensely scented oils for their pleasure. Homesick for his beloved Italy, Farnese had sent for essences to remind him of it. Before long he was obsessively blending these essences, creating wonderful fragrances – sumptuous, luxurious and exotic. Trevellyan, instantly enraptured by the Italian's skill, made him an offer for the whole business on the spot. Farnese, unable to believe his luck, accepted immediately. Trevellyan closed down the barber's shop and reopened it as an elegant emporium selling the fragrances that Farnese created, and costly accessories for gentlemen and ladies – ivory combs, crystal bottles and leather travelling cases. He renamed it Trevellyan, keeping Farnese on to develop scents and bring in custom. Farnese's eccentric ways and delightful wit brought hundreds of fashionable ladies and gentlemen to the shop, but it was the Great Exhibition of 1851 that marked the real start of the company's success. The Trevellyan stand featured an imposing mahogany glass-fronted cabinet with an impressive display of crystal-bottled eaux de Cologne, accompanied by beautifully fragranced soaps pressed into exquisite patterns, talcum powders and hair oils. From the musky scents of India, the zesty aromas of the Mediterranean, to the delicate bouquet of the English countryside, Farnese had developed an irresistible and inspired range of Trevellyan scents. It was the successful launch they needed and from then on the business prospered.

Could he ever have guessed what he'd begun? wondered Jemima. *Could he have imagined that over a hundred and fifty years later, his company would still be so successful and famous all over the world?*

The company had passed on from father to son and in the early twentieth century it saw its greatest breakthrough. Just before the First World War, Trevellyan launched the scent that was to define it over the next hundred years. With the upsurge in nationalistic pride, the time was exactly right for a fragrance that came to epitomise Englishness and all it stood for. That fragrance was *Trevellyan's Tea Rose,* a rich floral bouquet, delicate enough for the day and intense enough for the evening. Ladies and shop girls alike went mad for it and the desire for *Trevellyan's Tea Rose* grew into a craze. Its gentle scent was redolent of a civilised life in happier times; it evoked afternoon tea, village greens and pretty girls cycling down country lanes. It was said that soldiers soaked handkerchiefs in it, so that in the misery of the trenches they could, with just a sniff, be transported back home to the safety and warmth of their girl's arms.

Trevellyan's Tea Rose rode the wild wave of popularity to become an established classic. There were plenty of other Trevellyan fragrances, along with colognes for men such as the *Chatsworth* – created especially for the Duke of Devonshire – and *Leather & Willow*, as well as soaps, powders, bath oils and other unguents. But while all of these were successful, it was *Trevellyan's Tea Rose* that made the company's fortune. Trevellyan was stocked in Selfridges during its glory days and quickly became a bestseller in department stores across the world, with unprecedented sales in New York. It was said to be the favourite of the Duchess of York and Lady Diana Cooper; even the silent-screen siren of 1920s Hollywood Gloria Swanson had demanded personalised bottles be sent to her studio. Queen Mary refused to travel unless it was with at least two bottles of the famous fragrance, which was lavishly sprinkled over her pillows wherever she slept.

Tea Rose, Tea Rose, thought Jemima idly. *It's funny how much that smell has shaped my life. And yet – I can't stand it.*

It was the smell of her mother's bedroom, that pink satin creation with its swags and swathes and glass and crystal.

Really, Mother was born about fifty years too late. She would have loved being a social butterfly of the twenties instead of a woman out of step with her time in the seventies and eighties.

While the rest of the world was embracing power dressing and shoulder pads, eating in glamorous restaurants and jetting round the world with no care for the consequences, Yolanda and Cecil Trevellyan were living a life that could have been from fifty years earlier. Cecil ran the company, Yolanda ran the home.

They were childless until miraculously, it seemed, at the age of forty, Yolanda became pregnant with Tara. Two more girls quickly followed, with Poppy arriving when her mother was forty-six. She had thought she had begun the menopause and didn't realise she was pregnant until six months had passed.

The Trevellyans were torn between sadness that they had no sons and delight that they had any children at all. Their daughters would be brought up to be strong, successful women who could run the company when their turn came.

But the parents forgot one important thing: the girls had their own personalities, their own dreams and desires. The forty-year age gap loomed between the parents and their children, between a mother who had been old-fashioned for her own generation, and her daughters of the eighties and nineties.

When did it all start to go wrong? wondered Jemima. *Was it Jecca? Was she the problem? Ha! If only it were that simple. Who am I kidding? It was wrong from the start. It must have been. Oh, Daddy . . . why? Why did it all have to happen? We only wanted you to love us, or to show us that you loved us. Was that so very hard?*

The Jaguar pulled under the great stone gate with its pretty hexagonal lodges on either side, and rolled smoothly down the long drive. The drive at Loxton was impressive but it was nothing like Herne's. This was true English grandeur: a leafy avenue lined with ancient trees surrounded by lush green parkland and at the end, the house rising softly upwards, so natural in its landscape that it seemed as if it had always been there.

Jemima remembered her first glimpse of the house. It had been at dawn. She and Harry had driven from a ball together, three hours in Harry's ancient Roadster with only a strapless ball gown and some Gina heels to protect her from the cold – oh, yes, and Harry's dinner jacket. The house stood cloaked in mist against a dawn sky. The rising summer sun had quilted the sky with pink and gold and gilded the ancient walls and dozens of brick chimneys with a rosy light.

'Oh my God!' Jemima had exclaimed. 'What a magnificent house!'

'It's a castle, actually,' Harry had said with a grin, turning to her. She had been in love with him then, pure, fizzing, tummy-turning-over love. It was hard to remember how it had felt, now that their relationship had deteriorated so badly.

She'd loved Herne then, before she'd realised what it really and truly meant. It had looked like a fairytale, the kind of castle the heroine is taken to at the end of the story, where she will live happily ever after – but that was a disguise. The truth was that Herne was a burden; it was a parasite, ready to suck away the lifeblood of anyone who lived there, as they grappled with what caring for this great lump of stone, brick and glass entailed.

And yet Harry loved it with a passion that he'd never been able to show for her.

The car pulled up in front of the house, its windows glowing in the darkness. The door opened, illuminating the stone steps in front, and the housekeeper came down to greet them.

'Lord Harry, welcome home.' She bowed her head slightly in Jemima's direction. 'Your ladyship.'

'Hello, Teri.' Jemima coolly stalked past their house-keeper into the front hall. Teri had always hated her. They all did – all of the staff who'd worked here since before she and Harry had married. She knew what they thought of her: that she was a flighty, fluff-headed socialite who cared only about fashion, money and parties. They all worshipped at the shrine of Harry's mother, the late viscountess, who'd been an angel on the earth, helping the poor, opening hospitals, raising money for the sick, and, above all, had been loyal to Herne to her very last breath.

Well, they can fuck off, all of them. I'm not changing my ways, especially not for a pack of bolshy servants.

Jemima had less than no interest in acting the lady of the manor. She did what she had to do and then scarpered back to London as fast as she could, back to the life she knew and where she felt secure.

How could she be happy in this huge, draughty, dark house, with a husband who loathed her guts? No way. She remembered one time early in their affair when Harry had brought her to Herne. He'd been showing her round the house when some bell or other had summoned him away. He'd left her in front of a painting of the River Thames at Abingdon and told her to wait there; he'd be right back. She'd lingered for a while in front of the picture, studying every aspect of the old church and the riverside, the swans and the boats.

Then she'd started to become wary of the quiet and gloom, and wondered where on earth she was, and where Harry was, and how she would find him again. She began to walk down the corridor but must have missed a turning somewhere and ended up in a dark, narrow little hallway lined with locked doors. The house became suddenly frightening, menacing. She thought of the people who had once lived in this place, the ghosts that perhaps lingered on, and she began to spook herself. Turning back the way she'd come, she started to run along the corridor, breathless and cold, but found herself again somewhere entirely new, somewhere she hadn't been before.

'Harry! Harry!' she'd cried, almost sobbing. Where was he? Then she'd burst through a heavy red baize door and appeared on the grand walkway above the great marble staircase. She ran down, relieved to recognise her surroundings. She found Harry, talking away to Guy in the estate office. He always forgot the time once he and Guy got talking about all the business of the day. She'd fallen into his arms and he'd hugged her tightly. Burying her face in his neck, she had at once been comforted by his sweet, musky smell, his rough wool jumper holding the scent of bonfires and pine needles. The fear vanished. She was safe again.

Now she knew Herne much better. Although there were plenty of rooms she'd never entered and whole wings she'd only wandered round once, she was unlikely to get lost. But she'd never forgotten how threatened she'd felt that day she lost Harry. Whenever she was at Herne, she could never entirely shake that fear away. It was why she couldn't wait to get back to London.

She went straight to her bedroom. It was the one room in the house that Harry had allowed her to redecorate. She had been given free rein and had indulged herself with creating a simply gorgeous boudoir, and it was now the only room in the whole castle where she felt comfortable. Her vast white bed dominated the room. The stone walls were freshly replastered and painted a soft chalk white, and the ornate plasterwork on the ceiling had been picked out in black, so that it was dramatically accentuated against the white. Her bedroom was part of the original Elizabethan house with walls six feet deep and arched stone windows with tiny, diamond-shaped panes of glass – beautiful but draughty in winter. Thick oatmeal velvet curtains with an oversized purple damask pattern shut out the cold and the icy stone flags on the floor were covered in a pale sisal wool carpet and then finished off with lush white rugs. A chaise longue designed by Philippe Starke curved sensuously at the end of the bed. Jemima had had her pick of the most exquisite antique furniture in the house and her bedside table was a heavy Jacobean carved chest, the contemporary glass and silver lamp on top of it providing a wonderful contrast against the dark wood.

She sat down for a moment in front of her Linley dressing table, a simple piece of sycamore with rosewood stringing and burr ash inlay.

Mixed emotions coursed through her. Today she had buried her mother. Today she had discovered the final twisted trick the old woman had been hiding up her sleeve. Today she had had to face what life might be like without her juicy allowance from Trevellyan.

No. That will never happen! I won't let it!

She stared at her white face and wide blue-grey eyes. Was that fear she could see in them? It couldn't possibly be. Jemima Trevellyan was rarely cowed by anything. She laughed at authority and courted danger. She was a risk-taker, a game player. Wasn't she?

But suppose, for a moment, she lost it all. Suppose she lost the independence that her Trevellyan money gave her . . . what would she be left with? A life at Herne with Harry. No Eaton Square flat to escape to. No more shopping, parties, excitement. Perhaps the press and media, which she had always scorned, would lose interest in her and there would be no more diary pieces or two-page spreads on her fabulous life and celebrity friends. Or worse, perhaps they would write fake sympathy pieces about her fall from grace and publish photographs of her in last season's clothes, shopping in the village without make-up on.

She shuddered.

The worst of all was that if it was all taken away from her, it would be given to Jecca.

Evil, fucking, despicable Jecca, who'd done her best to destroy the family.

Jemima felt her fist clench. *How could Mother have done it? She hated Jecca more than any of us! What made her decide to give her Trevellyan?*

She blinked at her reflection. *But only if we fail,* she reminded herself.

Her iPhone chirruped from her bag. She scrabbled inside and picked it up. Tara's name was illuminated.

'Hello, Tara.'

'Mimi, where are you?'

'Herne.'

'When are you coming back?'

'Tonight, I think.'

'Tonight?' Tara sounded worried. 'It's so late already. Are you going to drive?'

'I was planning to.'

'Mimi, I don't think you should. You've had an incredibly exhausting day; you can't drive from Dorset to London, it's too much for you.'

'You know how I feel about staying here. I can't bear it.'

'I know, darling . . . but really, you can come back first thing tomorrow. What's another twelve hours? You'll be asleep for most of that.'

Jemima thought of the four-hour drive ahead of her and then of the beckoning bed in the mirror behind her. 'All right. I'll stay till tomorrow. But I'll be off first thing.'

'Good. That's what I was ringing you about. We need to meet with the Trevellyan board urgently. I've summoned Victor and his team, and the finance and account directors. We'll meet in the boardroom tomorrow afternoon at four. Can you be there?'

'Darling, all I have is an oxygen-blast facial, very easy to cancel. What about you? Your diary is a tiny bit more difficult, isn't it?'

'Don't worry about that. This is an emergency. Roz

has cancelled everything for me. We have to get this mess sorted out right away.'

'For once, I'm in complete agreement.'

'Good. Poppy will be there too. I'll see you at Trevellyan House tomorrow afternoon.'

'Bye, darling.'

'Bye. Sleep well.'

6

Poppy Trevellyan stood in the middle of the chaos in her bedroom and wondered what on earth she would wear.

She was spoiled for choice, that much was certain. Like her sisters, she adored clothes, but while Tara and Jemima took their pick of the most exclusive designers in the world, Poppy's tastes were somewhat different. Her outfits came from market stalls, second-hand shops, antique markets and junk outlets. She loved the thrill of rifling through a rail or a pile of garments, and discovering the treasure that might lie under a mountain of forgotten nylon and Crimplene.

Who do I want to be today? she wondered. Bearing in mind that she was going to an office, perhaps she ought to be suited in tailored lines and sober tones.

No. I saw enough of that yesterday at the funeral. And Jemima and Tara do suits all the time. I need something else . . .

She began to search through her wardrobe, flicking

through dresses, shirts, skirts and trousers. She found what she was looking for: some tweed shorts, jaunty and sexy with cute little turn-ups. To go with these she found a seventies canary-yellow polo neck and a black swing cardigan fastened with three giant buttons down the left side. To finish it off, she selected her favourite purple patent knee-high boots with stack heels.

When she was dressed, she twirled in front of her long mirror. *Just the thing for a lady of property*, she thought.

She laughed out loud. The very idea that Loxton Hall and everything it contained belonged to her was ridiculous. While all Jemima and Tara worried about were things like the furniture and jewellery, Poppy could only think about the stupid practicalities of the whole thing.

What kind of council tax would she be liable for on a twelve-bedroom Victorian Gothic mansion? She daren't even imagine.

Would she be expected to pay the staff wages? There was Alice, their housekeeper since they were children, and her husband Tony who'd always looked after the maintenance of the house. Then there were various cleaners, the gardeners and the temporary help from the village.

What kind of insurance was required? How often would the drains have to be checked and the radiators siphoned, or whatever it was that happened to radiators?

These silly questions floated into her mind before all the others. But in reality she knew that she would never have much to do with the house. It was part of her mother's contrary nature that she had given it to her youngest daughter, the only one she could be sure didn't really want it, just as she had probably taken pleasure in denying it to Tara, the one who yearned to be acknowledged by their mother, to be given the responsibility for something their mother cared about. As for Jemima – she probably couldn't care less about the house but doubtless wouldn't have minded some more cash and the family diamonds!

Poppy scrunched her dark hair into a loose pony-tail, and finished the look off with some oversized dark glasses.

I know what I'm going to do. As soon as I'm in that boardroom with all those lawyers, I'm simply going to give Loxton back. I don't want the damn house. I've spent my life trying to escape the trappings of the family name and all that it stands for. Mother's not going to force me back now.

Grabbing her vintage Dior pouch bag, she closed the door of her flat and ran quickly down the stairs. The one thing she had allowed her money to buy her was this flat, in an area she couldn't possibly have afforded if she really was the poor artist she pretended to be.

She'd always loved London's Bloomsbury, with its faded Georgian grandeur and atmosphere of creativity and learning. It was the old stomping ground of Virginia Woolf, Dylan Thomas and other literary greats, and it was full of old bookshops and antiquarian print galleries. Close to the British Museum, the British

Library, and university and hospital buildings, it seemed to house the heart of the city's intellect. Its aura of old glamour had a distinctly artistic air, being home to the Courtauld Gallery, the Royal Academy of Dramatic Art, and many distinguished music and literary venues. But it was an extremely expensive place to live. So Poppy had allowed herself to dip into her trust fund far enough to buy a two-storey flat at the top of a Georgian townhouse in an old square built around an enchanting private garden.

The upstairs floor had a spacious attic room with a glass ceiling that let in masses of daylight and Poppy used this as her design studio. She felt that having this work space justified the money she had spent on the basis that she could now begin to achieve her ambition of making her own way in the world without needing to use her famous Trevellyan name.

But it had been four years now since she had graduated from the Royal Academy Art School and she was no closer to finding what she really wanted to do in life. She had studied fine art but after graduating, she'd decided that she didn't want to spend her life painting pictures at an easel. She had flirted with lots of other artistic outlets, and still painted from time to time, but she was drifting.

It didn't help that her painful break-up from Tom, her boyfriend of almost five years, had completely stifled her creativity.

Poppy pulled the front door closed behind her and looked up at the sky. The rain clouds of yesterday had completely vanished and it was a bright, blue spring day. She would walk to Trevellyan House, she decided. She couldn't bear using the Underground on such a beautiful afternoon and she was strict with herself about using taxis too often. It was something she and Tom always used to argue about.

'Why do you bother?' he would say, exasperated. 'Considering how much money you've got, it's ridiculous to say it's expensive.'

'But it is,' Poppy would retort. 'And besides, it's bad for the planet. We're all going to have to get used to using our legs a bit more in the future, so why not start now?'

Tom would grumble about it but he wasn't about to change Poppy's mind. She didn't like the fact that Tom knew about her money. She had managed to keep it quiet all the way through her college course by enrolling as Poppy Thompson. She and Tom had been on the same course and she had noticed him the moment he walked into the art school on their very first day. He had a confidence and air of command about him that attracted her, and she was in awe of his artistic sensitivity. He seemed so knowledgeable for his years and he critiqued her painting in the kind of language that impressed her. She was utterly bowled over, but it wasn't until the second term that they finally got together after a night out pub crawling through Kentish Town. Only after they'd graduated did she finally tell him her real name and the fact that she was worth several million.

Their relationship had never been the same after that. First, there was the awkward issue that she had lied to him – or, at least, not confided in him sooner. Then there was the cold reality of her wealth. It seemed to drain Tom of all his previous generosity towards her. Suddenly, she was expected to pay for everything and not only that, Tom's tastes changed as well. No longer was he happy with breakfast at the local caff. He didn't understand why they couldn't go to the Wolseley and have eggs Benedict and champagne. A wonderful vintage shirt found by Poppy at a market stall was no longer a great birthday present. He wanted something from Paul Smith or Dolce & Gabbana – after all, she could afford it, couldn't she? The happy, balanced nature of their relationship became uneven and tense. Whatever she did irritated and annoyed him, and he was constantly snapping at her. And yet, he said he loved her. He still made love to her, passionately. And she still loved him, just as she always had. But gradually she'd become sure in her heart that there was no future for them.

I always knew my Trevellyan money would kill something beautiful, she thought bitterly. *And now it has.*

Tom had not taken the news well. He had become addicted to the luxuries her wealth could provide, just as she had feared, and he didn't want it taken away from him. Eventually, after trying to persuade her to come back to him, he'd turned on her in anger.

'If you hate your bloody money so much, why don't you stop bloody well whining about it and give it away!' he'd yelled, red-faced.

'Don't you think I want to?' she shouted back. 'It's not that easy. It's all in trusts and controlled by lawyers and directors and my parents. I can't just give it away. Perhaps one day, when I've got more control, I'll be able to. Until then, there's not much I can do about it.'

'Oh *poor* little rich girl!' sneered Tom, his eyes scornful. 'My heart bleeds for you. You know what I think? You're a fucking hypocrite. You could just walk away from it all if you really wanted to. But you like pretending to be better than it all, pretending you despise money, but actually it's there for you like a lovely big feather bed, ready for you to fall on when things get tough.'

His words stabbed her like a knife but she remained calm, her voice only trembling slightly. She stood up resolutely. 'I'm sorry, Tom. It's over. If I didn't really think so before now, you've definitely made me sure. Goodbye.' With that she walked out, leaving him fuming impotently, while she hid the tears behind her sunglasses, hitched the handles of her bag over her shoulder and left with her head held high.

That was over a year ago. She'd heard from mutual friends that Tom was going out with someone else now. An American girl called Chandler or Chelsea or something. Apparently her daddy was someone powerful in Washington and exorbitantly rich, so Tom had obviously got a taste for girls with money. Perhaps she would make him very happy by spending all her money on him, or just handing him armfuls of cash.

Poppy went down the stairs of her building, thinking hard. Last week, when she'd heard the news about her mother, she'd felt as though she were on the verge of collapse. It was yet another blow, after losing Tom and feeling that her creative juices were drying up. She'd begun to wonder how much more she could take.

Now this extraordinary bequest had landed on her – not just the house, but the business as well. No matter how bad she felt, she was going to have to summon all her strength and deal with it.

Feeling as though she were on the brink of something unknown, Poppy walked out of the elegant Georgian square and headed west.

7

London might be one of the most expensive cities in the world to live in, but Poppy still loved it. Every time she walked through it, she was seduced again by its charm. Yes, it was noisy, dirty and crowded, and there were buildings of such hideous monstrosity that she could only hope future generations would forgive their creation. But it was so rich in beauty and history and glamour that it would take more than a few nasty steel and concrete horrors to dent its attraction.

Leaving behind the faded delights of Bloomsbury, she headed towards the more affluent part of town. Skirting Oxford Street with its High Street chains – although admittedly the biggest and most impressive versions – and throngs of tourists and shoppers, she veered towards Marylebone, with its chic little shops and boutiques and trendy bars and restaurants. She liked this part of town and might have lived here if the Bloomsbury garden square hadn't taken her heart first. She wandered down past Harley Street and

Wimpole Street and crossed Oxford Street almost at Marble Arch. Now she was heading into Mayfair, where every car was a giant SUV, a sleek black Daimler or a jaunty Porsche, and where the streets seemed to smell of money. Here, although Poppy did not feel she belonged, she was certainly less conspicuous. Trustafarians with bank accounts at least as big as hers mooched about, wondering what to spend their money on today. Russian wives with bright blonde hair and excessive fur coats climbed into chauffeured Rolls Royces, off to spend more of their husbands' billions in Harrods and Harvey Nichols. Short men with gold jewellery and suits whose vast expense could still not conceal the size of their bellies trotted from glossy black front door to glossy silver Lamborghini and Poppy knew that their money made her inheritance look like a drop in the ocean.

Trevellyan House was in the exclusive area of Mayfair just before Piccadilly. Here could be found the kind of shops that only those in the know frequented, such as Thomas Goode, the exclusive china and glass shop that had been making fine china and porcelain for the crowned heads of Europe since the seventeenth century, or Purdey, where dukes and earls and all manner of gentry bought guns and hunting gear. Here were the galleries exhibiting old masters for sale; the most exquisite Persian rugs, held up like paintings for their superb workmanship, texture and colour to be admired; jewellery, glittering in the windows of the most expensive shops in the world. In nearby Bond Street were the famous fashion names: Chanel, Tiffany,

Gucci, Versace, Prada, Ralph Lauren, Asprey and a host of others. On the more discreet streets of Mayfair, luxurious boutique hotels nestled next to the kind of shops that cater to the needs of the very rich. And here was Trevellyan House, the hub of the Trevellyan empire, one of the last great luxury brands to remain in private hands.

On the ground floor was the shop. It was not the original Piccadilly barber shop that Samuel Trevellyan had walked into over a hundred and fifty years before – as Trevellyan fragrances had begun to grow in fame, the premises had quickly become too small and this large Mayfair house had been purchased. On the ground floor was the shop, a beautiful room where the many fragrances, soaps, oils and accessories were displayed in walnut cabinets. The polished floorboards were covered in dark red Turkish rugs while leather armchairs and a Chesterfield club sofa gave the clients somewhere to rest while they absorbed the delights of the Trevellyan fragrances and made their choices. Lamps and antique mirrors created a subdued, elegant atmosphere.

On the floor above had been the old workrooms, where the fragrances had been made by hand. Once, there had been long tables where white-coated craftsmen followed Farnese's recipes to conjure up the delicious aromas used to scent the perfumes, oils and soaps sold downstairs. Now all of that had been moved to a factory in the Midlands where bottles were filled and packaged on a conveyor belt, then boxed up and sent to destinations all over the world.

The shop was just as Poppy had always remembered it. It had never changed – still as scrupulously tasteful and as quietly restful as a gentlemen's club. She looked in for a moment before heading upstairs to the Trevellyan offices where the real action took place. Despite its importance in her life, she had only visited Trevellyan House a few times, mostly when she was young and her mother had brought them all to London on a shopping trip. They'd come by to visit her father in his imposing office where he sat behind a vast leather-topped desk, making what seemed to young Poppy to be terrifyingly important decisions. That was all she knew of Trevellyan House, apart from the odd glimpse of the boardroom, with its long table and stiff-backed chairs.

She walked into the reception area, noting the oil portrait of old Sam Trevellyan, in his high collar and black coat, a pair of fearsome sideburns descending his face. Opposite was a more modern oil sketch of her father, catching him in three-quarter profile, his mouth downturned and his blue eyes a little bulbous. He did not look happy to have inherited Samuel's success story.

He never looked happy, Poppy thought sadly. *I wonder if he and Mummy are together now?*

She felt a pang of affection as she looked at her father's face. He may not have been the perfect father, but she'd still loved him. Her earliest memories were of his distance and inapproachability; for a while when she was very little, she'd thought that the nanny was her real mother and that her parents were some kind of owners of the house whom she had to be nice to. Of course, she'd realised soon enough that Cecil and Yolanda were her father and mother, but for years she received little affection from them in comparison to what the nanny gave her. That quickly changed after Poppy's illness. She'd become the favourite from then on, and was given a lot more attention by both her parents. While Cecil was never exactly demonstrative, she'd come to realise that he loved his daughters dearly. In return, she had loved and trusted him. He became a source of support when relations with Yolanda grew strained as the girls became teenagers.

His real failing, thought Poppy, looking up at the portrait, was that he hadn't been able to hold the family together. He hadn't been able to save them from Jecca.

Poppy approached the desk. The receptionist behind it raised her eyebrows. 'Yes?' she said frostily, eying Poppy's shorts and patent boots. 'Can I help you?'

Poppy took off her sunglasses. 'I'm Poppy Trevellyan. I believe I'm expected?'

The receptionist leapt to her feet, flustered. 'Yes, yes, of course, welcome, Miss Trevellyan. Lady Calthorpe and Mrs Pearson are already here. Please follow me and I'll show you to the boardroom.'

Poppy followed her along a corridor and into the boardroom. Tara was sitting at one end, poring over some files, while Jemima was standing at the window talking quietly into the phone she had jammed to her ear. Victor Goldblatt was rifling through papers in his briefcase and other lawyers and directors were sitting about sipping coffee and chatting discreetly among themselves. Poppy noticed a striking young man who she remembered seeing chatting to Jemima at the wake. So he was a Trevellyan man. She'd assumed he was one of her sister's society pals. He wasn't cut from the usual Trevellyan business cloth, that was for sure.

Tara looked up. 'Darling, you're here. Wonderful. Now we can start. Would you like some water or coffee or something?'

'I'm fine, thanks.' Poppy put her bag down on the table and sank into a chair.

'As soon as Mimi's off the phone, we can begin,' Tara said, standing up and shuffling some papers. She was looking quietly chic as usual. Poppy knew that Tara was a favourite with her personal shoppers not only because money was no object but because her skinny frame made clothes look fabulous on her. Today she was wearing an Alberta Ferretti black wool tulip skirt that only someone with fantastic legs could carry off. She'd teamed it with black Chanel heels and an ivory silk blouse with a hint of padded shoulder, giving her a strong, businesslike silhouette.

Jemima, meanwhile, had obviously had enough of dressing up and was wearing dark Paul & Joe jeans, a cashmere striped T-shirt and a vintage YSL jacket in navy blue, along with a big pair of Tom Ford sunglasses. There was a tension about her that made it seem as though something might be wrong. She finished her call and dropped her phone into her bag, a yolk-yellow oversized clutch.

'Right,' she said, turning to the table. 'Oh, you're here, Poppy. Good. Perhaps we can get started. I've driven all the way from Dorset this morning, and had to cancel a very hard-to-get appointment with Dr Thraksi, so I'd like to get on with things.'

'Very well,' said Victor Goldblatt smoothly, looking at her over the top of his glasses. 'Please sit down, Lady Calthorpe, and we'll begin.'

The three sisters sat next to each other along one side of the conference table, facing the solemn-faced, suited men on the other.

One of the elderly men Poppy had also seen at the funeral cleared his throat and began to talk. 'I'm afraid I don't have the pleasure of knowing you ladies very well. I've met Mrs Pearson' – he bowed to Tara – 'but not you, Lady Calthorpe, or you, Miss Trevellyan. So I think some introductions may be in order. You know Victor Goldblatt, of course, the head of Goldblatt Mindenhall, whose relationship with Trevellyan goes back many years. They have ably represented and advised us for a long while. With him is Ali Tendulka, a very talented young lawyer who has recently joined Goldblatt Mindenhall and whom we are very happy to have as part of our team.'

So that's who he is, Poppy thought. *Not really Trevellyan after all.* She noticed that Ali Tendulka was glancing over at Jemima, who didn't seem to be aware of him at all.

The older man continued, 'On my left here is Simon

Vestey, the head of finance and to his left is our accounts director, Paul Glanville. Also, on my right, from our marketing and sales departments, William McKay and Ian Kendall. Our head of publicity hasn't been able to join us today unfortunately.'

As their names were mentioned, each man murmured and nodded.

It's like the war of the sexes, thought Poppy. *Typical for a boardroom to be full of men.*

'Simply lovely to meet you all,' said Jemima in a smooth voice, the kind that Poppy recognised as meaning trouble. 'The only thing is – who the hell are *you*?' She pulled off her glasses and eyed the old man at the head of the table with a steely grey gaze.

'Of course, of course, I should have said at once. I'm Duncan Ingliss, the managing director of Trevellyan.'

'The man in charge.' Jemima stared at him, twirling her glasses between her thumb and forefinger.

'Yes, my dear. It has been an honour to navigate this splendid old company through the last two decades.' He smiled condescendingly at Jemima. 'I hope you will see fit not to rock the boat and to allow me to continue at the helm of this dear old girl, as your father would have wanted.'

'Well, Mr Ingliss, I'm sure you're more than well aware by now that our *mother* clearly did not want any such arrangement and consequently this ship has just got a new captain. Three captains, to be precise. So, you'd better forget about steering anything and tell us exactly what's going on, because I, for one, want to know why on earth we'd suddenly be expected to take over the running of a company that's supposedly doing so well under its current management!'

Poppy bit her lip, realising suddenly that Jemima had just put in a nutshell what had been bothering her since the reading of the will. This task could not possibly be an easy one, or what was the point of setting it? She felt a tingle of panic as she considered that it might not just be difficult – it might be nigh on impossible.

Tara shot Jemima a warning look. 'This has come as quite a shock to all of us,' she said calmly. 'As far as we understand it from the terms of our mother's will, we are now joint chairmen and chief executives of Trevellyan.'

'That is correct,' Victor put in.

'Well, there are several questions that come to mind at once, not least what our financial liabilities are in respect of this inheritance . . .'

'We have the company accountant here,' interrupted Ingliss. 'I'm sure he can answer any questions that you have.'

'Well, I'm not an inheritance tax expert,' said Paul Glanville, looking nervous. 'I'm mainly concerned with the financial aspects of Trevellyan on a day-to-day basis . . .' He trailed off under the pressure of Jemima's expectant glare.

Tara seemed impatient. 'Look, we all know that there are breaks on capital gains tax for businesses who are restructuring. I'm sure there are plenty of ways that stock can be reassigned in order to maximise efficiency. But my question is whether the company counts as part of my mother's estate or not.'

Much to Paul Glanville's obvious relief, Victor Goldblatt leaned forward to respond. 'The intricacies of your mother's personal affairs were looked after by Sebastian Fenwick. He is joining us later. I've already discussed the matter with Sebastian, and he has told me that tax will not be an issue here. The requisite trusts and offshore holding companies were set up years ago to make sure that liabilities would be limited. Besides which, you and your sisters have been directors of Trevellyan for some significant time.'

'We have?' Jemima looked startled.

'Yes, indeed. You receive an annual package of salary and share options and bonuses. Each of you joined the board of Trevellyan on your twenty-first birthdays.'

'You mean that piece of paper Daddy got me to sign in the library?' asked Poppy. She looked puzzled. 'He didn't say anything about my becoming a director of the company.'

'Or me,' said Jemima, frowning. 'He told me it was in order that I could get my cash, but not that I'd be a director.'

'I knew,' Tara said quietly. 'At least, I knew I was a director. He had to tell me, when I was made a partner at Curzons. I had to be aware of my professional position so that I could declare any possible conflicts of interest.'

'You knew and you didn't tell us?' Jemima turned to her sister.

'Well, I knew about me . . . I wasn't sure about you.

Besides, what did it matter? As far as I was concerned, it was simply a standard procedure to keep tax liabilities down and smooth the way for the Trevellyan money to come to us. I had no idea it was ever going to have any significance.'

'What did you think would happen when Mummy and Daddy died?' Poppy demanded, her face flushing as she realised all too late that they were on the brink of sounding like a bickering, childish threesome. She could feel the patronising condescension of the businessmen opposite.

'I don't know.' Tara's voice faltered. 'I suppose I left it to them to make the decisions. After all, they never asked my advice or told me anything about the company.'

Jemima stared down at the table and said, 'I don't know how I feel about having been a director without knowing it.'

'Your parents didn't wish to bother you with the daily intricacies of running a company,' Ingliss said, clearly enjoying how quickly Jemima had fallen off her high horse.

'Well, they've damn well bothered me with it now,' Jemima snapped. 'The reality is, Mr Ingliss, that it falls to us to increase Trevellyan's sales, and not just increase them, but triple them in one calendar year, or the tap stops running, just like that. So I'd like to know exactly what the position here at Trevellyan is. What kind of mountain are we facing?'

Ingliss looked over at his finance director, who coughed and stood up.

'Ladies, I'm Simon Vestey and I'm going to give you a quick overview of the current status of Trevellyan. Could we dim the lights please?'

The lights were lowered. A wooden panel on the back wall slid smoothly away to reveal a plasma screen which instantly lit up. The word 'Trevellyan' appeared in the trademark flowing gold script on a dark blue background and a rush of romantic violin strings soared upwards.

'Trevellyan,' breathed a female voice in an American accent. 'The home of luxurious fragrance for more than one hundred and fifty years.'

A montage of film followed, lingering lovingly on the Mayfair shop and its gentlemanly good taste.

'For decades, connoisseurs have come to Trevellyan for the most sumptuous scents and exclusive grooming accessories in the world,' purred the narrator. 'From its birth in a Piccadilly barber shop in 1848 to today's international success story' – there were shots of Trevellyan concessions in the celebrated department stores of London, Paris, New York and Tokyo – 'Trevellyan has always been a byword for quality. Favoured by royalty and stars alike, it is one of the most recognised and admired brands in the world of luxury.'

A bottle of *Trevellyan's Tea Rose* appeared on a plain blue background. The narrator began to talk about the history of the perfume and its long life as a favourite scent across the world.

'For Christ's sake, turn this crap off, *please!*' Jemima jumped to her feet. Someone flicked off the film and the lights came up. 'Spare me the goddamn PowerPoint presentation! Do you think we don't know this shit? It's been drummed into us since birth.'

Ingliss smiled and made a soothing gesture. 'Now, now, Lady Calthorpe, please keep calm. Of course, you have more reason than any of us to know about the great heritage of Trevellyan. I simply wanted to make the point that we too, the current board and team of directors, know and understand the brand as well as you do. I want to reassure you that it is in safe hands and that we are going to do all we can to make sure that sales continue to rise. Of course, the increase you're talking about it is . . . hmm . . . well, I'll make no bones about it – it's ambitious. It'll be a momentous achievement for us all. But I'm confident that we can do it, and that Trevellyan will remain in family hands for a good many years to come. Now, if you'll let Simon continue, he has some excellent results to share with us.'

Sensing that Jemima was about to take no further nonsense from Ingliss, Tara quickly stood up too. 'Now, now, gentlemen,' she said coolly. 'I hope you aren't going to underestimate us.'

There was a pause as the businessmen exchanged glances.

'What on earth do you mean?' Ingliss stared up at the two sisters, his eyebrows raised, his expression disingenuous.

'I'm not sure exactly what you know about us but I'm a partner in Curzons Private Equities. I manage a portfolio worth billions of pounds. I'm used to analysing companies and their markets, and I'm used to following my instinct and betting on winners. That's why Curzons is one of the leading hedge fund managers in the world. Now my sisters and I came here today to get a lucid picture of the state of Trevellyan. We all know my mother was not about to ask us to raise the sales of this company by a wildly astronomical figure if the company was doing just fine. I want to know about the bottom line and I want to know about it now. I don't expect to be fed a load of corporate PR bullshit. Do you understand?'

She sat down gracefully and cocked her head expectantly. Jemima followed her example, sitting down and fixing the directors with her best icy stare. Duncan Ingliss looked uncomfortable. 'Of course, Mrs Pearson,' he said, and coughed. 'In that case, I'll ask Ian to report on sales.'

Ian Kendall nodded importantly, his bald head glimmering in the boardroom light. He blinked at the women sitting opposite him.

'No fucking PowerPoint, please,' muttered Jemima. 'Just tell it like it is.'

'Yes, yes, of course. Now . . .' He shuffled papers in front of him and then fingered his tie nervously. 'Right. OK, the overall sales position this year appears to be . . . er . . . continuing the trend we observed last year in that . . . er . . . well, home sales have followed the . . . um . . . current fashion in a year-on-year decline and export sales have also suffered owing to the strength of the pound against other major world currencies, particularly in our core markets of the United States, Europe and Japan. So . . . um, overall, the current picture is . . . disappointing.'

'How disappointing?' snapped Tara.

'We're not making a loss, are we?' asked Jemima disbelievingly.

Ian Kendall shuffled some more papers. 'Um . . . no. No, we're not making a loss but . . . well, further significant cutbacks will be necessary, perhaps in our operational costs and overheads, if we're . . . um . . . if we're to stay in the game.'

There was a long silence as the sisters absorbed the news.

'You'll have to excuse me,' said Poppy in a small voice. 'I really don't understand how business works. Are you saying that things are bad? That Trevellyan isn't selling any more?'

'It looks like it, Poppy,' said Tara. 'I'll need to examine the figures in detail but the kind of language our head of sales here is using is not what you hear when the pie is full of cherries.'

There was a movement at the side of the board-room table. It was Ali Tendulka, leaning back in his chair. 'May I interrupt for a second?'

All eyes turned to him. He let them stare at him for a long moment. His dark brown eyes met Jemima's surprised gaze for an instant – they both knew that she had been studiously ignoring him but now she was forced to acknowledge him – then he said, 'Gentlemen, when I was brought in by Victor to work on the Trevellyan account, I made it my business to do some very thorough research. And I mean, thorough. I'm fully aware of the situation this company finds itself in and I suggest you stop dicking these ladies around and start putting them in the picture. Because if you won't, I will.'

The tension in the room ratcheted up several notches as Ali's words sank in. The sisters glanced at each other. Only Tara appeared calm and unruffled. Jemima looked bewildered and Poppy scared. Ingliss took off his spectacles and began to rub them with a soft cloth. 'Very well. We won't beat about the bush, ladies . . .'

'You're not beating anything near *my* bush,' murmured Jemima under her breath.

'. . . things are looking difficult for Trevellyan. In fact, we have been seeing a pattern of decline for some years now. Even while your father was in charge, it was evident that the world was changing and that it was turning its back on Trevellyan. Things are even worse now. Your mother did all she could to keep the company going, and there are still lucrative sales pockets in our global market. But here, sales are down forty per cent on last year. We can carry on supplying our core market but we are unlikely to see any further growth, as things stand. In those terms, the brand is almost dead.'

'Dead?' echoed Jemima.

'What does that mean, exactly?' demanded Tara. 'And how has the company managed to last so long if it was in decline when our father was alive?'

'Simple. Trevellyan owned sites in some of the most exclusive premium retail areas in the world. We have sold them off, one by one, as and when we needed a cash injection. That is why there are no longer any

Trevellyan shops – bar the one we are sitting above, of course. We moved to concessions. We are stocked in the best department stores in the world, and have luxury outlets in most major airports. We cut our overheads massively that way. There have also been substantial cost-cutting exercises here at headquarters and at the factory.'

'And yet . . .' Tara frowned and tapped a pen on her notebook. 'Yet there was always enough money for shareholders? Enough money for us? Our mother never hinted in the slightest that our financial interest in Trevellyan might be under threat.'

'Your mother made sure that your allowances, bonuses and dividends were always paid,' Duncan said gravely. 'Even when the company could ill afford it. I believe she also disposed of substantial private assets – some investments, and property here and abroad. Some jewellery and furniture.'

Tara looked shocked but she said nothing.

Jemima had turned white-faced and her hands were shaking. 'Exactly when were you planning to tell us all this, if Ali and Tara hadn't wormed it out of you? What's your role in this decline?' Her voice began to rise. 'I want some fucking answers!'

'Mimi, stay calm, please. It won't help. Can't you see what Mother's done? We'll talk about it later. There's plenty of time for that. But first I want to hear as much about our current position as I can.' Tara pointed her Montblanc fountain pen at Simon Vestey. 'You can go first. I want a full briefing on current staffing, product costs, sales, marketing spend and a market analysis. And if you haven't got this to hand, I'll want a comprehensive overview of the entire company sent to me by tomorrow lunchtime at the latest. Understand?'

The men nodded. They seemed subdued by Tara's businesslike tone.

'Good. Then let's get started.'

8

'Where are we going to go?' Poppy pulled her cardigan about her more tightly against the cool spring wind gusting down the Mayfair street. The three sisters stood on the pavement outside Trevellyan House.

'Back to my place,' Jemima said. 'It's closest. We can hail a cab.'

'Oh, blast.' Tara was examining her BlackBerry. 'I've been emailed and called about a million times by Roz. I need to get back to the office.'

Jemima said crossly, 'No, Tara. You can't just leave us. We have to deal with this, and we have to deal with it now. Didn't you hear what they said to us in there? This is serious!'

Tara stared at her sister, frustrated. 'I know the most pressing thing in your life is whether or not you've made it to the top of the waiting list for another Birkin bag, but some of us actually work for a living and I have responsibilities elsewhere. I have to go. Anyway, I don't know what the hell we have to talk about until they get me that company information. Without that, we'll just be flailing about in the dark.'

'I can think of a few choice things we could mull over,' replied Jemima tartly. She shot Tara a look as if to warn her not to start pulling rank. Tara might be the oldest but Jemima had always been the natural leader. Biting remarks and sarcasm came naturally to her, and she readily used her wit and sharp tongue to put her sisters in their place. If Tara had academic brilliance and Poppy had artistic skill, then Jemima had decided she would turn herself into a beauty. But she was no airhead. She wanted to be the only kind of beauty who counted: a gorgeous girl with a bright mind. She might not be the most educated of the sisters, but there was no way she lagged behind them in intelligence.

Tara sighed and buttoned her Miu Miu coat, slipping her BlackBerry into her handbag. 'I don't want to fight. One thing's for certain, we have to be united over this. We've got enough people against us without adding each other to the list.'

'What do you mean?' Poppy asked fearfully. Her large green eyes widened. 'Who's against us?'

'No one, no one. Come on, Pops. You come home with me. We'll have some tea and try to start making sense of this mess.' Jemima grabbed her sister's hand.

'All right. We'll talk later. There's a chance I'll be home in time to see the children. Then I'll have to catch up with what I've missed today. Then I'll call you.' Tara saw a taxi trundling towards them, its light glowing. Without a moment's hesitation, she'd hailed the black cab and called out 'Bye!' over a tense shoulder as she retreated into the taxi.

Jemima's flat in Eaton Square was her favourite place in the whole world. It was where she felt entirely at home and entirely relaxed.

She had bought it not long after returning from her finishing school in Gstaad, an idea of her mother's that she had gone along with under threat of losing her allowance if she didn't. Although she had moaned horribly at the whole idea of leaving England, she had at first enjoyed her time in Switzerland, skiing and learning various ladylike arts alongside the daughters of various other European, American and Middle Eastern wealthy and titled families. By the time her first year was up, however, she was already bored. Most of the girls there were prim and proper, only concerned with the correct way of getting in and out of a sports cars and plotting who they should marry with the help of the Forbes rich list and the Almanac de Gotha, the index of the titled families of Europe. Jemima didn't care about that. By the end of her two years she was longing to cut loose and desperate to get back to London, where everything seemed to be happening. For the Gstaad girls, the height of naughtiness was sneaking out at night to the local nightclub where they drank white wine and were chatted up by the ski bums and ski instructors. It was all too tame for Jemima. She knew instinctively that London had much more adventure and excitement to offer her.

Coming back at the ripe old age of twenty, she had

at first shared a flat with some of her finishing-school friends but it became increasingly tedious. Her friendship with them quickly ebbed as they busied themselves with trying to fill in time before they met the billionaires they were going to marry. Most of them signed up to art or design courses and took them terribly seriously, staying in and going to bed early during the week so they wouldn't be too tired to study and attend lectures the following day. Jemima couldn't understand it. They had more money than they could ever spend, along with youth and good looks. Why weren't they having more fun?

She decided she needed her independence. When she found a flat for sale in Eaton Square, she made up her mind to have it the moment the estate agent mentioned the exclusive address and the walk-in wardrobe. It was far more money than she had available so she'd had to go to her father for funds. With a winning mixture of cajoling, pleading and explaining what an excellent long-term investment it was, she had got her way, as she usually did. The day she collected the keys, she had spun happily about the empty flat, squealing with excitement, unable to believe it was really hers to do whatever she wanted with.

The flat had seen some wild nights since that day. Through her roaring early twenties there had been no shortage of extraordinary parties, some lasting three or four days. Famous actors and actresses, musicians, models, playboys, princes and lords had all enjoyed the hospitality of the Eaton Square flat at some point. The young rich had flocked there, along with the newly famous or the just extraordinary: a grungy band from some Camden pub where Jemima and her friends had spent a drunken afternoon; artists; waiters and chefs from their favourite restaurants, pressed into coming back 'to carry on the party'; even the odd waif and stray from the street. Anyone was welcome. Huge quantities of drugs and alcohol were consumed, a great deal of sex was had, hearts were broken, friendships were made and dissolved and tragedies were narrowly averted, like the time when one of Jemima's friends, drunk almost to the point of blindness, simply climbed over the third-floor balcony and plummeted to the ground below. He had been so drunk that he'd fallen without tension, and had been lucky enough to land on a pile of bin bags left out for the rubbish men the following day. He'd broken both legs but lived to tell the tale.

It was not long after she moved into Eaton Square that she first caught the attention of the press, who had discovered a new appetite for beautiful young heiresses who seemed to live a gilded life. The media was hungry for details about Jemima and her friends, but fortunately no one ever gave away what really went on behind the doors of Eaton Square. The worst the paparazzi ever managed to snap were photos of the weary-eyed party-goers finally stumbling out of Jemima's building.

Of course, once she became a respectable married woman, the wild parties stopped almost completely.

Jemima and Poppy rose sedately to the third floor in the antique cast-iron lift, then Jemima opened the glossy red front door and led Poppy in.

'Sri? Are you here?' Jemima dropped her coat over the hall chair.

'Yes, Miss Jemima?' Sri appeared from the kitchen, wiping her hands on her apron.

'Could we have some tea, please? Thanks so much.' She went before Poppy into a grand, high-ceilinged sitting room. Three sets of French windows opened out on to a white balcony that gave a magnificent view of the garden at the centre of the square, which was in the heart of Belgravia, London's most exclusive postcode. Opposite Jemima's building was a mirror image of vast, white stuccoed mansions, most divided up into elegant flats; a few, owned by those whose wealth began in the hundreds of millions, were still houses.

Jemima had not long ago redecorated the flat and had spared no expense. She had had enough of Victorian Gothic at Loxton, and found her mother's penchant for silks, satins and ribbons sickly. She equally disliked Herne Castle which was a bona fide country house: shabby, dark, full of fabrics, textures, paintings and patterns, no wall left uncovered, no window unswagged, no table without a clutter of photographs, vases, bibelots and lamps. Jemima just couldn't bear that typically English old-fashioned décor any longer – it was too unchanging, too stuck in the past. She yearned for space, light and simplicity. When the flat, battered by all the high living and wild parties, had started to look worn out, she'd taken the opportunity to embrace the beauty of contemporary style and living.

The sitting room was her favourite room: welcoming,

restful and calm. The pale walls had only one or two carefully chosen paintings. Some beautiful black and white photographs in stark black frames ran along the far wall opposite the windows. One long grey velvet sofa faced a plain white one across an enormous glass coffee table on a white Mongolian sheepskin rug. The basic monochrome colours were lifted by small splashes of colour: a row of lily-green cushions, a red cashmere throw, a giant dark jade glass vase spilling pale hydrangea heads.

'Sit down, darling.' Jemima kicked off her shoes and relaxed on to the grey velvet sofa, tucking her feet up under her. 'Sri's bringing us tea, although I don't know about you but I could do with something a bit stronger. I'm feeling distinctly shaken up.'

'I'm afraid most of it went over my head.' Poppy sat down at the other end of the sofa, easing her patent boots off and rubbing her toes which were now throbbing from all the walking she'd done that day.

'We'll have to wait for Tara to give us her expert opinion, I've got no more of a business brain than you have. But even I can see that it's all looking pretty terrible.' Jemima looked sombre for once. 'I've teased you for years for trying to live without the family money – but now it seems as if you might have been the clever one all along. If what that Ingliss man said is true, we might have to get used to surviving without.' She frowned and shook her head. 'You know, I really can't believe it. We've been living in a dream world. Our parents have conned us – they've conned the whole world. Everyone thinks we are vastly rich heiresses –

that's what *we* thought we were – when the truth is, they've been selling every asset the company owns just to keep the façade going.'

'But can Trevellyan really be in so much trouble?' Poppy said wonderingly. 'I still see our perfumes everywhere, in all the best shops.'

'That doesn't mean people are buying them. Tell me the truth –' Jemima leaned forward and stared her sister in the eye. 'Would *you* buy *Trevellyan's Tea Rose*? Or *Vintage Lavender*? Or *Antique Lily*? If you had one, would you buy your boyfriend *Leather & Willow*?'

There was a long pause. Poppy looked down at her hands.

'No. I thought not. I wouldn't buy it either. It's grandma stuff, isn't it? It's what you picture soft-cheeked old ladies dabbing behind their ears and on their wrists before they go out to their bridge club. That's who I imagined was still buying it. But maybe all the old ladies and gentlemen who used to buy that stuff are dying out – and no one is taking their place.'

'But the US . . . Japan . . . Europe . . .' Poppy stammered.

'Yes, yes, it's been drummed into us how much everyone abroad loves our stuff. But do they really? Of course, there'll always be people who buy something because it's got the Royal Warrant on it – and thank God the Prince of Wales still likes *Chatsworth* or whatever it is he orders by the bucket load. But will that keep us going? Just look at what we're up against!'

'What?'

'The major luxury brands, of course. And think

about it – every actress and Z-list celebrity is launching their own scent nowadays. Britney Spears or whoever is just the start of it – there's competition like never before. No wonder Trevellyan is going down the pan. You know, now I think about it, I can't believe how I ever believed it would go on being the golden goose it has been for so long.' Jemima sat back, her eyes glittering. Then she jumped up. 'Come on. Come with me.' She pulled Poppy to her feet.

'Where are we going?'

'You'll see.' She led the way out of the sitting room, down the corridor and into her bedroom. From there, she went to her bathroom and opened the door. 'Look in there. What can you see?'

Poppy stepped into the room tentatively, almost as though she expected someone nasty to jump out at her. She looked about at the mermaid-blue mosaic tiles, the power shower, and the curved freestanding copper bath. 'Your bathroom?' she hazarded.

'No shit. But what do you see?'

'The bath . . . the lights . . .'

Jemima huffed impatiently. 'For goodness' sake, Poppy, I know you're an artist and therefore lost in a fog of creativity, but is there any need to be so dense? What have I got on my shelf and in my cupboard? Look, I'll give you a clue . . .' She marched over to her bath and pointed to the inset shelf. 'Origins, Liz Earle, Clarins, Clinique, Benefit, Dr Sebagh, Aveda. Now, in my cupboard . . .' She went to the twin copper sinks and pressed a hidden spring in the surround of the mirror above them. It obediently sprang open and revealed a cornucopia of the most expensive cosmetics in the world: Crème de la mer, Dr Hauschka, Bliss, La Prairie, SK-II and other high-end brands. 'Let me know when you spot anything with Trevellyan on it.'

Poppy turned to look at her anxiously. 'You're right. But you're different, you can afford anything you like.'

Jemima shook her head. 'Everyone is aspirational these days. No woman thinks "Oh, I'm only good enough for a supermarket own-brand, I'll leave all the good stuff to the rich." She thinks "I'm worth it" – it's been drummed into her enough times. She wants to be Keira Knightley wearing *Chanel N° 5* or Eva Green wearing *Midnight Poison* or Kate Winslet wearing *Trésor*. She doesn't have any reason to want to wear Trevellyan, particularly not *Trevellyan's Tea Rose* which she probably sees in her granny's cabinet. And as for being rich – well, you may not be able to afford a Mercedes or an Yves Saint Laurent crocodile handbag, or a house in Kensington – but you can sure as hell afford a bottle of perfume.'

'When you put it like that . . .' Poppy leaned back against the wall. 'Oh, God, what are we going to do?'

'We're going to have a struggle on our hands, that much is for sure.' Jemima looked thoughtful. 'But there's no reason why we can't give it our best shot. Come on, let's go and have our tea. You never know when inspiration will strike. Anyway, I can't believe it's really as awful as Tara and those old boardroom codgers seem to think it is. Everything will be fine, I'm sure.'

9

Tara shut her office door with a sigh. It was going on eight o'clock – not a late night by City standards but she usually tried to get away by six-thirty at the latest. The meeting at Trevellyan had completely screwed her day up and her usual clockwork arrangements had gone out the window.

Roz's chair was empty and her desk deserted. Tara depended utterly on her assistant, and luckily Roz was a gem. She was reliable and loyal. *What would I do without her?* she wondered. A black mood of depression had settled on her.

I'm not going to see the children, she thought wistfully. One thing that kept her going through every day was the thought of getting home in the evening to see her babies. Edward was almost five now, and Imogen was just three. Although Robina, the nanny, was a stickler for routine and for children being in bed by seven o'clock, Tara had managed to persuade her to keep the children up and let them start their bath at seven.

It meant that she would have to speed down to the car at six-thirty, hoping that her driver could make it back across London, through the rush-hour traffic, to her Holland Park house in time for Edward and Imogen's bath. Her driver was superb and knew exactly how to guide the long sleek Mercedes through the traffic, overtaking, undertaking and using bus lanes (goodness knew how many fines they'd had for that) in order to get Tara home.

Then she'd run up to the nursery bathroom where the children would be splashing together, putting bubbles on each other's heads and squealing with pleasure. She'd get down on the floor and no matter what designer dress or shirt she was wearing, she'd roll up her sleeves and start playing with them.

All too soon, Robina would appear with the towels strictly commanding, 'It's time for bed, children.'

But Tara would always take over for the bedtime routine. Drying them, dressing them in their pyjamas, scrubbing their teeth, reading them a story and tucking them into bed. Often, she would linger in their bedroom, sitting in the armchair watching the children until sleep finally overcame them, unable to tear herself away from the peaceful comfort these moments allowed her. She only ever saw them fleetingly in the mornings, when Robina brought them down to breakfast just before she dashed out for an early boardroom meeting, so these bedtime hours with the children were precious to her – they were all she got until the weekend.

Tonight, she wouldn't even get that.

Her driver was waiting for her in the company car park, leaning against the car and reading a newspaper. When he saw her, he hastily threw it into the passenger seat, put on his cap and opened the back door for her.

'Thanks, John. Sorry to keep you waiting.'

'No problem, ma'am. I'll try to get you home asap. Maybe there's still a chance you'll be able to see your kiddies.'

Tara smiled wanly. 'They'll be fast asleep, I'm afraid.' She slid into the soft leather seat and pulled her belt on. A moment later, the car was gliding out of the car park and into the London night.

'If you don't mind me saying, ma'am, you work too hard,' John said from the front seat and he signalled to turn left. Tara could see her favourite view: the great, grey-white dome of Saint Paul's Cathedral, floodlit against the inky sky, and beyond it, the river, with the bridges and embankment strung with twinkling lights.

She sighed and leaned back. A wave of exhaustion washed over her. 'You know, I do mind, John. I'd really prefer it if we didn't talk. I'm sorry, but I need a few moments to zone out.'

'Understood,' John said with a sympathetic smile. He'd been driving her for three years now and it was impossible to upset him. The glass panel that divided the front and back seats rose smoothly upwards, cutting them off from each other.

She let herself relax a little as the responsibility for getting her home fell to him. The route took them through the City, up the Strand, around Trafalgar

Square and up to Piccadilly. From there it was past Hyde Park and down towards Holland Park and home. The streets were packed with traffic. It seemed that there was never a time now when London wasn't busy. Some nights were all right, and they got home in good time. Others – when they hit jams or road works – filled her with stress and frustration. It was something in her life that she couldn't control. No matter how much money she had, she couldn't buy herself a quick, trouble-free ride home.

I guess only a helicopter could do it, she thought. But that was impossible, even though she was tempted. Where would she land a helicopter at home? On the chimney? It was ridiculous. The garden might just be big enough but the neighbours would never allow it – their shrubberies would get an unplanned trim every time she got home from work.

The journey home at least gave her time to think in peace. Even if she could still be reached by her BlackBerry, and had the computer screen mounted into the back of the front seat showing the state of the markets still open and trading, she was virtually alone. As the city sailed past the darkened windows, she could lean back and ponder for a while.

Today, she felt bleak. If yesterday's funeral had drained her emotionally, kicking her back to that place where she was never good enough, today had made her feel bone tired. It didn't take a genius to grasp that Trevellyan was in trouble and that it would fall to her to sort it out. What help could Jemima and Poppy be? She loved them both dearly but she was all too aware that they would be next to useless. All through their childhood, it had been the same. Tara was the sensible eldest sister – she'd had to be, responsibility for the younger ones had been hers. If they went out to play dressed by their mother in completely unpractical party frocks, it was Tara who would be in trouble for letting Jemima and Poppy get dirty. She became used to trying to hold the other two in check and, as they got older, digging them out of scrapes. Jemima, with her expulsions and bad behaviour, needed Tara as a diplomatic envoy to her parents. Poppy, babied and mollycoddled, used Tara as an alibi when she wanted to escape from home for a while. When Tara was at Oxford, Poppy often came to 'visit', though Tara didn't see much of her from the time she arrived to the time she left. She'd be off drifting round art galleries and colleges, visiting friends and making new ones. It was the same for both of them: happy to use Tara when they needed her, but mostly absorbed by their own wants and desires. Tara could see all too clearly that her younger sisters would happily shift most of the Trevellyan burden on to her capable shoulders. And what could they offer anyway?

Jemima knew everything there was to know about dressing up, shopping and parties. She could arrange flowers, decorate a room and be the perfect hostess. But what else had she ever achieved? And then there was the problem of her disintegrating marriage and her compulsive affairs. Tara had had high hopes that marrying Harry would sort Jemima out, give her a purpose in life. After all, there was that great house to be maintained, and with a title she had extra clout. She could devote herself to doing some good in the world. But no. For reasons Tara did not entirely understand, the marriage had quickly begun to sour to the point where Jemima could hardly bear to be in the same room as her husband. It meant that she was reverting to her old party-loving self but with an added ferocity. It was no secret that she was getting laid all over London and New York as well. Tara had heard the rumours and had read them too – veiled saucy titbits in the gossip columns making it quite clear that Jemima was not one to let her marriage vows stop her having fun. So if she expected Jemima to devote herself to sorting out the problems with Trevellyan, she guessed that she was going to be sorely disappointed. The only spark of comfort was that Tara guessed Jemima was more shrewd and switched on than she appeared.

She couldn't say the same of Poppy. Dear little Poppy – all her life she'd been petted and spoiled and as a result, she sometimes appeared helpless and naïve. Tara knew why it was: Poppy's big green eyes, so quick to fill with tears, had always won their father over to whatever she wanted and even managed to melt their mother's frostiness. And it was not all an act. As a girl she had been lost in a world of her own, busy playing make-believe all the time. Tara always felt that Poppy had been protected against the harsher realities of the world and for all she protested that she didn't want her money and that she was more interested in saving the planet than going shopping, she'd never really had to strike out on her own. It was down to the great scare of Poppy's childhood, when she'd fallen seriously ill and they'd thought they were going to lose her. After that, their parents had pampered and petted her. She became the light of their mother's life, the only one able to make her eyes soften and those stern lips smile. It was hard for the other two, but they learned to forgive Poppy for it – her kittenish charm was too hard to resist for long. Besides, there was someone else they were able to unite against . . .

Tara sighed and stared out of the window as Hyde Park passed by without her seeing it. Poppy thought of herself as independent but she wasn't really. How could she live in Bloomsbury, daubing away on her canvases or whatever else it was she did, without the help of the family money? There was no way she would be any use whatever when it came to Trevellyan – she just didn't have the first clue, or even care, about business.

It made the fact that Poppy had been left Loxton all the harder to swallow. Tara bit her lip at the thought of it. Rationally, she knew she didn't need or want Loxton. She didn't care for the house itself and her memories of her childhood there were not particularly fond ones. But she couldn't help feeling wounded by the fact that it had been denied her, lock, stock and barrel. Not a single piece of it had been held over for her. Mother hadn't left her so much as a brooch or a necklace to remember her by.

She drummed her fingernails against the seat and shifted anxiously as she remembered her trip to her mother's bedroom and the missing jewellery. Had it been sold? All of it? Or had someone removed it for safekeeping and had it sent to the bank? It was a puzzle, but one Tara was determined to solve. Her mother might have had few friends and little affection to show her daughters but she did love something passionately, and that was jewellery. She had a desire for it that put Elizabeth Taylor's in the shade. And she had sometimes used it to blackmail her daughters.

'I shall leave *you* my diamonds,' she'd say to whoever was in favour that day, though Tara suspected that secretly Yolanda would have preferred to take them with her into the next world. In fact, she probably regretted leaving her jewels behind more than she did her daughters. On Jemima's wedding day, Yolanda had put one of her most magnificent pieces, the great pearl and diamond choker, around Jemima's neck herself, smiling at the brilliant sparkle of the diamonds nestling between the luscious, creamy sheen of the pearls. The bestowal of the choker was a mark of how Jemima was in high favour that day, although there was no question but that it would be going back to Yolanda the minute it came off her daughter's neck. Poppy had been lent the emeralds and Tara the amazing diamond and sapphire necklace and earrings. Those stunning party pieces lived in the bank most of the time; their mother only kept her personal favourites in her bedroom: a few ropes of pearls, the diamond earrings, some cocktail jewellery, her rings and the locket.

Tara was certain her mother would have taken great

care of what would happen to the jewels. Yet there was nothing about them in the will, unless they were included in Loxton's contents. To treat her precious stones so carelessly was entirely out of character. So where were they?

'Here we are, ma'am,' said John through the intercom. They had drawn up in front of the impressive white façade of her Holland Park mansion. He got out and opened the door for her.

'Thank you, John. See you tomorrow.'

'See you tomorrow, ma'am.'

She walked up the stone steps to the front door and rang on the doorbell, so tired she couldn't even be bothered to find her keys. The lights were on in the basement flat. Robina had obviously retired for the evening, so the children were definitely asleep. Well, she could hardly be angry about that. It was getting on for nine o'clock – if Edward and Imogen had been up, she would have been furious with the nanny for not putting them to bed.

The door was opened by her housekeeper, who greeted her politely and stood aside to let her pass.

'Dinner is almost ready, madam. John told us that you were on your way home.'

'Thank you, Viv. Is my husband home?'

'In the study.'

'Thank you. Oh, could you bring me a glass of wine, please? Some of that Menetou-Salon if there's some open. Or the Chablis if not.'

'Of course.' The housekeeper glided quietly off down the corridor.

Tara dropped her briefcase, shuffled off her coat and kicked off her shoes, leaving them where they fell. Someone else would pick them up. What did she pay all these people for after all, if not so that she could do what she felt like from time to time?

She darted up the stairs as quickly as she could, up to the second floor and along the soft, carpeted corridors until she came to the children's bedroom. She listened at the door for a moment, then opened it and slipped in.

At once she could smell the delicious warmth of their sleeping bodies. Was there anything nicer in the world than the scent of her freshly bathed babies in their clean pyjamas? She went over to Edward's low white-painted bed and knelt down next to it. She put her face close to his head, inhaling his sweet warmth, and tenderly stroking his fair head. His face, softly illuminated by the glow of his nightlight, was as perfect as a sleeping cherub's, lashes swooping down on his cheeks and little bow mouth slightly open. She stayed there a long while before kissing him and whispering, 'Night, night, darling'.

Then she padded across the room to Imogen, who sighed and turned in her sleep. She hadn't been long in her big-girl bed and she had chosen one with a fairy canopy above it and two small curtains of candyfloss pink gauze. While Tara didn't like to give in to the absurd amount of pink little girls were encouraged to adore, she couldn't help letting Imogen have her way. Now she was tucked up under her patchwork quilt, a tiny princess in her miniature bed.

Tara knelt beside Imogen, smoothing her daughter's hair and gazing on her peaceful little face. *Her sleep is so untroubled*, Tara thought. She had no idea of the big, complicated world that awaited her. Imogen gave another little snuffly sigh and turned over, snuggling back down again.

'Sleep well, darling. See you tomorrow,' Tara breathed. Then she tiptoed quietly out, closing the door gently behind her. She returned downstairs to the hall, wondering where Gerald was. Walking across the hall, she went to the study door and listened at it for a moment. She could hear the sound of the television and Gerald's voice booming over the top of it. Opening the door, she walked in.

The room was very much in Gerald's taste: fake-old with a touch of brash. Brand new dark wood panelling covered the walls and along them ran library book-shelves, where hundreds of leather and gilt volumes were shut away behind wire doors. Gerald had bought them by the metre and not one had been taken off the shelf since the day they'd been put there. The room was oppressively masculine: hunting trophies adorned the walls, though Gerald had not so much as shot a rabbit, model yachts sat in full miniature sail on lacquered side tables and antique golf clubs were displayed in museum-like glass cases. Among all this, the huge Bang & Olufsen plasma screen television looked jarring, a piece of twenty-first-century technology sitting oddly in an Edwardian club room like a space ship surrounded by vintage cars. CNN news was playing while Gerald sat at his desk, staring at his computer screen, one hand clamping a telephone to his ear.

'Yes, yes, that's just as I said! Well, tell the board I won't take any of their whingeing. I intend to do it my way. That's the way I've always done it and I have an infallible instinct, as everyone knows.' He caught sight of Tara and waved at her. 'Yes, all right, old man. I'll see you tomorrow. Goodbye.' He put the phone down and stood up. 'Hello, darling, how are we?'

'We're fine, or least, I'm fine, if that's what you mean.' She went over for a kiss. He brushed his lips across her cheek, leaving a faint wet trail.

'You're late back,' he said reprovingly as he sat down again and picked up a crystal tumbler, swilling what Tara knew would be a Scotch and soda. 'The children missed you.'

'I know. I've just looked in on them.' She perched on the slippery seat of a leather armchair.

'Well? What were you doing?' He fixed her with a steely gaze. It was always like this: he wanted to know every detail of her day and precisely where she had been when. Once it had made her feel safe. Now it was increasingly disturbing.

'I told you we had the meeting at Trevellyan today. Once that was over, I had to go to the office. I'd missed so much, what with being away yesterday as well, that I had to stay late to catch up. I'm exhausted.' Tara felt herself droop and she sighed. How long had it been since she had really felt rested? She couldn't remember. The pressure was always on to keep going, to work harder, to stay on top of everything and succeed. She had to cope, she knew that. Taking a deep breath, she looked up at her husband.

'And what is the situation with Trevellyan?' he asked.

'Not good.'

Gerald raised his eyebrows. 'Really? How bad?'

'I'm going to find out the details tomorrow but I think very bad.'

'You surprise me.' He sat back in his chair and put the tips of his fingers together.

He always manages to look like a tycoon, thought Tara. *It's as though he's studied the part for a film role or something. And it never quite rings true.*

Her husband leaned forward, plucked a large cigar from the ashtray in front of him, put it in his mouth and sucked at it. A plume of heavy smoke floated from his mouth. He liked to smoke cigars – Winston Churchill was one of his great heroes and Tara always suspected that Gerald was trying to emulate him at every opportunity.

'Your parents struck me as competent people, very competent. And Trevellyan is a quality brand, everyone knows that. What on earth can be so wrong?'

Tara prickled. Everything Gerald said sounded like a criticism these days. Now he was implying that she had misread the situation. 'I don't know the full facts yet,' she replied coldly. 'I'm getting a rundown tomorrow.'

Gerald nodded slowly. 'Well, I'm sure it can't be as bad as you think. But if you need any help or advice, you know I'm always happy to do whatever I can.'

'Thank you, darling. And how was your day?'

'Productive, very productive! My team have done some excellent work today and I'm more convinced than ever that we'll be able to put together a very strong bid for the Fothergill group – or at least, a large part of it. That will give us the foothold we need for further growth. It's all very exciting. I shall tell you more over dinner.'

There was a quiet knock on the door and the house-keeper came in bearing Tara's glass of wine on a small round tray.

'Thanks, Viv. God, I need this!' Tara scooped up the glass and took a swig. 'Is dinner ready?' asked Gerald.

'Five minutes, sir. Please come through to the dining room whenever you're ready.' Viv went out.

'Come. Let's go through.' Gerald stood up and pushed his smoking cigar down into the ashtray. He went over to Tara and took her arm.

He always seemed to like these moments best, Tara reflected as they walked together towards the dining room. He revelled in the timeless traditions of the dinner table. He loved to see the silver candlesticks with their creamy-white candles casting a soft light on to the wine glasses and cutlery and napkins, all laid out just so. It had to be absolutely perfect, or he could fly into one of his terrible rages. The whole house was kept immaculate by the staff, and everybody rushed about to make sure that nothing was out of place, especially when Gerald was expected home. The children had already been taught that messiness was one of the cardinal sins: even their playroom was returned to perfect order, every toy in its place, every jigsaw in its box, every DVD in its case and shelved alphabetically, the moment they had stopped playing.

The dining room had the mellow light of a few lamps and the dinner candles. They sat at either end of the dinner table, the way that Gerald liked it, and Ashby the butler came round to serve them in the way he had served the gentlemen of the Travellers Club on Pall Mall. It was this record of excellence that had made Gerald hire him. Although Gerald hadn't managed to be put up for any of the most exclusive clubs yet, he had hopes that he might one day be a member. Until then, having Ashby put chops in front of him the way they had been put in front of lords, bishops, MPs and any number of other grand people made him very pleased indeed.

'How is that sister of yours?' he said as they started on their vichyssoise.

'Which one? Is there any more wine, please, Ashby?'

'Oh. Jemima, of course.' Gerald spooned some soup into his mouth.

'Of course. She's fine. The same as she was yesterday, I suppose.' Gerald had a mild obsession with Jemima that Tara found irritating. Any other wife might worry that her husband was entranced – and why not? Jemima was a beautiful woman who gave out an extraordinary buzz of active sexuality, even Tara could see that. But she was fairly sure that it wasn't Jemima's curves, long legs or honey-blonde hair that interested Gerald. In fact, it wasn't even Jemima herself. Gerald loved the fact that Jemima was a proper lady, married to a proper lord, and he was always trying to get closer to Jemima in the hopes of sucking up to Harry. He could never really understand why Harry didn't seem to want anything to do with him. His greatest desire was to be invited to Herne on one of Harry's shooting weekends, but it seemed very unlikely to happen.

When they were first married, Tara had been quite blind to Gerald's monumental social climbing. She hadn't seen his pompous side at all. Instead he had seemed warm and caring, and had enveloped her like a great blanket, making her feel cosy and secure. He had also taught her to enjoy sex in a way that had been entirely new to her. None of her previous boyfriends had been able to arouse her very much at all, she had always felt far too painfully self-conscious. She longed to be voluptuous and naturally sexy, like Jemima, instead of thin and boney, and had never been able to relax enough to get much satisfaction from the whole thing. It had been enough, she hoped, to lie back and let it happen, and the boys didn't seem to mind it that way. Gerald, though, had been a whole different story. He wasn't happy unless he had raised her to heights of enjoyment she had never known existed. Once he had made it clear to her that he couldn't be satisfied unless she was, and that seeing her in ecstasy gave him the wildest pleasure of all, she was finally able to feel liberated in the bedroom.

Watching him slurp up his soup now, his cheeks flushed from the whisky or three he had enjoyed in his study, his hair brushed forward over his bald patch, she could hardly believe that he was the same man who had sent her into such wild delight. It didn't happen much these days.

I can't really blame him, she thought. *I'm exhausted most of the time. And he works so hard as well. No wonder neither of us is ever in the mood. Yes, that's it. We're just never in the mood.*

She didn't want to look at the darker truth that lurked below the surface.

10

Meet me at the Ritz, 3 p.m. for emergency meeting read Tara's text message.

Standing in the entrance of her Eaton Square mansion block, Jemima jammed her dark glasses on then made her way quickly down the front steps, her head bowed. She'd learned various tricks for avoiding any paparazzi who happened to be around, and one was to present a very dull picture: show hardly any face, have a neutral expression, give nothing of any interest. She'd heard that Madonna reduced the value of her unwanted paparazzi pictures at a stroke by cleverly wearing the same outfit all the time: a very unglamorous tracksuit, shades and a cap. The result was that she was often left in peace as she went about her daily life as endlessly identical photographs were worth very little.

Jemima didn't think she could quite manage the tracksuit routine, but then, she didn't suffer to quite the same extent. The pursuit had been terrible a few years ago when she'd been going out with a very famous and very druggy rock star. She hadn't been able to go anywhere without a posse of photographers trailing her every move. They printed pictures of her wherever she went, from Glastonbury, where she watched her lover and his band on stage while wearing ripped-off blue denim dungarees over a tight pink T-shirt and turquoise lace-up wellington boots, to high-octane society occasions. She was pictured looking elegant in white Ralph Lauren and a classic Lock of Saint James's straw hat at Ascot, or in a Donna Karan little black dress and black cashmere wrap, leaving Le Caprice or the Wolseley. Her fashion sense was hailed in dozens of magazines, her luxurious life envied and pored over. If she and Billy walked down the street together, it was always with a pack of photographers backing away from them, snapping and shouting, and the next day they'd be plastered over the papers and gossip mags.

Will she take Cocaine Billy to Royal Wedding? screamed the tabloids when they discovered she'd been invited to the same nuptials as Prince William. She didn't take Billy – they were already on the verge of breaking up. Jemima had never been one for drugs; she'd done her fair share of experimentation and still enjoyed dabbling from time to time – plenty of Kensington, Belgravia and Notting Hill dinner parties ended up with crystal bowls of white powder being passed round after the main course instead of pudding – but luckily for her, she had avoided being sucked in. Watching Billy's raging coke habit spiral out of control, she saw all too clearly how quickly the enjoyment of a party buzz could turn into a dangerous obsession. For a while, she didn't want to do any drugs at all and once that happened, there was no future for her and her famous boyfriend, who was so deeply into drugs, moving from cocaine to crack and heroin, that it was becoming apparent he would probably never escape his addiction before it destroyed him. Even so, it was he who dumped Jemima.

'No offence, love, cos you're a fackin' great bird, yeah? It's just that you're a bit fackin' borin' these days. And I was born to party, yeah?' Billy had slurred.

'OK, Billy,' Jemima said, hiding her relief. She patted his hand. 'You take care, all right? And you know where to find me if you ever need any help.'

'Help?' Billy stared at her with his hugely over-dilated pupils. 'What kind of help? You mean, if I need to score?'

'Oh, no, darling. Quite the opposite.'

Billy looked blank, as he did so often. Jemima kissed the top of his head and left, hoping that he might somehow elude the clutches of the early death that she feared must await him.

She'd assumed that once she and Billy had broken up, the press would lose interest in her. They did, to an extent. She no longer had to face packs of press photographers wherever she went, but the interest was still there, flaring up whenever she was spotted at some society gala, charity fundraiser or fashion show, looking stunning and fabulously well groomed. Every now and then, she would hear the whirr of the shutter or see a battery of flashes in the darkness and know that she'd been papped. The next day, she'd see her image on a gossip website or a tabloid page, always describing her as Billy's ex and heiress to the Trevellyan millions.

Her marriage, called the society event of the season, had reawakened the press attention and turned into a media scrum. From the moment the engagement was announced, the media worked itself into a tizzy about the beautiful heiress and the lord who lived in a castle – it was too good a fairy story to miss.

Ironically, she met Harry at the very wedding that the press had been so interested in, when they'd assumed she would be taking Billy. Something about him had attracted her at once. Perhaps it was because he was different to the louche, monied crowd she'd been hanging about with for too long. He arrived looking formal and proper in a morning coat, unlike so many other guests who'd taken to disregarding the dress code and turning up in whatever took their fancy: bottle-green velvet lounge suits, pinstriped numbers with open-necked shirts, even jeans. Harry stood out, handsome in his exquisitely cut coat and dark charcoal striped trousers, the sober grey tones brightened by his jewel-coloured embroidered waistcoat. He was tall and fair with piercing blue eyes and an air of robust good health that only comes from hours striding outdoors in the countryside. There was also the unmistakeable set of stubbornness about his chin. He evidently knew his own mind.

All through the wedding, Jemima had been aware

of him, watching him from the corner of her eye even when she'd been holding court at her table, surrounded by the all usual hangers-on and a few new ones, mostly red-faced old duffers who'd had a couple of glasses of champagne and fancied chatting up that gorgeous young thing they'd read about in the papers.

Harry wasn't like that. He didn't seem the least bit interested in her, which only served to fuel her curiosity. Did he have a girlfriend? She couldn't see him with anybody. Was he gay? She didn't think so. Men like him weren't gay, in her experience, though there was always a chance she was wrong. He was sitting at a nearby table, and during the speeches she watched him carefully. His serious face suddenly lit up with laughter when the best man cracked a joke, and she loved the way it transformed him. Then and there she made up her mind to have him.

It was much later, on the dance floor, that they got close to each other. Close up, she was overwhelmed by his masculinity. Most of her friends were fey: skinny artists or boys who took too many drugs to be hungry. The ones who were most well built tended to be gay guys who went to the gym to work lovingly on their six pack and biceps. Very few of her straight male friends were like this: he towered over her, solid and muscular, and she loved how vulnerable and feminine that made her feel. Knowing what she now knew of Harry, it was pretty amazing that she'd managed to score with him. But by dint of Herculean flirting, at one in the morning, they were standing behind the marquee, its white walls dotted with blue, yellow and red from the lights, the boom of the discotheque pounding round them, snogging as fiercely as teenagers. Harry tasted so damn sweet – she'd never forgotten it. Perhaps she was too used to kissing guys who'd just smoked a packet of cigarettes, downed a bottle of Jack Daniel's and put away a few tabs of this or that, but Harry seemed so fresh and clean. It was delicious, just kissing away, feeling her stomach swoop over with lust.

She'd expected him to come back to the hotel with her that night but, as dawn rose over the big house where the wedding was held, he kissed her hand, took her phone number, murmured goodbye into her ear and saw her safely off in a taxi.

'Hey, Jemima, you scored last night!' crowed one of her friends who'd been at the wedding and who called as soon as was decent the next day.

'I know. He's rather hunky, isn't he? I never knew I could fancy a blond. I mean, Billy had blond streaks, but you know . . . all dyed. But this chap was so deliciously old-fashioned, you just wouldn't believe it!' Jemima rolled about in her hotel bed, thrilled by the memory of her kissing session the night before.

'Yes, but . . . ! I have to say congratulations, darling.'

'Really? Why?' Jemima sat up, pulling the sheet about her chest. She was more used to people being congratulated for getting off with *her*, rather than the other way round.

'Don't you know who that was?'

'His name's Harry.'

'Yeah, Harry Calthorpe.'

'So? I've never heard of him. Who is he?'

Her friend laughed. 'He's *Viscount* Calthorpe. He owns a fuck-off great castle in Dorset, darling! He's the real thing. Eton, Oxford, running the estate – he's one hundred per cent genuine aristocracy. You've only gone and bagged a lord! God, Cressida will be bloody *green*, her mother's had him earmarked for her since birth. But he's so hard to get at because he never goes to anything, he's a complete recluse. Hates parties. Hardly ever comes to London and when he does, he locks himself away at Whites where no girls can get at him. He hasn't been out with anyone since he broke up with Meredith Buckley-Squire at the Caledonian Ball five years ago. So, well done, Jemima. We were all beginning to think no one would manage to snare Harry Calthorpe.'

'Oh.' Jemima frowned and twirled her finger in the rumpled quilt.

'Well – aren't you pleased?'

'I don't know. I don't care either way, to be honest.'

When the call was finished, Jemima lay back down and stared up the ceiling. So her mysterious paramour was a lord. She'd met plenty of braying boys in her time and not cared much for them. But after a while, most of them had disappeared into corporate City life, and out of her glitzy, artistic, beautiful-people orbit. Of course she met various titled people at the society bashes she went to – *Tatler*'s Little Black Book party, at which she was a star guest, was full of them – but she was sure enough of her own importance not to need the social boost of being associated with some Lord this, or the Earl of that.

Of course, after the wedding, Harry didn't call for ages. It was not at all what Jemima was used to. She was quite tempted to track him down and make the first move herself, but something told her that it wasn't the best way to handle someone like Harry. She had the feeling that if she tried to pursue him, he would freeze and vanish, like a hunted fox. So, for once, she had to be patient. When he finally called, it was to invite her out for dinner.

'I thought we'd go to Rules,' he said, 'my father's favourite restaurant.'

Jemima, who dined out almost every night, had never been there but she had a sneaking feeling of what to expect and, sure enough, Rules turned out to be an extremely traditional restaurant where the waiters wore black tie and every table groaned with stark linen, heavy silver and wine glasses engraved with the restaurant's name. The walls were ornamented with hunting prints and antlers, some with old tweed hats hanging off them. The menu was classic – lobster bisque, oysters, ribs of beef, game, and old-fashioned rib-sticking puddings.

'Is this your favourite too? As well as your father's, I mean,' she asked, looking round at the other diners, who appeared to be either tourists or old chaps. Her Prada dress, vertiginous heels and highly groomed appearance looked very exotic here – it was not at all what she was used to. The restaurants she went to had the paparazzi outside, not the hoi polloi inside.

'Well,' said Harry, smiling, 'perhaps it's seen better days. My pa used to love it here but that was a while ago now. He was a big Graham Greene fan, and apparently one of the novels has a scene or two here, so don't be surprised if you see some bookish types staring about. Food looks good, though.' He looked worried. 'Don't you like it? We can go somewhere else if you'd rather.'

'Don't be silly, it's lovely. Of course we should stay.' Jemima leaned over towards him, raising an eyebrow flirtatiously over the top of her menu. 'On one condition. Afterwards, we go to one of my favourite hang-outs. Deal?'

'Deal. As long as it's not too racy.'

'You've already said deal so you can't back out now. Don't worry, I'm not going to frighten you.'

Two hours later, full of roast beef and sticky toffee pudding, they arrived at Annabel's, the Berkeley Square nightclub.

'Oh,' Harry said, obviously relieved. 'This is all right. My old man used to come here as well.'

'Yes – but that was then, and this is now. Annabel's is so wonderfully private. We can have fun in peace.' Jemima grinned at him.

So they went in to dance and drink and talk cosily in a discreet corner. Harry was recognised by some old school friends who could scarcely believe that they had just seen Harry Calthorpe dancing in Annabel's with a beautiful society girl. Then, when the night was over, he saw her into a taxi home, just as he had after the wedding, courteously refusing her purred invitation to come back to Eaton Square with her.

My God, she'd thought in the taxi on the way home, high on champagne and that curious mix of hormones that fizz through someone who might be about to fall in love, *he's playing hard to get!*

She was fascinated by him – by his impeccable manners, his peaceful life, his attitude towards the things that so absorbed her. He was completely uninterested in London life and parties and who was who, who was sleeping with whom, who was richer than whom, where the perfect holiday destination was this year, who had been invited out to so-and-so's private island. It washed over him. As Jemima told her friends, 'Darling, he simply doesn't give a shit.'

Everyone loved the romance of it: the beautiful party-loving girl and the old-fashioned lord who would prefer to wade thigh-deep in an icy river and fish than to go to the most exclusive parties or the grandest society events.

'You'll change him, Jemima,' they told her. 'What an amazing couple you'll make!' And she believed them. That was the trouble.

It had all seemed so perfect; even the first time they slept together had been a whole new experience for Jemima. Because Harry hadn't leapt into bed with her at the first opportunity, as every other man she'd met had, she'd assumed he was inexperienced and probably a rather clumsy lover, but she'd remained hopeful.

They'd been seeing each other for about six weeks when, at the end of an intimate evening in a small but delicious restaurant near her flat, he'd leaned across the table, taken her hand and said quietly, 'How about if we have our coffee back at your place?'

Her stomach had somersaulted. At once she felt

nervous, self-conscious and deliciously excited. 'Yes
. . . yes please,' she said, stuttering a little.

'Good.' With a discreet gesture, he summoned the
bill, paid it and the next minute they were walking
together in the cool Belgravia night, strolling to her
flat and to the moment she'd been waiting for. She
could hardly speak as they went back, his large hand
holding her small one.

Is this really me? she wondered. How many men had
she slept with after all? She'd lost count years ago, and
didn't give a fig anyway. As long as it was fun and they
both wanted it, who was counting? Sex had become the
same as any pleasure: there for the taking. Sometimes
it was good, sometimes it was bad. Sometimes she had
a strange, drug-fuelled, zany experience – mostly those
were with Billy – sometimes she couldn't remember
what had happened the night before. Occasionally she'd
had delicious life-enhancing sex with someone sweet
just when she'd needed it. Sometimes she'd had the
depressing experience of sex with someone she liked
but who never called her afterwards, though that was
rare. *So why the hell am I so nervous?*

She knew it was because Harry had built up to this
moment. He'd made her realise that he didn't sleep
with just anyone, that she was special to him. That
made her gulp, and hope that she would be worth it.
It also made her hope desperately that he would be
worth it too.

As she poured him his coffee, she was surprised to
find she was trembling and that she didn't know what
to say. When she handed him the cup, it shook violently

on its small saucer, and their eyes met and they laughed. That broke the ice and dispelled just enough of the tension so that she was no longer frightened. He placed his coffee aside and instead tenderly pulled her on to his lap and kissed her. It felt like the most natural thing in the world and Jemima's nerves subsided.

Jemima quickly discovered he was no unpractised lover, as she had worried he might be, nor did he let her dominate proceedings as she sometimes did. Instead, their bodies fitted so naturally and easily that afterwards she found herself almost moved by the rightness of it.

From that moment on they were rarely apart. There was no denying that she had fallen in love with Harry, and she was sure that he had fallen in love with her.

But Harry had another love: his home, beautiful Herne Castle and the acres of land that surrounded it. He was fanatical about the great outdoors and nature and farming. His primary concern for years had been to restore and preserve Herne, and to live a quiet, peaceful country life there. It was a side to Harry that Jemima had been told of but didn't see until the night he drove her to Herne for the first time, in the early hours of the morning after Bea Ogilvy's ball. As they arrived the sun rose behind the large old house and she could see in his eyes that he was desperate for her to love it too – and she had. The whole scenario was just too romantic for words: the house falling so gracefully and beautifully apart, while its handsome owner passionately tried to save it.

'I want to help you,' she said fervently, as they stood on the terrace on a fine summer's evening, looking out over the velvety green fields, the dusky woods and the golden wheat fields beyond. 'I want to help you save Herne, if I can.'

He hugged her tightly and then looked at her, his face alight with joy. 'You are amazing, do you know that? Really amazing . . .'

Four weeks later he proposed and she had no hesitation in accepting. It was a grand London wedding, packed with famous guests. She wore a dress designed exclusively for her by Jasper Conran, a delicious vintage-style gown in oyster silk that was demure but with a hint of forties cheesecake glamour that showed off her tiny waist. Then there were the jewels. Her mother insisted she wear the pearl and diamond choker worn at her own wedding day, and Harry had resurrected his mother's family tiara from some safe for her to wear. It was very impressive but it was heavy and didn't go with her dress quite as well as she'd hoped. Still, she looked ravishing and felt ecstatically happy as she got dressed in her suite at the Ritz, with Poppy and Tara bustling about her in their brides-maid dresses in shades of palest water-lily green.

'This is the happiest moment of my life,' said their mother tearfully as she looked at Jemima, standing in all her bridal radiance.

The sisters glanced at each other, unsure of what to say. Their mother was anything but sentimental and, as far as they knew, had never cried over any of them. But here she was, welling up like a big softie.

'It's not much to do with me, though, is it?' muttered Jemima to Tara as they prepared to go downstairs to the huge ivory Rolls Royce waiting to take them to Saint Margaret's, Westminster. 'She's just so happy to be mother-in-law to Harry, she can't hold it in. Awful old snob.'

'Shhh,' Tara replied, pulling her wrap round her shoulders. 'Who cares whether it's her happiest moment? It's you who matters. And you look amazing.'

'Yes, amazing!' breathed Poppy, coming up on Jemima's other side. 'Honestly, you've never looked so beautiful. I just wish Daddy was here to see it.'

Jemima stared at her, blinking away a sudden hot burst of tears, not wanting to ruin her make-up, applied so carefully by the very sweet make-up artist. 'I know. Me too.'

'We'd better hurry,' Tara urged gently. 'It's expected you should be a bit late but if you carry on much longer, the whole day will run behind.'

Jemima took a deep breath, then smiled broadly at her sisters. 'Then let's go.'

A press pack of photographers awaited her as she went quickly from the Ritz entrance to the car, and another at the church along with a crowd of well-wishers, oohing and aahing at the glamorous guests and their fabulous clothes. They sighed with delight when they saw the gorgeous bride emerge from her cream Rolls Royce, and her beautiful bridesmaids fuss about her, checking the dress and adjusting the veil. They shouted congratulations and good wishes as she was handed her bouquet of ivory-coloured roses and, now just a little white-faced and nervous, advanced into the church.

She walked down the aisle on the arm of her Uncle Clive, her mother's brother, to where Harry was waiting for her, tall and handsome, admiration and love in his eyes. The service passed in a rapid blur of emotion, beauty and music, then she and Harry walked back down the aisle in a burst of joyous organ music. Now she was the Viscountess Calthorpe, chatelaine of Herne Castle, entitled to wear a coronet with sixteen silver balls at the coronation of a sovereign. To her embarrassment, her mother gave her exactly such a coronet as a wedding present.

Then it was back to William Kent House at the Ritz for a grand reception. She and Harry left after a few hours, bound for a honeymoon in Scotland and then Tara's home in the Bahamas but she'd heard that the party went on into the night and, for some, into the next day as well, when the pictures of her in all her bridal splendour appeared on the morning papers.

The wedding was a huge success. It was the marriage itself that had proved the problem.

11

She was reminded of her wedding day as the taxi pulled up in front of the hotel. It was hard to believe that it was only four years ago. Now she was returning with her life transformed: marriage to Harry was a disaster and her inheritance looked about as sound as a three-pound note. It was obvious that everything she'd believed about her family, its status – financial and otherwise – and her own future was going to have to be rethought. Would she need to start working for her living? A shudder of horror went through her as she walked through the revolving doors and into the round reception area.

'I'm meeting Tara Pearson here,' she said to the smartly uniformed hall porter.

'Yes, madam. She's here already, waiting in the suite.'

'The suite?'

'Yes, madam. She's reserved one of our larger suites. Would you like to be accompanied there?'

'No, just tell me where it is. I'll find it myself.'

A few moments later she was walking into one of

the hotel's plushest suites, with a drawing room giving a pleasant view over Green Park.

'Jemima, hi.' Tara was sitting on a chintz sofa, a laptop on her knees and sheaves of paper on the table in front of her.

Jemima took off her glasses. 'Dear old Ritz,' she said. She gazed round at the classic interior of floral fabrics, heavy curtains and elegant antique furniture. 'It never changes. That's why I love it, even if it's decorated more to Mother's taste than mine.'

'I haven't been here since your wedding. It's good to be back.' Tara looked at her sister over the top of her black-rimmed glasses. Her hair was swept back into a smart chignon and she looked very businesslike. 'I wanted somewhere private and close to Trevellyan, so it seemed a good idea to have the first executive meeting about the future of our company right here.'

Jemima strolled about, eyeing the antique furniture and oil paintings. 'It reminds me of Trevellyan,' she commented. 'So old school. So old world.'

Tara nodded.

The door opened and Poppy burst in, panting, her curls awry.

'Oh God, I'm late again, aren't I!' she cried.

'Don't worry, darling, I only just got here,' Jemima replied. 'You haven't missed anything.'

'Hi, Pops.' Tara smiled at her sister. 'OK, we need to get cracking with this. Ingliss had all the information I wanted sent over and I went through as much as I could last night. I'm afraid I've got some serious things to tell you about where we all stand.'

Jemima fell dramatically into an armchair. 'Oh, shit, we're bankrupt, aren't we? That foul old bitch has ruined us all!'

'Oh no. It can't be true . . . not dear old Trevellyan.' Poppy looked horrified. 'But how on earth could it happen? It just doesn't make any sense that one day everything is fine and the next it's total disaster.'

Tara looked at them both solemnly. 'We're not bankrupt. But we're bloody close.'

'Am I going to need a drink for this bit?' asked Jemima.

'No. You're going to need a clear head. We all are.' Tara looked at Poppy. 'You'd better sit down.' Poppy obediently dropped her bag and sank into a chair. 'We thought Mother was quite the miracle worker, didn't we? When Daddy died, she turned from useless socialite who'd never done a day's work in her life to hard-nosed businesswoman, taking over the running of the company and making a success of it. But it seems that wasn't quite the real story. The truth is that Mother failed dismally. It's true to say that things weren't great for Trevellyan when Daddy was in charge – I don't think he was really cut out for a career in the perfume industry. We always knew he'd probably have been much happier playing the piano or teaching or something. But at least he understood the basic principles and that you can't drain a company dry, that it doesn't go on for ever without careful planning. You need a strategy – a business has to change in response to the times, just as Trevellyan always used to. The only thing is, Daddy didn't know how to do that. He didn't understand his times at all so he concentrated on Trevellyan's core market, the one he did understand – the old duffer brigade. He cut back a bit to make up for the fact that Trevellyan was no longer growing, but he kept it steady. Then Mother took over.'

Poppy's eyes grew wider. 'What happened?'

'In a word, disaster.' Tara consulted some of the papers in front her. 'Assets – gone. Sales – vanishing. The company – totally on the slide. And I'm afraid it seems to have been down to her Chairman Mao approach to things. No one dared give her any advice – if she didn't like it, she sacked them and avoided tribunals by paying them off with great wedges of cash, years of private health care, cars . . .'

'I imagine half of them were vying to get sacked, then,' commented Jemima.

'By the end, yes. Trevellyan's a sinking ship, to be honest, and everyone there must have known about it. I suppose whoever is left is just hanging on to see what they can get out of it. They're still paying good money to the board of directors. And, of course, to us. In fact, it's our allowances, salaries and dividends that are bleeding the company white. So here's the reality check. All Trevellyan money stops. Right now.'

Jemima gasped and turned pale, one hand flying to her mouth in shock.

Poppy shook her head and half smiled to herself. 'All of it?'

Tara took off her glasses. 'Yes. We should be able to negotiate new salaries as directors of the company in due course, if we actually manage to make any money. But for the moment we're going to have to do it for the love of it.'

'Hold on a second, Tara,' said Jemima. Her voice was tight and low, with a tiny tremor in it, as though she was fighting to keep control. 'It's all very well for you to say we're not going to have any more money. You've got a job that pays you a ludicrous amount and Gerald is absolutely loaded. Losing the Trevellyan money means everything to me and Poppy. It's all we've got.'

'I don't mind!' piped up Poppy, looking more cheerful than she had for weeks. 'I think it will do us good to live without it for a bit – to provide for ourselves for a change.'

'Don't be so bloody stupid!' Jemima hissed furiously. 'You're so fucking naïve, Poppy. La, la, la – look at the lovely trees, paint a pretty flower! That's you, isn't it? Well, guess what, it isn't like that. You've never had to worry about real life because of the Trevellyan money. Now you'll soon find out what it's like to be poor and I don't think you're going to like it one little bit. I know I'm not.' She turned to Tara. 'Don't you see what kind of a situation I'll be in if you take our money away from us? I'll be broke!'

Tara's expression was stern. For once, she was the older sister, able to pull rank on Jemima. Her business credentials gave her the power she'd never had before. 'You don't seem to understand. I'm not taking away the Trevellyan money – there is no money. There's nothing to give you.'

'I don't believe you!' cried Jemima. 'It can't be as bad as you're saying!'

'All right, say you go on getting your money. In six months to a year, it'll all be over. For good. Trevellyan will be bankrupt. Everything will go to the bank, or be sold off to companies like the one I work for. There are still a couple of assets that people will be drooling to get their hands on – prime Mayfair property, for one. But if you forgo your money now and work with me and Poppy to get this thing going again, then we'll all have Trevellyan, and an income, for the rest of our lives. Now what will it be?'

Jemima jumped up and stalked to the window. The other two watched her as she stared out at Green Park, stretching away towards Buckingham Palace. People were wandering across the grass, enjoying the brief spring sunshine. Children ran about while mothers sat on park benches chatting. Life was going on as normal, even though, for the Trevellyan sisters, it had utterly changed.

'It's not as bad as you think,' Tara said quietly. 'You own your flat. You must have something in the bank. You've got lots of things you could sell if you had to. You'll just have to cut back for a while. No more expensive trips. No more shopping and self-indulgence.'

Jemima's fists clenched. 'There's the small matter of my credit cards.'

'How much do you owe?' asked Tara.

There was a pause. 'Eighty on one. Forty on another.'

'What's the problem?' Poppy chirped up. 'That's nothing.'

'She means eighty thousand,' Tara said coldly. 'So that's a hundred and twenty thousand on credit cards. Somewhat *prolific*. Your interest payments must be about twenty-plus grand a year.'

Jemima stared steadfastly out the window, then muttered, 'Well, you know what the bank is like. My banker is always ringing me up and offering me more credit. It's so easy to put on a couple of flights, a bit of shopping, the New York hotels . . . it adds up so fast. I always mean to pay it off, but I keep forgetting.'

There was silence for a moment and then Tara said slowly, 'I would advise using any savings you've got to reduce that debt as far as possible. If you haven't got the income coming in, I can see that meeting repayments might be difficult. Let me know how it goes. If you really are desperate, you can come to Gerald and me.'

Jemima whirled round, her eyes ablaze, and said sarcastically, 'Oh, thank you, Tara. How kind of you! Shall I send all my bills to you, then? And what about the money I spend keeping Herne going every month? Will you pay for that too? How lovely for you to have so much money.'

'Wait!' cried Poppy. The others looked at her expectantly. She had a big smile on her face. 'I don't know what you're both so worried about. I have the answer. It's so simple.'

'OK,' Tara said slowly. 'That's very good news. There must be something I've overlooked. What is it?'

'Loxton!'

Tara frowned. Jemima's face cleared. 'Of course, Loxton!'

'We can sell it,' Poppy explained. 'Or, at least, I can. We'll sell it – it must be worth millions. And put the money into Trevellyan so we can get it going again.' She sat back in her chair. 'Ta-dah! Problem solved.'

'She's right. Well done, Poppy. What a relief,' Jemima said, smiling again. 'I thought I was in deep shit there for a moment.'

Tara bit her lip. Jemima noticed. 'What? What is it, Tara?'

'I wish it was that simple. Of course it occurred to me that we could sell Loxton, and you're right, it's worth several million at the moment. But there's a problem. Well, two problems.' The other two looked at her questioningly. 'The first is that Mother neglected to make the estate over to you in good time, Poppy. There's an inheritance tax bill to pay on the estate and all the contents of the house. The taxman will be popping round to tot it all up anytime now but we can expect a bill of at least three million, by my reckoning. Perhaps more, depending on the current market value of some of the furniture and artworks.'

Poppy gasped. 'Three million pounds! How am I going to find three million pounds?'

'Exactly.'

There was a pause as this information sank in.

'So she'll have to sell anyway,' said Jemima flatly. 'That much is obvious. But at least there'll be something left after the taxman has taken his bite, won't there? I mean, they don't take it all.'

'No.' Tara picked up another document. 'But that's where Mother's second little surprise comes in.'

'Second?' muttered Jemima. 'I'm losing count of her little surprises. I bet she's chortling away down in the inferno.'

'In the course of shoring Trevellyan up by selling off assets and properties, she also mortgaged Loxton. She didn't quite mortgage it up to the hilt but she managed to mortgage it just enough that by the time we've sold it, paid the tax and repaid the bank, there will be precisely nothing left. Perhaps enough to pay off the staff and tidy things up a bit, but nothing significant. Certainly not enough to make a dent in the Trevellyan mess.'

Jemima came back to the sofa and sank down into it. 'Oh God,' she said in a quiet voice. 'This is really serious, then.'

Tara nodded.

'So Loxton has to go, no matter what?' said Poppy.

'I'm afraid so, Pops. As soon as possible. We'd better instruct an agent to put it on the market immediately.'

'What about everything inside? The furniture, the paintings . . .'

'We could try to sell it intact. We should get quite a bit more if we do that. It might give us enough to hold Trevellyan up a bit longer. But –' Tara gazed seriously at her sister – 'that really is your inheritance. That's all there is. If you sell Loxton's contents and put the money into Trevellyan, I can't guarantee you that you won't lose it all anyway.'

'And what about me?' Jemima asked icily. 'I don't

have bloody anything! Pops, I think you should sell the lot. Send the contents to Sotheby's and we'll use the money for the company.'

Tara held up her hand. 'Shut up, Jemima. This is Poppy's decision. It doesn't matter how you feel about it, the fact is that she owns the contents of Loxton and it is her decision, and hers alone, what happens to them.'

Poppy looked at her sisters with her wide green eyes, running a chestnut ringlet round her finger.

'Of course I'll sell them. I think we should each choose a few things from the house, things we really want and that we'll treasure. And the rest should go to auction and we'll use the proceeds to save our company. It's definitely what I want.'

'Good girl,' Jemima said approvingly.

'That's extraordinarily generous.' Tara smiled. 'Thank you.'

'I'd have done the same,' Jemima said quickly.

'I'm sure you would. But there's one thing I have to ask you both.' Tara paused and looked uncomfortably at them. 'Do either of you know where Mother's jewels are?'

Poppy and Jemima stared back at her, both taken aback by the question.

'Aren't they in the house?' asked Poppy. 'That's where they always were.'

'No. They're not.'

Jemima frowned. 'They must be in the bank, then.'

'I'm looking in to that. But everything's gone from her dressing table, save one or two trinkets. Anything of value has gone – and so has her silver locket, her wedding and engagement rings and a few other things of sentimental value. She always kept those in her room, so someone's removed them.'

'Who?' asked Poppy.

'I don't know, obviously. Perhaps Mother sent them away herself.'

'Why would she have done that?' wondered Jemima.

'Goodness knows. But whatever her reasons, we need those jewels. They're potentially worth hundreds of thousands, and rightly, they belong to Poppy.'

'To all of us,' Poppy said loyally.

'We need to start looking for them,' Tara said.

'Let's add that to our To Do List,' said Jemima with a giggle. 'Let's see. Find cache of missing jewels. Sell family home and everything in it, so reducing selves to penury. Save family company before it goes bust.' She laughed.

Tara giggled too. 'And sue whoever it was who failed to get Mother's inheritance tax issues sorted out.'

'Why not?' said Jemima with a shrug. 'I reckon I can fit that in on Thursday. I won't be able to afford my massage and pedicure now, so I'll pop over to the lawyer's instead.' Then she said soberly, 'Oh God. It's all so huge, I can't quite take it in.'

'Don't worry, girls. We can face it and we can win.' Tara smiled. 'I know it.'

12

There was a knock at the door and a porter came in bringing a tray of tea things. A delicate china stand held a variety of sandwiches and cakes, and there were piping hot silver pots of tea.

'Thank goodness, I'm starving,' said Jemima. 'Clever you, Tara.'

'I thought we might need something to keep us going.'

'Ooh, cucumber sandwiches, my favourite.' Poppy pounced on the little rectangles with slivers of green peeping out of the bread.

'You can really count on the Ritz, can't you?' Jemima said, through a mouthful of smoked-salmon sandwich. 'It knows how to do a proper tea. Remember Mother and Daddy bringing us here when we were little for tea in the Palm Court? I thought I'd gone back in time. All that pink and gilt and green fronds and tinkling piano music. It was like stepping into the 1920s. Want a sandwich, Tara?'

Tara shook her head. 'Just a cup of tea, thanks. With lemon.'

Jemima checked the tea had brewed then poured it into the bone china cup and passed it to Tara, with the plate of lemon.

'OK, girls, it's time to start using our little grey cells,' announced Tara. 'Now we know the true situation, we have to decide how we're going to get Trevellyan back on track.'

The others looked blank.

'Sorry, darling,' said Jemima, until my blood sugar is back at reasonable levels, I'm no use to man or beast. You're the businesswoman. You must have the ideas.'

'I'm afraid we're going to be rather useless,' added Poppy apologetically. 'You're so good at these things, Tara. It's what you do for a living. I'm happy to provide some extra cash by selling the Loxton things, but I don't think I'll be much help otherwise.'

'And you know me,' said Jemima. 'Very happy to spend money. Not a clue how to make it. Sorry.' She shrugged.

Tara put her teacup carefully back on its saucer. 'And that's that, is it? Sorry, Tara, could you possibly fix it for us? We don't know about facts and figures and business, we're such helpless little kittens . . .' Suddenly she leaned forward, her eyes blazing. 'Haven't you listened to a word I've said? If you've ever had to prove yourselves, that time is now! You're both intelligent, talented women and yet you've learned to be helpless. Useless! Your own words. You should be ashamed of yourselves.'

'What do you want us to do?' Jemima said, startled by Tara's outburst. 'I can barely type. I can just about send an email. That's about it.'

'I did filing once,' volunteered Poppy. 'Will there be much call for that? If so, I'm sure I can help out.'

Tara laughed, a trace of bitterness in her voice. She leaned back in her chair and folded her pale, slim hands in her lap. 'If you could hear yourselves! The Heiresses . . . the aristocratic lady and the artist. That's your idea of business, is it? Typing and filing! Do you think Richard Branson does much typing and filing? Of course not! Business is about ideas. It's about instinct and understanding. It's about taking the knowledge you've got and using it. Jemima, what's your area of expertise?'

'Um . . . parties. Shopping. Shoes. Being somewhat high maintenance.'

'Yes! All vital to a luxury goods company! You see? We're going to need everything you know about how and why you and all your friends go shopping. And, much as I hate to remind you, you happen to be news-worthy. People like to read about what you're up to – where you go, what you do, who your friends are. Some of them – God help them – even want to *be* like you. We can use all that. Trevellyan is going to need an ambassador, someone to spark publicity and interest. That, your ladyship, could be you.'

Jemima looked interested but her tone suggested she was still not convinced. 'Yes . . . yes, when you put it that way . . . I suppose I *could* do something along those lines.'

'You'd better believe it. Trevellyan is going to need a major new relaunch. Some fresh ideas and a new image.' Tara pointed her pen at Poppy. 'That's where you come in.'

Poppy looked blank. 'I don't know the first thing about scent. What am I supposed to do?'

Tara sighed with exasperation. 'Haven't you been listening to me? Of course none of us know anything about running a perfumery business.' She paused for a moment, obviously trying to hold in her impatience at Poppy's helplessness. Then she regained her enthusiasm. You may not know about scent but you know about how things should look, what works together. You know me – virtually colour blind. I wouldn't know good branding if it came up and bit me. But you would. And I want you to start thinking about things like packaging and the look of Trevellyan. What works and what doesn't? You're going to need to do some research, too. I want you to immerse yourself in the world of luxury fragrances. We need to know everything we can about the world we're dealing with. There's just so much to be covered I wouldn't know where to start on my own . . .' Tara stopped and frowned. Some of her energy seemed to seep out of her. 'I've been feeling pretty miserable about all this. I just knew you'd both try and foist this on me but there's no way I can do this alone. I have a more than full-time job already and as it is I don't see enough of Edward and Imogen. I've thought hard about it – you're not useless, you can both make a huge difference if you put your minds to it. I don't intend to just let you give up. You need to help me. You can do it.'

Poppy went over and gave Tara a hug. 'We've been horribly selfish. We haven't given a thought to how busy you are. Of course we'll help. We'll do all we can, won't we, Mimi?'

'I think we've spent more time together in the last four days then we have since we were children,' Jemima said drily. 'Let's just hope we can maintain this *entente cordiale*. But I'm willing to do it if you are. What have we got to lose?'

'Exactly.'

'What if we fail?' Poppy said.

'Home to dreaded Herne Castle, until Harry kicks me out, which will probably be sooner rather than later. Then, God knows. I'll have to sell the flat, I suppose, if only to clear off the credit cards.' A look of pain passed over her face. 'I love my flat. I don't want to live anywhere else.'

'It won't come to that,' Tara said with determination. 'I mean it. We can do this, we can turn the company around. We just have to learn very, very fast. And we have to start treating it like a job. That means I want you both in offices in Trevellyan House from Monday. I've told Ingliss to arrange it. Three offices for the new chief executives.'

'Every day?' asked Jemima, alarmed.

'Every day.'

'*All* day?' queried Poppy.

'A full business day. Nine till five, minimum. It'll come as quite a shock to the system, girls, but it has to be done.'

Jemima looked sulky. The air of goodwill and positivity that had previously filled the suite was distinctly reduced. 'That's totally unrealistic, Tara. I don't get up until at least nine-thirty. Then I've got all my appointments. My hair, my masseuse, my personal trainer . . . It will wreak havoc with my diary and it's really not fair to them to mess them around like that. I can't possibly fit it in. I could probably do a couple of afternoons a week. And I can work from home, I suppose.'

'I've got about as much confidence that you've got the discipline to work from home as I have that you can fly a jumbo jet. You've not trained yourself, you don't know how to work. No. We've only got twelve months. We have to make sacrifices. If it means you have to paint your own toenails for a while, then so be it. Anyway, it's not like you'll be able to afford any of those luxuries for the foreseeable future.'

'What about me?' Poppy said in a small voice. 'What about my painting?' She looked up at her sister with anxious eyes. 'I need time to be creative.'

Tara turned to her younger sister. 'Sorry, love, but that means you too. You'll just have to channel all your creativity into rebranding Trevellyan. You can take up the painting again when we've done what we have to do, I promise.'

'What about you?' demanded Jemima crossly. 'What sacrifices are *you* making? Will you be in Trevellyan House five days a week, nine till five? I doubt it!'

Tara stood up and strode over to the window, looking out as Jemima had done earlier. The light was fading a little now in the late afternoon and people were heading home. The office workers were beginning to emerge, pouring down the Underground or climbing on buses to begin the long commute home. The other two watched as Tara turned towards them, her face tight.

'I'll be making my own sacrifices, believe me,' she said in a low voice. 'Now, I think we've done enough for one day. Have a good weekend. I'll see you in Trevellyan House on Monday at nine o'clock. Then we begin.'

13

Poppy approached the iron railings of the Soho club, weaving her way among the smokers congregated outside. There were notices up asking smokers to keep away from the doorways and not to scatter their used butts on the pavement, but it didn't seem to make much difference.

Not for the first time, Poppy was glad she didn't smoke. In fact, she'd managed to stay clear of most vices in her life. She wasn't a great drinker – a bad experience with vodka, whisky and claret when she was a teenager had gone a long way to putting her off – and she'd found the idea of drugs simultaneously frightening and tedious. Her imagination was already so vibrant, she was almost afraid of what might happen if she took mind-altering substances, and she had a healthy suspicion of anonymous white tablets or packets of unidentified powder. They reminded her of Nanny's dyspepsia tablets and the bicarbonate of soda she would make the girls drink if they had upset tummies and which Poppy had loathed.

The tediousness came from the behaviour of the people she knew who did indulge in such vices. She had one boyfriend who'd smoked cannabis cigarettes like others smoked Marlboro Lights and after a while she'd realised that he was far more interested in this pursuit than he was in her. And she got bored waiting for him to reply to her questions: short conversations seemed to take hours as his raddled mind moved at a snail's pace. His good looks and artistic talent weren't enough to compensate for it, so Poppy dumped him.

The reverse was true for the effects of other substances; she'd had many a good party ruined when collared by some coke-fired friend who'd pin her in a corner and talk her to death, eyes glittering brightly and mind racing at super speed. Or it was an E-head, full of love and affection for her, desperate to hug her, dance with her, and confide what a fantastic person she was.

No, drugs had never appealed to her. Her favourite vice – she felt a little embarrassed to admit it even to herself, as it sounded too little-rich-girl cliché for words – was champagne. It didn't have to be vintage, and she was just as happy with a good prosecco on occasion, but she loved nothing better than a glass of champers fizzing with those adorable bubbles, and the bitter-sweet biscuity taste on her tongue.

She went down the steps to the door of the club and let herself in. A sophisticated twenty-something girl greeted her and took her name.

'Your guest is here,' she said. 'Waiting for you in the bar.'

'Thanks.' Poppy made her way along a dark corridor and into the basement bar. It was dominated by a huge fireplace where a great fire roared away despite the spring warmth outside, its faux logs and ash looking very realistic.

She saw Margie at once, sitting at one of the long polished refectory tables, her head bent over a magazine. Poppy went over.

'Great to see you,' Margie said cheerfully, planting a resounding kiss on her cheek as Poppy leaned over to say hello. 'You're looking good – been anywhere nice?'

'Sadly no. I just met up with my sisters,' Poppy said. But she left it at that. She didn't want to tell Margie anything about the Trevellyan business. For tonight, she wanted to escape it. Besides, when she started telling Margie about her other life, her Trevellyan life, the whole thing sounded so outlandish and extraordinary, and it created a distance between her and her old friend, whose completely normal Yorkshire upbringing was a million miles from Poppy's.

'Oh? How are they?' Margie said politely, although Poppy could tell that she wasn't really interested. She had an inbred distrust of anyone with money, and titles were the work of the devil as far as she was concerned, but she'd always made an effort not to let that get in the way of her friendship with Poppy. They'd met at art school and had hit it off immediately, despite their different backgrounds. For Poppy, Margie was pure gold – a friend who liked her despite her wealth and background, not because of it.

'They're fine, thank you. Can I get you a drink?'

Margie nodded at a bottle next to her. 'I'm on the beers, thanks, and you can certainly get me another if you're buying.'

'I'll have the same,' Poppy said, deciding not indulge her champagne vice tonight as Margie scoffed so hard whenever she did. She went to the bar and came back with two bottles of Belgian beer.

Margie said sympathetically, 'Listen, love, I was so sorry to hear about your mum. How was the funeral?'

'Gruelling.' Poppy slipped on to the bench next to her friend. 'But OK. It was pretty bad while it was happening, but I've felt better since.'

'That's what funerals are for, I suppose,' soothed Margie. 'Closure.'

'Yes, I suppose so. I know that Tara felt better too, just like me. We were both terribly upset. But you know, I just couldn't believe how little Jemima appeared to care. She really seemed pleased that Mother is dead. I wouldn't have thought it of her.'

'Maybe it's an act,' Margie suggested. 'You know, to protect herself.'

Poppy considered this. 'You could be right. Jemima's spent her whole life ranting about how mean Mother was to her and how much she hated her. I suppose she could hardly start wailing and sobbing once she was dead.'

'Sometimes these things are delayed. It can take a while to realise that someone is really gone for good.'

Margie put her hand on Poppy's and smiled. 'Maybe your sister will come to terms with it over time. Don't be too hard on her.'

'You're being very understanding.' Poppy smiled back. 'Especially as I know how you feel about Jemima.'

'Oh, I don't know the woman! I might consider her over-privileged and having far more than it's right for one person to possess, but she's still a person with feelings, isn't she? I have got a heart, you know, even if you think I'm a rock-hard Northerner who'd like to line your sister's lot up against the wall and have done with it!'

Poppy laughed. 'You're making me feel better already. Thanks for coming out to see me.'

'Are you mad? Course I'd come out and see you, you nutter. Why wouldn't I?'

'Well, I know you sometimes get together with Tom and his lot on a Friday night . . .' Poppy's gaze moved to the table and she stared hard at a crack on it.

'Yeah, well, not tonight.' Margie took a swig from her bottle of beer.

'How is Tom?' Poppy asked, after a pause.

'OK.'

'Is he painting?'

'Yeah. He's got an exhibition in New York.'

'New York?' Poppy echoed, impressed.

'Yeah, he's really chuffed. It's some prestigious gallery in the centre of town, so he's painting like mad to get ready for it. They want fifty pictures at least.'

'Fifty . . . that's brilliant.'

'It's great, but you know what a perfectionist Tom

is. He's getting ever so precious about it all. You know how he works with egg tempura? Well, he's started using only organic eggs, as though it'll make a blind bit of difference, and it's costing him a fortune! Still, I expect Channing pays for that. It was her dad who swung his exhibition for him, too – he'd never have got that if it wasn't for her.' Margie laughed and then stopped, looking guiltily over at Poppy. 'Oh, Christ, love, I'm sorry.'

'It's fine,' Poppy declared, trying to hide the fact that every word was simultaneously fascinating and painful. Hearing about Tom was always difficult. 'I'm fine to talk about it, really. I'm over it. Tom can do what he likes. So I take it Channing is the American girlfriend?'

Margie nodded. 'She's nice and all, but she's bad for Tom. She hero-worships him and it's unhealthy for his ego, which is inflated enough as it is. She thinks he's the world's greatest living artist.'

'Tom must like that.'

'You'd better believe it! And she's always ready to hand over wodges of her allowance to make it happen. Naturally, Daddy will do anything to keep his little girl happy, and he's totally taken in by Tom's brilliant-artist routine as well.' Margie rolled her eyes. 'I wouldn't mind so much if he really *was* the next Picasso or something, but we both know he's not, don't we?'

'Yes,' Poppy said softly. She was suddenly seeing an alternative future, where she had been the one supporting Tom, making his dreams come true, turning the two of them into an important couple in the art world.

With her money and his unshakeable self-belief, perhaps they could have done it . . . She shook her head. *It wasn't what I wanted,* she reminded herself. *I need to be creative in my own way, not pay for Tom to indulge himself.*

'Actually, Poppy,' Margie said in a low voice, 'there's something I need to tell you.' She stared at the table and fidgeted awkwardly.

'What is it?'

'I wasn't sure whether now was a good time, what with your mother and everything, but I can't not tell you now we're talking about Tom. It would be like lying to you.'

'Yes?' Poppy felt a shiver of apprehension. She wrapped her fingers round the cold beer bottle in front of her.

'Sorry about this, love – but Tom is engaged to be married. He proposed to Channing last week and she said yes.'

It felt like a bucket of cold water being emptied over her head – a sudden, unpleasant shock.

'Are you OK?' Margie said gently, putting her hand on Poppy's arm.

'Yes . . . yes, I think so,' Poppy said a little shakily. 'It's weird, I shouldn't care. Because I know we weren't right for each other and maybe he and this Channing are the ideal couple . . . but it still hurts. I feel angry that he's happy again, and I'm not.'

'You'll meet someone else, you know you will.'

'I hope so. Otherwise I'm going to be alone a long time!' Poppy managed a rueful smile. 'My life is so confused at the moment, Margie. Mother dying has created a whole load of problems you wouldn't believe. More than ever, I feel like I need someone to lean on. I'm tired of being on my own. I miss Tom, even though I shouldn't. I still love him in some ways.' She bit her lip, trying not to let her emotions overcome her.

'You're going to meet someone else,' declared Margie. 'Someone fantastic. I can feel it in my water. And in the meantime, do you know what I think?'

'No – what?'

'I think you need some champagne. I know you can't stand beer. Come on. It's my treat.'

14

'Let me get this absolutely clear, Tara.' Eric Bonderman stared at her with his most steely gaze. 'You want to take a what?'

'A sabbatical.'

'Right. You want to leave your job for six months –'

'At least,' put in Tara. 'I'll need at least that long.'

'At *least* six months. Well, what the hell are we going to do without you? Who is going to manage your funds?'

'I don't know, we'll find someone. And I'll still keep an eye on everything, when I can.'

'Very good of you,' Eric said coldly. 'What on earth makes you think I'm going to agree to this?'

'I suppose because you'll have to. I need this time. I'm not taking an extended holiday, though God knows I deserve some time off. I'm not going to work for a rival, even though I've been approached by headhunters on at least five occasions in the last eighteen months.' Tara stood up and began pacing about Eric's luxurious office with its unrivalled view of the City. She was wearing a tight, dark grey pencil skirt and a magenta chiffon blouse with billowing sleeves. She made a striking figure and Eric tried hard not to stare at her slim legs as she marched about his office on her high heels. 'You know I've made a great success of the funds I've managed, and I've also come up with some hot tickets that have generated you and the company a lot of money. I've done it by spotting companies that are tottering and that can be rebuilt. Now I've got the chance of a lifetime. Right on my doorstep is my own company. It's falling to pieces and I can go in and turn it round. It's a priceless opportunity – not just to save my family's business but to test my instincts, and try out my ideas. I've done everything in theory up until now – now I've got the chance to do it in practice.'

Eric leaned back in his leather armchair. 'You mean that perfume house your father owned?'

Tara nodded.

'Why do you want to waste your time on that?' Eric asked, waving his pen about to show his bafflement. 'You're never going to make real money on it. It's small fry.'

'It might be now, but it's got huge potential.'

'Huge potential to suck up a load of money and sink without trace, taking your career with it.'

Tara stopped and faced him, her hands on her hips. 'Come on, Eric. A businessman as astute as you must appreciate the worth of the luxury goods market. And it's just about the only part of the retail industry still experiencing growth at the moment. The massive amount of money flooding in from the Russians, Indians and Chinese is keeping it very buoyant.'

He shrugged. 'Sure. But that's high-end stuff. Yeah, of course there's money in it. Any fool knows that. But you've got to be right at the top, where the rich come out to play. And I don't mean to offend, but your family shop isn't exactly up there with the big boys.'

'I can get it there.'

Eric made a quizzical face and grinned. 'Yeah. OK. Look, you're not serious, are you? I mean, who tries to relaunch a tired old business during a global economic downturn? Or do you know something I don't?'

'I've never been more serious. And I have another name for a global economic downturn – "opportunity". When others pull in their horns and stop playing, I get excited.'

His grin faded. 'Don't be stupid, Tara. This is a ridiculous waste of time, I'm telling you.'

'And I'm telling *you*.' Tara scooped up her coat and headed for the door. 'From Monday there'll be someone else in my office – I'll sort out who over the weekend. I'll be gone for at least six months. Make sure you arrange with payroll to stop my salary.'

'Hey!' shouted Eric angrily as she reached the door. 'What makes you think there'll be a job to come back to?'

'There will be,' said Tara, looking at him over her shoulder. 'We both know that. I'll be in touch.'

*　　*　　*

She felt a thrill of excitement as John drove her up and out of the company car park. It was like being let out of school before the long summer holiday. Of course she would have to devote the next couple of days to finding someone who could cover for her but she had a favour she might be able to pull in for this. And she would still be monitoring her funds and the markets, she knew she wouldn't be able to help herself. But now, she would also be marching into Trevellyan on Monday morning and taking charge. She would show them – she'd show the ghosts of her parents just who she was, and what they missed when they ignored her.

The Friday night traffic was thick and slow moving. John used all his skill to guide the great car through the throng, powering silently away, getting across amber lights by the skin of his teeth and generally doing his best to get Tara back home.

He succeeded brilliantly and they pulled up in front of the house bang on seven.

'You star, John, thanks.' Tara didn't wait for her driver to open the door. She was tip-tapping up the front steps before he'd even got out of his seat. 'You have a great weekend, OK? Give my love to Philippa. And I'll see you here at seven-thirty on Monday. We're going to Trevellyan House.'

John waved back, and pulled the big car back out into the road.

A few moments later, Tara was running into the bathroom.

'Mummy!' squealed Edward with delight. 'You're home.'

Imogen jumped up, covered in water and bubbles, eager for a hug, babbling excitedly as she told Tara all about her day, which involved the park, the swings and her friend Millie.

Tara laughed, not caring that her chiffon blouse was now drenched and clinging forlornly to her thin frame. 'Tell me everything, darlings,' she said, grabbing a face cloth with one hand as she knelt down next to the bath.

They spent a wet and silly twenty minutes, giggling and playing, until Robina came in and told them it was time to get out and prepare for bed. She took Imogen, while Tara wrapped a warm towel round Edward and heaved him from the bath. It was hard to believe that he was almost five already. It seemed as though it was only five minutes ago that she'd brought home that tiny little bundle from the Portland Hospital and set about learning to be a mother. Of course, she'd had help right from the start; first a live-in maternity nurse and then a full-time nanny. Robina was the second after the first had left to go back to Australia. She was brilliantly capable and seemed very happy looking after the little ones. Tara would have liked to have spent more time at home with the children when they were babies but she'd had to go back after six months' maternity leave. Her job demanded it and she'd known that if she wanted to be taken seriously, she was going to have to get back to the office as soon as possible. Even on her leave, she'd been on the internet a couple of hours a day, chasing leads, emailing and monitoring the world markets. A few times, she'd rushed into the office, leaving the nanny and Edward at home.

When Imogen had arrived two years later, it had been easier. She hadn't been as flooded with hormones as she had with the first, and yet it was still a terrible wrench to leave her little girl and return to the office. She had a feeling that there would be no more babies, and that she had lost her last chance to spend long happy days with her children, watching them grow up.

Still, Robina was doing an excellent job, the children were happy and healthy and she, Tara, was providing a wonderful role model of what women could achieve if they wanted. That was the thing – she didn't want to be a stay-at-home mum. She valued her achievements and her job too highly to let them go. But she also longed for her babies sometimes, and hoped very much that they didn't love Robina more; after all, it was Robina who fed them, took them to the park, comforted them when they fell over, looked after them when they were ill. During the week, Tara talked more to them by phone then she did face to face.

But I'm doing this for them, she told herself as she carried Edward through to the bedroom. *The children are the best part of me and Gerald, and I want them to be proud of us. I want them to see what I can do – Trevellyan is going to be the way I prove myself, I know it and it's their future too.*

Tara let herself out of the children's bedroom, blinking in the hall light. Reading three bedtime stories in a row by a dim light (a very sleepy Imogen had only

155

lasted the first one before dropping off), and then soothing Edward to sleep left her feeling completely dopey too.

Robina came out of the nursery at the same time.

'Hi, Robina, how was the day?' Tara asked with a smile.

'Very good, thank you. They were very well behaved. Imogen and I collected Edward from school as usual and we all went to the park for a good run around with the Wilson nanny and her children. Then home for tea.'

'Oh, excellent. And Robina . . . everything is tidy downstairs, isn't it?'

Robina gave her a knowing look. 'Oh, yes. It's all spick and span, don't worry.'

'Thank you. You know how Gerald prefers things . . .'

'I certainly do. Now, if there's nothing else, I'll go to my flat.'

'Of course. Go and relax, you deserve it.' Tara smiled again. She always tried to be as nice as possible to Robina, dreading the day when the nanny would hand in her notice for some reason. That wouldn't be for a long time yet, with any luck, for Tara and Gerald provided a very luxurious private flat under the house and a snazzy little car. Robina had every evening off and most of the weekend, a fat salary and trips abroad with the family whenever she wanted to go along, so there was no reason at all to leave.

Except Gerald, of course. But Robina seemed to understand about that, which was a great comfort.

Thinking of Gerald reminded her that she was going

to have to tell him about Trevellyan. He was not going to be pleased, she knew that. *I can avoid it tonight at least,* she thought. *He's out at some big dinner for important newspaper types. I can enjoy a light supper in peace in front of the television. Bliss.*

She would put off the evil moment until some time during the weekend, perhaps on Sunday morning. Gerald would probably want sex as usual, and just afterwards, when he was feeling relaxed and good humoured, was always a sensible time to broach awkward subjects.

She went down the wide staircase, her stocking-clad feet making no noise on the thick honey-coloured carpet. The house was so quiet. It glittered in the light of the chandelier that hung from the hall ceiling: mirrors, gilt, china, polished furniture, all reflecting the lavish golden glow.

Well, all she wanted now was a couple of poached eggs on thick, hot, buttery toast, a glass of cold white wine and something mindless on the television. She wouldn't think about Gerald quite yet. It wasn't time.

15

Jemima picked up the text as she left the Ritz on Friday afternoon. It was from Harry.

Hope you haven't forgotten we are due at Rollo's tonight for the weekend.

'Oh fuck with a capital fucking F!' muttered Jemima as she marched out of the hotel. She quickly fired back a message. *Yes, I had bloody forgotten. Can you tell them I'm ill?*

A few minutes later, when she was in a taxi heading back to Eaton Square, Harry's reply appeared in her inbox.

No. They know you're not. Don't be so rude. Meet me there at 8.

Jemima groaned.

Every now and then, they were forced to appear somewhere as a couple, pretending that everything was OK between them. Harry had a tight-knit circle of friends. His closest pals, all friends from school, probably knew him better than she did and almost certainly knew the truth about the relationship, even if Harry never talked openly about it and she suspected he didn't. He was far too English, upper class and male to start discussing his private affairs with anyone, no matter how much he was suffering. Then there was the wider group, also from school and some university friends. They were the only people Harry was interested in knowing. He would accept their invitations, go to their balls and house parties, enjoy himself and consider that he had a raring social life, thank you very much.

When Jemima complained that he only ever saw the same people all the time, he would ask her what on earth was wrong with that?

'I know them, I like them. Why would I want to go and meet a load of new people I've got nothing in common with and whom I will very likely detest?' he would ask.

'Because it's *fun* to meet new people!' Jemima would insist. But Harry was immoveable on the subject.

Rollo was one of Harry's school friends. He had a big rambling country house in Gloucestershire and a sparkling, blonde Sloaney wife called Emma who was only twenty-two and made Jemima feel haggard and ancient. Emma loved nothing more than pulling on a tight pair of jeans, a tatty cashmere sweater and some old boots and running about with a lot of dirty, smelly dogs, all the time still managing to look like a model.

And now they were invited to one of Rollo's dreaded house parties. Jemima gritted her teeth and considered how she could pull out but she knew in her heart that she had to go. Harry had made it quite clear that there wasn't another option, as far as he was concerned, and although they were on bad terms, she wasn't quite ready to bait him that far. It was galling because she'd had a fun weekend planned, with a charity cocktail party and dinner with friends, and a long lazy Sunday morning doing her beauty routine and gossiping on the phone. Besides, according to Tara, she was going to have to start work next week. Work! For the first time in her life. Surely she deserved a bit of time to herself before she launched herself into that. But it looked as though there was no alternative.

At the flat, she gave Sri the weekend off, threw some clothes into a Louis Vuitton weekend bag, selected a couple of evening dresses and hung them in a dress bag, packed some shoes and a bit of jewellery, and considered herself ready.

As she loaded her luggage into her car, she felt the spring breeze lift her hair and realised it was still light. The days were lengthening and the warmth was returning after a long spell of cold weather. Her spirits rose: maybe a speedy drive up the motorway to Gloucestershire wasn't such a bad thing. She'd leave the roof down while it was still light, plug in her iPod and sing along to her favourite tunes all the way. If anything was going to cheer her up, it would be that.

Racing down the motorway in her Lamborghini, Jemima didn't feel her spirits lift in quite the way she hoped. First she was getting closer and closer to Harry and that always made her uneasy, filling her with the sense that she was gearing up for a fight. Secondly, she couldn't shake her sense of apprehension.

On Monday, she, Poppy and Tara would start their mammoth task of trying to get Trevellyan back on its feet. How on earth could they succeed? She simply didn't have the first idea how they would start. Thank God they had Tara, who at least knew about the world of business. But what did she know about scent? What did any of them know?

The odds were stacked against them, that was for sure. And if they failed, then it would mean everything had changed. It would mean she would have to look at her life and, more importantly, at her marriage and decide what on earth she was going to do.

As darkness fell and the traffic became streams of red and yellow lights, she decided that this weekend, she'd try and look at Harry through fresh eyes and see what life would be like if there were no Eaton Square and no money.

She got lost on the way to the house. Harry had always driven her in the past and in the pitch black with no street lights, the winding rural lanes were identical. The occasional sign popped up to point the way to some obscure little hamlet but she had to stop and study a map by the car's interior light before she finally discovered where she was. As a result, she was almost half an hour late when she pulled through the wrought-iron gates and came to a stop in front of the Queen Anne mansion.

Emma arrived at the door to greet her, with two

golden Labradors bouncing up and down behind her, barking excitedly. She looked beautiful in a figure-hugging black cocktail dress, all peachy young skin and bright eyes. A necklace of diamond daisies sparkled at her throat.

'Hi, Jemima, so lovely you could make it. Down, Zeus! Down, Hera! Honestly, you two. Don't worry, we've not gone in yet. Everyone's in the drawing room having drinks. Shall I take you up to your room? I'll give you a hand with your things.'

Emma took her dress bags and led the way upstairs, chatting happily as Jemima followed behind with her luggage. From the moment she had stepped in the house, Emma had not stopped talking and Jemima instantly remembered how tediously she gushed, over-larding everything with compliments that felt insincere and even faintly mocking.

'I'm so pleased you could come. I said to Rollo, "If Jemima comes, this will be the most sublime party, she's just the ideal guest!" No one can hold a room like you can, darling, you're so fabulously witty and amusing. It's like having Dawn French in Sophie Dahl's body. Really, I mean it. We've got such a lovely crowd this weekend, it's going to be such great fun. Do take your time dressing – there's no hurry and we can easily wait for you.'

'Thanks.'

Emma led her along a corridor and then opened a bedroom door. She shot Jemima a worried look. 'You're in here with Harry. I hope that's OK . . .'

'Of course. Why wouldn't it be?' Jemima went in

past her. It was a typical country house bedroom: comfortable and unremarkable, with faded florals and hunting prints on the walls.

'Oh, no reason, darling! It's wonderful you two are still love's young dream. Well . . . we're downstairs in the drawing room. Do you remember where it is?'

'Of course.' Jemima smiled. 'I'll see you there.'

'Good. I'll leave you to it.'

'Thanks.' Jemima watched the other woman leave and then sighed with relief. What was it that irritated her about Emma? Was it her youth? Her beauty – all healthy, outdoorsy, rosy Englishness? Or her incredible self-confidence and self possession? She didn't seem at all fazed by her older, richer husband, or this big house, or welcoming so many guests into it.

Perhaps it's because I trust her about as far as I can throw her, Jemima reflected as she climbed into the shower in the tiny bathroom and turned on the hot water. A few minutes later she stepped out and not long after that, she was ready, in a simple red silk shift dress, glammed up by five-inch Louboutin heels.

She found her way back downstairs easily enough and followed the buzz of voices to the drawing room. As she opened the door, she saw everyone inside, standing about, holding glasses. The men were in black tie and the women in cocktail dresses, sparkling and shining in silks and sequins. A few turned to look at her as she entered.

Oh God, she realised, *I'm really on enemy territory here. These are Harry's friends. I bet they're all against me.*

Emma came forward to rescue her again. 'Jemima,

how lovely. You look fantastic, of course. You're going to blow the socks off our rural crowd. Rollo, come and say hello to Jemima.'

A tall, well-built man detached himself from a group near the fireplace and walked over.

'Jemima,' he said, with a cool smile, and leaned forward to kiss her on each cheek. 'How are you? Harry's over here.'

'Yes.' She had seen her husband as soon as she'd come in. Rollo led her back to the group. 'Hello, darling,' she said, reaching up to press her lips to his face.

'Hello.' Harry put his hand on the small of her back and pressed it, in the approximation of a hug. 'Good trip?'

'Excellent, thanks.'

'Rollo's got some champagne for you.'

'Just the thing,' she said smoothly, taking the glass and sipping from it. The conversation resumed around her and she stood there, part of the circle and yet feeling absolutely alone.

Dinner was not quite so bad. She and Harry were at opposite ends of the table, Harry next to Emma. She was not next to Rollo – rather pointedly, she thought – but instead next to a slightly sweaty man who seemed inordinately excited to be beside her. A plain woman in a hideous purple wrap dress was looking daggers in their direction all the time, and she took this woman to be his wife.

'So, Steven, what is it you do? You must tell me all

about it,' she said in her most seductive voice, and then sat back and prepared to be bored as Steven went into great detail about his management consultancy career. Harry's end of the table appeared to be having much more fun. Emma's light voice could be heard, punctuated by laughs from the men around her. Harry's laugh was a sound Jemima had not heard much lately, she realised and, as Steven droned on, she listened with half an ear to hear what it was that was so amusing. But the buzz of other conversations and the tinkle of glass and cutlery absorbed the sound, and she could only make out odd words here and there.

'. . . has bought the house across the valley,' she heard Emma say. Then a little while later, '. . . will join us tomorrow, we hope. Filthy rich, of course.'

Who could they be discussing? she wondered, as the plates were cleared away by the discreet staff.

'That's what I always say, anyway. Don't you agree?'

She looked up to see Steven gazing at her, hopefully. 'Oh, yes,' she said confidently, without a clue as to what he'd been talking about. 'I always say the same myself.'

After dinner, they all returned to the drawing room, where port, brandy and Scotch had replaced the cocktails and champagne on the drinks table, and the smokers lit cigarettes and cigars.

Jemima took a glass of brandy and wandered over to the window. She pulled back the heavy curtain and looked out over the Gloucestershire night. The house was surrounded by thick woodland and she could see little but the black shapes of trees moving against the dark cloudy sky.

'Some of us are going hunting tomorrow, if you'd like to come. It's almost the last meet of the season.' Emma was standing next to her.

'No, thanks,' Jemima said quickly. 'I don't ride.'

'You don't have to ride. You can follow. Most of us are following.'

'No. It's kind but I'll just potter about here, if you don't mind.'

'Of course not. You must do exactly what you want. I don't want you to be bored, that's all.' There was a pause that began to grow awkward. Emma hurried to fill it. 'I was just telling Harry about our new neighbour.'

'Really? Who is it?'

'He's a frightfully rich foreigner. A businessman. I thought you might know of him. He's called Richard Ferrera.'

Jemima shook her head. 'No. Never heard of him. Should I have?'

'Well, he's in your line of things.'

'What do you mean?'

'Scents and soaps, you know. Things like that. Not just that, of course. He's at the high end of luxury goods. His company owns lots of major brands, I believe.'

'Oh?' Jemima looked at Emma, her interest piqued. A week ago, she would have made some flippant comment and thought no more about it. But this seemed serendipitous. A successful businessman in precisely the line of work she was about to become a lot better acquainted with. Perhaps he could be of some help. 'How exciting.'

'He's coming over tomorrow night,' Emma added, 'so I must introduce you both. I'm sure you'll have tons in common.'

'Thank you. I'll look forward to it.' *I'd better keep her sweet,* Jemima thought, *if she's going to be useful and introduce me to this chap.* She smiled. 'And how's life with you, Emma? Enjoying things here in the country?'

Emma laughed. 'You wouldn't believe how busy I am. I thought city life was frantic, but honestly, it's nothing to running this place and keeping up with the incredible pace of things here. If it's not the hunt and the ball committee and the charity work, then it's the village or the church or something that needs organising and doing, and somehow I'm always being asked. I think people assume I've got nothing much to do. They don't realise I have to spend a week in London every month, keeping on top of things.'

'I know how you feel. People think it doesn't take any effort at all to look one's best. They have no idea, do they?' Jemima smiled again, just sweetly enough. She cast her eyes swiftly about the room. She had a feeling that this was as exciting as this gathering was going to get. Harry's lot were notoriously straight-laced; they might have a bit too much to drink occasionally but it was very unlikely that anyone was going to bring out some coke or get the music going and really start to party. If she made a discreet exit, she was unlikely to miss anything. 'Talking of looking one's best, I absolutely must get some sleep. Would you mind awfully if I went to bed? I'm ever so tired after my drive and I really do want to be on top form for tomorrow.'

'Oh, no, no, no. Please do. Breakfast is at nine tomorrow, but come down whenever you like. Good night.'

'Good night. I shan't make a fuss. I'll just slip away and see everyone tomorrow.'

'Fine.' Emma stood back to let her pass. 'Sleep well.'

Jemima let herself out of the drawing room, murmuring a quick good night to the people who noticed she was going, and then hurried up the stairs, relieved to be alone again. Dinner had been an ordeal but surely tomorrow would be better. There was this curious businessman to meet and something told her he could be exceedingly interesting, one way or another.

She undressed quickly and slid into bed, the wine and brandy from dinner already making her feel sleepy. She hoped she would be fast asleep by the time Harry came up to bed.

Jemima awoke to the unaccustomed warmth of Harry's body next to her. She lay completely still for a moment, blinking in the early morning light. How long was it since the two of them had been in bed together? It felt so unnatural and yet she realised with a pang how much she'd missed the intimacy of being in bed with him. She tried to remember the last time they had had sex. It was months ago, she knew that. It must have been just before Harry had walked in on her and Guy that terrible afternoon. He certainly hadn't touched her since.

Slowly, she turned over and looked at his broad naked back and the fair hair curling at the top of his neck. She had the strongest urge to stroke his skin and feel the heat beneath it, but she resisted. Harry was only here because he had to be. They obviously had a houseful this weekend, so all married couples had to share. She imagined that it wasn't such a novelty for most of them as it was for her and Harry.

Harry stirred and turned over, still asleep. She looked at his face, able to study it at close quarters for the first time in a long time. *I loved this face once,* she thought. How did she feel about it now? *Distant. Angry. Resentful.*

As she was thinking this, Harry's eyes opened slowly and the next moment he was staring at her.

'Hello,' she said.

'Morning.'

They gazed warily at each other for a while.

'How are you?' Harry asked.

'All right. How are you?'

'Struggling on.' He rolled on his back and stared up at the ceiling. 'Thanks for coming.'

'That's OK.' She propped herself up on her elbow so that she was looking down at him. She idly admired his long straight nose and firmly set jaw.

His blue gaze slid over to her, his expression neutral. 'Tell me what's been happening. What's going on with your inheritance?'

'It's all rather strange. It turns out that Mother wasn't

169

quite as clever as we all thought. Trevellyan is in trouble – it appears the company hasn't been making money for a long time. Tara seems to think that between the three of us we can sort it out.'

Harry snorted. 'Tara I can understand – but you and Poppy?'

'What do you mean?' Jemima asked, indignant.

'Well . . . the two of you! What on earth do you know about anything?'

Although this was precisely Jemima's own worry, she felt offended that Harry seemed to have so little faith in her. 'Thanks a lot!' she said.

'Come on, Jemima, be realistic. You've got absolutely no experience in this sort of thing.'

'I'll get some.'

'You don't know anything about business.'

'Tara does.'

'Well, what are you going to bring to the party?'

'I've got plenty of talents.'

'I'd love to know what they are,' said Harry snidely. 'Outside the obvious, of course.'

'What do you mean?'

'I think you can guess.'

She sat up straight, pulling the sheet to her breasts, her face flushed. 'Listen, you bastard, you'd better hope that I'm good at something other than looking decorative, because if I'm not, it's all going to get a hell of a lot worse for you.'

Harry's eyes narrowed and he rolled over to face her. 'Yeah, right. My whole future hinges on your business acumen? I don't think so.'

'Trevellyan is broke, darling! I'm not going to be getting lovely, fat, juicy cheques every month any longer. There isn't going to be any spare money for Herne. I'm going to be broke.'

Harry looked disconcerted. He stared at her for a moment and then said, 'What about that flat of yours? It must be worth a packet.'

'Yes, it probably is. But if I have to sell it, the money ought by rights to go towards saving Trevellyan. It's certainly not going to come to you.'

Harry glared at her coldly, then climbed out of bed. 'I know it comes as a continual surprise, but it so happens I don't actually want your money. I didn't marry you for it, any more than you married me for mine.'

'What did you marry me for then?' snapped Jemima, her eyes angry.

He turned slowly to gaze at her. 'I can't believe you can ask me that.' He walked into the small bathroom and shut the door.

Jemima watched him go, furious. *I'll show him*, she thought determinedly. *I'm damn well going to show him.*

171

16

Poppy woke up early on Saturday morning, showered and put on her Chinese turquoise silk dressing gown.

Who am I today? she wondered as she thought over the surprises of the last few days.

The week before last she became an orphan, albeit not exactly friendless and alone in the world. She'd been an artist in her attic flat, discovering herself and living as independently as possible. Then, suddenly, she became a real heiress, not just an heiress apparent, but the owner of a magnificent Victorian mansion and all that came with it, from the lush grounds right down to the paintings and staff. She had inherited all the trappings of a civilised and comfortable life.

But now she was tottering on the brink of poverty. Well, perhaps not quite poverty. But, by dint of her inheritance, she was in debt to the Government to the tune of millions of pounds.

She went over to the mirror and looked at her reflection. 'Poppy Trevellyan,' she said seriously. 'You owe the Government three million pounds. Pay up. At once.' The idea was so ridiculous, she laughed.

So now she would have to sell her inheritance. Despite her protestations that she didn't want the old place, the moment she'd heard that news from Tara, she'd felt a deep shock of grief. Lose Loxton? The place she'd grown up in? Even though she'd only owned it for a few days, she had already become accustomed to the thought that it was hers. She'd imagined walking through it, possessing it. And now, just like that, it was gone again. She shrugged. 'Oh well,' she said out loud. 'It's not as though I really wanted it.'

Poppy opened the doors of her enormous Victorian triple-fronted wardrobe. So she was no longer a woman of property. Now she was a businesswoman: part owner and saviour of Trevellyan. But today, she was going to be creative . . . she was going to tune into the soul of perfume. She needed something to put her in the mood . . .

Two hours later she breezed into Harvey Nichols wearing an Alexander McQueen red-and-white silk printed halter-neck dress that she had seen in the latest collections and absolutely had to have, even though it broke her vintage rules. Every now and then she went wild in the dress shops, allowing herself a little splurge on new things and this was one of them, along with some high red sandals. Today, though, she wasn't here for clothes. She was here to smell.

The ground floor was devoted to cosmetics and perfumery. All about her were small white booths, lit by strong overhead lights to create an almost clinically clean feeling. Each booth was devoted to its own brand, the instantly recognisable lettering of the most famous brands immediately grabbing Poppy's attention: Lancôme, Chanel, Givenchy, Estée Lauder. The countertops showed off lavish displays of the cosmetics on offer, as alluring and eye-catching as jars of sweeties for children. Photographs of impossibly beautiful models suggested how you, too, could look if only you wore Yves Saint Laurent mascara, or the new Clinique lipstick. It was a dream, of course, but a powerful one. It was so easy to believe that it was a stick of coloured wax that had created the flawless beauty on show and that it could be so easily bought for oneself.

Poppy had wandered through departments like this hundreds of times, shopping for make-up, but now, for the first time, she really took note of the perfumes on display. She'd never thought much about it before, which was odd considering how pivotal it had been to her whole existence. For her twelfth birthday, her father had brought home a very special present. Held in a blue box and tied with a silk ribbon, it was an antique Trevellyan bottle and inside it was a clear liquid tinted with the palest green.

'Happy birthday, Poppy,' her father had said with a smile. 'I've had it designed and made especially for you.'

She sprayed the scent on her wrist, thrilled to feel so grown up, and inhaled the sweet smell of jasmine. Her own perfume! Made just for her! She loved it, and it made her feel special because none of the others had a perfume made only for them. Every Christmas and birthday after that, she'd received another phial of scent to put in her special bottle, while Tara and Jemima always got one of the established Trevellyan scents. Her father had named the perfume *Sweetheart* because, he said, they couldn't call it *Poppy* when it smelt of jasmine. She had worn *Sweetheart* all the way through her teens and then suddenly stopped when it felt too babyish. She moved away from Trevellyan fragrances altogether, and on to hippyish herbal scents – patchouli, fruit oils, exotic musks – and then to organic, earthy compounds. But now the smell of it made her feel so nostalgic that she could hardly bear to spray it on to her wrist, even though the old bottle still sat on her dressing table. She'd never found anything she loved as much, although she'd tried some other famous brands. Now she hardly wore scent at all.

She continued around the shop floor. Every well-known name had at least three or four perfumes, and was promoting its newest addition. On the Chanel counter, there was *N^o5, N^o19, Coco, Coco Mademoiselle, Allure* and *Chance,* just for starters. Over at Lancôme she saw *Trésor, Poême, Ô de Lancôme* and *Hypnôse.* More and more it dawned on her just how many expensive and exquisite fragrances were on offer. Beyond the little booths were rows and rows of shelves, full of yet more perfumes: Guerlain scents, perfumes from designers like Stella McCartney, Thierry Mugler, Prada, Gucci, Armani, Calvin Klein, Hermès, Tom Ford, Marc Jacobs, Dolce & Gabbana, Burberry ... the list went on and on. As well as designer scents, there were the famous names: actors, singers and celebrities who had launched their signature scent, or even several. Just scanning the shelves quickly, she saw fragrances by Britney Spears, Kylie Minogue, Sarah Jessica Parker, Paris Hilton, Jennifer Lopez, Christina Aguilera and Kate Moss.

Now that she thought about it, she realised that, of course, she'd always been aware of all the perfumes on offer to her and yet it felt as though her eyes were really open for the first time. The number of fragrances for sale was startling: the sheer range of styles was almost overwhelming.

'Hello, can I offer you a tester of our latest perfume for women?' A smooth voice broke into her thoughts. Poppy looked round. An immaculately made-up woman in a black suit was smiling and proffering an elaborately moulded scent bottle, a red-nailed finger poised on the atomiser.

Seeing Poppy hesitate, the sales woman rushed on. 'It's a gorgeous new scent from Erin de Cristo. It's called *White Melody* and it's a fabulous blend of citrus and white flowers, perfect for a summer's evening or to wear to the beach . . .' Without waiting for Poppy to reply, she pressed down on the top, sending a rich spray all over Poppy's arm.

Poppy bent down and sniffed. A tangy zing of grapefruit hit the back of her nostrils and she flinched a little at the power of it.

'That's the top note,' said the woman hastily. 'It will settle down in a few minutes and you'll get the really sexy flavours coming through.'

'Thanks,' Poppy said and smiled. *The beginning of my education,* she thought. *This is where I start to sort out what's what.*

As she walked round, she tried to push away the feeling of apprehension that made her want to run away from this strange new world. She was beginning to realise how daunting a task she'd taken on. She took a deep breath.

There's so much! she thought, as she noticed yet another a display of fragrances, these from the small perfumers – Miller Harris, Jo Malone, Floris – and artisan perfumes from French, Spanish and Italian companies, in beautiful bottles and stylish boxes. *Who on earth is buying it all?* she wondered.

She began to try samples of perfumes that caught her attention. Some were sophisticated and classic; others wantonly sexy; some androgynous, aimed at boys and girls alike. There were old-fashioned florals; modern, light fruity fragrances; and brash, hard hits of scent that screamed of money and sex and parties. There was something for everyone. She smelt and smelt until she was almost high on a rich and sultry mixture of civet, musk, vanilla, fruits and flowers.

Finally she came across the perfume she'd known all her life. Tucked away on a corner shelving unit was the Trevellyan display, offering just a fraction of the range. There was the famous *Trevellyan's Tea Rose,* and a couple of the other floral fragrances in their sturdy cardboard boxes. The design had never changed as far as Poppy knew: navy blue boxes with the flowing Trevellyan script in gold and the name of the scent.

Each box was illustrated with a quaint watercolour of whichever flower it was based on.

Poppy went over. She picked up the *Tea Rose* tester and examined it. It was plain and basic: a clear glass bottle and a gold-coloured atomiser top. It seemed very Puritan and uninspired after all the coloured glass, exotic shapes and modern stoppers she'd been examining. She took a small paper strip and sprayed the perfume lightly on to it, then waved it under her nose. The smell hit her like a punch: her head was full of pictures and places. It was so familiar, it was like being whisked back through time to her home and her girlhood. It was an intense floral scent, pungent with rose to the exclusion of almost everything else. As the initial blast died away she began to pick up something else but had no idea what it could be.

This isn't right, Poppy thought, frowning. *This isn't how our perfume should smell. It's too . . . I don't know. Wrong, somehow.*

What did it say to her? What did it convey? It made her think of old bedrooms, untouched for years. It made her think of air fresheners in the lavatories of old-fashioned hotels. It made her think of bowls of dusty pot pourri in tea rooms in sleepy English villages.

No. That's not right at all. I may not be an expert, but even I can tell that we aren't going to be selling a million bottles of this any time soon.

Poppy picked up her post from the table in the hall of her building. There was the usual sheaf of stuff, along with serious-looking letters franked with the name Goldblatt Mindenhall. Various legal letters had been arriving for her all week, with details about the transfer of Loxton to her name and the length of time that probate would take, and all the other hundreds of things she was supposed to be concerned with. The executors of the will, Uncle Clive and another distant cousin her mother had picked on for some unknown reason, were no doubt sorting it out. She would wait until someone actually told her that Loxton was now hers and then she could go about asking someone else to sell it for her.

'Money!' she said out loud. 'It's all so serious and boring. That's what I hate about it.'

'Me too,' said a cheerful voice behind her.

She turned and saw a man letting himself into the building behind her.

'But they say it makes the world go round,' he continued with a smile, 'and unfortunately, we all need it. Hi. I'm George Fellowes. You live here, don't you? I've seen you about.'

He held out his hand and Poppy took it. He shook hers firmly, his eyes bright and friendly.

'Oh, yes . . .' Poppy looked at him, blankly, trying to remember his face but unable to place him.

'Don't worry, you probably won't have clocked me. I'm only a temporary resident here anyway. You might know of my aunt, she lives on the second floor. She's away in New York and I'm borrowing her flat.'

'Oh, yes, Miss Fellowes. I've seen her a few times. I'm Poppy. Are you staying long?'

'A month or so.'

They stood looking at each other and smiling awkwardly, then both began to speak at once.

'Well, very nice to meet you,' said George.

Simultaneously, Poppy said, 'Do let me know if you need anything – oh.'

They both stopped, then laughed.

'I said, do let me know if you need anything. I'm on the top floor.'

'Thanks.' He gave her another broad grin, his brown eyes crinkling up. 'I will.'

'Bye.' She set off up the stairs, trying to appear interested in her post, conscious of George looking up after her as she went.

17

Jemima refused to join Harry for breakfast downstairs. Instead she lay in bed, reading magazines from the stack Emma had thoughtfully left on a table. Finally she heard a clattering in the hallway and cheery voices as everybody made their way outside, then a roar of engines as they drove away. The riders would have already gone to the stables, the others would follow in cars and on foot.

Gone off hunting, she thought to herself. *Good. At least I can get some peace.*

She had no interest at all in country sports. Harry and his friends loved them all, and were endlessly hunting, fishing and shooting depending on the season. Jemima couldn't keep track. It seemed that if you wanted to be accepted by them, you had to be just as keen as they were. At first, she hadn't minded giving it a go. All she had wanted to do was spend time with Harry and if it meant spending hours in the freezing cold, waiting for the beaters to send over the next drive so the guns could take their shots, that was fine. But before long, she'd begun to get bored by it. It wasn't something she was keen on trying for herself, delicious as she found pheasant, and as a spectator sport, shooting left a lot to be desired.

It was when she'd started to pass on days out standing in an icy river or following the hunt that the gap between Harry and her had first emerged. Spending long days on her own in the castle, she became increasingly bored. On the days Guy was around – charming, sophisticated Guy – it hadn't taken too long before a mild flirtation began. Jemima needed company. She needed to feel loved and noticed. Harry had left her alone too much. Could she really be blamed for seeking comfort from Guy instead?

She flicked through the glossy magazines idly. A picture caught her eye. 'Neave – the newest, most exciting face in the world!' exclaimed the headline, above a picture of a model.

Another one, thought Jemima dismissively. *They're always talking about some new face.*

She examined the model with only vague interest but her attention was caught by the girl's arresting appearance. With paper-pale skin and thick, glossy black hair, she had dramatic looks that would catch anyone's attention. But what made her stand out were her extraordinary green eyes, which slanted upwards like a cat's. *Can they be real?* wondered Jemima. *That colour's too amazing. She must be wearing contacts.* But there was something about their emerald richness that proclaimed that they were real. The other thing that stood out was the curviness of the girl's figure. For a model, she had a surprising amount of flesh, most of it on her hips and breasts. She had a properly feminine figure, even if she was still much skinnier than most women.

My goodness, she's very sexy, thought Jemima. *I bet she's going to make it really big. Good luck to her, it's an awful world.*

She knew several famous models. One had managed to keep her career going well into her thirties before launching a swimwear range and retiring with great relief from the front line.

'It's a bloody nightmare,' she'd told Jemima over lunch. 'Permanently hungry, endlessly frightened of losing your looks, terrified of sixteen-year-olds taking your jobs . . . I'm telling you, they've gotta pay you good money just to go through the agony.'

It was a world that had never held any attraction for Jemima. She had the feeling it was a lot more boring than it looked – and it looked pretty boring.

She glanced at the article that went with the picture – it was a short puff piece saying that Neave was an Irish girl who'd been discovered working in a Dublin department store doing a Saturday job. She came from a huge, poor family and had been thrust within a matter of months into a world of glamour and luxury, flying from London to Paris to New York, dolled in the best couture clothing in the world and becoming the hottest face on the catwalks.

I hope it doesn't ruin her, thought Jemima as she flicked

on. She noticed an advertisement for a new perfume: a pop princess posed provocatively against a dreamy background of stars, her hair blowing in a breeze, an enormous heart-shaped purple bottle in her hands. *Celebrity*, ran the strap line. *For the girl with stellar dreams.*

It looks vile, thought Jemima. But she could see how it would appeal to a teenager who wanted to be as much like her idol as possible. A few pages on and there was another full-spread perfume ad, this time for a trendy fashion label which was launching its signature scent. Picking up the rest of the pile of magazines she feverishly searched through each one. She was stunned at how many perfumes were advertised, and every ad was perfectly pitched at the type of woman who'd be reading that particular magazine. The pictures, always of impossibly beautiful people, were carefully targeted at their market. Chic monochrome shots were aimed at older, sophisticated women. Younger, bold images of unashamed sexuality were clearly intended to tempt younger women. *This is how you'll find a man*, promised the advert. *A spray of this and he won't be able to resist you . . .* Others were fun and quirky, featuring unusual-looking models. *This scent will enhance your enjoyment of life*, the ad declared. *You'll skip down the streets of Paris in the rain, quirky and stylish and captivating . . .*

Jemima shut the magazine. *Oh my God, I'm beginning to see our problem. What's Trevellyan's message? Remember the 1920s – now you can smell like you were there too. Hardly the most appealing invitation. Come to think of it, what kind of advertising do we do?*

She couldn't recall ever seeing Trevellyan feature in a magazine, certainly none that she would read. Did companies like Trevellyan advertise? She'd always assumed they didn't need to – the brand was famous enough already. But then, all the glossy ads she'd just come across were selling big names: fashion houses, hugely well-known actresses, established perfume brands.

Jemima leaned back against her pillows. *Oh my God. This is going to be much harder than I imagined.*

She moved through the drawing room, weaving her way among the guests, the same faces as the night before with a smattering of new people, probably local gentry delighted to have bagged an invitation to dinner at the big house. The men were once again in the uniform of dinner jacket and black tie, and the women were dressed up in their best evening frocks. Jemima knew she looked good in her new Oscar de la Renta white silk dress printed with a bold black floral pattern. The skirt was knee length, full and trimmed with tiny white feathers. The bodice emphasised her tiny waist and left her arms bare. With it she wore black high-heeled Gina mules, bold red lipstick and a necklace of glossy black pearls to finish the effect. Her blonde hair was pulled up into an elegant twist. She felt very 1950s New Look, and yet spot on the season's black and white themes; she knew that she stood out among the dowdier, last season dresses and basic black that she could see all around her. Only Emma, radiant in a green silk jersey Zac Posen dress, looked anywhere near as glamorous.

Everybody seemed to have the high colour and good humour that resulted from a day's hearty exercise in the countryside. Jemima had spent a very languid day, but her stroll around the gardens in the afternoon had given her a boost. Now, though, she had only one thing on her mind. Where was that neighbour Emma had told her about?

The other guests shot intrigued glances as Jemima walked purposefully about the room, the women looking at her stunning dress and no doubt wondering where she had got it and how much it had cost, the men admiring her breasts, tightly encased in white silk, and the slim legs emerging beneath the full skirt.

None of the new faces looked as though they belonged to a stinking rich foreign businessman. Winding through the room, she found herself at the quieter end, standing by the fireplace just as she had the night before. And there was Harry, a glass of whisky in his hand.

'Hello, my darling wife!' he said loudly as she came up to him.

'Hello,' she said stiffly. 'Good day out?'

'Splendid. Splendid. You were sorely missed. Shame you didn't ride today – we were all looking forward to seeing your fantastic arse in a pair of jodhpurs, weren't we, Rollo?'

'Harry!' hissed Jemima, as Rollo turned to face them.

'Shall I just freshen your drink, Jemima?' asked Rollo smoothly, as he took her glass and moved away.

'What did you say that for?' She noticed Harry's

eyes were a little glazed. 'Oh my God, you're drunk. Why are you drinking whisky at this hour? We haven't even eaten yet.'

'Because I bloody feel like it, sweetheart, that's why. You look pretty. New dress? What am I saying? Course it's a new dress! When isn't it a new dress? You kit the local charity shop out like a bloody boutique, don't you, with the amount of cast-offs you send their way. How much did it cost you? Looks *very* pricy.'

'Harry, shut up,' growled Jemima. 'I don't know why you're talking this way. Stop being so loud, everyone can hear you.' She had noticed ears pricking, subtle sideways looks. People were tuning in to what Lord and Lady Calthorpe had to say to each other.

'Am I? We can't have that.' Harry grinned at her as he steadied himself against the fireplace. 'They might think we're not very happy together. That would be . . . well, *terrible*.' He took a final slug from his glass and the ice clinked against his teeth. 'You look very pretty,' he slurred. 'But you'd better take care of that dress. There might not be much more where that came from.'

'For God's sake, Harry, everyone's listening.'

'Why be ashamed of it? You'd better start preparing everyone for the news that you're going to be broke. No more money in the Trevellyan chest. All gone. No more pennies for the little heiresses.'

There was a definite frisson as people caught these words. Jemima clutched Harry's arm. 'Shut up!' she whispered fiercely. 'You don't know what you're saying.'

187

'It's just the truth, darling. You're going to be stony broke. And then what are we going to do? Looks like we might have to face some unpleasant truths, doesn't it?' He leaned towards Jemima, lowering his voice. 'Looks like you'll have to come back to Herne. Just as well you can have your own wing, isn't it? We wouldn't want to do anything as upsetting as talk to each other, would we?'

Jemima stared at him, fighting the urge to scream at him and at the same time feeling terrified that she might break down at any moment in front of him and a room full of people just desperate to witness first-hand the cracks in their marriage. Harry was hardly ever drunk. She had no idea how to control him. What was he going to say next? Was he going to announce to this roomful of people exactly what he thought of her?

'Harry, old man, come and take a look at this amazing picture I've just bought.' It was Rollo back with her drink, calm and unruffled. He handed the glass to her. 'Do excuse us, Jemima.' He led her husband away.

She turned back to face the fireplace, wishing she could just disappear up it. 'Oh God, what an awful mess,' she whispered.

She could hear the muffled conversation start up again behind her. She was about to lift her head and face the room once more when the drawing-room door opened and Emma came in with a new guest. He looked so different to everyone else in the room that there was an almost audible intake of breath as he entered. Instead of black tie, which every other man in the room was wearing, he wore a crisply cut grey, double-breasted suit, quite wrong for the occasion and yet unashamedly fabulous. He was dark, with skin like coffee mixed with honey, jet-black hair and very brown eyes, and he moved with an easy grace that expressed confidence and toughness.

Emma began to move among the guests, introducing her companion. They swapped pleasantries but did not linger long with many of them, until they got to a pretty young girl Jemima had not noticed before. She must have arrived that afternoon, as she certainly hadn't been at dinner the night before.

'This is my sister, Letty,' she heard Emma saying. 'Letty, this is Richard Ferrera.'

Letty could be no more than twenty, and a delightful example of fresh young English womanhood. She looked just like Emma, with perfect rose-petal skin and a mass of blonde hair, but there was something even more enchanting about her – a kind of gawkiness that spoke of youth and sweetness and wide-eyed innocence.

'How charming to meet you,' she heard Richard Ferrera say in a smooth American accent.

Of course, he had to be American, thought Jemima. *What's Emma's game, inviting her sister along like this? She can't be trying to set her up with a rich husband, can she? The girl's hardly more than a teenager. Wouldn't put it past her, though – there's no one so keen to get everyone else married as someone who's only just got up the aisle herself, and very successfully at that.*

She watched the man as he chatted to the two girls. He had not a trace of self-consciousness, she noticed, even though many might feel cowed at this countrified, aristocratic gathering – particularly if they were wearing the wrong thing. But somehow, Richard Ferrera managed to convey the impression that it was the people around him who were all very strange, dressing up in dinner jackets and bow ties, and that they amused him, rather than the other way round. His confidence sat on him lightly but with the strength of steel. There would be no denting it.

Jemima was fascinated by him.

Really, he's rather attractive, she thought to herself. *A bit shorter than I usually like them, but he's definitely very muscular under that suit. No one can carry off a jacket like that, no matter how well cut, unless they have some excellent definition underneath.*

And, of course, she reminded herself, he was in the business that she needed to learn all about, preferably before Monday. How brilliant if she could swan in first thing and start telling everyone what they needed to do and how.

This fantasy was rather appealing and she was just losing herself in it when she realised that Emma was leading the very man she was fantasising about towards her.

'Jemima, may I introduce Richard Ferrera? He's our neighbour. He's just moved into the old Brettington estate and he has big plans for it. Richard, this is Jemima Calthorpe.'

Richard Ferrera shook her hand lightly and smiled. 'Lady Calthorpe. I've heard of you, of course. It's a great honour to meet you.'

'Not at all. I'm delighted to make your acquaintance.'

'Oh, Jemima, your drink is empty. Let me go and fetch you a fresh one,' Emma put in and slid quickly away.

Jemima smiled at Richard Ferrera. He was even more handsome close up. She'd always preferred dark men, they seemed so sophisticated – it was an aberration when she'd fallen for Harry. She liked that warm-looking skin, the melting brown eyes, so different from that chilly English look, all pale and pallid.

'Are you enjoying life in Gloucestershire?' Jemima asked.

'Oh, yes, it's beautiful. The house is extraordinary. It was built six hundred years ago. It's everything I imagined an English country house to be. But there is a drawback.' Richard Ferrera frowned.

'Oh?'

'It's extremely cold here, isn't it?' He leaned towards her fractionally, as though confiding a naughty secret, and smiled, revealing perfect white teeth.

Jemima laughed. 'Oh dear, yes. If you're not used to it, the British weather can seem very bleak. But I promise you, it does get warm here. The summers are lovely. Where are you from?'

'In the States, I live in New York.'

'Then you must be used to cold. I've never been so

freezing in my life as I was in New York one winter. The snow was six feet deep!'

'Yes, but we have this marvellous thing called heating. You wouldn't believe how it improves the quality of life.'

'I doubt many of the buildings in New York are six hundred years old, though. It's always a little more difficult to heat old houses, they're inherently draughty.'

'Fair point. But when I'm in New York, I'm working. When I'm relaxing, I go to my place in Mexico. It's amazing – my paradise. No need for heating there. I've got a place on the coast, looking out over the ocean.' He smiled and shook his head. 'I'd love to be there right now.'

'Sounds perfect bliss.'

'It is. I'll have to show you some day.'

'I'd adore that.' She smiled back flirtatiously. These little invitations were just part of social chit chat. They never meant anything. Still, a hacienda in Mexico, or whatever it was called, sounded divine. She'd never been to that part of the world. 'So what brings you to this chilly isle?'

'Work, of course. I'm looking for business opportunities.'

'What is your line of work, Mr Ferrera?' enquired Jemima disingenuously.

The man stared at her, as if trying to work out whether she really was ignorant of him. He had a fiercely direct stare, unafraid and absolutely uncowed. 'Call me Richard, please. I am in the business of luxury,' he said at last. 'Something I think you must know something about.'

'Really? Why?' Jemima said coyly, enjoying the low buzz of flirtation she could feel between them. How much did this man know about her, exactly?

'Look at your dress – it is Oscar de la Renta, isn't it? It's fresh off the catwalk. Your shoes are Gina, the pearls look very similar to some I saw in a Garrard's catalogue recently and you have the aura of a woman who looks after herself very well. I've seen you photographed at the best restaurants, the most expensive hotels in the world. It's obvious that you live surrounded by luxury every day. You are no doubt an expert on the subject.'

'It's true I like the nice things in life, and I don't see why I shouldn't have them if I can afford them. But true luxury? I don't know. I still have frustrations and difficulties in my life, problems that money can't allay. Then my life doesn't seem anywhere near as luxurious as people think.'

'Ah.' Ferrera raised his eyebrows at her. 'You are confusing luxury with some kind of perfect existence in which nothing happens, like lying on a huge bed all day long, served with iced grapes and wafted by fans. That's the wrong way to think of luxury. It's what provides comfort and sustenance to your soul while you make the difficult, treacherous and sometimes boring journey through life. Think about it – don't cool Egyptian cotton sheets of the highest thread count bring you pleasure and soothe you at the end of a long day? Doesn't the best luggage, handcrafted from superb leather, piped with beautiful colours, printed with your own monogram, make that endless journey a little easier to bear? Wouldn't you rather drink one glass of Château Lafite Rothschild 1982 than a whole bottle of some cheap Bordeaux? Do you see what I mean? Luxury is where the soul and the body meet to be caressed.'

Jemima laughed again, a little surprised at his fervency. 'How funny. Yes, I suppose so. I've never heard it described in quite that way though.'

'I feel passionate about it.' Ferrera smiled. 'When you come from a background like mine, you think very hard about what the world can offer you, and what luxury means.'

'A background like yours?'

Ferrera shrugged lightly, his dark eyes glinting. 'I wasn't born to all this. I'm from a big, poor, immigrant family and I grew up in New York. My dad died when I was little and my mom brought us up on her own. It was tough, I guess. But it made me all the more determined to make something of myself and to get a little of the good things in life.'

'And now you've got quite a lot of the good things,' rejoined Jemima. 'It's very admirable. I'm impressed.' She couldn't help but feel the contrast with her own background. 'You obviously worked hard and made a success of yourself.'

'Yes, I did. I admit it, I'm very rich and very successful. But I'm not finished yet, not by a long way.' He stared at her intently.

Jemima looked up from under her lashes. *He's flirting with me, I can feel it. Well, he's very attractive . . .*

Emma glided up. 'Are you two having fun? Jemima is one of our most dazzling society figures, Richard. She's in huge demand so we're terribly lucky to have her here. Don't you agree that she's absolutely delightful?' She smiled that saccharine smile that Jemima mistrusted so much.

Richard bowed slightly in her direction. 'Charming. A very lovely lady.'

'You're so kind.' Jemima smiled at him.

Emma gave Jemima her drink. 'Here you are, darling. I'm so glad you two are getting on. I've put you next to each other at dinner. I'm sure you've got tons to talk about.'

When they were all seated, she noticed that Emma had put her sister Letty on the other side of Harry, so that he was locked in by blondes.

She saw Letty lean in confidentially towards her husband, revealing a great deal of cleavage and the tops of her breasts as she did so, and heard her say breathily, 'Oh, Harry, I used to *love* hacking home from the pony club on a Thursday afternoon, with Mummy driving behind ever so slowly to make sure I didn't get into trouble.'

She rolled her eyes. *Christ, what's she up to? Don't tell me that ridiculous little thing is making up to Harry. Well, she's on a hiding to nothing with that one.* She was quite sure that Harry was not the type to be unfaithful, although she didn't know why – they had never talked about it. It was quite possible, she supposed, that he was finding some comfort elsewhere, since he had found out about her own indiscretion, but she found it hard to imagine. He was old-fashioned, so proper. But still – she regarded the young thing shamelessly flirting with her husband, and watched her toss her mane of golden hair, pout her pretty lips and lean towards him, and felt a stab of something unpleasant in the pit of her stomach.

'That's your husband, isn't it?' A soft voice sounded in her ear. It was Ferrera leaning in close to her. She smelt a warm gust of his cologne. It was a fresh, clean scent but with a masculine undertone, a spicy blend of citrus and sandalwood.

'Yes. That's Harry.'

'Is it a British custom to treat married couples as if they'd rather be at opposite ends of the room?'

She laughed. 'We don't put married couples next to each other. They are expected to sing for their supper by amusing other people for once.'

'By the look of things, it's that little girl who is doing her best to amuse him.'

'Oh,' said Jemima lightly. 'We don't mind about that kind of thing either. It rather spices things up. There's nothing so boring as a hopelessly devoted married couple.'

'Really?' Ferrera turned his dark eyes towards Harry and Letty. 'Where I come from, such blatant flirting might be considered a little impolite.'

'Hmm.' Jemima turned towards him. 'Let's talk about something else.' The staff began to move quietly around the table, putting down the hors d'oeuvre. 'Tell me more about your business.'

'All right. Have you heard of FFB?'

'No. Should I have?'

'Not necessarily. Let's try another. Have you heard of LVMH?'

Jemima shook her head.

'OK. But you've heard of Möet champagne, haven't you?'

'Of course.'

'And Veuve Clicquot and Krug. And Louis Vuitton and Givenchy and Marc Jacobs. And Guerlain perfumes, Dior perfumes . . . I could go on.'

'Of course I've heard of them all. They're very famous.'

Ferrera nodded. 'Right. And they are all owned by LVMH, a French company that owns over fifty famous names and luxury brands. Richemont is another similar company – they own Cartier, Chloé, Montblanc and Dunhill, among many others. It's owned by a South African family, the Ruperts. The other major player is PPR, another French company. Those French love their luxury, that's for sure. They own Gucci, which in turn owns a host of famous names, mostly designers such as Yves Saint Laurent.'

Jemima frowned. 'I had no idea. How strange that one company can own so many different things. I suppose I've never thought about the business side of shopping all that much – how it all works behind the scenes.' She picked up her lemon half in its little muslin bag and squeezed it over the pink Scottish smoked salmon on her plate.

Ferrera speared a piece of fish on the end of his

fork as he continued. 'No – but a lot of us do. Most of these companies operate by allowing their subsidiaries to work independently, using their talents and going in the direction they see fit. There is an incredible amount of money involved in it – the owners of those companies are billionaires. One of the wonderful things about quality is that people are prepared to pay great sums for it, not just because of the inherent worth of the thing itself, but because it's a source of prestige. Throughout history, humans have tried to impress one another, to give the impression that they have that touch of something special, something that puts them above the rest of the crowd. A man drives, let's say, a Porsche. It says many things about him, not least that he can afford a Porsche, which we all know is very expensive. It also expresses his style, his taste, his class. It is the choice he's made. It tells you almost everything you need to know about him.'

'Almost?'

Ferrera gave a dark, half-smile. 'You would also need to look at his shirts, his shoes and his suits – and perhaps his pen.'

'What if he doesn't have a pen?'

'That in itself says something that chills the blood.'

Jemima laughed, amused. 'And what make is your pen? You obviously set a lot of store by it!'

'I'm lucky enough to have one custom-made for me by Cartier.'

'And do you drive a Porsche?'

'No, I don't. I usually drive a Ferrari.'

'So what does that say about you?' she asked teasingly.

'I guess it means that I prefer Italian cars to German ones.' Ferrera smiled. 'The thing is, you will make your own judgements but you will not underestimate the power of the brand.'

'So what is that first company you mentioned?' she prodded.

'FFB is my own company. Ferrera Fine Brands.'

'Goodness, how impressive! Who do you own? From the sounds of it, there isn't a great deal left.'

'Oh.' He shrugged and she was struck again by how at ease he was in his own body. 'There's plenty left, believe me. There are classic brands to be acquired, ones that will stand the test of time and always endure. And there are the more up-and-coming names, to be spotted, pounced on and brought into the fold. Consumer taste is always changing and it's important to identify new trends.'

'So, tell me . . . who do you own?' Jemima delicately sliced a piece of smoked salmon on her plate and lifted it to her mouth.

'I own some big American names,' he replied. 'Have you heard of Montrose Home and Garden?'

Jemima shook her head.

'It's a very big quality mail order brand in the States. We own that. Also Greave's.'

'I've heard of them,' Jemima said, pleased. 'They make the most fabulous shoes, so comfortable! I've got a pair in my car for driving. In fact, I must have several pairs. And I bought one of their gorgeous bags recently too.'

Ferrera smiled. 'I take that as a huge compliment, Lady Calthorpe. I'm delighted you like them.'

'Of course I do. Everyone does. And please, call me Jemima.'

'You see, Jemima, I always wanted a fine leather brand, and now I've got one. Greave's are expanding all over the world, and I'm hoping to move into many new areas with them. The workmanship is superb and I believe they can challenge Louis Vuitton in the luxury luggage market. In a few years, they will, I'm sure. I take a personal interest in Greave's. Our other lines are very American – New York-based designers and so on.' He reeled off a list of names, some Jemima had heard of and some she hadn't. 'I'm keen to move into European brands at this point. There are some wonderful old French names I wouldn't mind getting my hands on.'

'Such as?'

'Such as Hermès. Now that would be a coup.' He made a face. 'But it's impossible. They are one of the last privately owned companies and they don't intend to sell. Still, I won't give up hope. Things may change. Chanel would be another – the Holy Grail, really. But again, the Wertheimer family don't really have any plans to sell that particular goose and all its golden eggs. There are others I have my eye on though.'

'Then why aren't you in Paris?'

'I often am. But as it happens, I don't speak French and I don't particularly want to live there. I can get there very easily from here whenever I need to. Besides,

I've also got some ideas for expansion into the British market.'

'Really? How fascinating. Do tell me what they are.'

'I hope you understand that I really can't do that, Jemima.' He looked her straight in the eye. 'You're being very sweet and innocent with me, but I ought to tell you that I know exactly who you are.'

'Do you?'

'Yes. You're part of the Trevellyan family. That's a famous luxury brand. I know that your mother recently died – please accept my condolences. It must be a very sad time for you.'

Jemima looked down at her plate, pushing her food around with her fork. 'Thank you, yes, it hasn't been . . . easy.'

'If you don't mind my saying, the word is that you and your sisters have inherited the company. Is that right?'

Jemima was surprised. She put down her fork. 'Yes. Yes, it is. But how on earth did you hear about it?'

He shrugged. 'I have my sources. So, do you and your sisters intend to continue running it?'

'What else would we do with it?'

'Well, you could consider selling it, I suppose.'

She turned to stare at him. 'Sell it? To someone like you?'

Ferrera gave his sexy little half-smile again. 'Perhaps. But it's vulgar to talk business at the dinner table, isn't it? I'm sure we'll get the opportunity to talk about it some time soon.'

'What if we're not for sale, like Chanel?'

'Talking can't do any harm, can it? And it might benefit both of us. This smoked salmon is excellent, isn't it?'

'Yes . . . yes, I suppose it is.'

'Now tell me, are there any good shows on in London at the moment? I'm going down there in a fortnight for a while. I'd love to hear your opinions.'

She realised that the subject was well and truly changed.

Jemima sat on the bed, fuming. The evening had started so well, and then turned into a disaster. Ferrera had been a charming dinner companion, and they'd talked about all the things he should see in London; the hottest exhibitions, the best plays and shows. Business had not been mentioned again.

She had begun to realise that Richard Ferrera was a seriously sexy man. She loved the smooth American accent and the ease with which he spoke. His beautifully turned-out style and well-groomed body was in no way soft or off-putting – he was resolutely masculine. She had felt herself become seductive around him, lowering her voice and widening her eyes, putting herself in appealing attitudes.

But immediately dinner was over, Emma had pounced.

'Richard, come and meet Sukie Forbes, she's a sweetheart and lives so close to you; you're virtually neighbours. You don't mind, do you, Jemima? Only we don't know when we'll be able to tempt Richard back . . .'

Ferrera had shot her an apologetic look but had gone off politely with his hostess to meet her other guests. That left her able to observe Harry at the other end of the table and the outrageous flirting that was going on down there. Despite the large meal, he was still very drunk. At home he drank, but rarely to excess, and it was strange to see him so obviously inebriated, talking too loudly and laughing manically at whatever nonsense that stupid girl was coming out with. Letty also appeared to be thoroughly inebriated but Jemima suspected that some of that was an act. Jemima watched, appalled, as the two of them tottered off as soon as Emma led the way back to the drawing room. When she arrived there with the other guests, she saw them at once, cosied up on a window seat together, chattering away like two giggly teenagers keen for their first French kiss. At one point, Harry even pulled the heavy curtains round them so that all that was visible was their feet – one pair of polished black evening shoes and two slender feet in strappy sandals – but they were too drunk to keep them closed for long.

Jemima made small talk with a more sedate crowd at the other end of the room, distracted by her husband's behaviour and feeling angrier and angrier.

Harry hauled himself to his feet and said loudly, 'C'mon, Letty . . . let's go for a walk.'

'Oh, yeah!' screeched Letty. 'Fabulous idea, Harry!'

And they stumbled out of the room together. A few minutes later, Letty's laugh could be heard echoing up from the lawn below the house. 'It's bloody cold!' she squealed.

'I'll warm you up!' roared Harry and from the sound of it, he started chasing her around.

The other guests were shooting sympathetic looks at Jemima.

'Just high spirits, I expect,' said one, trying to be diplomatic.

'Spirits certainly have something to do with it,' snapped Jemima. As soon as was polite, she'd excused herself and come up to bed seething with rage and embarrassment. For two hours there was no sign of Harry.

Now she heard him veering around in the hallway, bumping into walls. The handle of the door twisted as he struggled to open it, then finally he managed to stumble inside.

'Oh, 'lo,' he said, registering that she was there. 'Thought you'd be asleep.'

'Well, I'm not. I've been waiting for you,' she answered icily.

'I've been exploring,' he mumbled. 'Got a bit messy.' He looked down at his black trousers which were now streaked with mud and grass. 'Think these'll have to go to the cleaners . . .'

'What the fuck were you playing at?' she hissed, her anger bursting out. 'You were all over that little bitch! You made a total spectacle of yourself, everybody was watching.'

'Why should you care?' he asked, making his way carefully over to an armchair and then falling clumsily into it.

'Why? Because it was fucking embarrassing, that's

why! I'm your wife, I'm sitting at the same table, and you're all over some stupid little teenager, pawing her in a way that's frankly disgusting for everyone else to watch.'

'What's wrong, Jemima? Are you jealous?'

'Ha!' She laughed loudly. 'Jealous? No. Just humiliated.'

'What about you?' he said quietly, his eyes glittering. 'What about what you get up to?'

'I don't embarrass you in public.'

'Oh – that's all right then. Except you were all over that greasy American tonight, weren't you?'

'Don't be so offensive. He's not greasy. And we were talking about business, if you must know. You, on the other hand, were blatantly trying to manoeuvre that girl into bed and it was just a degrading spectacle for everyone.'

Harry got up and started to walk towards the bed. 'Can you really blame me, Jemima?' He slumped on the bed next to her. His eyes were bloodshot and the toxic smell of whisky emanated from him. 'It's not as though we're doing much frolicking in the marital bed, is it?'

'What you do in private is your business – what you do in public, when I'm there, involves me too.'

'You don't want me any more, do you?' he said quietly.

'I . . . I . . .' She felt suddenly unsure of both herself and him. 'Not when you're like this – you reek of booze. It's disgusting.'

He leaned forward swiftly, put his hand around the

back of her head and pulled her face to his. The next moment, he was kissing her, and she was pulling away as hard as she could, pushing at his heavy body with her hands.

'Harry, get off! Get off me, stop . . .'

'Come on, Jemima, please. We can't go on like this. This marriage is like a living death. It doesn't have to be this way . . . come on, please.'

'No!' she shouted. He pulled back and stared at her sadly. 'You've done nothing but humiliate me all night – why on earth would I want to sleep with you? Besides, you've probably been snogging that little cow outside – the two of you looked like juvenile idiots. And you stink. Get away from me!'

He stood up, swaying slightly, unable to look her in the eye. 'I'm leaving tomorrow morning,' she declared. 'I don't see why I should have to suffer that supercilious bitch Emma and her godawful boring friends any longer. I did it for you, so that we could keep up the pretence that there was something in this marriage, but you've made a complete mockery of that. So I'm going back to London first thing.' She stared up at him defiantly. 'Don't try and stop me.'

'I'm not going to.'

'Good. And you're not sleeping here tonight. You may as well go and find that tart and sleep with her, because I don't want you in my bed.'

His face hardened as he absorbed this. 'Do you really mean that?' he said, with only the hint of a slur.

'Yes, I do. Go and sleep with her. I don't care.'

He winced. Then he stared at her. Their eyes locked.

'All right. If that's what you want.' He threw off his jacket, turned, made his way slowly to the door, opened it and left.

In the moment's silence that followed Jemima was astonished to find that tears were pouring down her cheeks. She threw herself onto her pillows and sobbed.

18

The boardroom table was covered in packaging and bottles. The boxes were in the Trevellyan signature dark blue, a royal warrant picked out in gold on the top of each and the flowing golden script announcing the name of the scent it contained.

The bottles were all identical – plain rectangular glass with gold-coloured atomisers and on each a white label with the name of the fragrance. A glass container held dozens of paper tester slips, and used slips lay on the table in little heaps.

Tara, Poppy and Jemima stood around the table, picking up bottles, spraying the scent on to tester slips and waving them under their noses.

With them were the directors of Trevellyan, standing about with bemused expressions as the women sniffed, thought and reacted.

'This is horrible!' exclaimed Tara as she flinched away from the slip she was sniffing. 'God, I hate that smell. What is it? It's powdery and dry, with something chemical and nasty in it. Like loo cleaner.'

'That's *Albermarle*, for men,' Duncan Ingliss said helpfully.

'It's vile. Smell this.' She held the slip under Jemima's nose. Jemima sniffed and then wrinkled her nose in disgust.

'You're right. It makes me think of dentists.'

'This one's pretty,' Poppy ventured. 'It's *Antique Lily*.'

They all sniffed at the slip she was holding out.

Tara nodded. 'Yes, that's not so bad. I think we can all agree that the main women's fragrances are the most successful.'

'And a couple of the men's,' added Jemima. 'I like *Leather & Willow*. It's rich and woody and very evocative. I wouldn't mind smelling that on a chap.'

Tara threw her an amused look. 'That's what Daddy wore.'

'Is it?' Jemima smiled. 'How funny. It makes me feel safe, somehow.'

'It makes me think of home,' Poppy said wistfully.

'Perhaps we're not the right people to judge these scents,' Jemima said thoughtfully. 'After all, they're completely bound up in our lives. Other people won't bring this kind of emotion and memory to these smells.'

'That's why we'll have a focus group,' Tara said decisively. 'I want to set up a group of ordinary people to assess the perfumes, and then to give their impressions of Trevellyan and what it means to them. I think

it's vital to find out what people think about the brand.'
She turned to William McKay. 'Can you set that up?
I want it done immediately.'

The marketing director looked confused. 'I'm not
sure. I'll find out what it involves. It's not something
we've done before.'

'That much is obvious,' replied Tara crisply. 'Come
to my office later and I'll give you my contact at a brilliant market research company. They can take it on
for us. Fuchsia Mitchell can make anything happen.'

'What about the budget?' William McKay said uncer-
tainly.

'Just do it, and we'll sort that out later.' Tara looked
around the room. 'OK, I think we've done enough
smelling. Let's sit down and start talking.'

The sisters took their places at the top of the table,
where three notepads and pens were set out, along
with three tumblers and a jug of iced water. The Trevellyan staff took their places around the table, most
of them averting their gaze from their new chief executives.

'Right.' Tara sat back in her chair and looked gravely
around the room. She was every inch the capable businesswoman in her black suit and sharp white shirt.
'This is the beginning of a new regime. You can forget
the cosy little existence you've had so far – that's over.
The era of letting this company disintegrate while you
take it for all it's worth is finished. We're starting
afresh and we're going to damn well take this place
where it needs to go, which is back to the top. Now.'
She put on her glasses, as she always did when she

wanted to appear more serious, and stared at the Trevellyan directors. 'Who here is the production director, and who is in charge of product development?'

A man coughed nervously from further down the table and fingered his tie. 'I'm in charge of production,' he said in a soft Birmingham accent.

Tara looked at him over the top of her glasses. 'And your name is . . . ?'

'Bill Haverstock.'

'OK, Bill. Explain, in very simple terms, the set-up.'

'Right . . .' Bill swallowed nervously. 'Well, I run the factory. We're based on a trading estate outside Birmingham. We've got a small staff – the smallest possible, really, to run the operation. I've had to lay a lot of people off in the last few years and supplement the core staff with agency workers when it's been necessary. Our set-up is very straightforward. In one part of the factory we manufacture the fragrances according to the standard formulas. In another, we bottle and package. We have an office division running the general operation, the accounts and distribution. That's it, really. A lot of the operation is outsourced wherever possible, to keep costs down.'

'And the raw materials?' Tara asked, scribbling a few notes on her pad.

'We receive deliveries of the raw materials on an as-needed basis. Those are for the fragrances themselves. The boxes are made off-site by another company, as are the glass bottles and the labels.'

Jemima frowned. 'It's really odd, but all this seems very unfamiliar to me. I mean, we grew up with

Trevellyan perfumes in the house, and Mother had a decanter full of *Tea Rose* on her dressing table.' She reached out and scooped up a bottle of *Trevellyan's Tea Rose*. The bottle looked painfully simple and the label almost gauche in its old-fashioned simplicity. 'It was nothing like this. This looks like the kind of thing you'd buy in an ancient chemist shop or find in some seaside B&B. How on earth did we come to be selling this?'

Duncan Ingliss swapped a glance with Bill Haverstock.

'Um . . .' Bill looked even more nervous. 'There have been some changes over the years –'

Duncan cut in quickly. 'Yes, we have at times had to look at our overheads and the best way to cut costs. That's inevitably meant changing suppliers. About five years ago we moved to a new bottle supplier in order to keep the costs as low as possible.'

'So these are new bottles?' Poppy reached out and picked one up. 'I thought they didn't look much like they used to. Does anyone have one of the old ones?'

'There's a display in the foyer of our scents through the ages,' Duncan said. 'You'll see the old bottle there.'

'Could you get one please?' Tara said sweetly, and watched as Duncan hauled himself to his feet and went out of the room, clearly unaccustomed to doing such a thing himself. 'Well, it's obvious that the operation is being run on a shoestring. We won't be able to save ourselves much there – it's already cut to the bone.'

'I'm very glad you said that,' Bill Haverstock said, clearly relieved. 'I thought I was going to be sent back with the task of sacking yet more staff and cutting yet more costs. To be honest, I just don't know how it can be done. We're all already running as cheaply as we can.'

'Could I say something?' asked Simon Vestey.

'Yes . . . Simon – you're the finance director, aren't you?' Tara asked. 'Go ahead.'

'Cutting costs has been the only way we've been able to reverse our decline.'

'Reverse it?' Tara asked coldly.

'Well – stop it.'

'You may have slowed it down but you certainly haven't stopped it. And as for reversing it – please. It's quite clear that every time you've cut costs, sales have also dropped. It's been a relentless fall.' Tara shuffled through some papers in front of her. 'Now, I've done my best to learn about the fragrance industry in a very short time. It's not something I knew anything about. But one of the things that's abundantly clear is that it's a huge market, and the top perfumes and scents make millions. The market for fine women's fragrances is worth over five hundred million in the UK alone. Men's fragrances are close behind at around three hundred and fifty million. In this area of retailing, quality always does better than the mass market. We're a quality brand, so why is Trevellyan doing so bloody badly? We got a tiny amount of market share, and it's dropping.'

The door opened and Duncan Ingliss came back

in holding a small glass bottle. He returned to his seat and put the bottle on the table.

'Oh, it's lovely!' exclaimed Poppy.

They all looked at it. It was about ten centimetres high, a cylindrical bottle of clear, silvery glass with a faint pleat in it. The round lid was silver, flaring out prettily at the top.

'Yes, that's what I remember,' Jemima said, picking it up. 'That's the bottle I know. Why on earth are we using that one?' She pointed at the current bottle with its blunt angles and bland design. 'It looks cheap and nasty, nothing like this. This is the kind of bottle I'd like to see on my dressing table.'

'We're using the new design precisely because it is cheap,' Duncan said stiffly. 'The new bottles are mass produced and therefore the quality of glass is lower than the old style.' He gestured at the bottle in Jemima's hands. 'That bottle costs an awful lot to manufacture. We couldn't go on using such an expensive product.'

'But isn't that part of what you pay for when you buy a Trevellyan scent? The beautiful bottle? You can't charge people for a premium perfume and put it in that bottle. It's obvious that it only costs a few pence.'

'With great respect, Lady Calthorpe, you don't have the first idea about this business –'

'Perhaps not,' Jemima shot back, 'but I know something about buying scent and I can tell you that the packaging is absolutely key. What's blindingly obvious is that when it comes to perfume, a woman is as much attracted by the bottle it comes in as she is by the way it smells!'

Tara intervened before Duncan could reply. 'Let's leave that for a moment, though you've made an excellent point, Jemima, and one I want to come back to.' Tara leaned forward on her elbows and stared Duncan in the eye. 'You haven't yet told me who is in charge of product development.'

Duncan looked uncomfortable. 'Well . . . The truth is – we don't have anyone.'

Tara stared at him, surprised. She frowned and took her glasses off. 'What? There had better be a good explanation of why not.'

Duncan sat up straight. 'Listen, I'm beginning to get a little tired of this. It's a strange and unpleasant interrogation by people who don't know anything at all about our business. Mrs Pearson, we are not like the big fragrance houses. We don't launch new lines every year. We have an established set of very famous scents and we don't see the need to add to them. To be quite honest, we cannot afford to add to them. Launching new fragrances costs a great deal of money and we simply don't have it. We have instead put our resources behind promoting the perfumes we do have. After all, we have *Trevellyan's Tea Rose.* Very few perfume houses can boast a name as famous and resonant as that.'

'I'm sorry you're not enjoying this process, Duncan. I'm afraid it's going to get a lot nastier for you before it gets better. I can quite see the reasoning behind what you've done. But it's also clear it's not working.'

Tara gestured at the bottles all over the table. 'Now, it's precisely because we don't know anything about the business that our opinions are worth having. We've smelt the products and there are a lot of them we don't like. They're too old-fashioned. They don't smell right. We need to do something about that – it's the core of the entire business.'

'That's the funny thing,' put in Poppy. She had taken the old-fashioned bottle from Jemima and was examining it. 'They don't look right in these horrible new bottles – but you wouldn't expect that to affect what they smell like. And yet, they don't smell right either.' She reached for the bottle of *Trevellyan's Tea Rose* and sprayed it, this time on to her skin. She gave it a moment and then inhaled strongly. 'It doesn't smell the way I remember.' She turned to her sisters. 'Do you remember Mother wearing *this*?'

'I always hated it,' Jemima said frankly. 'And I still do.'

Tara leaned over and sniffed her wrist. 'I'm not sure. It does make me think of Mother. But I know what you mean, there's something not quite right about it.' She looked at the directors. 'Any reason why that might be?'

There was a feeling of tension in the air. 'Ladies,' said Duncan Ingliss at last, 'this is *Trevellyan's Tea Rose*, I do assure you.'

'There's no one here I trust to tell me the truth, I'm afraid. And I'm getting very tired of all this hostility and resistance.' Tara got gracefully to her feet. 'Now, I'm calling an end to this meeting. Might I remind you, gentlemen, that all of your jobs are now on the line. Unless we're completely satisfied with your performance, we will have no hesitation in dismissing you. Jemima, Poppy – I'll see you in my office in five minutes.' She stalked out of the boardroom, leaving them all gazing after her.

19

Tara sat down at her desk, boiling with rage and frustration.

Keep calm, she told herself. *It will get easier. It has to.*

She was used to a slick operation, where enthusiastic young people jumped to answer every question she had, to find her information she needed or to prove their dedication.

I'm used to a can-do culture, she thought. *I can't bear all this negativity. It's as though they're happy for this company just to die on its feet. It's obvious it needs some radical work to get it going again.*

Her office door opened and Poppy came in.

'Jemima's just getting some water,' she said, and sat down. 'Whose office was this?'

'I don't know. They've made three of the directors move out. I think there's been a bit of a reshuffle down the corridor. Some poor secretary has no doubt been moved on to a fire escape or something. I'll look into that in due course. Frankly, at the moment I'm tempted to sack them all.'

'They do seem a little . . . slow,' Poppy said tactfully.

'Poor old Trevellyan.' Tara made a face. 'Anyone decent must have left long ago. We've got some hard decisions to take, Pops. We're going to have to decide how much of our own money we're going to risk to prop this place up.'

'I don't mind putting everything in,' Poppy replied quickly. 'You know how I feel about that.'

Tara shook her head slowly. 'I appreciate the gesture, love, but I don't know if I can allow it. It's looking less and less likely that we'll be able to turn this place round. All of my initial ideas for cost cutting have just been thrown out. What we need to do is put money into this operation. I think it could be the only way to save it.'

Jemima came in, smiling broadly, clutching a water bottle. 'That was jolly good fun!' she announced, tossing back her fair hair. 'It's quite a revelation seeing you at work, Tara. You're really scary! I can tell that being head girl was excellent experience for this kind of work. It was like you were carpeting the prefects after you'd found them smoking behind the boarding house. Terrific stuff.'

'I suppose that's a compliment,' Tara said grimly. 'But I'm afraid it's a hell of a lot more important than I supposed.' She stared at her sisters for a moment. 'I don't know about you two, but I've got alarm bells going off all over the place. I have the distinct impression we're being lied to.'

'I know what you mean,' Jemima said, frowning. 'You could cut the atmosphere in that boardroom with a knife.'

'I'm going to bring some new people in,' Tara said decisively. 'We can't work with this lot.'

Poppy gasped. 'You're really going to sack them all?'

'No, not yet. I may need them around for a little while longer. But I'm going to bring in some people I know and ask them to start going through this place with a fine-toothed comb. The answers have to be here. I want every filing cabinet opened, every scrap of paper found and read, and every computer accessed.'

'Wow.' Jemima looked at her with respect. 'Can we do that?'

'We can do anything we damn well like.'

Jemima sat back casually in her chair. 'I don't know if this is the right time, but I wondered how we felt about possibly selling the company.'

The other two stared at her. 'Sell?' said Tara, surprised. 'What are you talking about?'

'Well, if we got a good offer for it, perhaps it would be the best way out. After all, none of us want to run this place. You've got a career already, Tara, and Poppy really wants to be messing about with paints. I'm certainly much happier shopping than I am sitting in a boardroom. If we sold this place, we could all afford to forget about Trevellyan and just get on with our lives. After all, do we really care about it?'

Her question, met by stunned silence, hung in the

air. At last Tara said, 'Why are you bringing this up all of a sudden?'

'I met a man at a dinner party on Saturday night – a very successful man, who is building up his company in this country. He owns luxury brands and he pretty much said that he was interested in buying Trevellyan.'

'Who?' Tara jumped to her feet. 'Who said that?' She stared down at the table. 'Christ, I might have known the sharks would be circling already,' she muttered.

'His name is Richard Ferrera and he owns a company called FFB.'

'Yes, I know him,' Tara said grimly. 'At least, not personally, but I've heard of his business interests. He's been phenomenally successful in the States. He seems to know exactly where the market is going and how to exploit it. I knew he was keen to go shopping for new companies – he's just had a massive cash investment, no one knows where from. What did he say?'

'Nothing really, it was almost social chit-chat. He just said something about us being able to help each other and that we should talk about it sometime. But I didn't talk to him after that – Emma Bonnington kept him to herself for the rest of the evening.'

'That was it?' asked Tara. 'What did you say?'

'Nothing. I just said something like, "What if we're not for sale?" and that was that.' Jemima took a swig from her water bottle. 'Honestly, Tara, don't get your knickers in a twist. He didn't make me sign anything, even though he was so handsome he could have wrapped me round his little finger if he'd wanted. Sultry Mexican looks. Yum.'

'I'm sure he could. Right. Just what we needed.' Tara sat down again and sighed. 'I don't know about you, Poppy, but I don't want to sell. Not yet.'

'Are we even allowed to sell?' Poppy asked. 'I mean, Mother's will said we had to turn the company round –'

'Yes, her motive there is becoming clearer and clearer,' put in Jemima.

'– or it all goes to . . . to Jecca.' The name came out as though Poppy had to force it. 'If we sell the company, does that mean she can't have it?'

'Hmmm. I expect Mother will have thought about that. We'd better talk to Victor about the will.'

Jemima burst out. 'What I still don't understand is why she picked Jecca! I mean, she could have picked Aunt Daphne or Uncle Clive or any of those pathetic Boyle cousins. She hated Jecca more than any of us – but she was willing to risk giving her Trevellyan. Why?'

'I think it's obvious,' Poppy said in a small voice. 'She wanted us move heaven and earth to save Trevellyan, so that we'd stop Jecca getting it. And I, for one, don't want to sell. I've got faith in Tara, in all of us. I believe we can do this. Perhaps this man, Richard Whoever, might be useful in other ways, but I don't want him to have our company. It sounds like he collects them as though they were stamps and I don't want Trevellyan to be something else he just sticks in his album.'

'That's two against one.' Tara smiled at Poppy.

'All right, all right,' Jemima said irritably. 'I was just making a suggestion. Christ, is it a crime to want an easy life now and then? So, we don't sell the company. Where do we go from here?'

Tara tapped her pen on the desk. 'What we need is someone who knows something about perfume. Someone who's got experience in the perfume industry. I just don't know who that someone is. But it will be my job to find out. Poppy – I want you to go to Loxton and get that bottle of *Trevellyan's Tea Rose* from Mother's dressing room – and any other Trevellyan scents you can find. Jemima . . .'

'Yes? What's my mission – should I choose to accept it?'

'I want you to be our eyes here. I want you to start going through the company files; most importantly, the ones in the sales, marketing and publicity departments.'

'What on earth will I be looking for?'

'I don't know. But you'll know it when you see it.'

'Very helpful. Thanks. That's about as appealing as a bucket of cold sick. Why does Poppy get to go to Loxton while I have to scrabble around in dusty filing cabinets?'

Tara frowned at her. 'No more complaining. Just do it.'

'All right,' said Jemima grumpily. 'Honestly – you'll be giving me a hundred lines next. I think you missed your calling as a school mistress.'

'That's enough. Let's get to work.'

20

Gerald was rutting away on top of her, gasping and panting. His face was a violent red and his eyes were shut tight with his exertions. A bead of sweat dropped from the end of his nose and splashed on her eyelid, making her eye sting.

Please, please, please, Tara begged silently. *Please hurry up!*

She wasn't sure how much longer she could stand it. Soon she might just have to scream at him to bloody well stop and push him away from her. She tried to help him along by running her nails up and down his back, the way he used to like it, but she wondered if he could feel much now through the great layer of fat that lay under his skin, soft and putty-like below her fingertips. She moaned in a pretence of pleasure, hoping it might spur him onwards, but really it was a groan of exhaustion and growing discomfort. She could feel herself drying up as his penis jabbed into her – soon she would be so completely unaroused that he wouldn't be able to enter her at all, her body would reject him altogether.

Gerald huffed louder, increased his pace and then he opened his eyes and they rolled upwards in his head, his mouth stretched in the bizarre grimace he always made at the approach of his climax, and he tensed.

At long bloody last! Tara thought with relief.

He gave a few final thrusts as his orgasm spent itself, then rolled off her, sighing heavily.

'Thank you, my darling,' he said after a few moments. 'Most delightful congress. I trust you were adequately satisfied?'

'Of course,' Tara said dutifully, though she wondered how he could possibly believe that she had been any such thing. A rush of sadness engulfed her. Was this really what her marriage had come to? It seemed so strange now to remember what their sex life had been like when they'd first got together; it was hard to imagine desiring Gerald as fiercely now as she had then. He had been less fat, certainly, but even then he'd been stocky and well rounded. Nevertheless, she'd found his fleshiness attractive – it was different from her own skin-niness and seemed to indicate Gerald's sensuality, his love of life, and his predilection for pleasure. He certainly cared more for her satisfaction back then – he would always delay his own orgasm until he was quite sure that she had already reached her own climax. The first years of their marriage had been very happy in that respect. She felt wistful just thinking about it.

'How is your grand enterprise at Trevellyan

proceeding?' Gerald enquired, sitting up in bed and drawing the sheet up below his flabby chest. His cheeks were losing their hectic red as he recovered from his exercise.

'It's more challenging than I anticipated.' Tara pushed herself up so that she was sitting, trying to ignore the warm trickle of Gerald's spending creeping down her thigh. Only a few minutes more and she could decently escape. 'But I'm confident we can all rise to it.'

'Even those feather-headed sisters of yours?' Gerald snorted. 'Jemima is designed to be looked at and admired, to be a magnificent hostess. She could be a great lady in society, bringing together the most important men of her day for parties and modern salons, like the wonderful *grandes dames* of the past. It's a crime to put her in a boardroom – like keeping a beautiful panther on a chain when it should be roaming free in the jungle.'

'I'll tell her you said so,' Tara answered drily.

Gerald continued on without hearing her. 'And Poppy – well, charming she may be, and pretty in her way, too, but she has something of the infant about her. She's no more suitable to run a company than Imogen is. No doubt, that's why your mother left her Loxton, it's quite obvious she'll be the one who actually needs it. She won't marry well and she certainly won't make her own money. She's like a needy child, yearning for guidance and protection.'

'Mmm. You can tell her that yourself. She's coming here later, on her way back from Loxton.'

226

'Don't be silly,' Gerald said loftily. 'It would destroy what little confidence she has, poor thing. It was one of your parents' few failings: to spoil that girl and wrap her in cotton wool. Anyway, I shan't be here to see her later, I'm afraid. I have a business meeting.'

'On a Sunday?' Tara looked over at her husband, surprised.

'I never stop working,' Gerald declared. 'My life is my work and vice versa. Tara, you know very well I never take weekends or holidays, I am always alert and functioning, always thinking of my enterprises. Now . . .' He leaned over to the house phone, picked it up and dialled. 'Yes. Coffee. At once. Then soft scrambled eggs and smoked salmon, granary toast, French butter. And don't forget – the cutlery on the folded napkin on the left-hand side of the tray. And no crumbs on the plate! I want it perfect this time.' He put the phone down. 'Did you want anything?'

'No.' Tara swung her legs out of bed. 'I'm going to have a shower and then join the children.'

'Very well.' Gerald settled himself against his pillows and reached for his book, a biography of Stalin.

Tara went to her bathroom. A moment later, she was under the hot gush of the shower, scrubbing Gerald away as fast as she could. Her revulsion for him was growing, she knew that. How long could she go on sharing a bed with him, going through this dreadful Sunday morning ritual of arid sex that left her unmoved and unhappy?

Her desire for him had never recovered from that one frightful night.

227

It was a few years before, not long after Imogen was born, that Gerald's tastes had begun to change – or at least, that he had begun to reveal them to her. He had always enjoyed the rough and tumble of love-making, dominating her with his physical strength, but it had been harmless enough and her pleasure had always been important to him. Gradually, though, things took a different turn: he began to get pleasure from beating her. He didn't punch her or want to give her a black eye or a bloody nose. Rather, he had wanted to tether her. At first it had seemed rather innocent, as he playfully tied her to the bed. He would bind her to the bedrail with silk scarves and blindfold her with another, then begin to whip her lightly with a slim belt he kept specifically for the purpose. It wasn't some-thing that aroused her, but she knew he enjoyed it, so she occasionally let him do it. She would writhe on the bed as the leather slapped across her bottom, crying out and begging for mercy, giving a good performance of being in agony even though it didn't hurt her terribly much. Gerald loved it, though. As soon as he saw the red lines rising across her buttocks, he would begin to breathe more heavily. When she cried out that it hurt, he beat her a little harder, panting more. But after a few minutes, he would be able to bear it no longer and had to drop his little stinging whip and push his short, thick penis into her. He always came within seconds after the whippings.

Tara grew to hate them, as Gerald wanted them more and more often. He no longer cared about her pleasure, or taking her to the heights of ecstasy. He only wanted to get out his belt and thrash her bottom until the welts showed, then enter her quickly and buck on her until he'd climaxed, leaving her miserable and unsatisfied.

Then, one day, a strange contraption was delivered, a large wooden frame with leather cuffs for her wrists and ankles, which he'd ordered off some specialist website. She was frightened of it from the first moment she saw it, but he persuaded her to let him tie her to it, telling her that he wouldn't hurt her, not really. It was just for fun. A game. Eventually, she agreed. He wanted it so badly and he'd promised faithfully that the minute she wanted him to, he would free her.

It had been terrible. When she was fixed on the frame at her wrists and ankles, he hadn't taken out the belt, as usual. Instead he had produced a bunch of birch twigs and begun to slap her with it lightly, watching as the blood rushed to the surface of her skin in response to the blows. She had gone along with it at first, moaning and screaming as usual at the slightest touch, waiting for Gerald to be overcome with excitement. But when she begged for mercy this time, he didn't stop. Instead he increased his pace, beating her harder and harder. Soon, the pain was real and unpleasant. Her buttocks were stinging badly, the twigs cutting into her flesh with a burning bite. She demanded he stop and release her. He ignored her and only increased the strength of his blows until she began to weep as the pain grew more intense. This only inflamed him more and as she begged him to stop and let her down, he began to thrash her seriously, until she could feel blood smeared over her bottom and thighs and the agony was almost making her faint.

He did not even enter her. The thrill of hitting her was so great that he came without touching her, the jet of sperm splattering her back and thighs as he moaned with delight.

When he released her, she could not look at him. She had crawled away to the bathroom to dip her poor, broken bottom in cool water and sob quietly to herself. Over the weeks it took for her skin to heal, she avoided him at every opportunity. He acted as though nothing had happened and seemed oblivious to what he'd done, while the frame vanished somewhere, probably hidden in some attic.

He had broken her trust and abused her, and it left her devastated and in turmoil. But she couldn't bring herself to talk to him about it; it was too strange and humiliating, almost unreal. All she knew was that her desire for him vanished in one moment, leaving her utterly unable to feel aroused by him.

It had killed her love for him, too, she knew that now, even though she had tried to forget and forgive, and cling on to whatever was left.

Then, one night, to her horror, he asked her to mount the frame again.

'No!' she cried, tears springing to her eyes. 'Never again! It's revolting. How dare you? How dare you ask me? You know what you did!'

He did not force her or even try to convince her. He simply said 'Very well, my dear' and it was never mentioned again.

She didn't dare think about how Gerald was indulging his lust for beatings since then. As far as she could tell, his appetite was satisfied by the weekly Sunday morning rut in the bed, with nothing more extreme than his fat body heaving on top of hers until he came.

How much longer she could endure even that, she did not know.

They were in the garden later when Poppy arrived. The afternoon had turned delightfully hot and sunny, a foretaste of summer in an otherwise wet and blustery spring, and Tara had taken the opportunity to catch up with the Sunday papers sitting on a rug under the old beech tree at the end of the garden while Edward and Imogen played nearby. Sometimes they squealed as they chased each other around; at other times, she would look up to see the two of them engrossed in something, their heads close together as they squatted next to a flower bed, observing the slow progress of a snail or watching a wood louse curl up into a ball when they prodded it.

She saw Poppy approaching down the long lawn, and folded away all the news pages before her sister reached them.

'Look who it is,' she called to Edward and Imogen, who rushed towards their aunt, yelping with joy, for hugs and kisses.

'Hello, sweeties,' laughed Poppy, trying to return all the kisses as fast as she could.

She disentangled herself after a few moments and headed for Tara, beaming.

'They're so adorable!' Poppy glanced over at her nephew and niece as they ran over to their playhouse, a perfect miniature Swiss chalet with an upstairs and a downstairs, all furnished in beautiful, to-scale furniture, right down to a tiny white porcelain sink. There was even electric lighting and running water. 'I wish I saw more of them.'

'So do I, darling,' said Tara lightly. 'We've just been enjoying some quiet time together before we go in for tea.'

'No Gerald?' Poppy looked about, as though she expected Gerald to pop out from behind a bush.

Tara shook her head. 'Working today.'

'He's tireless.' Poppy made a face. 'I'm exhausted by Monday to Friday – let alone Sunday too.'

'How was Loxton?' Tara asked, patting the rug beside her. Poppy sat down next to her. The soft spring wind lifted strands of her hair as she curled her arms round her knees and sighed.

'Oh . . . strange. Very strange to be there without Mother. Even odder to go into her bedroom to get the *Tea Rose* and for her not to be there. I half expected to see her sitting in bed, propped up on all those pillows with her tray next to her – that Georgian silver teapot she always used, remember that? – saying, "Ah, Poppy, my dear, to what do I owe the pleasure of this visit?"'

Tara smiled. Poppy had their mother's deep, syrupy tones down to a T.

Poppy smiled back, a little ruefully. 'But of course, she wasn't there. The place feels deserted. Just Alice in the kitchen, still keeping everything ticking over until I'm in a position to make some decisions about the old place.'

'Did you feel like you wanted to live there?' Tara asked, brushing her hair from her face.

'Live there? I don't think I could imagine anything worse. Just me, in that big huge place?' Poppy shuddered. 'I say just me, but of course, I wouldn't be alone. All the ghosts that are there ... I could feel the echo of the days we'd spent there, as tiny children through to teenagers, and the desperation we all felt in the end to escape. You must remember ... And not just our ghosts either ...'

'No,' Tara agreed. 'Not just ours.'

They exchanged a significant glance.

'Hasn't all this made you feel differently about the parents?' Tara asked after a moment.

'I don't know.' Poppy thought. 'Not really. It's just confirmed what I already knew. I suppose I always realised that something was wrong. I mean, even if they had been happy – well, Jecca changed that, didn't she?'

'So it was Jecca who caused all the unhappiness?'

'We'll never know,' Poppy said softly. 'Not now.'

Tara watched as her children called to each other in the playhouse. A tiny shuttered window on the upper floor opened and Edward poked his head out, calling to his mother and aunt to watch him. They waved and smiled and obligingly said they were watching.

After a while Poppy said, 'I always knew I was their

favourite. But it was only because I didn't challenge them, not like you and Jemima.'

Tara frowned. 'What do you mean?'

'Well, you were clever. And very grown up. They must have known you could see right through them, and that soon you'd be asking uncomfortable questions. And Mimi was so obviously destructively unhappy with the way things were and they didn't have the first idea how to cope. But me . . . you know I was always docile, always eager to please. Happy to be fussed over. I was the easy option.'

There was a long pause. Then Tara murmured, 'Maybe there's something in that, you know. It certainly explains a lot.'

'But they adored you too,' Poppy said hastily. 'I know that. They loved us all, even if they struggled to show it.'

'Maybe.' Tara watched Imogen run out of the little chalet and slam the front door behind her with relish. 'I guess that one good thing to come from it is that I always show my children how much I love them.'

'Good,' said Poppy fervently. 'Good. You must.'

Tara sighed. 'I just wish I had your certainty. That they loved us, I mean.'

'But this awful thing, this challenge to bring Trevellyan to life again . . . well, I think it's proof.'

'You do?'

Poppy nodded. 'Absolutely. I think Mother knew it would bring out the best in all of us.'

'We shall see,' Tara said grimly. 'You certainly have more faith in her clairvoyance than I do. Come on.'

She climbed to her feet, stretching up and sighing. 'Viv's putting out tea in the conservatory. Let's go and have some.'

Poppy got up as well. She smiled at her big sister. 'Yes please. As long as we can take those cute little things with us.'

'Try keeping them away from Viv's apple scones and you'll see a whole other side to those cute little things,' said Tara wryly. Then she called the children to join them as they walked back across the lawn.

21

It was a week later when a svelte, fashionably dressed woman, her hair a sleek, dark bob, stopped outside the famous old Trevellyan shop. She appeared to be admiring her reflection in the glass of the shop window. She was wearing an elegant, beautifully cut berry-coloured suit, with a sharp little jacket over a crisp white shirt, and a knee-length pencil skirt – an outfit of timeless chic. However, when she made a face at the glass and said, '*Dieu!*' it became obvious she was looking at the inside of the shop.

A moment later, she marched through the front door.

'May I help you, madam?' asked a shop assistant, coming forward to greet her.

'Yes, if you please,' she replied curtly in a strong French accent. 'I am 'ere to see the lady in charge.'

'Lady in charge?' The shop assistant blinked. 'You mean Mrs Armstrong? I'm afraid she's on a tea break . . .'

'No, no,' the lady said impatiently. 'Not Meesus Armstrong. Pierreson.'

'I beg your pardon?'

'Madame Pierreson.'

'I'm afraid I don't know who you mean.'

'The lady 'oo runs thees company!' cried the woman crossly, ''oo is your owner?'

'Oh, the owner! You must mean Miss Trevellyan – one of the Miss Trevellyans, that is.'

'If you say so.' The lady closed her eyes for a moment, then opened them to reveal a piercing brown gaze. 'Ooever it ees – please take me to her at once!' The piercing brown gaze was insistent.

A few minutes later, the French woman was standing in the reception area, peering at the displays of perfume bottles.

'Mademoiselle Deroulier?' Tara came into reception. 'I'm Tara Pearson.'

'*Oui* . . .' muttered the French lady to herself. 'You see – Pierreson, just as I said. These people are imbeciles.' Then she looked up with a smile. '*Bonjour.* I am Claudine Deroulier. *Enchantée,* Madame.'

Tara took in the woman's appearance from top to toe. She'd hoped for a typically elegant French woman and Claudine Deroulier did not disappoint. She was probably in her forties but she had an elegant agelessness that came from a lifetime of looking after her complexion and figure. Her thick dark hair brushed her jaw line in a chic bob, and her make-up was so expertly applied she appeared to be wearing nothing but the bright red lipstick that contrasted with her creamy, smooth skin. Her clothes were subtle but clearly very expensive. She carried a silver Chanel 2.55 bag over one shoulder, and her low pumps were also discreetly engraved with the linked Cs of Chanel.

'And I'm delighted to meet you. Thank you for meeting with us – it is a great honour. You come very highly recommended, Mademoiselle.'

'*Merci*. But I cannot say I am surprised – I am very good at my job. That is why you want me, I know that.'

'Absolutely. If you're ready, my sisters are waiting for us in the boardroom.' As Tara led the way down the hall, she said, 'I trust the hotel is satisfactory?'

'*Oui, oui*, very good. I am most comfortable. It is not quite as fine as the Crillon in Paris but it will do.'

'It is hard to match the Hôtel Crillon. I stay there myself when I'm in Paris.'

'An oasis of luxury in a terrible world,' agreed Mademoiselle Deroulier. She sighed longingly. 'I mees Paris already.'

'You left yesterday, didn't you?' Tara asked. She was impressed by the woman's excellent English, and found the strong French accent charming.

Mademoiselle Deroulier's smile dropped. '*Oui*. But to be away from Paris even for a day is like a lifetime.'

'How lovely to feel so strongly about your city. I don't think I feel quite the same way about London.'

'London 'as its charms but . . . I agree, it does not have the true elegance of Paris.'

'Here we are.' Tara opened the door and led the way into the boardroom. Once again a selection of the Trevellyan scents were laid out on the table, along with plenty of paper testing slips and refreshments. 'May I introduce you to my sisters?'

Jemima stood up and came round the table. In honour of their French guest, she was wearing white Yves Saint Laurent wide-legged trousers and a dusky pink Dior scoop-neck top, looking as fresh and spring-like as the day outside.

'Mademoiselle Deroulier, what a pleasure to meet you. I'm Jemima Calthorpe. Please call me Jemima.'

'The pleasure is mine,' murmured Claudine Deroulier. She looked approvingly at Jemima's outfit. 'Charming.'

'And I am Poppy Trevellyan.' Poppy stood up. She had decided to go a little wild today and was a wearing a leopard-print blouse with black trousers, her coppery hair brushed back in a long curling mane.

Claudine raised her eyebrows. '*Enchantée.* And you three ladies are sisters, *n'est-ce pas?*'

'*Oui, Mademoiselle. Nous avons herité la maison de notre père,*' said Jemima in pretty French. '*Un de nos ancestres a fondé la maison au dix-neuvième siècle et maintenant nous voudrions sécuriser l'avenir de nos parfums célèbres.*'

Claudine made a little bow. 'You speak French delightfully, but I beg that you will allow me to speak English. I treasure every opportunity to improve. Now, you say you have inherited this perfume company. I understand you need my help.'

'Exactly. Would you please sit down?' Tara gestured to the seat at the top of the table, where the fragrances were lined up.

Claudine went to take her place, sitting down and looking intently at the bottles ranged before her. 'Mmm,' she murmured, and muttered something under her breath that the sisters couldn't hear. She looked up at the three of them as they watched her. 'I can tell that your expectations today are very great – and rightly so. I am a master perfumer. I grew up in Grasse, the home of perfume,' she said proudly, 'and my father was a master perfumer before me. He worked for Givaudan and created some divine fragrances, classics, masterpieces! I'm sure you've heard of *L'été et la Mer*. A wonderful blend of citrus and aquatic. It was created in 1947.'

'I'm afraid not,' said Tara. 'You're going to find us woefully ignorant.'

Claudine looked puzzled. 'But you own a *maison des parfums*. How ignorant are you?'

'Very,' said Poppy. 'I hardly ever wear perfume, except for the jasmine one Daddy made for me. I've got a couple of Body Shop things I quite like.'

'*Body Shop?*' Claudine echoed incredulously. She turned to Tara. 'And you?'

'I wear scent,' Tara said quickly. 'I mostly wear *J'adore* by Dior at the moment, although not today. I forgot to put anything on this morning.'

Claudine's face cleared a little. She pouted and shrugged. 'Yes, *J'adore* has a been a great hit. Huge. It is on the wane, though. For me, it is a little ... predictable.' She looked at Jemima. 'And you?'

'I have to admit to a secret obsession with perfume,' Jemima declared. 'At the moment I'm very fond of Jo

Malone's scents. I'm utterly addicted to her Lime Basil and Mandarin.'

Claudine nodded. 'Yes, yes. A wonderfully innovative perfumer. Very modern and attuned to her clientele. I applaud her.'

'And I also love *L'Air du Temps* by Nina Ricci, *Joy* by Jean Patou' – Jemima was pleased that she had won in the perfume stakes, beating the other two hollow, and she gushed on – 'and pretty much all of the Guerlain and Givenchy fragrances. Also, just last week I bought the new Marc Jacobs scent, which I adore.'

'The newest one? The flower scent?' Claudine raised her eyebrows. 'Surely a little young for you?'

Jemima's mouth fell open and the other two giggled softly.

'I do not mean to offend,' Claudine put in quickly. 'It is simply that it is aimed at the . . . shall we say, less *sophisticated* market.'

A little mollified, Jemima said, 'Perhaps. It's something I would only wear on a summer's day.'

'Very wise.'

'And of course, I wear *Chanel N⁰ 5* when I'm feeling old-school glamorous.'

'But of course.' Claudine sighed. '*Chanel N⁰ 5*. We call it *le monstre*, you know. The monster has dominated fine fragrances for ninety years, always a bestseller. It is an extraordinary masterpiece, often imitated but never bettered. The dream of every perfumer is to create a fragrance that will topple the great *N⁰ 5*.' She smiled at the sisters. 'And perhaps now is that time. Explain what it is you wish from me.'

'Well ...' Tara leaned forward eagerly. 'Our company is on its last legs. Sales have plummeted ...'

'Oh yes, I know. A pity when something that was once great loses its way.'

'We know nothing at all about the perfume industry but what we do know is that, for us, the scents we have just aren't working any more. Some are better than others but we have no idea why some are so terrible – it doesn't even seem possible that they were ever fashionable. That's why we need you.'

'A nose,' put in Claudine. 'A trained, expert nose to tell you what you need to know.'

'Exactly. So first of all we want you to smell these scents and give us your impressions. But the one we are most concerned about is our signature scent.'

'*Trevellyan's Tea Rose.*'

'Yes.' Tara pushed the bottle towards her.

Claudine looked at it intently. 'I have not smelt this juice for a long time. My father had a bottle in his laboratory. He told me it was one of the finest of the rose florals. The rose is the queen of flowers, the epitome of the feminine, floral scent. It speaks to all women, I believe. But one must treat the rose with the respect it deserves. Now, this is a 1912 creation, I believe, *non?*'

Tara and Poppy looked blank. 'Yes,' said Jemima. 'You're quite right. I've been reading through all the company files this week and discovered quite a lot. It was first launched in 1912, with instant success.'

'May I have *une touche* please?' Claudine gestured for a tester slip. Poppy passed it to her. Claudine took up the bottle and sprayed some liquid on to the paper. Then she held it under her nose as the sisters watched her anxiously. Closing her eyes, Claudine took a long sniff of the tester, then put her head back, seemingly lost in thought.

'Well . . . ?' interrupted Tara, after some minutes had passed. 'What do you think?'

'In a word – *une calamité*. This is truly hideous.'

Jemima and Tara looked at each other, dismayed.

'How can a classic scent like this be hideous?' Poppy asked, worried.

'Simple.' Claudine made a face. 'Your ingredients are appalling. I cannot believe that this is the scent my father admired so much; it's terrible. The dominance of a cheap rose essence makes me feel ill, I'm not joking.' She shuddered. 'Really, it's an insult to my skill. Why have you brought me here to smell this?'

'We're as surprised as you are!' exclaimed Tara. 'What do you mean, cheap rose essence?'

'Exactly what I say. There is one simple question I must ask you, Madame,' said Claudine. Her face was cold and her voice tight with disapproval. 'Where do you buy your ingredients?'

Tara opened a file and scanned it quickly. 'According to our information, the fragrance ingredients come from *Maison Georges Montand* in Grasse.'

Claudine leapt to her feet. 'That is enough!' she cried. Her face was flushed and she was clearly furious. 'Georges is a dear friend of mine. His essences and absolutes are of the highest quality. His rose and jasmine fields are second to none. I've known fragrance houses attempt to buy his entire stock in order to stop their rivals getting their hands on his wonderful stuff. His jasmine sells at $12,000 a kilo! Do not insult me! Do not insult my friend, my colleague. Georges is like me – he is an artist. He would never supply you with the ingredients that are in this . . . travesty! There is a word for your perfume. *Merde*!' She tossed her head in the air and began to walk away.

'Wait, wait,' cried Tara, also jumping up. 'Please, Mademoiselle. There must be some mistake, some confusion. All we wish to do is discover where it is going wrong. I beg you to stay and help us.'

Claudine made a dismissive noise and continued for the door. Jemima got up and rushed forward to meet her before she got there. She put a hand on the French woman's arm and said quickly, '*S'il vous plaît Mademoiselle – nous avons besoin de vous et votre nez magnifique. Je vous implore de restez ici.*'

Claudine stopped and looked at Jemima. Her eyes settled on the pretty dusky pink top for a moment and somehow it seemed to reassure her. She murmured, 'Dior. You cannot be all bad.' There was a pause. 'Will you please admit that Georges cannot possibly have sent you the ingredients for *Tea Rose*?'

'Certainly. We wish to do all in our power to correct this frightful error. There is obviously a mistake in our information. Please forgive us. Remember we are new to this.' Jemima smiled, using all her charm to calm the other woman's anger.

'Mademoiselle, I think I may have an answer.' It was Poppy. She pointed to a large crystal bottle of scent sitting on the table in front of her. It was an antique, with a pink silk-covered bulb pressed to spray the scent inside. It was half full of a golden liquid. 'This is my mother's *Tea Rose*. I would like you to smell it.

Claudine narrowed her eyes. 'You want me to submit my precious nose to that stuff again? I don't think so. I'll need at least a day to recover from the last experience.'

'Please.' Poppy smiled her most winsome smile. 'You may be surprised.'

The French woman looked at her hard. She made a *moue* and then smiled, though still coolly. 'Very well. I have come a long way. I will give this perfume one more chance. You evidently have your reasons for asking me.' She walked over to Poppy and sat down in the seat next to her. '*Une touche, s'il vous plaît.*'

Poppy passed her a paper slip.

'*Merci.* Now we will see.' She squirted the slip with the liquid inside the decanter. Closing her eyes, she lifted it up under her nose and inhaled. Then she frowned and inhaled again. There was a long pause and then she inhaled again. At last she opened her eyes. They held an expression of confusion. 'But this is most strange. This juice is not the same as the one over there.' She pointed across the table to the small glass bottle of *Tea Rose*. 'This is quite different. It has structure, complexity . . . it was built quite differently to the other. The flower accord is pure tea rose: it is rich, real, velvety. And underneath I can find several other accords. There's jasmine. There are aldehydes, most definitely, which give it its sophistication. The other juice' – she grimaced – 'is cheap, nasty. It is rough. It has no tenacity. It will never last on the skin, let alone develop into a finer, true fragrance. But this is genuine.'

There was a silence as everybody absorbed this information. Then Tara said slowly, 'I'm sorry, Mademoiselle Deroulier, but I want to be quite clear that I've understood what you're saying. The *Tea Rose* in this bottle is not the same as the one that we are currently selling?'

'Absolutely. It is beyond a doubt,' declared Claudine. 'I would stake my reputation on it very happily. It is the difference between cashmere and acrylic.' She suddenly smiled openly at them. 'Quite a mystery, ladies.'

'Indeed,' said Tara. She looked grim. 'Quite a mystery.'

22

Poppy stopped by the garden in the middle of her square. Like many old-fashioned squares in London, the centre was a stretch of green bordered by trees and shrubs, fenced off with iron railings, copies of the key to the gate only available to the residents of the houses that surrounded it. It was a lovely spring evening, still light and the sky a gentle blue, pinking gently in the west. The grass was a vivid green and she could smell the leaves of the trees and the white blossom on the cherry trees.

She would go in, she decided. A few quiet minutes wouldn't hurt and she felt the need to gather herself. Besides, what else did she have to look forward to? Another quiet evening in on her own?

Friends were leaving her to herself at the moment, she noticed. No doubt they were trying to be respectful of the fact that her mother had died and assuming she needed time on her own and not to be bothered with frivolous invitations to dinners and parties.

She found the key to the garden gate in her vintage Kelly bag and opened it. Stepping inside, she felt herself relax a little. She walked over to one of the weathered wooden benches and sat down, looking out into the garden. It was hard to believe she was in the centre of London: the trees and hedges shut out the road almost completely and muffled the sounds of the traffic, not that there was much in this square. Tiredness bent her shoulders and she sighed.

I've never worked this hard in my life, she thought. *And it's not even been two weeks!*

Even at college she hadn't been required to arrive at nine o'clock and stay for the entire day. It was a new experience, and she couldn't work out if she liked it or not.

But I'm not myself, she thought. *I know that. The others don't seem to have noticed. I feel as though I've been through so much. Losing Mother.* She felt herself slump a little at the thought. Jemima's hatred for their mother was so overpowering that it seemed to infect Poppy and Tara as well. Poppy felt as though somehow she wasn't allowed to say that, actually, she had loved her mother, in her way. Yolanda Trevellyan had not been a very loveable woman, but she had tried to show affection in the only way she knew. And at the crisis in Poppy's young life, when she had fallen so ill with meningitis that the doctors had warned she would not survive, her mother had been there, spending every minute at her daughter's bedside. Then she had bequeathed her everything she owned – Loxton and everything inside it.

But we're going to lose that too, Poppy thought. Why did the idea fill her with such despair? After all, she hadn't wanted it. In fact, she'd dreaded being given it. But knowing now that it would be taken away, along with so much else, depressed her. Then there was all the administration that would have to be dealt with. Her Majesty's Revenue and Customs were in the process of assessing her mother's estate for taxation. Probate had already been applied for, and soon Poppy would be receiving the kind of bill that most people only read about in the business pages of the newspapers. It was terrifying.

That's why Loxton has to go, I suppose. There's no way we could keep it.

She picked at a piece of lichen on the arm of the wooden bench, admiring its silvery grey colour. *Tara could keep it for us, if she wanted. She's got the money and so has Gerald. But she won't. Why not?* She felt angry for a moment, then was astonished at herself. *I sound like Jemima! I'm the one who's wanted to get rid of my money all these years. And now I can. Now I can really begin to work, and I have a proper goal. To save Trevellyan.*

She could see that Tara didn't want Loxton and there was no reason why she should have to spend millions of her own money just to keep it for Poppy. Besides, if they wanted to save the company and make a go of it, the house had to be sold. It was as simple as that.

Life had turned so quickly into something full of loss and uncertainty. How could they save the company from ruin? It was obvious that none of them knew the first thing about their family business. Five minutes with Mademoiselle Deroulier had been enough to show them all the vast gap in their knowledge. When Tara had asked how much it would cost to launch a new scent, the woman had looked at them and said, 'You mean a new fragrance to challenge the great perfumes on the market? To rival the big houses?'

Tara had said yes, and Mademoiselle Deroulier had snorted and said briefly, 'Millions! Millions.'

There was just no way they could do it. The money simply wasn't there.

'Hello,' said a warm voice. 'Looks like we've had the same idea.'

Poppy looked up, startled, and saw the young man she had met in the hall a week or so ago. He was standing by the bench, wearing dark trousers and an open-necked checked shirt and a green jumper. Under one arm he had a book. He was smiling in a friendly way and she was struck by how boyish he looked, with his soft brown hair falling over one eye and his open expression.

'Oh. Yes. Hello.'

'Do you remember me? I'm George. I'm living downstairs from you in my aunt's flat.'

'Yes, of course I do. How are you?' She wished he would go away and leave her alone. After all, she'd come here for some peace and quiet, not for social chit-chat.

'Fine. Lovely evening, isn't it? Do you mind if I join you?'

Poppy forced a smile. 'Of course not. You're very welcome.'

'Thanks.' He sat down on the bench next to her. Taking the book out from under his arm, he showed it to her. 'Bit of light reading. It's the latest Booker Prize winner.'

'Oh.' Poppy glanced at it, not recognising the name of the author. 'You must be very clever.'

George looked amused. 'No, no. Not really. It's work, I suppose. I work in a bookshop near the British Museum, a really charming place. Our customers are rather heavyweight, keen on poetry, politics and the latest literary fiction. So I need to be able to talk intelligently about whatever's new.' He looked at her a little more closely. 'Hey, are you all right?'

'No,' Poppy said in a shaky voice. 'No, I'm not.' And she burst into tears.

'I'm terribly sorry about that,' Poppy said, handing George a cup of tea. She felt very embarrassed, even though he'd been unfalteringly kind and understanding as he'd comforted her. 'I really don't go about sobbing my eyes out all the time.'

George took the mug she was offering. 'Thanks. Please, don't worry. I didn't mind – in fact, I rather liked it. Apart from the fact that you're obviously unhappy,' he added quickly. 'Your mother's just died. It's no wonder you're feeling miserable.'

'I suppose I am. I'm not used to it. I'm such a happy soul usually, you see, and very self-reliant.' It had felt unforgivably girly to be crying in front of a stranger, especially when he'd pulled her into his chest and hugged her – even more so because she'd actually enjoyed being hugged by him. His warmth and sweet masculine smell had enveloped her and comforted her, and yet, it had made her cry even harder.

'I tell you what,' he said, putting down his mug of tea. 'Why don't we go out tonight and you can tell me all about it?'

'Well . . . I don't know.' She was doubtful. She'd already planned her quiet evening alone, recovering from all the emotions that were engulfing her days. The last thing she wanted to do was go out on the town.

'Have you got something else to do?'

'No, but –'

'Nor have I. And I saw that a little Italian place has opened not far from my work. It looks great. Let's go there together and have a bite to eat.'

Poppy thought for a moment. Why the hell not? George was charming, and so easy to talk to. 'All right, let's.'

He smiled at her. 'Perfect. I'll finish my tea and then leave you to it. I'll call for you at eight.'

Poppy smiled back. 'It's a deal.'

George was as good as his word. At eight o'clock precisely there was a knock on the door, and he was standing outside. He'd changed his shirt and put on a brown moleskin jacket, and run a comb through his hair, but otherwise he looked exactly the same: ordinary but comfortable and cheerful.

Poppy had quickly showered to refresh her tear-stained face, and then dressed for a casual evening out in wide-legged jeans and a white embroidered top, both of which she'd picked up in an offbeat little boutique in Islington. Over her top she wore a bright yellow cashmere wrap cardigan, and she'd tied her hair back.

'Gosh, you look ever so pretty,' George said as soon as he saw her, and she laughed because he sounded so old-fashioned.

'Gosh!' she exclaimed. 'Who says *gosh?*'

'Just me and my chums these days,' George joked. 'Careful, or you'll have me saying crikey next.'

They walked casually through Bloomsbury, passing tourists, students, office workers and every other type of city dweller. Chatting easily together, they strolled past the British Museum and through the small streets that led them down towards Oxford Street.

They found the restaurant after a few wrong turns. It was exactly what Poppy had hoped for: small and intimate, with red-checked table cloths and candles in Chianti bottles. They sat down and George impressed her by talking a few words of Italian with the pretty waitress ('Just your basic GCSE stuff, I'm afraid,' he said modestly). Then, as they ordered and waited for their food, they carried on telling stories about themselves. Poppy talked about her time at art school, and ended up telling him all about Tom and the breakup and Tom's subsequent engagement.

'Oh dear, you must think I'm quite a sad case,' she said. They had finished their antipasti and were waiting for their next course. 'One sob story after another.'

'I think it sounds as though you've been through a lot recently.' George poured a generous slug of red wine into her glass. 'When did you break up with this bloke?'

'About a year ago.'

'That's not very long, if you don't mind me saying. He's got engaged awfully fast. You were together five years or so, weren't you?'

'Yes.' Poppy sighed. 'And somehow I seem to have lost a lot of our mutual friends as well. I don't know what Tom told them but they've cut me out of the loop. I'm not as included as I used to be. Margie is the only one I still see. We all had such fun together, they were a great crowd. I feel rather ... lonely, I suppose. I only keep up with what they're all doing through Facebook these days.'

'Poor old thing.' George looked at her sympathetically. 'Then your mother dies. No wonder you're in a bad way.'

She smiled at him. 'You're very comforting, do you know that? You just seem to have an instinctive understanding.'

'I'm very in touch with my feminine side.' George grinned and she noticed the way his eyes crinkled at the edges when he smiled. He was quite attractive, she decided, in a boyish and very English way. She liked his height and his soft brown hair and his large, capable hands.

'That's enough about me,' she said. 'What about you?'

The waitress came and put their main courses down

in front of them: grilled lemon sole for Poppy and calf's liver for George.

'Oh, there's not much to tell. I'm just your typical eternal student. I was studying at King's for ages and ages. I stayed on after my first degree to take a masters, and then started a Ph.D., which eventually I rather gave up on. I've been living in shared flats and student digs for years. Then my dear auntie told me there was a job going in her friend's bookshop. Sylvester is as rich as old Midas and only really runs the shop as a hobby, and he needed a manager he could trust. So I took the job on and, you know what, I really love it. I think I've found my calling. Only thing is, although he pays me very well, it's still not much. I mean, no one works in a bookshop in order to get rich, let's put it that way. Then Auntie told me she was moving out of her place for a while and would I like to flat sit for her while she was away? Of course, I jumped at the chance – cycling in from Nunhead to the middle of London every day wasn't much fun.' He saw her expression. 'It's a district of London – quite far out. Close to Dulwich. I was lodging with a couple of friends.'

'Oh, I see.'

'Anyway, then I met you, of course. I couldn't help but notice that a simply ravishing girl was living in the flat upstairs, so I gathered up all my courage and introduced myself. I hope you didn't mind.'

'Of course not.' Poppy smiled at him. She could feel herself blossoming. Ever since Tom, there had been no one special. She'd had a date or two but nothing serious. *I'm used to being the one everyone ignores,* she thought. *Jemima is the interesting one – beautiful, glamorous, well connected, titled. And Tara impresses everyone with her incredible career and superwoman lifestyle. And I'm just the young one – fiddling about with paints and not doing anything very impressive.*

Then it suddenly occurred to her that she was the chief executive of a major company, independently rich since she'd inherited Loxton, and part of a crack team saving the family business. Perhaps she wasn't so pathetic after all.

They talked on in the candlelight, thoroughly absorbed by each other's stories. Over their espressos, George told her about growing up in the West Country, his happy childhood and large family.

'It sounds wonderful,' Poppy said wistfully, attracted by the vision of a warm, boisterous, normal family life.

'It wasn't perfect – nothing is. But it was very happy and there's something to be said for that.'

When the meal was over, Poppy was feeling happier than she had for months. They had slowly worked their way through two bottles of rich Italian wine, and she was full of delicious food and felt distinctly light-headed.

'How convenient,' George said. 'I can walk you all the way home. I've got the perfect excuse.'

'Mmmn,' said Poppy, realising that he had slipped his arm around her, and was holding one of her hands with his. It was a delightful feeling, and she revelled in it as they strolled, half drunk, back through the still busy city streets.

When they got home, it seemed completely natural to ask George up to her flat. She made them a coffee each, and when she sat down on the sofa, it also felt like the most normal thing in the world for him to sit close beside her. They got closer and closer until she was snuggling against his chest and his arm was round her, his hand lightly caressing her hair. Her heart was fluttering, her skin tingled and she longed more than anything for him to kiss her. Then he did. What began gently and softly soon became fierce and passionate. It seemed that under George's boyish exterior and shy demeanour was a man who desired her strongly and properly. She surrendered herself to the delicious sensations.

They lay together on her bed, the room half lit by an orange glow from the street lamp outside.

George ran his hand up over her naked body; her skin goosebumped at his tantalising touch.

'You're gorgeous, do you know that?' he breathed. 'That was simply amazing.'

'It was rather, wasn't it?' Poppy giggled. 'You know, I didn't go out tonight expecting to sleep with you.'

'No. It was a delicious surprise for me too.' He dropped a kiss on her collarbone, then looked at her anxiously. 'Was it all right for you? Did you enjoy yourself?'

'Mmm, you know, I really did,' she said luxuriously.

'Good. I mean, I thought you did, from the noises you made . . .'

They both laughed.

'You know, I needed this,' Poppy said softly. 'You've reminded me what life's all about. Thank you.'

'The pleasure was literally all mine,' George said, and kissed her again.

23

Jemima was doing her best to enjoy the luncheon party but it was hard going. Usually, she would have loved this kind of thing: a small gathering of twenty ladies, delicately tinkling silver forks on china as they pushed salad round their plates in the private room of an achingly fashionable Mayfair restaurant and kept eagle eyes on how much everyone else was consuming.

'Are you going to Monaco this year, darling?' one demanded of her neighbour.

'Yes, yes, we've been invited on Ferdinand Mazzorri's yacht. He has a mooring in the harbour every year and it's such fun! Though I have to put handcuffs on Reggie to stop him gambling away the family fortune in the casino, the wretch.'

They laughed, high-pitched trilling laughs.

I won't be going to Monaco this year, Jemima thought darkly, staring at a piece of pickled artichoke on her plate.

'We're going to Mustique, of course,' declared

another. 'The same as usual. I'd get bored if Selina wasn't such an amazing hostess. And of course, the Princess will be there.'

'Dear Princess,' purred another. 'I haven't seen her since the New Year party at the Delaforte place. How is she?'

I won't be going to Mustique either, thought Jemima bitterly, even though she had only been once and hadn't had a wonderful time. She listened on as the ladies discussed the parties and social events they'd be attending over the summer.

But I've got to work. The full extent of what her change in circumstances meant was beginning to sink in and she didn't like it one bit. Now, instead of heading off to the shops and boutiques of Knightsbridge as she did most mornings, she had to think carefully about what she wanted and whether she really needed it. It was an unfamiliar and unpleasant feeling.

And it turned out that when one had a job, one could rarely drop everything and head to New York for a party whenever one felt like it.

And there would be no more little treats in her favourite New Bond Street jeweller, where she was fond of picking up antique art deco pieces every now and then. A gold and ruby leopard bracelet had been her last find.

As the party continued, Jemima tried to perk herself up. The only thing worse than having to deny herself and economise would be the others finding out that she was in dire straits. No doubt many of them were hiding cracked marriages and strained bank balances behind their filled and Botoxed faces and beneath the collagen-plumped smiles. It didn't do to be found out, that was all.

The last thing she could ever bear being was an object of pity.

'What are your plans, Jemima?' asked Venetia Ffoulkes. 'Anything exciting?'

Jemima turned to her with a bright, happy expression and said, 'Oh Venetia, just the usual. It's such a grind, isn't it? Arabella's got me into organising a party for the regatta. And will I be seeing you at Cheltenham in Gerry's box as usual? I've got the most divine hat from Frederick Fox, you'll simply die . . .'

And on she went, chattering away as though nothing in the world were wrong.

Tara was trembling all over.

'For God's sake, Gerald,' she said in as calm a voice as she could manage. 'The children are asleep just down the hall.' They were in their bedroom, Gerald pacing up and down, stopping only to bear down on her as she sat huddled at the foot of their bed.

Her husband's eyes were blazing. 'Why the hell are you so fucking disobedient, you bitch?'

'Come on, darling, please . . . let's not argue about this.' She smiled, trying to break through his anger, to calm him down.

'Don't "darling" me, you fucking moron,' he spat. 'You think you're so clever, that you can just go your own sweet way and everything will be all right. You're a fool!'

'Gerald, I don't understand –' she began, but he cut her off.

'Well, why not try your fucking best? It's not thermodynamics, sweetheart!' His face was red with rage, his eyes screwed up with the force of his anger. 'Let me explain it to you again. You've left a successful career and an inspired boss to waste your time over some tired, clapped-out company, through sheer pig-headedness. It's obvious Trevellyan's day is over. Of course we wouldn't have dreamed of saying or even thinking such a thing while your mother was alive but now she's gone, it's time to face the truth. Trevellyan is finished.'

'I don't think so –' Tara began, but Gerald cut her off again.

'And now I hear the rumour that someone is prepared to pay you good money for this company! And instead of thanking your lucky stars and biting the man's hand off, you're planning to reject it!' Gerald's voice rose with fury.

He had come into the bedroom, bright-eyed and excited, hardly able to keep his enthusiasm in check, to tell her that he had heard that an American company was interested in acquiring Trevellyan. According to his sources, FFB were actively putting together a plan of acquisition, and were prepared to pay good money to add Trevellyan to their portfolio.

'Isn't that marvellous?' Gerald had said, beaming. 'Now you can stop this fool's errand and get back to Curzons, with a healthy little bonus as well! I suggest you get in touch with this fella who runs it – Ferrera, they said his name is – and start opening the negotiations.'

Perhaps her mistake had been to bat the whole thing away too carelessly. Gerald had obviously expected her to scream with delight, thank him for saving the day and rush over to the phone to make some urgent calls. Instead, she had just looked at him over the top of her reading glasses and said lightly, 'Oh, I know. We're not interested.'

She'd gone back to her magazine. A moment later, Gerald had exploded with the kind of rage she had not seen for a long while.

Now he was pacing again, up and down the room. 'How dare you treat me with so little fucking respect? You didn't even ask my permission to leave Curzons. Don't you think I should be consulted about these things? You've consistently failed to inform me about your activities, and you've consistently let me down.' Gerald was panting as though he'd been running a race, his fat frame gasping for oxygen.

'How?' Tara dropped her glasses and magazine and stared at him, her fists clenched. She was scared and shaking, but trying not to show it. 'How have I let you down?'

'How? Are you a simpleton?' Gerald pulled off his tie and then sank down into an armchair, facing her. 'You have left Curzons. You are receiving no salary. You've taken on the goddamned foolhardy mission of restoring your family fortunes, trying to save that miserable wreck of an outdated company. And you've done all this without once consulting me. Me, your husband. The man who has always known what's best for you. Well?' He sat forward, his fist pounding the table beside him.

'I haven't left Curzons, I've taken a sabbatical –'

'And Eric agreed to that, did he? Don't make me laugh. There's no way he'll keep your job open for you if someone better comes along. You've been stupid. Appallingly stupid. It's bad enough that we're getting nothing from your mother's will but a part share in a company that's almost finished, without you throwing away your job as well. And now you won't even sell the fucking thing, when someone is prepared to offer you decent money for it. God knows when you'll get someone else who'll do that. I'm telling you, Tara, this is your last chance.'

'I don't understand,' Tara said plaintively. 'I thought you'd be pleased. I want to put Trevellyan back on its feet.'

Gerald snorted. 'Come on,' he drawled. 'Do you really think that's possible?'

Her head drooped. She thought back over all the terrible surprises of the past fortnight. 'I don't know,' she whispered. 'I just don't know.' She had never felt so powerless, so ignorant and so helpless. And in her naïvety, she had thought her husband might understand, might want to help her. Instead, it had driven him into a rage of the kind of intensity she hadn't seen since the worst period of their marriage, just after Edward arrived.

'No. You don't know. You block-headed slut!' he

yelled, making her jump. 'Do you have any idea what you've done?'

'I don't understand,' Tara cried. 'What does it matter to us? We don't need the money!'

Gerald ignored her, jumping to his feet and pacing back and forth across the room again. Then he turned on her and shouted, 'Don't waste your time on this fool's errand, do you hear me? I'm ordering you to sell Trevellyan.'

'What?' She was stunned.

'You heard me. Sell it! Get out while there's still something to be salvaged from the wreck.'

'But I've told you, I don't want to sell it,' Tara said, trying to sound strong even though she was terrified. What on earth had provoked this reaction in Gerald? She knew that their relationship had been more difficult over the last few years but she had never seen him like this. As her career had blossomed outside the home, and she'd appeared stronger and more confident, inside the home, Gerald had cracked down, imposing more and more rules on the household. There were set ways of doing everything. Some ritual or other governed every aspect of their lives. But he had never lost control quite like this and it frightened her. Up until now she had allowed him to exercise control because she didn't want to think about what might happen if she defied him. Now it looked as though she had defied him without meaning to, and she was going to have to carry on defying him.

'I command you to sell it!' he shouted.

'No!' Tara cried. 'I won't. I can't. I owe it to the others.'

Gerald's face went puce. 'Do you intend to disobey me?'

She didn't dare answer. He raced over to the dressing room and opened the door. It revealed rails and shelves of clothes and shoes, all perfectly arranged and colour coded. Nothing was out of place. It was immaculate and spotless.

'Gerald, no,' Tara said, panicking. She had lived for so long with his mania for order and correctness that she had begun to rely on it herself, to feel distressed when things were out of place. She also knew what it meant when Gerald lost his temper.

He didn't appear to hear her. He rushed into the room, paused for a moment as though gathering his strength, and then attacked the clothes, ripping them from their hangers, clearing shelves with one swipe of an arm.

Tara jumped off the bed and ran over, shouting, 'Gerald, no, please, don't do that!' But it was too late. He was in a fierce frenzy, turning boxes over, shaking out the shoes inside, throwing her clothes into a crumpled, twisted mess in the middle of the room. Then he picked up a slim belt and held it in his hands, rubbing the leather across his palms. He turned to glare at her with a wild look that she knew all too well.

Oh God, she thought, with icy fear. *Oh God, no. Not this. Please. I can't bear it if this begins again.*

24

Tara looks terrible, thought Jemima. Her sister had come into work wearing a massive pair of dark glasses. When she'd taken them off, she'd revealed swollen eyes, her lids pinkish and dark bags puffed underneath.

'Are you OK? You look awful,' she'd said, concerned.

'I'm fine.' Tara had sounded short. 'I had a bad night. Imogen was awake and she kept me up for hours.'

'Bad luck,' Jemima said sympathetically. 'Is the little poppet ill?' She had a soft spot for her nephew and niece. She couldn't believe how sweet they were, considering Gerald was their father.

'She's fine. It's just one of those things children do. You wouldn't know anything about it.'

Jemima flinched.

'Oh Christ, Mimi . . .' Tara looked mortified. 'I'm sorry. I didn't think . . .'

'It's fine,' Jemima said stiffly. 'Really. Forget it.'

'No, I mean it, I'm sorry . . .'

'Don't we need to get on?'

The door opened and Poppy came in, breezy and smiling. 'Morning, girls! How are we all today?'

'Not quite as perky as you, I'm afraid,' Jemima said, raising her eyebrows.

Poppy sighed happily. 'I *am* feeling rather fantastic, as it happens –' She faltered as she looked over at her big sister. 'Oh my God, Tara, is everything all right?'

'I'm as fine as I can be, considering the mess we're in. Right, let's get started.' Tara fired up her laptop as Poppy shot Jemima a concerned look, but it was returned by a dismissive shrug.

Tara pushed on, wanting to avoid any more discussion about her tired, washed-out looks. 'Now, as you both know, we've got a major problem as far as our product is concerned. To be brutally frank, if Claudine is to be believed, we're selling a fake. The formula for *Trevellyan's Tea Rose* has been interfered with. I think it's perfectly obvious that this is something Mother has done. Her drive for cutting costs appears to have overridden all other concerns. To be honest, it seems to have sent her a bit barmy.'

'She probably realised she was on the brink of destroying Trevellyan,' Jemima said.

'Or at least, being at the helm when the ship went down,' Poppy agreed. 'Imagine. She loved this company more than Daddy did. Remember how taking over control of it after he died seemed to wake her up and give her a purpose in life? It was almost as though it took Daddy's place. It meant everything to her. No wonder she was willing to do anything to save it.'

'She loved being the boss,' Jemima added. 'Nothing thrilled her quite as much as dressing up for board meetings, do you remember? She'd become even more ram-rod straight and terrifying, issuing orders all over the place. At the time, I thought it was rather funny.'

'If only she'd seen that what she was doing was having exactly the opposite effect of what she wanted,' Tara said grimly. 'She must have realised that if she tampered with the scent, people would notice, that she would take away the only thing that mattered about Trevellyan – its quality.'

'She probably thought no one would notice.' Poppy's good mood seemed to have melted away and she looked glum.

'They probably didn't at first. Perhaps they just thought they'd gone off it. But in the end, they clocked that something wasn't right and that something they'd once loved no longer spoke to their senses, no longer ignited the nostalgic feelings it once had. It didn't speak of rich tea roses flowering in an English garden on a summer's day. It spoke of cheap flowers farmed in a field in some foreign country, and a perfume conjured out of synthetic notes.'

'So what do we do?' Jemima looked at her sister. 'What's the answer?'

'To be brutally frank, there aren't many options open to us. We're going to face an uphill struggle – the perfume's been debased and degraded. Its most loyal fans have abandoned it. Everything about it has been compromised in order to cut costs and keep margins as high as possible. If we want to save Trevellyan, our best option is to recreate the original perfume. To relaunch it. To create a new, exciting story around it and make it explode back on the perfume world like a shower of stars. But that's going to take a huge amount of work – and a huge amount of money. Which we haven't got.'

'What are the other options?' Poppy asked.

'There's only one other option.' Tara looked down at her screen, holding in a shudder as she remembered Gerald ordering her to sell Trevellyan. It was hard not to flinch at the memory of what had happened next. 'I don't think it's what any of us want, but I have to put all the choices in front of you. We sell the company. We sell up to someone who's got the money to invest in it, or to someone who'll simply break it up and sell off the assets, piece by piece.'

'And that will be the end of that,' Jemima said softly. She thought for a minute, examining her perfectly manicured nails, painted in a shade of softest shell-pink. 'Oh God. I didn't think I'd care. But I do.' She looked up. 'Can't we somehow find the money for the redevelopment? For a proper relaunch?'

'There's the Loxton money,' Poppy put in. 'Don't forget that.'

'We'll need it, Pops, but God knows how long it will take before we're in a position to empty the house and sell the contents, it could take months for probate to be granted. And anyway, the problem is, that could all just be a drop in the ocean.' Tara smiled, relieved that Poppy and Jemima weren't willing to surrender yet. 'I want to give this our best shot, and I think you do too. To that end, I've asked someone else to meet us. My hope is that we can persuade her to come on board.'

'Other than Claudine?' Poppy frowned.

'Yes. Claudine is a perfume expert, a nose. She's going to help us discover the old formula for *Tea Rose*, perhaps even rework it. She has plenty of experience in the fragrance world and I intend to draw on that as much as I can. But she's not a businesswoman. We need someone who can tell us what's going on. Someone who knows this world inside out. So I've recruited some help from the top.' Tara stood up, walked gracefully to the boardroom phone and dialled reception. 'Hi. Could you send Ms Asuquo in please? Thanks.'

Jemima and Poppy looked at each other and then at Tara, who smiled at them. 'Trust me. I know what I'm doing.'

A moment later, the boardroom door opened and the receptionist stood there. 'Ms Asuquo,' she said, and stepped back to allow the guest to come forward. In the doorway stood a tall figure in a bright red suit. She was stunning; at a glance she could be mistaken for Naomi Campbell, although her skin was darker and her physique more athletic. Her hair was pulled back, a tuft of afro curls bursting from the red silk ribbon tied into it, and her make-up was flawless.

'I hope I'm not making the biggest mistake of my life,' she purred.

Tara got to her feet. 'You're not. I guarantee it. Hi, Donna. Welcome.'

'Thanks.' She stepped forward and looked around the boardroom. 'I hate to break it to you, ladies, but this place has nothing on Erin de Cristo's digs. Where are the freshly picked white lilies? Where is the air-conditioning wafting your signature scent all about? I'm used to seeing trays of sushi and miniature French pastries when I go in for meetings.' She glared at them all, then suddenly broke into a charming smile. 'Hey, I'm kidding. Erin's great but she's very spoiled. So, am I right in thinking you need my help?'

'Completely,' Tara said, grinning back and thrilled to have completely blindsided her sisters who were currently sitting, mouths agape. 'Take a seat and we'll tell you all about it.'

An hour later Donna Asuquo had heard the entire story.

'I'm beginning to think that maybe I should get up right now and run,' she said soberly. 'You guys are in deep shit.'

'That's why we need you. That's why we want you to leave Erin de Cristo for us.' Tara looked at her earnestly.

'OK, I'll tell you why I'm here. I'm bored at Erin's, that's for sure. I've learned just about all I'm ever going to learn there, and it's all about perpetuating the myth. Erin has three or four juices that are always in the top twenty in the list. She's just bringing out new versions of her classics now and that's kind of uninspiring . . .' She saw the expressions on the women's faces. 'OK, juices are perfumes, I think you've probably got that.

And the list is the bestseller list, just like with books. Every week, every month and every year, we find out who's doing best in this crazy, cut-throat world. Erin's always paranoid about it but she doesn't have to worry. She's got some classics there. To tell you the truth, I'm getting frustrated where I am. Like most designers, Erin has licensed her scents to one of the big fragrance houses. They develop, create and distribute the juice – our role is comparatively small. I'm fascinated by it and I've learned an awful lot but now I want a bit of excitement and adventure, the chance to put some of what I've learned with her to the test. The only thing is . . .' Donna shrugged. 'I think this might be a challenge too far.'

'We're assembling a crack team,' Tara said hastily. 'As well as you, we've got Claudine Deroulier on board.'

'Oh?' Donna raised her eyebrows. 'Of course I've heard of her.' She reeled off a list of fragrance names, some of which the women knew and some they did not. 'She created some amazing juices. She's old-school French, isn't she?' Donna adopted a comical French accent. 'For me, eet is all about ze aart!'

They all laughed.

'But tell me,' Donna leaned forward, fixing each of them in turn with her almond-shaped brown eyes, 'what exactly is it you want to do?'

The sisters spoke over each other in their eagerness to reply, keen to tell Donna their story.

'We want to recreate our brand, reinvigorate it. We want to launch it so that everybody notices and so that

273

everyone in the world recognises and desires our scents,' Jemima finished. Either side of her Poppy and Tara held their breath, inwardly praying that Donna wouldn't do the sensible thing and leave.

'Hmm.' Donna smiled. 'So just the moon on a stick then.' She frowned. 'How about I tell you some of the realities of this business? For one thing, there are too many perfumes on the market. Hundreds are launched worldwide every year – new fragrances from the top brands, the famous names we all know so well. But not just those. Celebrity perfumes have become the latest big trend. In the industry we might consider them little more than commercial, one-note scents, hardly worth the cost of the bottle, but they're doing enormous business. It all started with Jennifer Lopez and her first juice, *Glow*. Since then it's been a crazy rush to bottle that precious celebrity essence. Look at Paris Hilton – before it was even officially launched in the US her perfume sold out twice in Macy's. Britney Spears might be on the edge but her perfume has made thirteen million dollars. The men aren't immune either – David Beckham has just launched his fifth scent. And if the celebs aren't selling their own, they're becoming the face of other people's, even the big Hollywood men. Davidoff just this year signed Ewan McGregor, and Dolce & Gabbana have Matthew McConaughey. And of course, we can't forget the girls – Jean-Paul Gaultier's snapped up Agyness Deyn, Calvin Klein's got Eva Mendes and Chanel has just signed Audrey Tautou.'

'Do you mean we need a celebrity?' asked Jemima, frowning.

'What I mean is, the competition is intense. And guess what – the market is flat. Perfume sales aren't growing much at all. It's partly because there's just so much on offer, and it's hard to retail perfume outside the Christmas and Mother's Day promotions. A lot of people see it as a gift purchase. Many women don't buy themselves fragrance or consider themselves to have a signature scent, if you like.'

'What about the celeb angle then?' asked Poppy.

Donna looked at her. 'Traditionally, fine fragrance has brought in a lot more money than commercial, mass-market scents. But that seems to be changing. Boots the chemist is increasing its market share and it tends to be a place where there are fewer premium scents on offer – bar a couple of really big names. The celebrity perfume doesn't focus on the smell – it focuses on the image of the person who supposedly created it –' Donna raised her eyes to heaven '– yeah, right! Like Paris Hilton got going with her test tubes and essences and started creating a formula. Of course, the premium fragrances have always used beautiful women to sell their perfume, but even their angle is now more along the lines of *Catherine Deneuve wears Chanel – so should you*. It's a significant market shift, this coming away from what's in the bottle and focusing instead on who you associate with the brand. It's hard for everyone to come to terms with.'

Tara looked serious. 'This can't be the end of the story. There can't just be huge designer perfume, like Chanel, Gucci, Dior and so on, famous fragrance houses like Guerlain – and celebrity mass-market scents. There's more to the perfume market than that, isn't there?'

'Of course,' said Donna. 'There are hundreds of more niche products on offer too. Up-and-coming make-up brands, like Laura Mercier, for example, are putting a lot of effort into launching their scent lines. And there are upmarket perfume houses like Les Parfums de Rosine, the House of Creed and L'Artisan Parfumeur in Paris. Not to mention Parfums Caron, Edmond Coudray and many more. There's Tocca in New York and Santa Maria Novello, an Italian perfume house very famous to those in the know. Serge Lutens is a great talent. He created his own perfume house after working with Shiseido and he's won so many awards at the FiFis.'

'FiFis?' queried Jemima.

Donna nodded. 'The fragrance Oscars. A very important deal in our world. So you see, there are very successful lesser known fragrance houses all over the place. Here we have new boutique houses like Miller Harris and Jo Malone. These people believe in quality and innovation. They seek a customer base who knows, appreciates and can afford their product – loyal fans who will return time after time, and also invest in the products that go alongside the juice – soaps, creams, lotions, candles, incense sticks . . .'

Jemima said excitedly, 'Perhaps that's the angle for us!'

'Perhaps it is.' Donna grinned at her. 'Cos if you're going to start challenging the big boys, you're going to need a hell of a lot of money. You know who the big boys are, the ones who really run the fragrance market? It's the huge, multinational corporations who develop the biggest perfumes in the world. Most fashion houses go to them to create new perfume, and those corporations have a lot of muscle.' She picked up the bottle of *Trevellyan's Tea Rose* that was sitting on the table. 'I know this stuff, of course – everyone does. That's priceless and I would say it's your most important asset. But I don't know anybody who wears it – and that's your greatest challenge.'

'Do you think we can turn this around?' Poppy asked quietly.

'I don't know. You can try. It's going to be a huge job.'

Tara leaned forward and pushed her glasses up the bridge of her nose. 'What we want to know is – will you help us?'

Donna didn't reply. Instead, she leaned forward, took the bottle of *Tea Rose* that sat on Tara's desk and squirted some of the original scent on to a tester. She raised to her nose and sniffed it. She closed her eyes for a second and then smiled approvingly. 'God, it makes me think of going to my first school dance. I wore this to it.' Then she looked earnestly at each of them in turn.

'I worked very hard to get where I am. It's not easy for a black woman to succeed in high fashion and beauty in this country. It's all very white European – it's almost exclusively the focus for everything: clothes, make-up, jewellery – and fragrance. My name doesn't

277

sound European and I certainly don't look it, so it was hard for me even to get my foot in the door. I came in through the PR route, and that's what I still love doing. I'm a marketer. I look at the business, I try to understand and predict it, I try to sell our product. Erin de Cristo gave me a chance when she took me on. I'm still not even sure I want to leave her company but when you called me, I couldn't help being interested in what you had to say. The top isn't always the most exciting place to be.'

When Tara spoke, her voice was so heartfelt, it almost vibrated with passion. 'Donna – we need you. We need your expertise. We know so little and you know so much. The rewards may be low at first but, if this thing turns round, I promise you it will be very worth your while.'

Donna thought for a minute. A wide smile broke over her face. 'You know, there's something about this crazy scheme that appeals to me! It's virtually hopeless, but . . . the raw materials are here. It's a challenge. I want to try my hand at doing something myself. This looks like the perfect opportunity.' She stopped and looked pensive again. 'Give me till tomorrow. Then I'll let you know. OK?'

'OK,' exclaimed Tara, with her most charming smile. 'We can't wait. We just hope it's going to be good news!'

'You know what?' Jemima was up and pacing the room. Donna had gone, leaving the sisters alone. 'For the first time since all this started, I feel really excited. As though a light has suddenly come on in the darkness. I can see which way we could go . . . a high-end, utterly luxury, utterly lovely brand. Very, very desirable and very chic.'

'You mean, do away with the leather armchairs, red rugs and dark wood?' Poppy's eyes were sparkling. 'Oh my God, how fabulous! This whole place could be redesigned – it would be so much fun!'

'Now you're thinking along the right lines,' Tara said. She also stood up, folding her arms and half smiling as she tried to contain her excitement. 'We should have seen this from the start. We can't go cheap. We can't do cheap. It isn't in our blood. What we do know is *expensive*. We need to work up from the foundations of the business and redevelop everything about Trevellyan. Start with the ethos and the vision, then move on to the look, our image and ultimately our products. If we're going to be for ever associated with Trevellyan we'd better make sure it reflects us. It's going to be ours now and we need to feel proud of that.' She looked at her sisters. 'We can brush away everything that's gone before and start again. A completely new beginning, a fresh start. How bloody brilliant will that be?'

'*Bloody* brilliant,' breathed Jemima.

'A dream come true,' said Poppy, and clapped her hands with delight.

25

The telephone rang in Tara's office. She scrambled to find it under the mass of paperwork. It felt like she was still barely scraping the surface of the Trevellyan mess – every day brought new discoveries and more nasty surprises.

'Hello, Tara Pearson,' she gasped into the phone when she finally managed to scoop it up.

'Hi, it's Donna.'

'Hi, hi! How are you?' Tara sat back, smiling, hoping the phone lines could transmit the positivity she was trying to push down them. 'It was great to meet you yesterday.'

'You too. You know, I found it really funny. There you were, the famous Trevellyan heiresses. Your sister Jemima – I've read all about her in the magazines. I've seen pictures of her at parties and launches, I mean, my God, I think she was at Erin's show in Paris and at the launch of the Bond Street shop. And there she was, hanging on my every word. And I could tell that Poppy was so keen to learn as well. As for your determination . . . well, you've got a backbone of steel.' Donna's voice was breathy and there was the sound of traffic in the background. 'But you're still just on the brink of some major change, there's so much to be learned and achieved. How long do you have to turn this all around?'

'A year. Max.'

Donna whistled. 'Bloody hell. Worse than I thought.'

'Yep. It is tight.'

'As a ferret's arsehole, darling. And what can you offer me?'

'What's your salary at the moment?'

'It's a hundred and five a year, plus benefits, bonuses, all the Erin de Cristo products I want, and big discounts on clothes.'

'OK.' Tara took a deep breath and thought fast. There was no way Trevellyan had the funds for that kind of salary. Not at the moment anyway. 'We can't quite match that. But I can offer you eighty and we'll make it up with performance bonuses based on results. There'll also be some share options which could prove valuable. We'd need to hammer out the details, obviously, but I don't think you'll be unhappy with our package.'

'Ok-aaayyyy,' Donna drawled. 'When would you need me?'

'As soon as you can?'

'I think I could swing it to start next week.'

Tara felt a rush of excitement. 'You mean, you're coming on board?'

'Yes, yes I am. You can count me in. I'm a sucker for challenges.'

'Donna, that's great! That's fantastic! Listen, let me know for sure when you can start and I'll get everything sorted for you at this end. And I want you to meet us for a celebration drink. I'll text you some dates and you can let me know what's good.'

'You bet. Hey, you're my boss now.'

Tara could hear the delight in Donna's voice. 'It's my privilege. We're going to make waves!'

'You'd better believe it.'

Jemima had been out scouting all morning, diligently researching the perfume market. Before she started, she popped into Smythson's to buy herself a big leather-bound notebook in duck-egg blue. The cover was stamped with the words *Interesting Facts* in silver letters. And she had seen a great deal to interest her. Now the notebook's first ten pages were covered in scrawls and notes and sketches of bottles. In her handbag she had dozens of paper tester slips in all sizes, some stamped with the name of the designer or fragrance, others plain and annotated by Jemima in pencil. When she opened the notebook, a heady gust of scent came out, rich with a score of different notes and flavours, a mixture of everything she'd been trying that morning.

'You know what?' Jemima said as she breezed into Tara's office. 'There are some amazing scents on the market. Today I tried *Jicky* by Guerlain – it was created in 1889. I mean, imagine!'

'Some of our scents were created in the nineteenth century,' said Tara, looking up. 'About four, I think, are still made and sold today.'

'I've got some strong ideas – some real inspiration. I've been all round the place. Bond Street, Oxford Street, Sloane Street – the bastions of luxury. Honestly, Tara, it's just too cruel. I couldn't do any shopping for myself at all! I daren't.' Jemima sat down and made a sulky face.

'How are your finances?' Tara asked. 'The allowances stop as of this month. I hope you're prepared.'

'I've done a bit of cancelling, let's put it that way. I've broken it to Josephine that I'm only coming for a cut and colour once every six weeks.' Jemima closed her eyes and shuddered. 'I'm sure people are going to notice immediately but what can I do?'

'And your credit cards? I hope you've got that sorted.'

Jemima shrugged. 'I talked to my banker. We cashed in some options, share thingies I'd invested in – apparently – and paid off the cards and got me a bit of ready cash.'

'That's good. Just don't rack up debt on credit. If you use it, clear it. That's all I'm saying.'

'Yes, yes.' Jemima sniffed. 'No need to preach. The point is, I've got enough put by to last me a while yet. But if we get to the end of a year and we haven't managed to turn this thing round . . . well . . . we'll see. I'm going to stay positive, that's all. And telling Harry he can whistle if he wants more money for Herne is going to be a distinct pleasure.'

'I've got good news,' said Tara. 'Donna called. She's going to start next week.'

'That's wonderful!' Jemima clapped her hands. 'Bravo!'

'And Fuchsia Mitchell called as well. She's going to come in and give me the results of the focus groups.'

'That was quick! Better and better . . .'

'Where's Poppy?'

'She went out to research bottles. She's got the names of some manufacturers and she's been talking to them about designs and costs and so on.'

'Good. But that means she's not going to be here for a rather important announcement.'

Jemima looked apprehensive. 'Which is . . . ?'

Tara picked up a piece of paper from her desk and handed it to Jemima, who scanned it quickly. 'What's this? A list of directors?'

'It's a list of everyone I propose to make redundant.'

Jemima whistled. 'That's quite a lot of people, Tara!'

'Yes. And I'd like to know what the hell most of them are doing.'

'What about redundancy packages? This is going to cost a fortune.'

'Not as much as keeping them on in the longer term. I'm going to negotiate each one separately and I'm going to resort to scare tactics. Each of these people presided over a period when sales fell dramatically – that's reason enough to be held up as incompetent. But worse, they also sanctioned the bastardisation of our perfumes, and that could possibly be of interest to various legal bodies. After all, if you sell an inferior product and pretend it's something superior, you are surely infringing the trade descriptions act.'

Jemima gasped. 'Are you serious?'

'I've no idea. But I don't think anyone is going to want to find out – do you?' Tara smiled. 'I'll be bringing in the lawyers tomorrow for the initial discussions and then we can start.'

'It'll probably be kinder to put most of them out of their misery,' commented Jemima, looking at the names of the condemned. 'Duncan has been sloping about the corridors looking like a spare part. He obviously hates what's going on.'

'That's why he needs to go. I'm going to reward loyalty and hard work, but I'm not going to tolerate the smallest iota of dissent. Discussion, yes. Disloyalty, no. I don't believe Duncan is really loyal to us and the company. So he has to go.'

'Spoken like a true business superwoman!' said Jemima, and saluted. 'I'm glad you're in command. I've some great ideas for what we can do with the scents . . . I mean, the *juices*.' She looked proud of using the vocabulary of a real perfumer.

Tara smiled, her face lighting up suddenly. Jemima realised how tired and worn her sister had looked over the past few weeks. She had scraped her hair back into a tight ponytail, and her suits had been in sober tones of grey, dark blue and black. She had even abandoned her killer heels for flat ballet pumps.

'We're not out of the tunnel, but I can see a kind of light at the end of it,' said Tara.

Jemima went over to her sister and hugged her. It was the first time she'd done that for years, she realised. 'We really appreciate this, Tara – all the work you're doing. You're the driving force here, we do know that.' She pulled away to look her sister in the face. Tara's eyes were sparkling with tears and her lip was trembling. 'God, are you all right?'

'Yes . . . yes . . . just tired, that's all.' Tara tried to smile but she couldn't hide the misery in her face.

'What's wrong? Something is. You'd better tell me,' Jemima said strictly. It was the only way she knew when dealing with emotional situations: she became businesslike and direct. 'Is it the children? Are they all right?'

'Yes, yes. Robina tells me they're fine.'

'Is it Gerald, then?'

Tara's gaze slid away. Jemima pounced.

'It *is* Gerald, isn't it? Oh God, what's he doing? I always knew he was a disaster. No one can be that pompous and not be fundamentally selfish and stupid.'

'Mimi, stop it. Don't say such awful things. He's my husband.'

'But that doesn't mean you have to be loyal to him beyond the call of duty! If he's making you miserable, then you need to talk about it. Come on.' Jemima lowered her voice to sound more gentle and caring. 'What is it? Who can you tell if not your sister?' Jemima sat in the spare chair opposite Tara, patiently waiting for her to open up.

There was a long pause. Tara fiddled with the button on her jacket, then she looked up almost fearfully. 'You remember Gerald's . . . problems?'

'Any one in particular?'

'If you're going to be nasty . . .'

'Sorry, sorry. No. Which problem do you mean?'

'You know how he likes things just so.'

Jemima rolled her eyes. 'Oh, you mean the way the house has to be immaculate? I've never met a straight man as house proud as him, that's for sure.'

'It's not just that he's house proud. He has a serious problem with it,' Tara said quietly, looking down at her lap. 'The whole house has to be exactly as he wants it, or there's trouble. I mean, huge rages. At first, when we were married, he just liked the place tidy. He used to instruct all the cleaners and staff as to precisely how he wanted things, even in the kitchen. I knew it was unusual – I mean, none of my friends' husbands dictated how the kitchen should be organised – particularly as he doesn't cook. But I didn't think it was a problem, just the way he is. He likes to be in control, that's not so strange, is it? But gradually, it's got worse and worse. In fact, the higher I've climbed in my career, the more his mania has grown. I honestly think he has a form of Obsessive Compulsive Disorder.'

'I thought that was hand washing and turning off lights a million times,' said Jemima, frowning.

'It can manifest in lots of ways. I've looked it up on the net, and it's a complex condition. It can be brought on by stressful situations.'

'What kind of stress does Gerald have? He's a highly successful businessman. He owns about two hundred newspapers across the world, doesn't he? He just has to let the whole thing run itself – at least, that's the impression I was under.'

'Me too,' Tara said quietly. 'He's always told me not to worry when I've asked him how the company is going. But I'm no fool. I know that print media is struggling in the high-tech, web-based environment. There are huge cutbacks in news outlets and in regional news capability. Gerald's papers are nearly all regional. It's why he wants to buy his way into a national newspaper in this country but he's running into diffi-culties – at least, I think he is. He won't tell me what's happening but the research I've done into his company indicates that things are not that rosy.'

Jemima looked frightened. 'But Gerald's our safety net!'

'That's what I thought. But yesterday he went ballistic, partly because I'd in effect resigned from Curzons. He went utterly mental. Besides terrifying me, it also made me fear the worst. Why should he care that I'm not bringing home a hedge fund manager's salary? He's supposed to be rolling in it.'

'And what have you found out?'

'Nothing yet,' Tara said grimly. 'The company is in apparent good health. But something is worrying me . . .'

'He's just bought an estate in Scotland, hasn't he? That's hardly the action of a man in financial trouble.'

'You don't know Gerald. It's precisely the kind of reckless, showing-off thing he would do in a crisis. It would deflect suspicion from the true state of affairs.'

'It sounds as though you don't really love him any more,' Jemima said quietly.

Tara stood up and walked to her office window. 'All my life, I've worked to be a success. I know bad things can happen, things that are outside one's control. But the essence of success is knowing when a risk is worth taking, and when it's not. I don't think Gerald understands that. He believes he's untouchable, destined for great things. He honestly believes he's superior to little people and that's a dangerous mindset. I used to be overawed by him, impressed by his confidence and the certainty he possessed that he was always right. Now . . .' She turned to face Jemima, fear in her eyes. 'I just don't know. It's beginning to look more and more like hubris to me. And I'm not sure I want to share my life with someone like that any more. Besides, there are other things in our relationship that aren't right.' She paused for a moment and then added quietly, 'He wants to control me too. He thinks he can.'

'So leave him,' Jemima said earnestly. 'You don't have to put up with his behaviour.'

'It's not that easy.' Tara's head drooped and Jemima wondered if she were crying. 'He's making my life hell. I can't tell you everything that's happened. But I'm not ready to leave him. What about the children?'

'Do you honestly believe it's healthy for them to live in that environment? Not a thing out of place? The whole house terrified of putting a foot wrong? Do you want them to grow up with a mother scared of their own father? I know our childhood wasn't exactly rosy, but one thing's for sure, our parents respected each other. Who knows if they loved each other right to the end – though I think Mother never stopped adoring Daddy – but they certainly never showed us anything other than a united front.'

'But the children are happy, honestly. He's their father, he adores them and they love him with all their hearts. I can't break up our home.' Tara turned round, wiping her eyes. 'Another Trevellyan mess, I'm afraid. Look at us. Both in miserable marriages. How did we manage to end up with husbands we don't love?'

Jemima stared at her for a moment, then averted her gaze. 'I don't know,' she whispered.

'At least we have the company,' Tara said stoutly.

Jemima gave a half-smile. 'Yeah. But a company doesn't keep you warm at night.'

26

Poppy clutched her sketch pad under her arm. In it were dozens of pictures of perfume bottles, She'd spent a happy afternoon in various department stores and perfumers, looking only at bottles and trying to understand what they said to her and to the average shopper. She'd found bottles shaped like stars or abstract shapes, like classical urns, with stoppers shaped like birds or diamonds or flowers; square bottles, round bottles, triangular bottles; clear or opaque; with accents of silver or gold, with labels and without, with ribbons, with jewels, with engraving. There was no end to the variety.

Then she'd gone to an arts club in Notting Hill where she was a member and spent a further happy hour drawing ideas for what she thought was the perfect bottle for *Trevellyan's Tea Rose*.

What is Tea Rose? she wondered. *Who is this scent for? What is it trying to say? What should the bottle convey?*

She ended up with some ideas she liked but she

realised that until the new version of the perfume was created, they wouldn't know the answer to any of those questions. *It's a process of evolution,* she thought. *As the scent evolves, we'll start to understand what we really want. At the moment, all we know is what we don't want.*

She decided not to return to Trevellyan House and instead walked back home, taking a detour through Kensington Palace gardens on her way, to enjoy some greenery and a break from the heavy traffic on the main road.

I wonder if George will be about, she thought idly as she walked. She knew he had a couple of afternoons off a week but couldn't remember which they were. She sighed happily. The night she had spent with him had been beautifully invigorating. For the first time she understood how sex could be good for your health: she felt alive, full of energy and generally happy. She had also not given Tom a thought since it happened.

Is that all it takes? she wondered. *One really good shag from a new bloke and suddenly, my broken heart is all mended? Who said women were fickle, eh?*

But it felt as though a line had been drawn under her relationship with Tom. Spending the night with George had shown her new possibilities. There were other men out there; funny, witty, caring, expert lovers, just waiting to be the next chapter of her story.

When she reached the square, she walked slowly, taking every step at half-speed. Then, when she got home, she climbed the stairs at a snail's pace, listening out all the time for the sound of anyone in the building. She passed by Miss Fellowes's flat, glancing at the door, but continuing up the stairs.

It was only when she reached the door to her own apartment that she realised the swooping sense of disappointment which descended on her could only mean one thing. That she'd been hoping to see George more than she'd realised.

Oh God, she thought. *So much for sex being good for you. I'd forgotten that getting rid of one obsession just leaves a vacancy for another. I can't believe it. I bet I never see him again.*

She was dressing to go out when there was a knock at the front door.

She breathed in sharply and stared wide-eyed at her reflection for a moment.

Her first thought was: *Is it George?*

Her second was: *If it is, thank God I'm already dressed!* She was wearing a flowery silk tea dress in bright blues and reds, with high cream Mary Janes. To go with the dress, she'd set her hair in a 1940s Veronica-Lake peek-a-boo style, so that she had a long dark sheet of wavy hair falling seductively over one eye. Fiery red lipstick and lashings of mascara finished the look.

Her third was: *But I'm going out!*

Heart thumping, she opened the door. Her stomach did a somersault. George was standing there in the hallway, a sweet smile on his face and a bunch of white ranunculus in his hand.

'Hello,' he said. 'I thought I'd drop by. I got these for you.' He noticed how dressed up she was and his face fell. 'Oh, you're going out. Of course.'

'Thank you – they're beautiful.' She took the flowers

he was offering. 'Yes, I've got to go to a private view. A friend of mine is exhibiting for the first time. It's very exciting.'

'Well, I hope you have a marvellous time. Perhaps we can meet up another evening.'

'Why don't you come with me?' Poppy said in a rush. 'Ally won't mind.'

'Oh. I don't want to impose. Honestly, I only came by on the off chance . . .'

'No, no, you must come. I mean it. It's just a view. The more the merrier. Especially if you buy a picture . . . Joking, I'm joking,' she said quickly when she saw the look on George's face.

'As long as you're sure I wouldn't be in the way . . .'

'I'm certain.'

'Then I'd love to.' He stepped into the flat as Poppy went about gathering her bag and finding her keys. Finally she was ready.

'Have I told you how devastatingly gorgeous you're looking?' he asked, taking her hand.

'No.' Poppy looked out sultrily from under her sheet of hair. 'But you can if you like.'

'I most certainly *do* like. I particularly like that 1940s look. It makes me feel like I'm back in fashion, briefly.'

George was wearing a tweed jacket, a bright yellow waistcoat and baggy chinos, with polished brogues. He could have stepped straight out of 1947.

It's a sign, thought Poppy. *We're obviously the perfect match.*

* * *

294

The private view was held at an exclusive Cork Street gallery. Burly men in black suits stood on either side of the door as the guests arrived. Just inside, a beautiful blonde gallery assistant took their invitation, ticked them off a list and asked them to sign the visitors' book. George signed in a flowing handwriting. He seemed entirely at home in the glitzy crowd. The men were debonair in suits, a mixture of old and new money, arty types and high-powered City boys who were looking to invest in paintings, as they needed something to spend their money on. All the women were extremely glamorous, from the pretty young things, mostly from wealthy backgrounds and trying out the art world as a career, to the fabulously well-turned-out forty-and-fifty-somethings. There were even a few knock-out old ladies, loaded with jewels and wearing expensive black dresses or vintage Chanel tweed suits.

Immediately Poppy arrived, she was surrounded by friends, and she spent a happy hour exclaiming, kissing cheeks, introducing George and talking non-stop, swapping as much news as she could in the short period of time before another friend dashed up to claim her.

'You're very popular,' murmured George into her ear as he pressed a glass of champagne into her hand.

'I didn't realise how many people would be here.' She smiled at him delightedly. She already felt a little high on the champagne, and it was lovely to see so many friends, greeting her so enthusiastically. She had begun to believe that no one wanted to know her after

Tom, that they had taken his side. And yet, there they all were, asking her where on earth she'd been hiding and saying how brilliant it was to see her again. Not one of them had mentioned Tom, but maybe they were being polite. After all, she was obviously here with George.

She caught a glimpse of him in a mirror. He was chatting comfortably to a group of people. She could see her own reflection too, standing just to one side of George. She looked pretty and her dress was still as good as it had looked in the mirror at home. But more important than that, she looked happy.

After the private view, they walked home together. On the way, they stopped at a Japanese restaurant and bought a big tray of sushi and sashimi to take home. Back at her flat, they sat cross-legged on the floor and ate with chopsticks. Poppy opened a bottle of champagne from her fridge and their ability to pick up the sushi and dip it in the soy and wasabi deteriorated accordingly, but it made them laugh. Ella Fitzgerald's voice came silkily from the stereo, and Poppy felt ridiculously contented.

When the tray was empty and the soy dish almost dry, they both knew what would happen. Poppy turned down the lights, kicked off her shoes and danced lazily to the music, singing along to 'Dream A Little Dream of Me' while George watched her, his gaze burning.

A moment later, he jumped up, took her in his arms and they danced slowly together. He was surprisingly good at it, pressing her tightly to him so that they moved in harmony. Her stomach swooped as lust bubbled through her.

Kiss me, kiss me, she thought. Then he lowered his mouth to hers and began to kiss her properly, pushing his tongue into her mouth, exploring her. He tasted warm and delicious and she responded quickly, pushing her hands inside his waistcoat and unbuttoning his shirt so that she could feel his smooth chest and run her hand up to the nest of soft hair under his arms. He smelt so sweet, all she wanted to do was bury her nose in his neck and arms, and inhale his smell. It excited her and set her heart racing.

'You feel amazing,' she murmured as she pulled his clothes from his body, until he was wearing only his trousers, that couldn't conceal his growing arousal.

She stepped back from him and smiled seductively, tossing her dark hair with a flirtatious shake of her head. Then she slowly unbuttoned her tea dress, and let it slip to the floor leaving her standing in her small white cotton briefs and bra. Stepping out of the dress, she went back to him, pressing herself against him so that the hardness in his groin rubbed against her stomach. He bent to kiss her again, wanting to touch her skin, run his hands over her naked back and over her white breasts which swelled up invitingly from her bra. But she teasingly pushed him backwards until he was standing against one of the dining chairs, then, more forcefully, pressed him down on to the seat. He looked up at her, his eyes intense with desire. She sat down on his lap, one slim white leg on each side, and returned to his mouth, kissing him deeply and pushing her groin against his trousers.

He was panting between their long kisses, desperate to caress her breasts, his mouth reaching for her nipples, eager to free them from her bra, but she kept him softly back, so that his desire for her grew stronger.

'You're teasing me,' he protested, longing to touch her flesh and rip her bra and panties away.

'All in good time,' she breathed. Reaching down, she unzipped his trousers and felt inside. She pulled out his stiff cock, smiling with admiration. She held the shaft close to her, pressing him against her panties tempting him with the damp heat within. He moaned softly. When he bent his head to her breasts this time, she let him use his mouth to push the fabric aside and release her erect nipples so that he could suck and pull on them, making them tingle delightfully while she ran her hands over his cock.

Pausing for a moment, she reached for the condom packet she'd put in her bag earlier and left in reach on the table. Handing it to him, she watched as he deftly opened it and rolled the sheath down over his cock. Raising herself up on the chair, she pushed aside the crotch of her panties. He drew his breath in sharply at the sight and tensed as she pulled his throbbing penis towards her. For a moment she remained poised above it, the tip just lost inside her and then, when they could both stand it no longer, she lowered herself on to him. George closed his eyes and gasped as he entered her, feeling her tightness yield to him, and they sat motionless for some time, enjoying the exquisite sensation of being joined together.

Then George wrapped his arms around her, taking her weight, and stood up, with her still impaled on his penis. He moved slowly into the middle of the room and then sank to his knees, lowering her on to the soft rug until she was lying on her back. Reaching down, he pulled at her panties until the seam broke, then he pushed them aside, and began to thrust inside her.

It was exactly what she wanted. At the pitch of anticipation, she was ready to let him take control and begin to move hard and deep inside her, filling her up exquisitely. She could feel his balls banging against her buttocks with every long, intense thrust and that alone made her tingle with excitement.

They moved in time together, her hips rising to meet him, to let him go as far as he could inside her. She raked the skin on his back with her nails and bit at his neck and shoulders, urging him on. Suddenly he exploded inside her, pushing in with intensity, slowing as his orgasm possessed him. When he'd regained himself, he smiled down at her.

'Did I leave you behind? I'm sorry, I couldn't help it, you were just too incredible. We'll have to do something about that . . .'

He moved his hand downwards, sliding his fingers into her and smoothing them upwards over her clitoris. She shivered jerkily as he touched her most sensitive spot, now highly aroused and ready. He sank his mouth on to hers, kissing her deeply at the same time as his fingers played over the hard bead of her clit, rubbing and rubbing, exerting just enough pressure to urge it to greater and greater sensation, until an immense wave of pleasure burst over her. She tensed and then gripped him to her, crying 'Oh, oh, God . . .' as the orgasm pulsed through her, releasing all her tension in a glorious climax.

Afterwards, while they were lying in each other's arms, Poppy murmured, 'Mmm, I really enjoyed that. It was utterly lovely.'

'Well, I'm glad to hear it,' George said with a smile.

Poppy laughed. 'You must have guessed from all the thrashing about and then coming embarrassingly loudly?'

'I suppose so – but one doesn't like to assume.'

'I think it's a safe bet when someone shouts "Yes, oh my God, yes!"' She rolled over to face him. 'You know, you're really very . . . hmm . . . what's the word? Surprisingly . . . well, let's say . . . a *very* good size.'

George grinned. 'So I've been told, but you know, it's hard for me to tell. After all, I've got no one to compare myself with.'

'You don't look at all the type.'

'What type should I be? A rippling hunky body builder or something?'

'No.' She laughed. 'I don't know. You just seem quite unassuming and I thought that if a man had a big cock, he was full of machismo and testosterone and "look at me, I'm so great, you're mine, baby, I'm going to take you to heaven and back" sort of thing.'

'No.' George picked up one of her hands in his large one and stroked it. 'I think you'll find those men are the ones with the small penises.'

She laughed. 'Well, I'm a very lucky girl!'

'Lucky in lots of ways,' George said, looking her straight in the eye. 'You've got all this for a start – a beautiful flat, your own dosh. And you're gorgeous, sexy and amazing. That's a winning ticket in the lottery of life, isn't it?'

Poppy stared at him for a moment and then said slowly, 'You might be surprised, actually. I might look like all I have to do is spend my money but it's not as simple as that.' She told him about Trevellyan, regaling him with the whole story, finishing up with the fact that she and her sisters had only one year to turn the company around.

George listened intently. 'What I don't understand,' he said finally, 'is why you've only got one year to do it. It sounds like you should have much longer than that. How on earth can you manage to revive a company in twelve months?'

'Because, according to my mother's will, if we don't manage it, the whole company will go to Jecca.'

'Who's Jecca?' asked George.

Poppy paused. She couldn't help hesitating before she discussed Jecca. It was so ingrained in her that Jecca was not to be mentioned that it was hard to overcome the inbuilt reluctance to talk about her. But what harm could it do to talk about her with George? Surely he was one of the few people who could listen without prejudice.

'Jecca is Jecca Farnese. Or, I suppose, Jecca Trevellyan. It depends which name she feels like using. She was adopted by my parents when she was just a baby. I suppose to understand why, we have to go right back to the beginning, to the start of Trevellyan. Years ago, when Samuel Trevellyan founded the company, he did it with the help of an Italian man, Farnese, who developed all the original fragrances for the company. He was an astounding talent, apparently, an inspired perfumer. His sons inherited his gift and they stayed in the company, running the laboratories, while my family ran the business side. But there was always a difficulty – the Farnese family were well rewarded for their work but they did not become as rich and successful as our family, even though the company could not have been built without their talent. As the years went by, resentment passed from generation to generation, getting stronger. Then, when my father was a young man, it looked as though the problem could finally be solved. He and Luca Farnese were close friends. They went to the same school and it seemed that the Farnese family had finally been accepted into British society. Luca and my father even went to Cambridge together. It wasn't long after my father left university that he met my mother and they married. But apparently my mother and Luca did not get on, because his friendship with my father abruptly ended. Luca left his job at Trevellyan and disappeared to Italy, where he was gone for many years.

'When Luca finally reappeared, it was on the doorstep of Loxton. He had come from Italy where he was desperately poor. He'd put all his money into trying to start his own perfume house and now it was gone and he was utterly destitute. He also had a beautiful young wife, Isabella. He threw them both on to my father's mercy.'

'What happened?' George asked, enthralled. 'Did your parents take them in?'

'I was only a baby when the Farneses turned up on our doorstep and I don't remember anything about it. But Tara remembers that night very clearly because it was dark and raining, and these wet, bedraggled people arrived – real orphans of the storm. They stayed but there were terrible rows between my parents, or so I've heard. My mother considered Luca Farnese had forfeited his right to any help and that he'd lost his money through his stupidity alone – I don't think there was any love lost between the two of them. However, my father felt that the Trevellyans were eternally in the debt of the Farnese family, because without their talent, we would have been nothing. So he was obliged to help Luca and Isabella.'

'How long did they stay?'

Poppy sighed. 'It all took a terrible turn. Once they were settled in the house – they'd been there a month or so – Luca Farnese got in his car and drove it off a bridge at high speed into the river which was at full flood. He drowned.'

'Poor bloke,' George said grimly. 'It's hard to imagine how desperate you have to be to do such a dreadful thing.'

'His wife was devastated and there was no question

of her leaving after that, of course. She had nowhere to go, no family, no money. And she was pregnant.'

'With this Jecca.'

Poppy nodded. 'Yes. When Jecca was born nine months later, Isabella stayed on. I have a vague memory of her. She was very beautiful with long black curly hair, and she sometimes wore a cross and beads round her neck. I can remember her singing to the baby in her own language, lulling her to sleep.'

'So, if there was Isabella, why did Jecca become a Trevellyan? Why was she adopted?'

'Because Isabella died.' Poppy felt a wave of unhappiness wash over her. Just saying the words brought back a feeling of horror, the sensation she must have felt as a young child at that time. It made her think of shouting and tears, anger and despair. She rolled on to her back and stared up at the ceiling, remembering.

'How did she die?'

'I don't really know. It was never talked about. I always had the impression that it was an illness. Something sudden and strange. But as I say, no one ever told me and I never asked. But Jecca stayed with us and grew up with us.'

'She didn't have other family?'

'Yes, but she didn't know any of them so perhaps it was decided she was better off with us. I'm not sure Jecca thought that, though. She always seemed so unhappy. We tried to treat her as one of us, as our sister, but it was never right. She looked and behaved so differently to us, for one thing, she was so completely

Italian. Jecca was always aloof, and when she wasn't aloof, she was angry. She and Jemima particularly hated each other. Jemima had always been Daddy's favourite but when Jecca arrived ... well, it was as though he decided to love her best because she was so alone in the world. He just worshipped Jecca. My mother always favoured me – I suppose I was her baby and I had an illness early in my life that seemed to give me special status. Tara longed for Mummy to love her best, and Jemima longed for Daddy to love *her* best. But she couldn't compete with Jecca.'

'So where is Jecca now?'

Poppy rolled over to look at him. 'I honestly don't know. She ran away when she was eighteen. She'd been in boarding school, but she left at sixteen. Daddy set her up in a flat in London – he always gave her whatever she wanted. Then, one day, she vanished. We never heard from her again. My father was distraught. He was never the same after she went. I'm sure part of the reason Trevellyan is in its current mess is because Daddy lost his passion for it when Jecca left. I always thought she must have gone back to Italy, to look for her mother's family.'

'Didn't she have her father's family in this country?'

Poppy shook her head. 'A few distant cousins perhaps. Her closest Farnese relatives emigrated to South Africa in the seventies.'

'So she could have gone there.'

'I suppose so. It's a mystery.'

'Have you tried to track her down?'

'No.' Poppy ran her hand over his chest. 'To be

honest, I don't care where she is. None of us do. We can't help but feel she was partly responsible for Daddy's death – he was literally heartbroken. She certainly changed Mother into a bitter old woman. She ruined our family.'

'So if the worst happens and she inherits the company, how is she going to find out? Who will tell her?'

Poppy shrugged. 'The lawyers will have to look for her, I suppose. I'm sure they have ways of finding missing heiresses. I just hope it won't come to that.'

George pulled her to him. 'Of course it won't.'

'Let's not talk about Jecca any more. I don't want to feel depressed.'

George grinned. 'Her name won't pass my lips. They're going to be much more profitably engaged.' He kissed her, then began to kiss gently down her chest towards her stomach.

Poppy sighed luxuriously, ran her fingers through his hair and lay back.

27

Jemima paused for a moment in the doorway of the bar at Claridge's. She loved this room: its opulent art deco cream, silver and red seemed the epitome of glamour. It made her want to toss her hair like a movie star and drink dry Martinis.

Tonight, she felt good. She'd decided to take a day out of the office and have her last splurge, so she'd spent the day being pampered, massaged, steamed and beautified. Her hair was a fresh gold, blown out into a 1960s style, and she was a wearing a silk cocktail dress in a vivid green with black detailing, also in a sixties style, with a neckline cut high and straight across the shoulders, small cap sleeves and a figure-hugging pencil-cut skirt. She'd accessorised with black Jimmy Choos and a black sequinned clutch bag.

She could see that Tara, looking more demure in a grape chiffon Burberry number with an embroidered cashmere cardigan, had bagged them a booth at the end of the room, so she sauntered through the bar towards her.

'Hello, Jemima! How on earth *are* you? Where have you been? Everyone's saying you've simply *vanished*.' Annabel Duff-Brown, a socialite whose love of gossip was only matched by her slavish adoration of titles, seemed to have appeared from nowhere and stopped Jemima a few paces in.

'Hello, Annabel.' Air kisses were duly exchanged. 'I've been busy actually.'

'Busy?' Annabel blinked. 'Aren't we all, sweetie? But is that any reason to miss the Grayson-Templeton bash? We all wondered where you were ...' Annabel suddenly cast her a sly expression. 'Are you spending all your time at Herne with Harry?' she said, dropping her voice to a husky whisper. 'How is that old rascal?'

'Fine, thanks,' replied Jemima coolly. She wasn't about to give Annabel what she so obviously wanted – a reaction. Jemima knew that the gossip must have been rife after the events at Rollo's. No doubt, everyone was enjoying chewing over the details – the drunken behaviour from Harry, the blatant flirting with Letty Whatsit, Jemima fleeing the scene first thing the next morning. She was sure it was providing lots of fun for everyone.

As for Harry, she hadn't seen or heard from him since that night. All she knew was that whenever she thought about him she felt a stab of such pain that she had to force herself to stop thinking and to close her mind to him. 'Listen, I can't stop. Do give my love to everyone. Bye, darling.' She carried on marching past.

Tara waved when she saw her. 'Hello. Poppy's here, she's just in the loo. Oh, look, here she comes.'

Poppy looked beautiful in an A-line leopard-skin-print mini dress, with loose long sleeves. She appeared unusually exotic, her mane of dark hair making her seem very feline.

'Gosh, you look good,' Jemima said, frowning.

'Do you like it?' Poppy did a twirl. 'I picked it up in my favourite second-hand shop in Kensington. It's real seventies!'

'It's not just your dress, though I must congratulate you for being bang on trend with that flowing, almost kaftan look, and the animal print. There's something else . . .'

'Yes!' Tara joined in almost accusingly. 'You've definitely got something about you . . . I noticed it yesterday.'

'You're having sex!' declared Jemima, sliding on to the red leather banquette and throwing down her clutch bag. 'There's no other explanation. I hope this doesn't mean the ghastly Tom is back on the scene . . .'

Poppy laughed. She knew it was true: her eyes were sparkling, her skin glowing and she was moving with the kind of sensuous stride that only comes from lots of very satisfying sex.

'No. Not Tom.' Poppy beamed at them, enjoying the fact that for once she was keeping her sisters guessing.

'That's the first time you've been able to mention

his name without welling up in I don't know how long,' said Tara, smiling at her sister. 'So sit down and tell us all about him.'

Poppy took her place, trying not to look all starry-eyed. 'He's called George and he's so sweet, you can't imagine. He works in a bookshop and he's like this old-fashioned gentleman, stepped out of a classic Gainsborough movie.'

'What a red-hot lover he must be,' joked Jemima.

'You'd be surprised,' Poppy said coyly.

'So how did you meet him?'

'He's staying downstairs from me.'

'Handy,' put in Tara.

Poppy nodded then said hastily, 'I mean, I don't know if it's serious or anything. It's all very early days. But we're having fun.'

'And plenty of it, by the looks of things,' observed Jemima. She looked around. 'Oh, you've ordered champagne.'

'I'm going to have it opened when Donna gets here, which should be any minute,' Tara said.

'Have you seen how many people are here tonight? Honestly, half of the London social scene is drinking Manhattans and whisky sours in this room. Annabel Duff-Brown just tried to ambush me, and where others lead, she most definitely follows.' Jemima stared around the room. 'It's strange, but I don't feel as much a part of their world as I once did.'

'You've only had a job for five minutes and you're no longer the It girl!' Tara laughed. 'What a radical change.'

Jemima looked impatient. 'But don't you feel it too? It's as though the whole of my life has transformed. I can't believe that I got all this money from a business I never gave a second thought to. Now I think about it, I feel a bit ashamed. Yes, it's lovely to have money, lots and lots of it. But I've realised almost too late that it's important to always understand how and why you have it.'

'Goodness!' said Poppy suddenly. 'Look!'

They all turned towards the door, where Donna had just entered. Ripples of admiration went about the room. She was magnificent in a coral Herve Leger bandage dress that displayed to perfection her slender figure and impossibly long legs.

'Wow, what a great dress,' breathed Jemima. 'I'd order one, except I don't think it could look half as good on me.'

'Ladies, good evening,' said Donna as she approached the table.

'Donna, hi.' They all jumped up to kiss her hello, admire her outfit and make sure she was comfortable on the banquette.

Tara signalled a waiter to open the champagne that had been chilling in an ice bucket beside her. When each of them had a glass of sparkling golden liquid at the ready, Tara raised hers to make a toast.

'To you, Donna. Thank you for joining us. You've taken a huge risk, we know that. We promise you it's going to be worth it. It may well be a bumpy ride, but with your expertise and our determination, I just know we're going to be a huge success. This is the perfect team!'

They all raised their glasses and touched the rims together.

'Thank you.' Donna smiled. 'I'm so excited. You are my kind of ladies, I can tell that already – your clothes are fabulous, for one thing. I can't wait to get started.' She sipped her champagne.

'We've got some ideas,' Jemima said, fired up with enthusiasm. The sisters had been in a meeting for the whole of the previous afternoon going through their vision for the new-look Trevellyan and, while it was far from finalised, they felt real progress had been made.

'Me too.' Donna pulled a leather notebook from her bag and opened it. 'Shall we get started?'

'Wait, wait,' protested Tara, holding up a hand. 'This was supposed to be a celebration drink, not a work summit!'

'Ever heard that thing about the iron and striking while it's hot? What's to wait for?' Donna shrugged, with a charming smile.

'OK. But a little social chit-chat first, please,' Tara begged, 'so I don't feel like I'm forcing you to work already.'

'Why did you decide to join us?' Poppy asked a little shyly. It was often hard for her to speak up when the three of them were with a stranger – the other two always seemed so confident and self-possessed, quick with words and eager to put their point of view forward. Poppy had always felt as though she understood images, colours and patterns better than she understood words. 'I mean, Erin de Cristo is such a big name. Her make-up line, her skin care, her scents . . . and the new clothing line as well. Why would you want to leave such a thriving company?'

Donna smiled at her. 'Good question. My boyfriend thinks I'm crazy. The truth is, I like being part of a small team – very creative, very organic, very capable. Those are the things I thrive on. Erin de Cristo's outfit is not going to be like that for much longer, I'm afraid, so I realised it wasn't a place I wanted to stay.'

'Why not?' Poppy asked.

Donna looked somewhat uncomfortable. 'This is top secret. I'm not supposed to say anything about what's happening.' She glanced at the sisters. 'Could you promise me this will go no further?'

'Absolutely,' said Tara, and the other two nodded.

'I wouldn't know what the hell to do with confidential information anyway,' Jemima said with a laugh.

'OK. I'm taking a risk here, but I trust you guys.' Donna looked at each of them in turn. 'The reason I'm going is simple – Erin is about to sell out.'

'Sell out?' echoed Tara.

Donna nodded. 'Yep. She's been approached by an American company to buy her out. Everything will belong to someone else – the name, the products, the licences, the premises . . . you name it. She says she's going to retain creative control but I've heard that the Chief Executive of this company is a control freak, and liable to interfere with the way things are run.' She shrugged. 'Lots of the big brands that are owned by a parent company are given free rein – it's what

313

keeps the magic alive. As long as they're successful, no questions are asked. My own feeling is that Erin may not be so lucky.'

'Which company is this?' Tara asked.

'It's called FFB. Do you know it?'

Jemima looked startled. 'Yes, I do. I just met the guy who runs it. He sat next to me at a dinner party the other week. Richard Ferrera. *Very* tasty.'

Poppy and Tara exchanged a look. They were both well aware of Jemima's inability to restrain herself where handsome men were concerned.

'Mmm. I wonder if that was a coincidence.' Donna raised her eyebrows. 'Did he talk business with you?'

'Not really.' Jemima frowned, thinking back to her meeting with Richard Ferrera. 'But he told me a bit about his company, and how he wants to rival the big luxury firms. He seemed incredibly focused and driven.'

'Did he mention Erin?'

Jemima shook her head. 'He mentioned Trevellyan briefly – he even suggested we think about selling to him.'

'Oh.' Donna took a sip of her champagne, thinking hard. 'OK. What did you say?'

'I said we weren't interested in selling.'

'I'm surprised. I wouldn't have thought Trevellyan would be big enough for him.'

'It has the name,' Tara pointed out. 'And with the right investment, it could be great again. That's what we're banking on, at least.'

Donna nodded. 'But still . . . It sounds like he might be out to get you.'

'I don't see how he could have known I'd be at the party, let alone organise sitting next to me.'

'Don't underestimate him,' warned Donna. 'I've met this guy. I saw him charm Erin. He knows exactly how to get what he wants and I'm sure he would use all sorts of methods to get where he wants to go.'

Jemima remembered his effect on her: he had been so smooth and polished without being in the least overbearing or off-putting. He seemed so polite, so intelligent. She had been seriously impressed by this man, who had come from such humble beginnings, pulled himself up by his own efforts and was so full of vision and determination.

'He said he wanted to get into the European market,' she said, recalling their conversation. 'He seemed very keen on the French and British labels.'

'I'm sure he is. The places where the last great luxury labels, with all their prestige, tradition and glamour, can be found,' commented Donna. 'No wonder he wants to go on a shopping spree round here. Can you ladies hold him back?'

'We own virtually the entire company – seventy-five per cent of it anyway,' Tara said. 'No one could buy it without our say so. We'd always have the casting vote.'

'Who has the other quarter?'

'Some of the board have shares. Family members. It's in dribs and drabs. No one else has the power, I can guarantee that.'

'Well, that's a relief,' Donna said, smiling. 'Or I might end up with Ferrera as my boss anyway.'

'That's not going to happen,' said Tara decisively. 'Absolutely not.'

'Good. I wouldn't want to go from the frying pan straight to the fire. Now, is there any more of that champagne? We need to celebrate.'

Jemima let herself into the flat. Sri had left the hall light on, so it wasn't as bleak as it might be, but she was still alone. She stood in front of the mirror and looked at herself appraisingly. Leaning in, she peered at her face. Not bad. Those oxygen-blast facials really did the trick: her skin looked dewy and soft and young. But who was she kidding? At twenty-eight, she was at the height of her beauty, she knew that. Soon, the late nights and champagne would start to take a toll on her, if she wasn't careful.

She pulled off her Kenneth Jay Lane emerald earrings and put them on the hall table, then kicked off her shoes and padded through to the sitting room, turning on lights as she went.

What the hell, I'm only young once, she thought, and opened the sleek modern cabinet that ran along one wall, pulled out a bottle of single malt, and poured herself a good measure. She took her tumbler over to the window and gazed out into the darkness. The square was full of lighted windows, little glimpses into other wealthy lives.

Why do other people's lives seem so happy and uncomplicated from the outside? she wondered. Then she thought about how she must appear to others: young, good-looking, rich, and married into the English aristocracy.

No doubt they all think I'm living some kind of dream. No one knows how miserable I really am.

She looked about the flat. She knew in her heart that it would have to go. From what Donna had said this evening in Claridge's, they would need all the cash they had to relaunch the company. This place was worth around five million. She'd have to sell, buy something more modest in . . . she frowned, trying to think of somewhere cheaper where she could bear to live but couldn't come up with anywhere. No doubt she'd have to find a tiny place on the outskirts of Kensington, or even be forced to use Herne as her only place of residence. Any money she could raise needed to go into Trevellyan. She sighed and took another sip of the whisky. It would be worth it. Anything to stop that bitch Jecca getting her hands on the company.

Just the mention of Jecca's name made her want to scream. She still couldn't understand how their mother could have contemplated risking Jecca inheriting the company, even if the threat of it was probably the only thing that could unite the three girls and focus their attention on the job in hand. After all, it was Jecca who had come irrevocably between her parents and destroyed their marriage. They could never agree on Jecca, because Cecil had adored her while Yolanda had loathed her, although she'd tried her best to hide it. Over the years, it had soured the relationship between husband and wife to the extent that they had ended up living separate lives, albeit under one roof.

Daddy gave Jecca anything she wanted. He loved her more

than he loved me, and I was his daughter, his real daughter.
Why couldn't he love me the same way? What did she have
that I didn't?

She remembered Jecca's tantrums, the fearsome
outbursts of anger that shook the whole house, the
screaming, the pounding, the breakages. Once, Jecca
had broken three pieces of the antique Spode tea set,
a treasured gift from Cecil to Yolanda. Jemima could
picture that day so clearly, seeing Jecca race down the
hall to the antique French china cabinet, yank it open,
and then, with an evil glint in her eyes, pick up the
delicate cups and smash them, one by one, on to the
stone floor. Yolanda had screamed a wild, piercing
scream and Jecca, who'd been on the verge of picking
up the rest of the tea set, had stopped, frightened by
the strange otherworldly noise. She'd known then
that she'd gone too far.

But Cecil had made sure that she was never
punished. God only knew how he'd squared it with
his wife.

But he'd do anything for her. Anything. And he never
cared how much she hurt me.

From the time she could talk, Jecca had taken a
delight in persecuting Jemima. It didn't matter that
Jemima was four years older, Jecca had never been in
the least bit afraid of her. Instead, she whispered mali-
cious things to her, hid her favourite toys, destroyed
her favourite books, turned people against her – her
only friend from the village had never wanted to play
with Jemima again after she'd spent the afternoon
with Jecca. Jemima would find her bed stuffed with

thistles, or nettles, or vile creepy crawlies. Her best dress was discovered one day covered in bright red stains that could never be cleaned off. No matter how often she told her father that Jecca was pinching her under the table at dinner, or stealing from her piggy bank, or spoiling the flowers she was pressing, nothing was ever believed. Jecca was never punished and she would sneer and laugh silently as Cecil admonished his daughter for telling tales.

'Jecca has suffered very much,' he would say gravely. 'You are a lucky little girl, Jemima. You have Mummy and me. Jecca's parents are dead. She only has us, so we must be extra kind to her.'

'Don't forget, you have to be kind to me,' Jecca would tease when Jemima, her face scarlet with fury and frustration, chased her and pushed her up against a wall. 'I'll tell Daddy if you're not.'

Jemima had to release her, furious but impotent.

The quiet, ceaseless torture went on for years. Then she escaped to boarding school, where at least she was free of Jecca – except in holidays when the younger girl would be waiting with the many tricks she had dreamed up during term time. There was the occasion, for example, when Jemima's treasured collection of vintage Barbies had vanished only to be unearthed months later by the gardener, who'd found them buried in a vegetable patch and irredeemably ruined. Her father had once given her a beautiful edition of *Alice's Adventures in Wonderland* for her birthday – it was found with all the Tenniel illustrations she so loved scribbled out with bright green felt-tip pen. And there was the time her favourite old teddy had his brown glass eyes pulled off. Jemima had cried bitter tears, knowing who had done all those spiteful things. Then, to her horror, Jecca asked to be sent to the same school as Jemima and there was no escape. The persecution began again, but this time with added awfulness. Now Jecca, with her whispering campaigns and sure knowledge of Jemima's weak spots, caused her real pain, turning the school against her. 'Jemima smells of cat's wee,' went one nasty little whisper. 'Have you smelt her? It's disgusting . . .'

Jemima knew she didn't smell and yet the rumour hurt. It damaged her. Girls sniggered at her in the dining room. The whispers continued: 'Jemima never washes her hair, she's got nits . . . Jemima's in love with the music master . . . Jemima's a slag, she's not a virgin . . .'

Her parents wouldn't listen and the school turned a blind eye to it, until Jemima forced them to notice and to expel her. She was found in the middle of the night, drunk on vodka, loudly playing the piano in the school hall wearing only her underwear, a cigarette burning on top of the piano. She left the school the next day.

'At least I went out with style,' she muttered to herself, as she was driven away by her irate parents, happy in the knowledge that Jecca was safely imprisoned in the school behind her.

Before Jecca, she was kind, quiet and obedient. After Jecca she'd realised that only bad girls get noticed, and now she had a taste for it. Her school career became a car crash: she left with four expulsions and a couple of exam passes to her name. The only thing for it after that was a finishing school for rich girls who didn't need to bother with a career.

And now here she was, with one last chance to stop Jecca from stealing her life once more.

So, if the flat had to go, then it had to go.

28

'First, I would normally need a brief, something to tell me what you want in this perfume I must create for you. In the industry, we are given sometimes pages and pages of notes, sometimes a picture, sometimes an object. Once, I was given a piece of satin ribbon and a copy of Shakespeare's *A Midsummer Night's Dream* with the instruction: put this in a bottle! Make it a scent.' Claudine smiled to herself. 'That one was easier than you might think. But here, we already have a juice. The classic *Trevellyan's Tea Rose*. So in this situation, things are a little different, *non*? You have your brief – it is in your mother's bottle. You wish me to recreate this scent.'

The sisters glanced at each other. Tara took the large perfume bottle and pressed the silken bulb, spraying scent on to her wrist. She inhaled, thought and then passed the bottle to Poppy.

'What's your analysis of this scent, Claudine?' she asked.

'It is a delightful piece. There are several rose accords in there, built round a musk and a heavy dose of jasmine. In fact, it has many, many ingredients. If you wanted this replicated exactly, it would be straightforward enough. We could put it through a very clever machine called a gas chromatograph that will identify all the constituent molecules and their percentages, and we could then rebuild it. What is notable about this is the quality, the richness, the tenacity . . . all hallmarks of a good juice. It develops on the skin, responds to the warmth of a body like a pearl necklace, gaining lustre and depth.'

'It's too . . . *rosy* for my taste,' declared Jemima.

Claudine fixed her with an impassioned stare. 'Rose is the most classic of the flowers. It is the foundation for nearly all the most treasured perfumes in the world. *Chanel N⁰ 5* is a classic rose scent, along with jasmine and aldehydes, of course. Les Parfums de Rosine sell only rose-based fragrances. The Different Company make one of my favourite scents, *Rose Poivrée* – fifty kilos of rose petals to create two hundred and fifty millilitres of juice. Some people adore rose in all its forms. For others, it can smell a little soapy, perhaps because it has been cheapened by overuse in inferior products.'

'Yes, that's how I feel too,' chimed in Poppy. 'It reminds me too much of bad soap.'

Claudine looked a little impatient. 'Very well. Which direction do you want to go? Zesty and fresh? Or rich and heady? Warm or cold? What is the story of this juice?'

'We don't know. We've no idea what warm or cold perfumes smell like,' said Poppy helplessly.

'We want something modern,' declared Jemima. 'Not too heavy. But it has to be classic and really very like the original *Tea Rose*.'

'A flanker?' asked Claudine. Then she explained. 'A reworking of an original scent. Like the summer versions of classic fragrances. Esteé Lauder's classic *White Linen* has been released in other versions.'

Jemima frowned. 'I suppose so. But flanker doesn't sound right.' Her face cleared. 'I know what the difference is. *White Linen* still exists, alongside the flankers, doesn't it? But in this case, we're not going to supplement the original, we're going to replace it. It must have all the depth and passion of the original version but with something extra. Something fresh.'

'But sophisticated,' put in Tara quickly. 'We don't want something girly and sweet. It must be something a glamorous woman, from twenty to sixty, would love to wear. Suitable for the day but also rich enough for the night.

There was a long pause during which Claudine looked at them as if to say 'You have no idea what it is you want!' Then she spoke.

'Then there is really only one answer. I will return to my laboratory, I will build some iterations and bring them back to you to sample. Yes?' She looked to Tara for approval, who nodded.

'How long will all this take?' Donna asked, frowning. She had been scribbling notes on to a piece of paper while they were talking.

'As long as it takes,' Claudine said frostily.

'This baby must be launched by November so that we're in time for the Christmas market. We're going to have to make a big, big noise if we want to get noticed. Jemima – I'll talk to you later about publicity and marketing. Poppy, we'll need to discuss packaging and the bottle, sooner rather than later, because we've only a few months to design, model and then order our bottle. As for the juice itself . . .' Donna looked up at Claudine, her face serious. 'Ideally we need samplers for the press in October. That means a final version of the juice can't come soon enough, especially if we're going to consider ancillary products.'

'What do you mean by that?' Tara quizzed.

'I mean body lotions, creams, soaps . . . all that stuff.'

'We might not have time for that. It might have to wait for next year,' muttered Tara. 'Just getting the juice sorted is going to be an Olympic-sized challenge.'

'Let's see how we go,' Donna replied. 'Claudine? What's the best you can do?'

The French woman narrowed her eyes and thought. 'I want to help you,' she said finally. 'I will do my level best. I will attempt to have iterations here for you next week. Then it will depend on what everybody thinks of them.'

'Thanks,' Donna said. 'We appreciate it.'

'Where's your lab?' asked Jemima.

'I share a laboratory with other perfumers just outside Paris.'

'I'd love to see you develop our juice.'

'Then you should come back with me, too,' Claudine said, unsmiling. 'If you want to.'

'One of us should go to Paris anyway,' Donna said quietly. 'We're going to need to look at distribution there. I want someone to go in and start charming the big department stores. It's absolutely vital we tell them what we're doing and get them involved.'

'Then why shouldn't that be me? I'm sure I can handle it if Donna tells me what we need. I'll do whatever's necessary and make the time to visit you in your lab.' Jemima smiled at Claudine. 'We can book our Eurostar tickets today.'

29

'Hello, ma'am. Good day?' John gave her his usual comforting smile as he closed the door.

'Not bad, John, not bad,' Tara replied, though it wasn't exactly the truth. Today she had realised the extent of the job in front of them. Up until now, a calendar year had seemed like a long time. A discussion with Donna earlier in the day had highlighted how little time they really had. It was late April now and they had barely six months to launch.

'Without a November launch, there's no way you can get the Christmas market,' Donna had explained. 'And without that, you're fucked. I mean it. You will sell perhaps fifty per cent less than you otherwise could. So by November, we not only have to have everything finalised in terms of the juice itself, we also have to have a marketing, advertising and PR campaign well under way. That means we have to move fast.'

Tara knew now how big the job was. The only

comfort was that, from her figures, she could see that increasing sales by the amount they needed was not as difficult as it sounded. They were looking at a base of very low sales indeed.

'We need to reinvigorate the US market as well,' Donna had said. 'That's going to be very costly. Hugely. I mean, if we had several million to spend, it would help.'

'We haven't got that.'

'It's a problem we have to consider. Without the States, you won't be able to move towards the really big money.'

'I'm beginning to wonder why anyone gets into this crazy business!' Tara had declared, throwing up her hands.

'Are you kidding? The profit margins on perfume are fantastic. If you get a hit, you'll be rolling in it. If you hit the jackpot in India and China, you could make twenty million dollars in the first quarter. The big houses make oceans of money from their perfume, believe me.'

'What did Erin make?'

'Erin's scents bring in almost fifty per cent of her gross profit.'

'Really?' Tara blinked. 'That much?'

Donna nodded slowly, a smile creeping across her lips. 'That's why we all do it. It's why we all battle it out and spend so much trying to persuade people that the dream inside our bottle is their dream – the rewards are mind-blowing.'

Donna had gone on to sketch a future that included

not just a range of bestselling perfumes, but deals with top hotel chains to supply fragrances and toiletries, luxury soaps and perhaps a move at some point into further accessories, leather goods, scarves, even cosmetics.

It was all incredibly exciting. But it was also a huge mountain of work with no guarantee of success.

The afternoon, however, had been grim. She, Poppy and Jemima had presided over the firing of the major directors of the firm, calling them in one by one to face them, like the aristocrats facing the revolutionary tribunal. There was only one outcome and they all knew what it was. Tara finished each painful interview the same way.

'We want to thank you for your contribution to Trevellyan, but you'll no longer be needed. We'd like you to collect your things and leave the building immediately. And could you please return all company property – mobile phone, laptop, car keys – at once.'

Two lawyers from Goldblatt Mindenhall observed and minuted each interview, one of them the dark young man Victor had brought with him that first day.

Most of them had taken the sacking quietly. It had obviously been expected but none of them looked exactly happy about the outcome. Only Duncan Ingliss had proved trouble, as they had feared. He'd gone scarlet and spluttered with outrage, making Tara fear he might be a candidate for a heart attack.

'You can't do this!' he'd shouted. 'I've given twenty-five years to this company! I own shares! Your father trusted me!'

'I should think you'd be ashamed to admit all those things,' Tara said coolly, 'seeing as the company's decline over the last twenty-five years has been somewhat extraordinary.'

'I shall challenge this,' Duncan spat. 'I shall take this to my lawyers. I will see you in court.'

'I hope not, Duncan. We've created a redundancy package for you that is more than generous under the circumstances. I wouldn't want to see a court take that away.'

Duncan had left, apoplectic with rage but powerless. What could he do against the combined will of the Trevellyan sisters?

Tara leaned her head on the cool glass of the car window. At least that was something to be glad about – she had feared that they would never be able to work together but so far everything was going well. The ideas they had thrashed out together were good ones. She was looking forward to presenting them to Donna. The question was, when the hard graft really started, would the sisters still be able to work in harmony? Tara sensed that Donna was banking a lot on Jemima, her fame and her contacts. She could see that Donna was well aware of Jemima's newsworthy potential and wanted to exploit it. That was all very well, but it was a question of whether Jemima would play ball or not.

As soon as she walked into the house, she could sense the tension. She ran quickly upstairs to the nursery to find Robina and the children. They were not in the bathroom, as she was expecting, and she felt a quick rush of horror as she hurried to the nursery. She got to the door and tried to open it but it was locked.

'Robina? Robina, are you there?' She rattled the door.

A moment later it opened and Robina looked out. 'Come in,' she said quietly. She was pale and her expression was strained.

'Is everything all right? Are the children OK?' She hurried past the nanny, through the nursery playroom to the connecting door into the children's bedroom. Opening it, she saw that they were tucked into their little white beds. Imogen was asleep, but Edward was still awake, clutching his favourite bear and staring up at her by the glow of the nightlight.

'Hello, Mummy,' he said quietly.

She went over, knelt by the bed and hugged him. 'Hello, my darling. How are you?'

'I'm all right.' He regarded her solemnly, his blue eyes wide. 'Daddy isn't well. Robina said we should stay in the nursery tonight and not have our bath.'

'Yes, darling. Daddy's not well today,' she soothed, fighting the panic and anger that were building up in her. 'Don't worry, he'll be fine tomorrow. Did you have a good day at school?'

Edward nodded, but said nothing.

'Good boy. It's time to go to sleep now. Good night, darling.' She hugged him again and kissed his soft cheek. He brushed his hand down her face.

'Can I give you a butterfly kiss, Mummy?' he asked.

'Of course.' She put her face next to his so that he could flutter his eyelashes against her cheek. 'Thank you, what a lovely kiss.'

He smiled at her, sighed and closed his eyes. She pulled the quilt up around him, and quietly went out of the room, shutting the door gently behind her. Robina was sitting in her armchair.

'What happened?' Tara asked quietly.

'I'm not really sure, to be honest. Mr Pearson was here when we got back from collecting Edward this afternoon. He seemed fine then. We had our tea in the kitchen as usual, and after that we came up here to play and watch television. Then something happened and Mr Pearson just went mad. I spoke to Viv in the kitchen on the phone afterwards' – Robina nodded towards the internal phone that connected the nursery with all the major rooms in the house – 'and she said that it was a phone call that sent Mr Pearson so crazy this afternoon. It was awful. We could hear him roaring round the house. Apparently he's torn the study to pieces. Then we heard him coming up here. Well, I couldn't let the children see their father in such a state and I was a bit frightened myself, so I locked the door. A few minutes later, he was shaking and kicking the door, demanding to come in. But he was swearing terribly and was obviously not himself, so I refused.' Robina looked at her nervously. 'I hope I've not acted out of place.'

'Of course not, you did absolutely the right thing. How long was my husband trying to break in?'

'Not too long. But the children were very agitated.

Imo was crying and Edward was dead white.' Robina looked at her lap for a moment then glanced up. 'I hope this isn't going to happen again. I'll have to reconsider my position if it does. I didn't feel right at all about Mr Pearson acting like that.'

'It won't happen again,' Tara said strongly. 'I promise you that. Thank you, Robina. You did the right thing today. Please do go and take the rest of the evening easy.'

She went downstairs, full of apprehension. Their marriage had always been one in which Gerald was the leader, the mentor. She followed and learned from him. He had encouraged her in her career and told her she could do anything she wanted. The approval he'd given her had been what she'd always craved, and it helped her to blossom. She went ahead and had children earlier than she had planned because Gerald was so much older than she was and she knew he didn't want to wait. The house they'd bought had been the one he'd chosen and it was decorated to his taste. And then, it had all started to go wrong. His need for control had focused in on the minute aspects of their existence and every facet of his family's behaviour was dictated by him. Then he had begun to crave those beatings, to find pleasure in punishing her. It made her skin crawl to remember it. No – Gerald had changed in almost every way. It was virtually impossible to reconcile her husband of today with the smiling, generous, encouraging man she'd fallen in love with.

What could have triggered this outburst? she wondered.

It had to be his business. Perhaps he'd been thwarted once again in his efforts to break into the British media. It was hard to get established in such a small world, it was always going to be a struggle. Was that enough to tip him over the edge like this?

At the study door, she stopped and listened. There was no sound from within. She opened the door and couldn't prevent herself from gasping at the sight inside. The room was torn to pieces, just as Robina had said. The antique books had been pulled off their shelves and were lying in crumpled, battered heaps on the floor. The model yachts were smashed and torn, their miniature riggings hopelessly tangled. Trophies had been swept to the floor along with the contents of the desk and tables. For a normal person, this would be a devastating mess. For Gerald, with his mania for order and tidiness, it was the equivalent of sitting in hell.

But there he was, hunched in his armchair, surrounded by the debris, calmly watching the news on the plasma screen, the sound turned down almost to mute as usual.

'Oh, hello darling,' he said in a normal voice but without turning to look at her. 'Welcome home.'

'Gerald – what's happened?' she whispered.

'I'm just watching the television. I want to see if I'm on it.'

'On it? Why would you be on it?' She stepped forward into the mess, picking her way through the things on the floor. 'What's happened?' She sat down in the chair opposite him. He continued to stare at the screen in front of him. She realised how unwell he looked. His skin was pasty and grey, his eyes bloodshot. His lips were dry and his hands were trembling. He seemed so much older, washed out, and very tired. *Is this my husband?* she wondered. Gerald had always been so colourful, so much larger than life. He looked half his old self now. *When did this happen? Did I let it happen?*

'Something rather bad has occurred,' Gerald said calmly. 'This afternoon I wanted to run away. I wanted to take the children and go as far away as I could. But I can't get away, I know that. They'll get me eventually.'

'Who? Who will get you?'

He looked impatient and tsked. '*They* will, of course.'

Oh God, he's gone insane. Who does he mean by "they"? 'Are "they" people, Gerald? Or something else?'

He shot her a look and almost laughed. 'You think I'm mad, don't you? I wish I were, darling, I wish I were. It might be a defence – "not of sound mind". We'll have to see.'

'Defence?'

'Yes. I'm afraid so. I've got myself into a spot of bother. When I say "They are coming" I mean the authorities. Our dear boys in blue. The police.'

Fear rushed through her, turning her hands numb and freezing her all over. 'The police? But why?'

'A matter of a little loan, my dear, that was not strictly above board.' He sighed heavily. 'To be quite frank, I've used some money that didn't actually belong to me in order to further my business interests here.

335

Of course, I intended to repay it but before I've been able to do that, the board in South Africa has been advised that there is a deficit of some one hundred million dollars in the pension fund. And they've got very shirty about it indeed. It's all very unreasonable of them.'

Tara gasped. 'Oh, no, Gerald, you haven't!'

He looked cross. 'I'm not going to be nagged and scolded by you. Understand? This has nothing to do with you. It's my problem and I'll sort it out.'

'What are you talking about? How can it be *your* problem? What about our house, our family, every- thing we own?' She felt dizziness whirl round her head. The implications of what he was saying were so enormous, she could barely take them in.

His eyes flashed suddenly and he roared, 'If you hadn't been so goddamned stupid and given up your job, it might have been all right! There would have been other money, access to more funds. But now . . .' He was deflated again, like a balloon shrinking slowly downwards. 'Who knows what will happen now. A court case. My assets frozen. I don't know.'

'Where has the money gone, Gerald?' she asked quietly.

'I needed it for investment,' he said irritably. 'I need cash to be a serious player in the media business, to buy my way in. And I've got to look the part, I have to have the toys, or they won't accept me.'

'You mean, the Scottish estate . . . did you pay for it with the money you . . . borrowed?'

'Yes, yes. But that was nothing, just a drop in the

ocean.' His offhand tone only fuelled her fury. She felt sick with shock. She had always known that Gerald was ruthless and believed himself above the rules made for everyone else, for the little people. But she had never dreamed he could be so stupid and selfish – not to mention immoral – as to stoop to theft. She saw in a flash how he would have persuaded himself that it was perfectly all right and convinced himself that it really was a loan he intended to repay and not a terrible breach of trust.

'Do you know what a pension fund is, Gerald?' she asked quietly, white anger building in her.

'Of course –'

'No, do you *really* know its true worth? It's hours, days, months, years of hard toil by people who never get near a fraction of the sums you play around with every day. We're talking about honest people who've worried all their lives about how to pay their mortgage and their bills and put food on the table. These are ordinary people who worked in your companies, making you richer, doing the right thing by saving for their old age. Every penny, every dollar, belonged to someone else, someone who has no other way to buy food, heat or light, who is trusting that at the end of their lives, the money they've salted away so carefully will be there. And you . . .' Tara's voice started to rise '. . . you've stolen it! Worse than that, you've squandered it away. You've taken their food and drink and security and you've spent it on a fucking Scottish house you don't even need! You stupid bastard! What were you thinking?'

'It was Daniel who advised me to do it!' Gerald said, looking almost frightened of her for the first time in his life. 'And Terence! If anyone should be blamed, it should be them. They were the ones who came up with the idea.'

She looked away from him, hating his cowardice. Couldn't he take responsibility for this, at least? 'But how did you get your hands on it? I'm just amazed this was allowed to happen. What about the board? The reports to the regulators? The auditors?'

'It was fairly complicated,' conceded Gerald, with a touch of his old pomposity as though he was rather proud of his achievement. 'A complex structure of companies and trusts was needed to release the money.'

'And you were going to sneak it back the same way, were you?'

'Yes. We thought it out very carefully. It was Terence's masterstroke, really. No one would lose out. Everyone would get their money back.'

'Once you'd got yourself a big, lucrative piece of the media pie and had started to make some money.'

Gerald nodded. 'That was the plan.'

Tara shook her head. 'And now it's in smithereens.' She couldn't believe how foolish Gerald had been, how selfish. 'How did it come to light?'

'That is something I intend to find out.' Gerald crumpled again, looking scared and defeated. He put his head in his hands. 'Oh Christ, Tara. I can't believe it's come to this.'

'Nor can I,' Tara said soberly. She stared at her hands

clasped in her lap. She no longer recognised the man sitting opposite her. She couldn't even bear to look at him. He was a violent, unpredictable man, who'd wrecked havoc on her life, on the lives of her children and on the lives of those employees whose pensions he'd stolen. All this time, as her love for him had faltered and died, she had wondered how she was going to escape him and whether she could bring herself to leave him and break up their family. But in the end, he had finished it for her, by indulging his own arrogance and greed. She was filled with a strange calm. 'The house is in both our names, isn't it? The children and I can stay here for a while, I expect, depending on what happens.' She stood up and took a deep breath. 'But I don't want you here any longer.'

'What?' Gerald lifted his head and stared at her, incredulous.

'You heard. You'd better leave.'

'I can't believe my ears! So much for the fucking supportive wife!' he shouted. 'I'm in trouble and you don't want to know. After everything I've done for you! I've made you, I've fucking *created* you, you thankless bitch.'

'I didn't want it to end this way any more than you did. But you must have known we couldn't go on much longer. Not after the way you've been behaving. The other night was appalling. I don't know if you even fully realise what you've done.' She stared at him and he had the grace to drop his gaze.

In his madness, he had taken the belt in his hands and begun to lash out at her, not caring if he flicked her in the face, or caught her across the arm. Her protests had just spurred him on, and he'd growled a curious, throaty growl that made her skin go cold. When she'd turned and run, he'd chased her down the hall until she'd locked herself in the guest bedroom, refusing to open it despite his roars of anger outside in the corridor.

She knew then that their marriage was over. This just confirmed it. It opened the door to freedom, at last.

'It's one thing to attack me. But when you frighten and threaten our children, when you tell me you want to run away with them . . . I can't ignore that. I can't tolerate this any more. The children and I can't live in fear of you for the rest of our lives. I want you to leave immediately.'

'You're nothing without me,' he snarled.

'We'll see. You can go to my City flat and stay there. I'll call John now while you're packing. If the police come, I'll tell them that's where you are.'

'I can't believe it.' He looked amazed. 'You're serious. You're really throwing me out in my hour of need.'

'You brought this upon yourself. It's not safe for us to be around you. I'm sorry, Gerald. I know you need help and I'll try to make sure you get it. But the children come first. Now, I'm going upstairs to start collecting your things.' She moved calmly and confidently across the room, hoping he couldn't see how frightened she was inside. He was a stranger to her now. A man who would pound at the nursery door, terrifying the children inside. A man who would steal the retirement fund of his employees and spend it on a house he didn't need. A man without self-control and with no understanding of the effects of his actions.

It's over, she thought, as she walked out of the room. *I don't love him any more. He's never coming back here.*

The thought filled her with relief.

30

'I've gathered you all here this morning because I've got some things to tell you,' Tara announced. The entire company was gathered in the boardroom, looking apprehensive. Rumour had been sweeping the building since the day before when various directors had been called in only to exit the building hastily not long afterwards. No doubt there were exaggerated stories doing the rounds. Tara needed to nip all that in the bud. She was wearing a bright colour in a strong fabric to accentuate her positivity and upbeat attitude: a bold magenta pink Dior wool suit edged in pink leather, the skirt split at the side to the thigh, and black stilettos. Her dark hair was loose and flowing, her face perfectly made up. She looked every inch the confident, beautiful businesswoman.

'Before we start on what's happening here at Trevellyan, I want to let you know something you're all going to find out in the next few days anyway. My husband, Gerald Pearson, has had a warrant for his arrest issued by the South African authorities concerning serious financial misconduct in relation to his business interests abroad. No doubt it will be all over the newspapers, cases like this often are. I want you to know that I have absolutely no knowledge of my husband's companies, and no dealings with them. My husband and I have separated and nothing in his case will have any effect on Trevellyan whatsoever, so please, don't be alarmed by it.' She smiled at the assembled crowd.

'That's that out of the way. All very dull gossip. Now for the exciting stuff. What we've got planned for Trevellyan. First, the factory is stopping production of *Trevellyan's Tea Rose*. The other scents will be manufactured but there will be changes coming up. I'll tell you more about those in due course. Second, the shop below us is closing.'

There was a gentle groan from her audience. They had been expecting something seismic and here it was. Tara held up her hand.

'But not for ever. It is closing for a refit. The designs will be available for you to see very soon.' *Once we've decided what they'll be,* she added mentally. This all sounded a lot more organised than it was in reality. 'I'm sure you've noticed by now that we're making some big and necessary changes. Some of you have already met Donna Asuquo –' she gestured towards Donna, who nodded her acknowledgement – 'she's come in to help us relaunch our business. It's an exciting time. We'll be creating a whole new look for Trevellyan and recreating our most famous scent for the contemporary woman.

343

We're going to be a boutique perfumer with global appeal. We'll be re-establishing ourselves to sit alongside the very best and most glamorous of the perfume names. We'll be expanding our market share wherever possible, particularly in the Asian markets. Alongside this global appeal, we'll also offer an intensely personal service. Here, at our shop, there will be the opportunity for customers to design their own fragrances, to enjoy treatments based on our products, to buy gifts and treats for themselves. We'll also have a strong web presence – an Internet gift-ordering service, special pages devoted to our scents with downloads, a free sampling service, gift offers, loyalty inducements and much more. Our key notes will be quality and luxury. Trevellyan has lost its way in the last few years. The people who helped that happen have gone now and in their place we have some new faces. Claudine Deroulier is our expert nose, working for us on a freelance basis. Donna has joined us from the phenomenally successful Erin de Cristo and is running our brand relaunch. Jemima will be heading up our publicity and marketing campaigns. Poppy is focusing on design and packaging. And I'm managing the business aspect and the overall operation, so if you have any questions, it's me you should come to, OK?

'All your jobs are safe at the moment, and I intend to keep it that way for the foreseeable future. The girls who work in the shop will move upstairs while the refit's taking place. No one is about to be turfed out. The worst of it is over and from here on we're back on the up. It'll be hard work, but we've got a fantastic team and I know we're going to enjoy this journey to success together. To toast our new beginning, we've got some champagne on the table over there, along with coffee and orange juice for those who think it's a bit early to indulge. The patisserie have sent in some delicious croissants and pastries, so please help yourselves and we'll all be circulating among you to answer any queries you have. Thank you for listening.' Tara paused, then remembered something she intended to add. 'Oh, yes, I almost forgot. From today, I'll be known as Tara Trevellyan. Thanks.'

There was a scatter of clapping that built up into full-scale applause. Someone cheered. Jemima and Poppy smiled at her encouragingly.

She had won them over. They were all on side.

'My God, Tara, you were brilliant!' Jemima rushed to her sister and hugged her. Once they'd talked to everyone who wanted to chat and the last croissant had been polished off, they'd left the boardroom for Tara's office. 'And so brave. It's terrible news about Gerald, terrible.'

'Thank you.' Tara returned the hug. 'It's a shame that it all had to happen at once like this but, to be honest, we couldn't go on. It had become too horrible. Once I realised that he was capable of breaking a trust like the one he has, I knew I could never trust or respect him again.'

Poppy came up to add her hug. 'I'm so sorry. How are the children?'

'They don't know much about it at the moment. For them, life is going on much as usual. I don't think they really mind much that Daddy's gone away for a while. He gave them an awful fright yesterday.' Tara looked miserable for a moment. 'It's certainly not what I hoped for them. Divorce. A father in court for grand theft, potentially facing a prison sentence.'

'They've got you,' Poppy said softly. 'You adore them, they know that.'

'Yes, but I'll be providing for them on my own for a while at least. This puts a serious spin on what we're doing. I've got no safety net, no funds to draw on if Trevellyan needs them.'

'We're all in the shit now.' Jemima grinned. 'We've got nothing and everything to lose. We have to go for it.'

'Of course we do. And if I thought for one minute that we couldn't make it, I'd be out of here, begging Eric for my old job back. But we can.'

'You're being very strong,' said Poppy, holding her sister's hand. 'I admire you.'

There was a knock on the door and Donna came striding in.

'Well done, Tara. That was exactly the right note. Everyone seemed very reassured and happy in the boardroom. Now, we'd better get going. We need to make some big decisions today.' She sat down and waited until the others were seated as well, then tapped her pen in a businesslike way. 'Right, first things first. We're all agreed that our focus initially has to be *Trevellyan's Tea Rose*. It's our most famous scent, it's what we're known for. But first off, we have to change the name. Don't be offended, ladies, but Trevellyan is not as sexy a name as, say, Gucci or Guerlain or Hermès . . . any of those high-end foreign names. Trevellyan says quality, robustness, time-honoured tradition, and all that. But it doesn't say *sex*, and if we want to reach a new audience, that's what we have to say. The emphasis today is on sex appeal.'

'When wasn't it?' said Jemima drily.

'Exactly. Now, Fuchsia Mitchell got back to us with the results of the focus group. It won't surprise you to learn that people view this company as "reliable but unexciting". They might consider buying its products for an elderly relative, someone very traditional. They found it "comforting" and didn't want to see it disappear, but weren't keen on buying its products themselves. The group consisting of twenty-something women, the single ladies with relatively high disposable incomes, and a strong interest in fashion, beauty and their own attractiveness . . . well,' Donna made a face, 'they'd barely heard of our brand. It doesn't feature in any magazines they read, any images they see, it's never mentioned. That crucial customer base is entirely missing. The focus group of older women, mid-thirties to fifties, mothers looking to treat themselves . . . they'd heard of Trevellyan, considered it high quality and appreciated its prestige, but had no interest in it for themselves. They saw it as more of a "tourist" brand – something very British that was now aimed more at those visiting from abroad.'

'It's good to see it all down on paper,' commented Tara, 'but I think we could all just about guess this from the start.'

'Right – but it helps us focus. We need to raise the profile – that means advertising, courting the press, holding events, coordinating a launch. We also need to come up with a look that will appeal to our target audience. Which brings me back to the name.'

'What are you suggesting?' asked Jemima.

'We have to drop the Trevellyan part of *Trevellyan's Tea Rose*. At the very least it has to be *Tea Rose*. The question is, do we change it further, to indicate that the perfume has been redesigned?' Donna looked at Poppy. 'What do you think?'

Poppy frowned. 'You mean, like *Tea Rose Two*, or something?'

'Or . . . *Vintage Tea Rose*?'

Poppy shook her head. 'We already have *Vintage Lavender*. And *Antique Lily*.'

'*Tea Rose Revisited*?' put in Jemima, then said quickly, 'No, that's wrong.'

Tara had a try. '*Beyond Tea Rose . . . New Tea Rose . . . After Tea Rose . . .*'

Jemima giggled. 'After Tea Rose. Sounds like it can only be worn after tea!'

'When Estée Lauder wanted to recreate *White Linen*, they called it *Pure White Linen*. Dior add a different word in front of *Poison*, so it's now *Midnight Poison*,' Donna explained.

'*Pure Tea Rose*,' muttered Poppy. 'No, it's just not working . . . You know what, I think we should just

348

stick with *Tea Rose*.' Before she could be interrupted, Poppy carried on, surprising herself with how assured she suddenly felt about her ideas. All that research was finally paying off. 'English perfume names never sound as good as French ones, so I don't think we should try to get all fancy with ours. If we drop Trevellyan, then we've got a new name and it's pretty. Let's do the rest of the talking with the design – the bottle, the box – and the advertising.' She looked at the others almost nervously. 'Actually, I've already been thinking about what the new Trevellyan colours should be. We all agree, I think, that the navy blue and gold have had their day. Those colours are more regal than sexy. Fashionable women today treasure femininity, but not girlishness. They look for sophistication rather than something twee. Now if *Tea Rose* is our signature scent, that's where we need to start. So . . . I took a trip to a rose breeder and I came back with these.' She bent down and lifted a box from beside her chair and placed it on the table. Opening the box, she carefully lifted out some long stems, each one with an exquisite rose bloom on the end of it. 'These are tea roses.'

The others exclaimed at the gorgeous flowers, which came in hues of soft pinks, dusky roses, pale yellows and ivory whites. Their formations varied from strong, traditional-looking, furled-back petals to soft, bunched, crinkled petals folding in on a yellow heart.

'They come from an original variety that was supposed, not surprisingly, to have a fragrance reminiscent of tea. They are a great favourite of rose breeders, considered by some to be the most superior of flowers, both in beauty and fragrance. They've been bred and interbred for well over a century, and there are stunning varieties, as you can see. Just about every shape and colour you can imagine. But the gardener I spoke to told me that they are best in the colours of the dawn – those rosy, gold-tinged pinks. Look at this, I love this . . .' Poppy picked up a stem. The rose was creamy white with the faintest hint of a mauvey pink at its heart. The petals in the centre were tightly furled, rolled in like tiny shells. Around them, another row gathered protectively, the valley in the centre of each petal hiding pinkish shadows, and then another, until the rose opened out into a beautiful pillow of petals. 'This is called the *Devoniensis*, or more commonly, the Magnolia Rose. You can see why, with these waxy white petals tinged with the merest breath of purple.'

'Exquisite,' agreed Donna.

'Look at this one!' Jemima picked up another flower. 'This makes me think of old-fashioned country gardens. It's like a Dog Rose that's been stretched out.' Her rose was wide and flat like a saucer, its delicate petals yellowy pink with a hint of apricot, a nest of golden stamens at its centre. She smelt it. 'Oh, that's gorgeous.'

'I love this,' Tara said softly. She reached for the rose. It was the palest, most delicate pink, its outer petals curling back to display a mass of smaller folded petals, like the lightest tissue paper scrunched up and held in a cup of wafer-thin porcelain. 'It reminds me of weddings and . . . yes, like the other one, of country gardens, and summer days.' She sniffed. 'I really *can* smell tea in this! I'm sure I can. Oh, it's lovely.'

'That's a *Gloire de Dijon*,' Poppy explained. 'I like it too.'

'So do I.' Donna took the stem from Tara and observed the flower carefully. 'We're going to have to be careful if our inspiration is to come from these roses that we don't end up going too girly and English country garden about the whole thing. We can't come out looking sickly or saccharine. We have to get that balance exactly right, especially if we're considering using pink as our signature colour.'

Poppy looked over at the *Gloire de Dijon*. 'You're right, but taking that flower as our inspiration, I think we could go as pink or as white as we wanted. Obviously we want to avoid a pastel pink or anything remotely Barbie. That would be all wrong. But a kind of off-white-pink might be feminine without being garish.'

Jemima looked thoughtful. She was looking at the mass of stems and the mixture of colours they produced. The room was full of a strong rosy fragrance. 'If we're too subtle, we'll go the other way and achieve nothing. Look, pink is pink is pink. It says one thing – girl. Female. It's also one of the colours of the rose, so it's suitable for a scent called *Tea Rose*. Obviously, we're going to go with pink but I think Poppy's right. Anything pastel or too chalky will be all wrong. We want subtle, soft and yet strong . . .'

'How about a *nude* pink?' suggested Poppy. 'Something that has almost a beige or grey base, rather than a creamy white one?'

'That's a good idea,' Tara said. She nodded. 'Yes, I like that. It sounds more sophisticated.'

'So we take this slightly country wedding look,' Poppy was enthusiastic now, able to see the colour she meant inside her head, 'and give it a slick of urban grime, grey it up a bit, make it look like it's *lived*. An off-pink pink, closer to the colour of skin . . .' She glanced at Donna and blushed. 'I mean, of white skin, obviously.'

'Don't worry,' Donna said lightly. 'I know what you mean, it's fine. I really like your idea. You're right that we need something strong. It's going to be the colour we use in the shop, perhaps on our packaging, our stationery, everywhere . . . we need a good colour.' She frowned. 'I'm not sure about dirtying it up, though. This is going to be a home of beauty and hygiene. We don't need sparkling white, but we definitely need to be saying "fresh and clean" and not "a bit grubby".'

'Don't worry, we will. I'll get some colour swatches to show you what I've got in mind.'

'It's a shame Claudine isn't here,' Tara said. 'She could smell some of these lovely flowers.'

'I'm meeting her later at Saint Pancras,' Jemima said, picking up the *Gloire de Dijon*. 'Why don't I take her this for her inspiration?'

'Good idea.' Donna looked at Poppy. 'And that was a brilliant idea, actually getting tea roses. Well done.'

There was a knock on the door and one of the receptionists came in. 'Mrs Pears . . . Sorry, I mean, Miss Trevellyan. I thought I should let you know that I've been getting a lot of phone calls for you while you've been in your meeting.'

'Really? Who from?'

The receptionist looked apologetic. 'It's the press, I think. And I'd better warn you there seem to be quite a lot of reporters and photographers outside.'

They all jumped up and rushed to the office window. Sure enough, below them was a small crowd of reporters in macs and leather-jacketed men carrying cameras.

'What do you think they want?' asked Poppy fearfully.

'I'm afraid it's not Jemima this time,' Tara answered grimly. 'I think it's me. The news must have broken about Gerald. God knows how long this little story is going to enthrall them.' She looked round at the other three. 'Well, we wanted interest in Trevellyan, ladies. It looks like we've got it.'

31

Tara was right. The news had broken that the South African authorities had issued an arrest warrant for Gerald Pearson. He'd come out to face the press that morning, accompanied by his lawyer. Bulbs flashed and television cameras recorded him making his statement – if there was one thing the media loved, it was the sight of a wealthy and powerful man toppling off his pedestal.

When Tara left Trevellyan House that afternoon, she had to run the gamut of the press.

'What's your reaction to your husband's imminent arrest, Mrs Pearson?' shouted one reporter as photographers pushed their cameras into Tara's face.

She blinked in the light of the flashes and said nothing. The questions kept coming.

'How do you feel about the prospect of your husband going to prison?'

'Is it true you've thrown him out?'

'Is that any way for a loyal wife to behave? Most

women would stand by their husbands in times of crisis, wouldn't they?'

Don't let them get to you, Tara told herself, gritting her teeth. Using all her willpower not to shout back that these strangers knew nothing the hell about her life, she forced her way through them to the pavement, where John was waiting with the car. He helped her in, pushed back the photographers and journalists and managed to get into his own seat.

'Quite a fuss there, ma'am, if I may say so,' he said, glancing at Tara in his rear-view mirror.

'You can say that again. And it's just the start.'

She was right. At home, another posse of cameramen and journalists were waiting. When they saw the car arriving, they rushed towards it, holding out microphones and jostling for a position close to her.

'What have you got to say?' they shouted. 'Give us a comment! Did you know about your husband's activities? What do you think about his arrest?'

The barrage of questions hit her like a hail of stones. Television cameras shone lights in her eyes. She felt panicked as she emerged among the crowd.

'Hey, get off her. Make way! This lady needs to get inside to her children,' bellowed John, as he pushed reporters out of the way and guided Tara through to the house. Viv was waiting to open the front door and let them both in before slamming it shut in the faces of the prying press.

'Thank you, thank you. I don't know what I would have done without you, John,' Tara gasped.

'You're welcome, ma'am. Honestly, they're like

beasts, aren't they? How would they feel if it was them being hounded like that?'

'They're all trying to earn a living, I suppose,' she said, shrugging off her coat. 'Now, please stay here for as long as you like. Viv will make you something to eat. I'm going to see the children.'

She went up the stairs, feeling an amazing sense of liberation. The fear and tension that usually filled the house was gone. Gerald was gone. His brooding, dominating presence had left them. She felt three inches taller.

But this is only the start, she reminded herself. *There's still a long way to go.*

Later, she watched the ten o'clock news on her own in the sitting room. The children had had a happy day, though Robina said that there had been a couple of wobbly moments.

'Edward knows something's happened to his daddy, but he's not sure what,' Robina had told her, so at bedtime, Tara had talked very softly and reassuringly to her son, telling him that Daddy loved him very much but had had to go away for a while. They would see him soon, she promised. Edward seemed content with that, and went happily to sleep.

But while she was revelling in the freedom of being able to put her dirty supper plate on the coffee table and leave it there, the news Tara had been dreading all day came on to the screen.

'Today, a warrant was issued for the arrest of press tycoon Gerald Pearson. He is suspected of fraud and is accused of diverting millions of pounds of his company's money into his own pocket,' intoned the news presenter over archive footage of Gerald in black tie, attending a grand dinner where the Prime Minister was present. 'South African authorities have threatened to seek his extradition if he does not return there voluntarily and face questioning. Police in this country are understood to be investigating aspects of Mr Pearson's business interests here, along with his property acquisitions.'

The screen showed Gerald emerging from Tara's flat, his lawyer standing discreetly behind him. He looked drawn but he smiled bullishly at the cameras and said loudly, 'I'm utterly innocent of this outrageous charge and I look forward to proving it in court.'

There's no fool like the fool who fools himself, Tara thought. *Can he really believe he'll get away with this?*

It was strange to see him on the screen and to realise that only twenty-four hours ago, he'd been here in this house.

Never again, Tara resolved. *Never again will he step foot in this house. Maybe we'll leave here. I've never liked it. This was Gerald's house, not mine. Too beige. Too boring. Too immaculate.*

She was startled to see herself on the television, her face screwed into a grimace, pushing her way through the press.

'Mr Pearson's wife, Tara Pearson, one of the well-known Trevellyan sisters and heiress to a large fortune, had no comment for reporters but it has been rumoured that she and Mr Pearson have recently separated.'

'Large fortune?' she said out loud. 'I bloody well wish! Well . . . I suppose we'll always be the heiresses, even if we lose everything.'

She sat back on the sofa and thought hard. She'd have to decide what she'd do now that Gerald was to be arrested. He was still Edward's and Imogen's father and they needed him. That tie would bind them together for ever, no matter how much she wished to be free of it.

Jemima was rather thrilled by the novelty of not being the focus of attention for once. When she left Trevellyan House, the cameramen took a few snaps of her and then lost interest and she was soon striding down New Bond Street, passing all the delectable shops and wondering if she dare go shopping.

But what's the point? I'm going to Paris this afternoon, the capital of shopping!

She felt cheerful and upbeat. Today's meeting had achieved a lot of things. Donna had been supportive of all their ideas. The shop below would be completely refitted, with a beautiful, light airy room at the front, displaying the fragrances and other products. Behind this would be some treatment rooms and a perfumery, where customers could explore scent, commission their own fragrance or experiment with mixing essences for themselves.

They agreed that the old gold script had to go, and that the new Trevellyan font would be simple, stylish and modern. Donna had immediately rung up some designers she rated highly and asked them to come up with ideas for the new look. She'd also set up meetings with fitters to commission designs for the shop and treatment rooms.

She's so can-do! marvelled Jemima, as she admired a pair of tight black trousers in the Gucci window. *She makes things happen. It's inspiring.*

On impulse she popped into Fenwick to have a quick browse. The big names were all very well, but sometimes she found something utterly charming that no one else had or could recognise. 'Oh, this is a Sophie Vertiga,' she'd say airily, as if everyone would have heard of the new designer.

She was flicking through a rack of Issa dresses when she heard voices in the nearby fitting room.

'Do you know who I just saw downstairs?' drawled one. 'Only, like, Jemima Calthorpe!'

'Really?' replied the other, who was evidently having a little trouble getting into her outfit, if the puffing were anything to go by.

'Yeah – she must be feeling pretty grim, with her husband doing the dirty on her with Letty Stewart.'

Jemima froze, one hand on a vivid purple silk mini kimono dress.

'What, old Harry Calthorpe?' said the other voice, surprised. 'He's not the type, is he? From what I've heard, that is. I don't know him.'

'Yeah, he's not but apparently he's panting like a randy old dog over Letty and she's thrilled to bits. Fancies being the second Lady Calthorpe something rotten, or so I've heard. She can't wait to get her teeth into the whole rigmarole: country house, hunting, tweed skirts.'

'Isn't she a bit young for all that?'

'She's one of the new old fogies, you know, like Prince William and his gang. And let's be honest, what else is she going to do with herself? She's got one A level, in decorative needlepoint or something. She was always going to be on the lookout for a husband and if she's found him early so much the better.'

'Can I help you?' said a voice in Jemima's ear.

She gasped and spun round. A girl with a Fenwick badge stood next to her, looking at her questioningly.

'No, no . . . I have to go.' She pulled her bag on to her shoulder and walked as quickly as she could across the shop floor, down the escalator and out into the sunshine, but the day suddenly felt bleak and black and her previous high spirits had been dented.

Jemima had managed to recapture some of her good humour by the time she bowled up at Saint Pancras to meet Claudine. The sun was shining, she was on her way to Paris. Life was an adventure.

So what if Harry is sleeping with that horrible tart? she asked herself. *Let him. I can't be a hypocrite about it. I've had my own fun, after all. And if he wants a divorce . . . well, there's nothing to stop us now. Mother's dead, and she was the only one who cared about it.*

She pushed away the sense of panic and hurt that the very mention of the word 'divorce' sent spiralling inside her. She simply didn't want to think about it – so she wouldn't.

Saint Pancras was bright and bustling. She picked up her ticket and found Claudine waiting for her at the check-in gates, looking demure and stylish in another of her Chanel suits, this one in a black and white tweed, a small Gucci suitcase next to her.

'Ah, you are here. *Bon*,' Claudine said with evident relief, offering each cheek in turn to be kissed.

'Of course I am. Did you think I was going to be late? I'm early, look!'

'You are only just in time,' replied Claudine severely. 'We are supposed to check in at least thirty minutes beforehand.'

Jemima shrugged. 'Oh, they always let you on, you just have to charm them.'

'They may let beautiful English titled ladies on,' sniffed Claudine, 'but they are not quite so obliging to small French women with very heavy suitcases.'

Jemima laughed. Claudine always had that way of expressing herself, as though she disapproved of every-thing, but Jemima could tell that it was simply the older woman's habit. Her deadpan delivery sometimes hid the wry wit Jemima had spotted several times and her prickly irritation was often an act. She could tell that below the surface crossness, Claudine was teasing her and flattering her at the same time as telling her off for being so slapdash. She had grown to like the French woman, admiring her strong intelligence and outspokenness, and the confidence she had in her own taste and opinions. Claudine spoke her mind, valued her own expertise and would not tolerate fools, that much was certain.

They went through the gates, and then past the security check. Jemima wore a simple travel outfit of Miss Sixty jeans, a vintage Jean-Paul Gaultier T-shirt and a black Jil Sander jacket, along with Stella McCartney boots. She carried a large printed velvet bag into which she'd tossed everything she thought she'd need for two days away, leaving room for a couple of new purchases.

Twenty minutes later they were in their leisure select seats – the Eurostar equivalent of first class – stretching out and settling down. A few minutes after that, the train was gliding smoothly out of the station and through London, on its way to the coast.

The atmosphere was a little awkward at first but they did their best to relax with each other. Jemima made small talk, asking Claudine how she had enjoyed her stay in London. The French woman said it had been fine, that she had always admired the city but that she couldn't wait to get back to Paris.

'Do you live in Paris?' Jemima asked.

Claudine nodded. 'I have a small flat there in *Le Marais*. I adore the Marais. It is the most civilised part of Paris. The laboratory is in the suburbs, so I make the reverse journey of most Parisians – I live in the heart of the city and take a train to the *les banlieues* for work.'

'Is it your own laboratory?'

'It is one I share with some other perfumers. Friends of mine have set up a company, a very exclusive artisan perfumery. They wanted me to join them, but . . .' She made a face. 'I like to work alone. For many years, I was part of a large company, a designer of fragrances for the famous names. It was OK. They paid me very well. I won some big commissions for them. They call us "ghosts", the noses who build the juices that are sold under other people's names. The great Italian designer who pretends he creates his fragrances? *Puh!* The real talent lies in the shadows, with the artists who blend a thousand molecules, or just twenty, to realise the designer's vision. That was me. Then I decided I would find some independence. I am not too good in the corporate world and we perfumers are curious creatures – we are highly strung, creative, competitive, paranoid . . . not much fun, in other words. Although I prefer to work alone, I need the equipment that any perfumer must have: costly materials, a computer, lab technicians to mix my formulae . . . I cannot afford that on my own. So I went into partnership with my friends, part funding and sharing the facilities we all need.'

'A very good idea,' Jemima commented.

'Now I receive briefs from all over the place. I submit my *essais,* that is, my idea for realising the brief in scent, and occasionally I win a commission. Often I do not. But, *eh,*' she shrugged, 'that is the crazy world of perfume. Luckily a hit will fund all my misses.'

'That's why you could come and work for us.'

'*Oui.* I am my own mistress. I do what I please. I am interested in what you are doing. I wish to see the art of perfumery survive.' Claudine smiled tightly.

The train steward came by, handing out menus.

'Are you hungry?' asked Jemima.

'No. For me, just black coffee.'

'Tea for me. I know. Very English. I can't help it. If it's the afternoon, I have to drink tea and that's that. Oh, I almost forgot, I have something for you.' Jemima reached into her Mulberry bag. 'I hope it's not crushed. I only wrapped it in tissue . . . here it is.' She pulled the *Gloire de Dijon* rose stem out of her bag and put in on the table in front of Claudine.

The French woman looked surprised. She opened the tissue paper and revealed the rose, still radiant, its pale pink beauty undiminished despite a few bruises on the outer petals and a slight limpness. The fragrance rose up between them, stronger for the slight crushing, sweet, rosy and faintly tea-like.

'Oh. Well, thank you.' She looked up at Jemima, frowning slightly. 'What a kind gift.'

'It's beautiful, isn't it? I thought you'd like it. It's inspiring, I think.' She beamed at Claudine, who smiled back, more relaxed now. 'Now what are you doing for dinner tonight? I'm staying at the Hôtel de Vendôme and I thought you could join me there.'

Claudine's face fell. 'I'm busy tonight, I'm afraid. I'm dining with a friend. It was arranged this afternoon.'

'Not to worry. I can look after myself tonight. Why don't I come and visit you in your lab tomorrow afternoon and then we can go from there back into town and have dinner then? You can tell me how things are progressing.'

'Yes, yes. I could do that.'

'Good. We can sort out the details later. Now where's that tea and coffee? I could do with a drink.'

The train sped on its way towards France. Jemima and Claudine chatted a little more, then Jemima pulled out the latest *Vogue* but before long she was sleepy and soon dozed off. By the time she woke, the train was racing through the French countryside and it was growing dark outside.

'We'll be there soon,' Claudine said, in her mysterious way. 'Another half an hour.'

'It's so amazingly fast, isn't it?' Jemima yawned. 'Mmm. I tell you what, I'm not used to working so hard! The last few weeks have been quite a shock to my system. Now, you must give me your numbers and the address of the lab.' She pulled out her phone and carefully stored all the numbers Claudine dictated to her.

Claudine leaned forward and stared at her intently. 'I am truly sorry I cannot dine with you tonight. I hope you do not take it personally.'

'Of course not.' Jemima laughed. 'You were bound to have something else to do. I was silly to think you might be free. I'll call up some chums. I shan't be lonely, don't worry about that. Even if I'm alone, I'm sure some slimy types will try and keep me company. It is France, after all. Men are so dreadful.'

'*Oui.*'

'Are you married, Claudine?'

'*Non, non.* I am not married. I do not have a boyfriend.'

'Good,' declared Jemima. She thought of Harry and his panting over Letty Stewart. 'Take my advice, and don't.'

Claudine stared at her.

'Actually, I think I'll see if Marie-France is in. I knew her at school in Gstaad . . .' Jemima started scrolling through her address book and making calls, as Paris drew closer.

32

At the Gare du Nord, Claudine and Jemima parted ways. Claudine descended into the Metro while Jemima went to the taxi rank, hailed a cab and directed the driver to the place Vendôme, a classically beautiful Parisian square dominated by the towering column of bronze that stood in the centre, on the top of which a statue of Napoleon, dressed like a Roman emperor, stood staring balefully out over the capital. The buildings that lined the square looked like miniature palaces with high arched windows, Corinthian columns in camel-coloured stone, and the steep-pitched square grey roofs that so distinguished Paris's architecture. Here, style and money – lots of it – met in graceful harmony. The Hôtel Ritz at number 15 had for its neighbours Guerlain Perfumes, Bulgari, Armani, Cartier, Schiaparelli, Van Cleef & Arpels and Chanel, among many others. The rue Saint Honoré, with its fabulous shops and boutiques, ran along its southern side, and beyond that lay the famous Tuileries Gardens.

Jemima walked into the lobby of the Hôtel de Vendôme. Smaller and more intimate than the Ritz, it was still opulent and luxurious. The foyer was a grand mixture of coloured marbles, leather, dark wood and a vast crystal chandelier, but all on a tastefully manageable scale. Jemima was greeted courteously in perfect English and led upstairs to her suite. There she was able to look out on the Parisian skyline, admiring the opulance of the wealthiest square in Paris.

This is a treat, she decided, taking in the stylish little sitting room with its green velvet chaise longue, the bedroom and sumptuous marble bathroom. *Tara might not like the fact I've got a suite, but honestly . . . it is business!*

She spent a happy hour enjoying a hot shower and making herself up for the evening. Tonight, in a gesture of solidarity, she too was wearing Chanel, a pale peach sequin-covered tulle knee-length dress, the sleeves cut in two waves, so that they appeared to come from one piece of material draped mysteriously and yet elegantly round her shoulders. She pinned a large, diamond star-shaped brooch on one hip and slipped on high silver strappy sandals. When she'd finished dressing, she put the last touches to her face, and spun round in front of the mirror.

I feel glamorous. I feel like a movie star. Damn Letty Stewart. I'm going to have fun.

She put her phone, credit card and lipstick into a sequinned bag, picked up a cashmere wrap and headed downstairs.

* * *

The perfectly trained staff knew who she was, and their respectful gaze told her that they recognised her dress as high fashion, the kind very few women could afford, and treated her accordingly.

'This way, *milady*,' murmured a uniformed man, leading her to the bar and to a table. 'You are waiting for somebody?'

'Yes. My friend Pia de Longueville is meeting me here.' Marie-France had been delighted to hear from her old friend Jemima, but to her eternal despair, she was at her château in the Loire and unable to meet her that night. Pia, another of her Gstaad friends, had answered the call instead. After a misspent youth frittered away partying far too hard, she was now the fashion director of a glossy magazine and the epitome of an elegant Parisian career woman. A late drink at the Hôtel de Vendôme was just her style.

'Will you have a drink while you are waiting?'

'Yes please. Champagne.'

The waiter bowed and a moment later was back with a glass of champagne which he placed carefully in front of her.

'Thank you.' Jemima took a sip. She was aware of the admiring glances she was getting from the men sitting in the bar, and enjoyed the feeling of being watched and lusted after. She knew she looked good and she also knew she looked expensive and therefore important, not to be trifled with. These men might desire her but they also had to respect the fact that she wore the signs of money: not just the jewels, the clothes and the shoes, but also the inimitable confidence that comes with the knowledge of a place in the world.

After a few minutes, her phone lit up. She had a message. It was from Pia.

Darling, I will be late! I'm so sorry, work crisis. Please wait, I will be there.

Jemima stared at the phone crossly. She was hungry and wanted to eat. She had nothing to occupy her time with, no book, no magazine . . . how annoying of Pia! Should she return to her room and wait there? After all, there was no telling how long a work crisis would last. Or just give up on her and go out alone? But that was rather depressing.

'Oh, damn it all. It was all going so well,' muttered Jemima irritably. 'I suppose it's too late to find someone else.'

'Lady Calthorpe, hello,' said a charming voice.

Jemima looked up with surprise at the face of Richard Ferrera.

'Excuse me,' he said with a smile that showed his perfectly straight white teeth. 'I couldn't help but notice you as you came into the bar. Do you remember? We met at Emma Bonnington's house a while ago . . .'

'Of course I do,' Jemima said, recovering her composure. 'How lovely to see you. What are you doing here?'

'I've just been at a business meeting, in one of the conference rooms. I was about to order a drink to cap the day off. I'm a big fan of the bar here. They make a wonderful Martini.'

'You're not staying in the hotel, then?'

Richard shook his head. 'I'm at the Ritz.'

'So we're neighbours, then. How nice,' Jemima said lightly. 'Would you like to join me?'

'I'd love to.' He sat down next to her, beckoned over a waiter and ordered his drink. It came almost immediately. 'Well, what a delightful chance, to meet you here.' He raised his glass to her. 'To serendipity.'

She lifted her champagne glass to him. They both sipped their drinks.

'I hope you're not drinking alone,' he said.

'Not now. But I was about to be abandoned, I'm afraid, at least temporarily. My friend Pia has had to stay late at work. We were going to go out. Now I suppose I shall order room service and watch television until she turns up.' She made a disappointed pout.

'Now that would be criminal. You look totally divine, far too wonderful to go back to your room alone. Please, allow me to take you to dinner at the Ritz. I have a table booked.'

'Surely you're meeting someone else ...'

'No one that can't easily be cancelled,' he said smoothly. 'Business can wait. I've had enough of it for one day anyway.'

'Well, if you're sure ...'

'I am.'

'Then, thank you. I will.'

How lucky, she thought as she walked across the place Vendôme on Richard Ferrera's arm. *Just when it all looked bleak – here's a knight in shining armour. But I must be careful,* she reminded herself. *This man might have ulterior motives. I must make sure I don't give anything away.*

Ferrera had made a quick quiet call on his mobile in the foyer of the Hôtel de Vendôme while Jemima sent Pia a text telling her not to worry about their date – they would rearrange. Then he offered her his arm with a smile of practised charm. Jemima could understand in an instant how he had come so far in the world. His style and confidence were steely strong.

It's amazing that he grew up in the New York slums – he doesn't betray for one second that this isn't what he was born to, she thought. She admired it and respected it. Somehow it meant more than her own gilded background. *I've never had to work for anything,* she thought almost guiltily. *I've always had everything I wanted, and never feared not fitting in.* It was difficult to imagine what breaking into the world of privilege was like for those who came from outside it. She had the distinct impression that the achievement had bred ruthlessness inside Richard Ferrera.

'Do you know why this restaurant is called *L'Espadon*?' asked Ferrera as they were led to a table in the dining room. The room was heavy with luxury, decorated in a classic French style in hues of gold, peach and dusky pink. Vast crystal sconces lit the room between huge arched mirrors swathed with yards of velvet so that they looked like windows. A wisteria tree, drooping beautiful purple blossoms, appeared to be growing in the middle of the room.

'*L'Espadon*? It means swordfish, doesn't it?' A waiter

pulled a chair out, and Jemima sat down elegantly at their table. Ferrera took his place opposite.

'Yes. Charles Ritz loved to go deep-sea fishing for swordfish with friends like Ernest Hemingway. When he wasn't out at sea with the real things, he liked to practise his fishing by casting a line down the grand staircase here. So they renamed the restaurant in honour of his favourite catch. Do you speak French?'

'It's almost all I've got to show for two years at finishing school. That and the fact I'm rather good at skiing. And skiing instructors, come to that.'

Ferrera laughed. 'You are disarmingly frank.'

'About some things. It's an English habit, I think, to enjoy shocking people just a little.'

'I can't pretend to understand the English, or your country. It's a very confusing place. America, however, is much more straightforward. Your background, be it Italian, Irish, Jewish, African American or, like me, Mexican, whatever, pretty much dictates the kind of home cooking you like. But it's what you achieve in life, what you choose to do with your talents and abilities, that defines you. That's what gets you respect, not your heritage. It doesn't seem that way in your country.'

'You mean we're obsessed with class?' Jemima shrugged. 'Maybe. But show me the society that isn't. Don't forget our society is a few centuries older than yours, so we've got a lot more subtleties and nuances – plus titles, of course – to contend with.'

'Maybe. It just seems that are more chances to make something of yourself in the States.'

373

'That, if you don't mind me saying, is crap. It's the same everywhere. Money will buy you advantages in life. It isn't fair, and we all have a duty to try and sort out the inequalities in our societies so that every child has an equal chance, no matter what background they come from. But the truth is, a child born into the underclass in America has as big a mountain to climb as one born poor in Britain.'

Ferrera smiled at her. 'Maybe you're right. I can see we both have our corners to fight. But it's too early in the evening and the night is too beautiful for such a serious debate. Tell me what you are doing in Paris.'

'I will, right after I look at this divine menu. I'm starving.'

They ordered their food, the sommelier brought the wine Ferrera had selected, and then they were free to chat.

'I'm here on business too,' Jemima said.

Ferrera raised his eyebrows. 'Oh? What business is that?'

She played for time, taking a sip from her wine glass. *How much shall I tell him?* she wondered. 'We're looking at our distribution here in France. I'm meeting with some of the major stores tomorrow.'

'Oh? Are you planning new moves?'

'Just building on our success, of course,' Jemima said in a careless tone. 'It doesn't do to become complacent.' Ferrera nodded in agreement.

Their starters arrived – foie gras with a rhubarb chutney for Ferrera, asparagus in a froth of hollandaise with tiny poached quail's eggs for Jemima.

Ferrera cut a small sliver of foie gras. 'I have heard that dramatic changes are happening at Trevellyan. Many of your directors have left and some are making a big noise about how unhappy they are. They say that you and your sisters know nothing about the perfume business and are bound to fail.'

'They would say that, wouldn't they? They're the failures. They just don't want anybody to think that. Much more convenient if they make out that we are the useless ones. But everyone will see the truth in due course.' Jemima picked up an asparagus spear and dunked the top of it into the soft yolk of an egg.

'Fighting talk.' Ferrera smiled. 'Erin de Cristo tells me that she has lost a valued member of staff to you.'

'Yes, we're thrilled that Donna Asuquo has come to us. She's top notch.'

Ferrera waited for her to say more but she simply smiled and said, 'It's charming here, isn't it? I can't help loving the dear old Paris Ritz almost as much as our London one.'

'So,' he prompted, 'are you launching something new?'

'You know I can't possibly tell you anything about that,' purred Jemima. 'All very highly confidential. But everything will be revealed in due course.'

'I'm sure it will.' Ferrera pushed away his plate. He had eaten fast but with impeccable manners. 'You know, I'll come straight to the point. I know your company is in trouble. I know you need funds, badly, especially if you've got plans for a new perfume. What would you say if I was to make you an offer to buy Trevellyan?'

'You mean, become a partner?'

'No, I mean, own the company outright. I could keep you and your sisters on to run it – if your performance were satisfactory, of course. You would still be at the helm, but it would belong to me. Just think', he said quickly, 'of what you'd be able to do with the kind of money I'd be willing to pay for Trevellyan. With that sort of cash injection, you'd be able to realise all your dreams for the company, and retain a financial interest in it.'

Jemima frowned. 'It's an interesting proposition,' she said slowly. 'But of course I'm in no position to tell you if we'd be open to that or not. I'd have to speak to my sisters and we'd have to consider it very carefully.'

'Of course. This is not a business discussion. This is simply idle chat that might plant a seed – a seed that could grow into something very exciting and profitable for us all.'

Their main courses came: stuffed veal sweetbreads for Ferrera, and medallions of lamb for Jemima.

'Oh, yum,' breathed Jemima, gazing at her delicious-looking dinner. 'Let's tuck in.'

Ferrera laughed loudly. 'I can't imagine an American girl saying such a thing!' he said. 'It's very refreshing.' He eyed her plate. 'Are you going to eat that potato?'

'Why? Do you want it? Hands off, buster, it's mine.'

'It's carbohydrate, though.'

'Excellent major food group.'

'No American girl I know would touch it, particularly not in the evening.'

'Bugger that. We were brought up to eat what's on our plate.' Jemima shrugged. 'There's no point in fetishising food – it just makes you obsess about it. Banning something is a sure fire way to make you crave it. I just try to be moderate in all things.'

'Sensibly said.'

'Besides, as long as you work off the calories with some intense physical activity, the kind that raises the heart rate and leaves you gasping . . . well, everything's fine.' She looked at him flirtatiously under her lashes.

He leaned in towards her and said softly, 'I know a wonderful place not too far from here. It has fantastic music, old-time swing. We could go there later, have a drink, dance a little. What do you think?'

'It sounds great. I'd love to.'

After dinner, they walked through the atmospheric Paris streets to the nightclub. It was in a basement and inside it was all faded glamour: rubbed red velvet, a battered wooden dance floor, waiters with long white aprons round their middles carrying small trays of drinks: Pernod, Scotch, Ricard. This was a club for serious, late-night drinkers. On the raised stage, a small band of elderly men in drooping bow ties played beautiful songs from the thirties and forties.

They sat at a table in the near-darkness, a small tealight providing their only illumination, and Ferrera ordered drinks: a fine cognac for each of them. The band played 'Smoke Gets in Your Eyes'.

Jemima sang along and then said, 'Only it doesn't

any more, does it? The smoke. Once this place would have been filled with a fug of Gitanes. It doesn't feel quite French without it.'

'I know what you mean. But I prefer the fresher air. Would you like to dance?'

He led her on to the dance floor where they joined a few other couples. He held her close and they swayed to the soft sound of the music.

Jemima felt the thrill of the physical contact. *How long was it*, she thought back, *since that man at mother's funeral?* She felt a sudden yearning for comfort, for a man's arms around her, to be caressed, touched, made love to.

Could I? she wondered. *This man isn't like the others.* She sensed vaguely that she could be out of her depth with Ferrera, that he might not be as fleeting as the men she casually picked up, enjoyed and then never saw again. But lust was creeping inside her. It was the feel of his powerful muscles beneath his perfectly cut Armani suit, his rock-hard thighs moving against her as they danced. He was the exact height for her – Harry had always been too tall – and his smooth hands held hers justly firmly enough. She could smell his fresh, citrus scent and see the softness of the brown skin of his neck just below his ear. Sensing the strength and power in him was an aphrodisiac. As the brandy soaked into her bloodstream, she felt her resolution not to get too close to Richard Ferrera waver. *Could it hurt? One night? God, I need a damn good shag.*

She pushed gently against him, to let him know that she was responding physically to his nearness. He looked down at her, his dark brown eyes inscrutable, and they carried on dancing.

It was after one in the morning when they emerged from the club. Jemima knew she was drunk, but she was high on it and happy. *Here I am in Paris, with a gorgeous man. It's perfect.*

They walked down to the river and looked at the lights of the city twinkling on the surface of the Seine.

'You're a very enigmatic man, Mr Ferrera,' she said dreamily, resting her head on the soft wool of his jacket.

'Please call me Richard,' he murmured. 'I'd hoped we'd got past the formalities by now.'

'So had I. But even if I call you Richard, I won't feel as though I know you any better.' She looked up at him. 'You've listened to me chatter on all night and hardly said a thing yourself. You've talked about business, of course, and what you think about the President's foreign policy, and how you're learning to understand London society . . . but there's not much about the real you.'

'What is it you want to know?' Ferrera looked down at her and smiled.

'Oh . . . where do I start?' She sighed happily. What she really wanted to know was if he was thinking the way she was: that there was only one way for a romantic evening like this to end. For the whole evening, she'd been drawn to his quiet poise and the sense of great passions swirling just below the surface. Surely he must feel some attraction for her, or why were they here? 'Are you married?'

'No. I was married once. Let's just say I'm very happily divorced.'

They drifted over to the edge of the water near a lamp-post. Ferrera stared out over the river and said nothing for a such a long time that Jemima began to worry she had offended him by asking him if he was married. Perhaps it was too personal – but they'd been flirting discreetly all night.

'It's a beautiful evening, isn't it?' she said at last. 'Paris is so romantic.'

'It certainly is. It's a city for lovers, that's for sure.'

'Oh, yes.' She smiled to herself. So she had been right – this evening was a long flirtation. She felt a quivering anticipation. *Will he kiss me now?* she wondered, eager for him to turn and touch that handsome mouth to hers as they stood close together, watching the dark water ripple past. But he didn't.

'Shall we go back?' he asked after a while, and they walked on, Jemima trying to hide her disappointment and still hoping that he might make his move when they were closer to the hotel.

At the place Vendôme, he walked her to the door of the hotel and dropped a kiss on her cheek but did not attempt anything more.

'Good night,' he said. 'It's been a wonderful evening. What a lucky chance it was to meet you.'

'I think so too,' she said softly, seductively. 'Would you like to come upstairs for one last drink?'

He stared at her for a moment, then smiled and

shook his head. 'I must go back to the Ritz. It's very late and I have a breakfast meeting. Listen, I'm throwing a big party in London in few weeks, to celebrate a business acquisition. I'd love you to come. And your sisters too, of course. You're all welcome.'

'Thank you,' she said, with a small sigh of regret. She knew the chance had been and gone. 'You know where to reach me. Good night.'

She turned on her heel and walked into the hotel.

Ferrera went upstairs to his suite. When he opened the door, he saw a beautiful woman in a yellow silk gown standing at the window, her back to him. Hearing him come into the room, she spun round, her eyes furious.

'Where the fuck have you been?' she spat.

'I told you. I took her to dinner.'

'That was hours ago! Where have you been since then?'

'We went dancing . . .'

'Oh how very fucking romantic!' She strode about the room, flinging her arms about dramatically. 'While I wait here all alone! Dumped, for that bitch.'

'Don't be ridiculous. It's business. It had to be done. You will see the results, I promise.'

'Did you kiss her?' she hissed, whirling about to stare at him, her dark eyes blazing.

'Of course not,' he said coldly.

'Did you?'

'Do you think I'm lying?'

'I don't know what to believe! She's capable of anything . . .'

'Jecca.' He walked towards her and held out his arms. 'You mustn't let your personal feelings interfere like this. We want to achieve our goal, don't we? I'm doing this for you, after all.'

She pouted sulkily and let him take her in his arms. 'I know . . . I know. It just makes me sick, that's all. Knowing that you were with her. You don't know how she treated me in the past. She bullied me all through my childhood, because I wasn't good enough to be in her precious family.'

'I know what they made you suffer,' said Ferrera quietly. 'Believe me, I've not forgotten.'

33

Poppy spread out the Pantone colour cards on the table in front of her and stared hard at each one.

'Which one do you think?' she demanded.

'Eh?' George looked up from the window seat where he was buried in a book. 'What did you say?'

Poppy frowned in mock crossness. 'I can't believe it. We've been going out for only a week and you're already ignoring me!'

'Don't be silly,' he said, putting down his book and getting up. He went over and hugged her. 'I couldn't ignore you if I wanted to. What are you doing?'

'I'm trying to choose a colour for our new signature fragrance. I've narrowed it down to this range of pinks. I want to show the others the perfect colour at our next meeting – but I ought to take three possibles at least.' She pointed at her current favourite: a matt pink with the faintest hint of pearl and beige. 'What do you think of this one?'

'I'm no judge, I'm afraid,' he said apologetically.

'And I don't think I'm your target market either, so my opinion doesn't count for much.'

'Hmmm. You're right. Well, I'll take this and this and this.' She scooped up the colours she'd chosen and filed them in her drawing pad, where she had the working sketches for the final bottle design. 'All ready for work on Monday.'

'So what shall we do for the rest of the day? It's a gorgeous sunny morning. I thought we could go to the zoo ...'

Poppy put her arms round his neck and kissed the tip of his nose lightly. 'That sounds lovely but actually I have another plan. I have to go to Loxton – my parents' house. It's going up for sale and I have to deal with some things there. I wondered if you'd like to come with me. We could stay the night. It might be the last time I'm there.'

'Wow. I'd love that. I feel honoured.' George smiled at her.

'You are. But you also have a car.'

They drove down to Loxton, taking an hour to clear London and its heavy traffic, but once they were free of it, they sailed on into the countryside and made good time to the house.

'This is some house!' said George as they approached the red-brick mansion. 'Is this really all yours?'

'For about five minutes it is. We have to sell it to clear the mortgage and the death duties. But it's where I grew up.'

They pulled up in front of the house and went in.

It was exactly as Poppy had last seen it. Nothing had changed. But she knew that someone had been to value the contents so the lawyers and taxmen could assess the duties payable. Goldblatt Mindenhall were still sending her serious-looking letters every few days to keep her abreast of developments.

'Crikey!' said George, looking at the marble floor, heavy antique French furniture and the staircase swirling away to the upstairs. 'Who's that?' He was looking at the life-sized oil painting of Yolanda.

'My mother,' said Poppy softly. 'The matriarch. The one who got us into this mess. I still don't understand why she didn't get the inheritance properly sorted out after Daddy died so we wouldn't have to foot such a massive tax bill. It makes me think that for some reason she changed her mind about the whole legacy at the last minute. Maybe I wasn't supposed to get Loxton originally.' She shrugged. 'We'll never know, I suppose.'

'She looks quite a character.'

'She was.'

'How did she make her hair stay up in that huge bouffant?'

'Industrial quantities of hairspray. I'm not joking, she was a walking fire hazard. Now, let's go and grab a cup of tea and then I can get to work.'

They found the housekeeper in the kitchen. She made them tea and put out slices of homemade cake.

'I got your letter, Miss Poppy. The bed in the green bedroom is all made up.' The housekeeper glanced at George, whom she had clearly not been expecting. 'I hope I've got enough food in.'

'How are things here, Alice?' Poppy asked, sipping her tea.

Alice shook her head. 'Quiet, miss. Most of the staff have left now. It's just me and Tony in the lodge now and I understand we'll need to be out once the house is on the market.'

'Have you got somewhere else to go?'

'Yes, yes. A new position with a lovely family in the North. They're big in shipping, I believe. We're planning to take a little break on the coast with my brother's family before that, and then we start in the summer.'

'You've been such a wonder here, Alice, looking after Mother right to the end.'

'Least we could do,' Alice said gruffly. 'Your mother wasn't easy but she was fair and we were very touched to be remembered in her will.'

'We're going to wander about, Alice. You mustn't worry about cooking for us tonight – we'll look after ourselves. The same goes for tomorrow morning.'

'Very well. I'll pop in and tidy up tomorrow afternoon. I believe the agents are coming?'

'Yes, they want to take photographs before the house is emptied.'

Alice shook her head. 'Hard to believe there'll be no more Trevellyans at Loxton.'

'I know. But everything has to change some time.' Poppy looked about the kitchen, where she had spent so many hours as a girl, making toast or hot chocolate or just chatting with Alice. 'I'm sure a new family will be very happy here. And you know what? I think this place deserves a change.'

They spent a happy afternoon, wandering about the house. Poppy gave George a grand tour, showing him everything from the plush ground-floor reception rooms to the dusty attics full of rubbish.

'There must be all kinds of treasures here!' George exclaimed, looking at the trunks, suitcases and boxes of books, knick-knacks, photographs and old toys. 'Look at that funny little pedal car!'

'That was mine, when I was a toddler.' Poppy smiled. 'Funny, it used to be much bigger than that.' She laughed. 'Or so it seemed to me.'

'You're not throwing all this stuff out, are you?'

'What else can I do with it?'

'Oh no, you mustn't. You'll regret it.' He looked at her, his face fervent. 'You must store it.'

Poppy put her hands on her hips and made a face. 'But look at it all! I'll never have the time to go through it.'

'One day you will. Then you'll be glad you've kept it.'

'Mmm.' She looked at the dusty boxes. 'Maybe. Well, let's get on and I'll think about it.'

The afternoon passed by as they went from room to room, Poppy putting bright yellow stickers on the items to be valued and then sold by the auction house.

'You're putting stickers on everything!' said George, watching as Poppy stuck yellow circles on pictures, lamps, china, furniture and antique books.

'We need the cash. Anything that can go for a decent sum has to go. It's not like we want these things. I don't even like most of them.'

'Do you really need the money?' George looked disbelievingly. The effect of seeing Loxton and everything inside had obviously made him regard the family as hardly short of a shilling.

'We really do,' said Poppy firmly. She stood in front of her mother's great portrait for a moment, gazing up at the idealised smooth skin, glittering eyes and great swoop of hair. Yolanda's floor-length gown was a mist of floating chiffon, the jewels at her throat and wrist seemed almost a third bigger than their real-life models and her waist at least a third smaller. *The painted equivalent to airbrushing*, she thought. Her mother had never looked like that. She had just wanted to.

Poppy leaned forward and pressed a yellow sticker on to the frame, pushing it down hard to make sure it stuck. *There*, she thought. *Goodbye to all that. It's time to look ahead now.*

The press did not seem to be losing interest in the Pearson story. By seven o'clock in the morning, photographers were camped outside, waiting for Tara to emerge from the house so that they could take pictures of her.

She had been on the phone to Gerald's lawyers and to her own, trying to find out what the situation meant for them all. Gerald's lawyer, Harold Jamieson, told her that the most likely outcome was that Gerald would return voluntarily to South Africa and turn himself in.

There was a further development: Gerald's company had launched a suit against him for the return of funds they claimed he'd stolen. His assets would be frozen while the case was decided.

'You're going to have a complicated few months,' Harold told her. 'How entwined are your finances with Gerald's?'

'Thankfully not too much. He's never involved me in his business and I've never involved him in mine. Most of the properties are in single names – the Cape Town house, the Scottish estate, the New York property are all in Gerald's name. The City flat and the bungalow in the Bahamas are mine. This house is joint property and so is the Cotswold house.'

'Obviously any assets that can be shown to be yours will remain your own. Joint assets may need to be sold and the money divided, just as in a divorce.'

'How handy. Two birds with one stone,' said Tara drily.

'Sorry?'

'Gerald and I have separated. I'm sure he's told you. I'll be seeking a divorce in due course.'

'I'm sorry to hear that, Tara,' said Harold soberly. 'Are you sure? This is going to put an enormous strain on Gerald. A criminal trial at the same time as losing his wife and family . . .'

'He really should have thought of that, Harold, before he decided to raid the company piggy bank, shouldn't he? It's a bit late to start saying how sorry he is. I suspect he's only very, very sorry he got found out.'

'I see. Well, have your solicitors send me the appropriate correspondence in due course.'

'Thanks, Harold. I will.'

It was a Saturday and she was determined to enjoy it. No work today, she decided. She would take the children out. They would go to the park with their bikes, play at the playground and have an ice cream in the sunshine. Then somewhere nice for lunch and in the afternoon, perhaps she'd see about taking them to the pictures, or rowing on the Serpentine, or skating in Hyde Park. There were so many lovely things to do. She pushed the thought of Gerald out of her mind.

They had to face the press when they came out of the house but with John making a path for them and the children holding tightly on to Tara's hands, they got past them without much trouble. The presence of the children seemed to make the journalists hold back a little.

They would usually have walked to the park but to shake off the press, John drove them there in a circuitous way. Then they were free to enjoy the spring sunshine. The children ran off, delighted, to the playground while John unloaded the bikes from the boot.

'Have a great day, ma'am,' John said sincerely.

'Thanks, we will.'

And they did. Imogen had just learned to ride her bike with the stabilisers on but she was still a bit wobbly and tried to keep up with Edward, who whizzed away on his little two-wheeler, proud that he could ride it without help. Tara walked along behind them both, enjoying the sound of their piping voices and merry laughs.

'Come on, Mummy!' shouted Edward. 'Try and be faster!'

'Mummy, Mummy,' cried Imo, 'I can't see!' Her helmet had slipped forward over her eyes and she was pedalling slowly towards the edge of the path and a large rhododendron bush. Tara darted over and rescued her, laughing as Imo's big blue eyes were revealed from under the helmet.

'I got lost,' she explained.

'Don't worry, darling, I found you,' Tara said, dropping a kiss on her head.

This is good, she thought, as Imo pedalled off again, her tongue poking out with the effort of making the bicycle go the way she wanted. *We need more of this. Hell, I need more of this. They're not babies any more. They're growing up so fast. I can't miss all of it. I just can't.*

That night, when the children were in bed, exhausted after a wonderful day full of treats, Tara sat down at her computer and began to search through property websites.

34

'Goodness, look at this! It's not what I expected.'

'What did you expect?' enquired Claudine. She and Jemima were standing in the door of her office.

Jemima frowned. 'I suppose I imagined a sterile laboratory and you sitting there in a white coat, mixing potions from glass bottles.'

'I have some essences.' Claudine gestured to a row of small phials on her desk.

'Yes, but – apart from that, it looks just like an ordinary office. The desk, the books, the computer . . .'

'The computer is now our most essential piece of equipment,' said Claudine solemnly. 'I use it to create my formulae. Then I email it to the lab down the hall, the technicians mix me a sample of what I've created and send it to me to smell. Then I'll make some changes to the formula and start again.'

'But where do you keep the smells?' asked Jemima, surprised. 'How do you know what to put in?'

Claudine smiled and tapped her head. 'In here. I

know a great, great deal about scent, about what molecule smells like what and what its properties are – how it reacts, how long the smell will persist, what will degrade or damage it. I spent years at the Givaudan school analysing scents, learning them off by heart. I know in my sleep how to create the basic recipes for scents. I can mix you the smell of chocolate with two molecules. At school, I learned to construct new smells. "Create me a violet frozen in ice!" our tutor would say. Or he wanted the smell of a coffee drunk on a summer's morning in the place de la Bastille. Or the scent of grey clouds massing over a mountain. Building is part of it, breaking down another. He would ask us to find the constituent parts of a strange scent we had never smelt before. It was like learning a language, the vocabulary, the grammar, the rules . . . That is why I know what to put in my formulae.'

'Amazing,' breathed Jemima. 'What an incredible skill.'

'Yes,' agreed Claudine. 'Incredible.'

'And have you come up with something for us today?'

'I have begun to build something,' said the French woman cautiously. 'I have a sketch I am happy with. But I will need to continue tomorrow. I will bring at least three *essais* for you to try.'

'How exciting. I can't wait. Is there really nothing I can smell now?'

'No,' replied Claudine bluntly.

'What about those little bottles?' pressed Jemima.

Claudine glanced at them and relented. 'Very well.

You may smell one. They are essences and absolutes: refined, essential smells, the building blocks of fragrance. Some are natural, some synthetic. Natural essences are obtained by using heat and natural absolutes are the result of cold extraction, using solvents. Synthetics, of course, are developed in laboratories.'

'We want only natural ones in our scents,' said Jemima quickly.

'Why?' asked Claudine icily.

Jemima was taken aback by her reaction. 'Well . . . Natural is good, isn't it?'

'Suddenly you are an expert on perfume?' demanded Claudine irritably.

'No –' She had forgotten for a moment how sensitive Claudine could be about her area of skill but she had learned not to take any of the crossness to heart. She found Claudine's highly strung nature rather funny, though she tried not to show Claudine that as it would only make her even more prickly. The best way round it, she had discovered, was to remain sunny and charming, and Claudine's irritation would melt away.

'Then please allow me to be the judge. As it happens, synthetic molecules can be the most divine of fragrances. The very first were created here in France over a hundred and twenty years ago and some of the greatest perfumes in the world have been built with them. In fact, I believe that when synthetics were discovered, the creation of perfume truly began. Some synthetics are superior to the natural version, and often far cheaper not to mention more friendly to the environment.' She stared at Jemima. 'Or would you prefer all the precious sandalwood forests of India to be destroyed so you might wear your favourite scent, huh? Or the sperm whales murdered, so you can have natural ambergris?'

'Of course not –'

'Synthetic molecules can be cheaper, more stable, more persistent, less prone to warp or degrade in different formats. But if *you*, *Madame*, believe they are inferior, then perhaps I ought to throw away my synthetics! Despite the care, love and skill that has gone into refining them, they are not good enough for you!' Claudine's voice was rising and she put her hands on her hips.

Jemima burst out laughing. 'Honestly, Claudine, you're so touchy! You must ignore me, I know nothing. If you say synthetics are good, then they absolutely must be.'

Claudine huffed a little but she was obviously mollified. Her irritation vanished as quickly as it had come.

Jemima picked up a small phial. 'Now, can I smell this?' She took off the lid and sniffed. Her face changed as she registered the intense purity of the smell. 'Oh my God, it's incredible. It's the smell of violets. So strong, so . . . distilled!'

'Yes. That's right.' Claudine looked pleased at her reaction.

'But should you be putting violets in? We're trying to make a rose scent, aren't we?'

Claudine began to look cross again, then she

laughed. 'You will still try and tell me my art? It is something I'm experimenting with, to do with achieving the scent of tea, if you must know.'

'Oh! How clever . . .'

'Now, I think we should get out of here. I've had a long day. Are we going to dine tonight?'

'Yes, I'd love to.'

'Good. I'd be honoured if you would come back to my apartment and I will cook for you.'

'Thanks.' Jemima smiled at her. 'That sounds lovely.'

They took the train into Paris and then the Metro to the Marais district. Claudine's flat was in a stunning eighteenth-century building that had once been the town house of a French aristocrat.

'No one too rich or powerful,' said Claudine as they went up in the little lift. 'They built on a more fabulous scale than this.'

'It's beautiful.'

'I like it.' She led Jemima into the apartment. It was simple, restrained and stylish, decorated in earthy colours of stone, grey, warm brown and honey. The only bright colours came from the large works of abstract art on the walls.

'What a beautiful flat,' said Jemima sincerely.

'Thank you. Now please make yourself comfortable. I will fetch you an aperitif for you to enjoy while I prepare dinner.'

Five minutes later, Jemima was stretched out on the sofa, a Campari and soda on the table next to her, leafing through French *Vogue. Funny how quickly my*

French is coming back, she mused. *Although today was quite a baptism of fire.*

She had met senior managers of three of Paris's most prestigious stores. It had been hard work interesting them in the Trevellyan brand.

'There are new launches every day, *Madame,*' explained one, a man in a grey suit and brown-rimmed glasses. 'The public are becoming difficult to interest in new perfumes. There is too much on the market.'

'This is a luxury scent, not just another celebrity-endorsed run-of-the-mill fragrance.'

They had shrugged. They were French and not about to take lessons in luxury from an English woman. Luxury was French by its nature – the world knew that.

'What is the story of your perfume?' asked someone at one of her meetings.

'It's the new version of what was an old classic. A reworking into something entirely new for the contemporary woman.'

'What will it smell like?'

'Like a tea rose but very sophisticated, fresh and modern.'

'No, I mean, which successful perfume?'

'Oh . . . I don't know.'

'Mmm. Well, send us a sample when you have it, and details of your campaign. Your current scents perform decently for us – nothing extraordinary though.' The managers seemed bored by her. She was determined to grab their attention and get their support.

At her last meeting, disheartened by another luke-warm reception, she said impulsively, 'You will be very impressed, *messieurs,* by our campaign. We intend to launch simultaneously all over the world. We have someone very famous lined up to be the face of *Tea Rose.*'

There was a flicker of interest. 'You have?'

'Yes.'

'Who?'

'That', declared Jemima, 'is a secret until the very last minute. But you will be extremely excited when you discover who it is.'

'An actress?' They looked eager. 'A Hollywood star?'

'I can't say any more.' Jemima tried to look mysterious and yet fully in control.

'Stay in touch,. *Madame,*' said the manager as he showed her out. 'We will be interested to find out more in due course.'

It was the most positive meeting she'd had all day.

Now Jemima leafed through the magazine, mentally crossing out all the actresses who had already been signed up to front other brands. Scarlett Johansson, Jennifer Lopez, Keira Knightley, Nicole Kidman, Kirsten Dunst, Chloë Sevigny, Charlize Theron, Kate Winslet, Uma Thurman . . . anyone with any style was taken, or so it seemed.

She was struck by a fashion spread in the middle of the magazine. It was that same model, the one her attention had been caught by before. What was her name? Her looks were unmistakeable; the curvy lusciousness, the dark hair and the startling green cat's eyes. Neave. That was it. The stunning new Irish star – no doubt her name, Niamh, had been changed to a spelling more friendly to the American market on the recommendation of her management. She was truly gorgeous. It was no wonder that everyone seemed so captivated by her.

Jemima picked up the magazine and rushed through to the kitchen. 'Look at this woman, Claudine. Isn't she fabulous? So stunning! Look at those legs, those hips. You don't see many models like this, do you?'

Claudine left the saucepan she was stirring and looked at the page Jemima was proffering. 'No, no,' she murmured. 'She is certainly lovely.'

'I wonder if she would consider being our face – the face of *Tea Rose*. She's a new star – I've read that she's everywhere in the States and that studios are begging her to take screen tests. People are fascinated by her.'

'It is a good idea,' agreed Claudine.

'Yes, yes . . .' Jemima went back to the sitting room, lost in thought.

Claudine served up a truly delicious dinner.

'I can't believe you cooked this yourself!' exclaimed Jemima. 'It's just too good. Like something in a restaurant.'

They ate onion soup, thick and dark, with croutons and cheese, and then *coq au vin*.

'So French,' Jemima said, delighted.

'Simple food. I love to cook.'

'Exactly what I needed. Thank you.'

'You are most welcome.'

During dinner, Claudine seemed to relax and open up a little, talking about her childhood in Grasse where she would go out on a summer morning and pick jasmine flowers for the fragrance houses. The scent of those early morning flowers began her lifelong obsession with perfume. 'From the earliest recorded time, man made perfumes, we've always been fascinated by them. The Ancient Egyptians, of course, made balms and unguents from herbs and spices. By Roman times, there were popular brands, even perfume shops. A Roman perfumer named Megalus created a perfume called Megalium, made with balsam, rush, reed, behen nut oil, resin and cassia.' Claudine shrugged. 'Perhaps it was tolerable. I prefer the sound of Susinum, built with honey, lilies, cinnamon, saffron and myrrh.' She frowned. 'Perhaps one day I shall try to recreate it. It would be interesting. To smell it would truly be to travel in time, don't you think?'

'Why do you love perfume so passionately?' Jemima asked, sitting back. She was surprised by how much she was enjoying the evening, how relaxed she felt.

Claudine smiled thoughtfully. 'I love it because it always makes me feel so alive. The miraculous scents of the world . . . I adore them. Every day I'm reminded of the beauty of creation, the beauty of life. The structure of scent is so complex and so variable, no one really understands how it works. All I know is that it is deeply entwined with our pasts – a smell can bring back a time of one's life more intimately and immediately than a photograph or a diary – and with the poetry of existence. We all have our favourite smells – fresh mown grass, the sweet yeasty scent of a bakery in the early morning or the wind blowing saltiness in from the sea. And we all have our least favourites. For me, I despise the smell of hot asphalt when they are mending the roads – I cannot bear it. And I dislike the geranium, one of the few flowers I rarely use in my juices. But I still admire the millions of molecules that work together as one to create its odour – and despite the complexity and the minuscule balance of its fragrance, each and every flower will carry the same scent. Isn't that miraculous? That is why I love it.' She raised her eyebrows. 'Shall we go back to the sitting room with our coffee?'

'Yes. Let's.'

They entered the small but elegant room. Jemima went to the window and looked out over the roofs and lighted windows of the Marais. Claudine came and stood beside her. Jemima was filled with a sense of rare contentment. It was the peace and quiet, the sense of being far from her troubles and all the worry and stress that had engulfed them in the last month or so. What was happening with Gerald was frightful and bound to throw Tara off course. How could she possibly concentrate with her husband facing a possible trial and perhaps even a prison sentence? Then there were her own problems . . . she had to think seriously about her financial position. If Trevellyan wasn't able to pay her soon, she would start to be in trouble. And when she got back home, she would have to face Harry sooner or later, she knew that. She couldn't go on avoiding him for ever.

But not now . . . not tonight. I'm taking tonight off. My phone is switched off. No one knows where I am. I'll face everything when I get back to London tomorrow.

She was suddenly aware that a hand was resting softly on her arm and that it had begun to rub gently along towards her elbow.

Then the hand moved to her hair and began to play lightly with it, smoothing the ends and stroking it.

'Claudine?' she said cautiously, turning slightly towards her.

'Shhh,' whispered the other woman. 'I hope you don't mind.'

'Well, I –'

'Jemima, I want to kiss you. May I?' Claudine leaned in towards her and before Jemima could say anything, she had risen lightly on tiptoe and placed her lips lightly on hers. Surprised, Jemima said nothing. The kiss went on and she felt Claudine's mouth open and caress her own lips. It was beguiling: so soft and gentle that it was like being kissed by a leaf or a petal.

Then Jemima came to her senses and pulled away, shaking her head. 'No . . . no . . .'

'Why not?' Claudine's eyes were shining. 'I know you feel the same, from everything you've said. You are like me, *non*?'

'What? You mean, I'm a lesbian?' Jemima laughed. 'What on earth made you think that?'

The light died in the other woman's eyes. 'From what you've done and said . . .'

'I'm not sure –'

'You gave me a rose, a present ... you asked if I was married and said I should not, that men were dreadful. You admired the model in the magazine, her hips and legs. You wanted to have dinner with me, just the two of us – you *asked* me.'

Jemima was full of surprise and embarrassment. 'Oh, Claudine ... the rose was just part of our brief. I'm sorry if you thought I was coming on to you. Oh dear, I can see how it might have seemed otherwise. I am sorry. I'm afraid I'm not a lesbian, aside from a little experimentation when I was younger. I only laughed because I'm such a tart that it's rather funny anyone should think I hate men.'

Claudine dropped her gaze. 'I am mortified,' she whispered.

Jemima understood at once that the whole evening had been a seduction routine. *Why the hell didn't I realise? I've been through a few in my time! God, I'm an idiot.* She remembered the night before when she'd wanted to seduce Richard Ferrera, how she had sent him subtle signals that she was available to him. He had let her down, but gently.

'Please don't be mortified. It wasn't your fault in the least. I'm very flattered that you find me attractive.'

'But of course. You are lovely,' Claudine said frankly. Her eyes flicked down over Jemima's body: the full round breasts, small waist and long legs. The sight seemed to fill her with renewed confidence. She reached out and stroked Jemima's cheek. 'Is there no chance that you could let me show you a more beautiful way to make love?'

'It's tempting,' Jemima smiled. Apart from practising French kissing once or twice with girls in the boarding house at school, her one real experience of another woman had been when she'd been high on coke and champagne and had gone to bed with a famous model and her boyfriend. They had been too out of it to end up too entangled in a full-blown sex session but Jemima remembered enjoying the other girl's soft kisses and the pressing together of their bodies. It was not something that repelled her, it was just that she had always preferred men. 'But . . .'

'But?' Claudine moved closer and touched her lips to Jemima's again. 'It is not a crime, you know, to share warmth, comfort and pleasure with another human. We are both grown up. If I were a man, would you sleep with me?'

'Probably . . .' It was true she did find Claudine attractive. The older woman was so immaculate and stylish, so confident and self-possessed. Her skill and quick mind, even her very French temper, were fascinating. Jemima could not help thinking that the other woman would be just as skilled at teasing pleasure from her body as she was at conjuring beautiful scents from tiny molecules. She would understand the power of small but perfect movements. Jemima could feel the pent-up lust from the previous night waken and tingle lightly all over her body as she imagined what it might be like to allow Claudine to seduce her.

'Then why not let yourself? What is to stop you?'

'We work together. It wouldn't be right.'

'I'm not your employee. You are not abusing my

position. I am my own mistress, remember?' She ran her lips along Jemima's jaw line, brushing one hand lightly over her breast. Jemima shivered. Without meaning to, she was enjoying the delicate, bird's wing touches.

'Shall I stop?' The soft hand was rubbing gently across one breast, skilfully arousing the nipple beneath Jemima's lace bra.

'I don't want to lead you on,' whispered Jemima. 'And I'm not sure how much I would be able to . . . reciprocate.'

'I shan't expect a thing in return. I only want to give you pleasure. You won't owe me anything.' Her low voice was persuasive, seductive. The lips were back on hers, pressing softly, begging to be let in.

I hope I don't regret this, Jemima thought as she opened her mouth. Claudine kissed her fully, slipping her tongue inside her mouth. She tasted warm and rich, of red wine and honey. *This doesn't feel as strange as I thought it would.*

'Trust me,' whispered Claudine insistently. She led Jemima to the rug before the fireplace, and pulled her down on to it so that they were both sitting facing one another. Then she returned to kissing her, a little harder now, and with deft hands quickly unbuttoned her blouse and pushed it back, revealing Jemima's breasts.

Jemima felt the hot rush of arousal. Whatever was happening to her was too delicious and intense to stop. She felt entirely passive, entirely in Claudine's hands, and the sensation was novel and pleasant.

Usually she was an active, even dominant partner in sex. Tonight, she was ready to be worshipped.

Lying her back, Claudine began to kiss lightly down Jemima's body, massaging her soft skin as she did, neatly pushing away her clothes and unzipping her skirt until she was lying only in her underwear. The heat building up inside her was intense as Claudine released her breasts from her bra and began to suck gently on each nipple in turn, grazing them with her teeth, getting more and more persistent until each one was rock hard and hypersensitive.

Jemima's breathing grew faster and faster and her heart was pounding. No one in her life had spent so long adoring her breasts, titillating them, bringing her to such a pitch of excitement. She closed her eyes, allowing herself to think only of the sensations she was enjoying, as Claudine began to slide further down her body.

She knew what was coming, and the anticipation of it was almost unbearable, like a terrible ache. Then Claudine reached her panties, slid them quickly off, parted her legs and dipped her head downwards.

The feel of her soft, warm tongue exploring her made every nerve in Jemima's body tingle but the pool of sensation was greatest in her stomach and groin, where heat and desire were building together into an intense feeling. Without being aware of what she was doing, she spread her legs wider and put her hand on the top of Claudine's head, as if to prevent her from stopping the delicious licking and sucking that was sending huge waves of pleasure through her body.

Oh God, I'm going to come at once . . . I won't be able to hold . . .

Reading her body expertly, Claudine stopped tickling her clitoris and moved further down. Jemima gasped. She could feel Claudine's fingers entering her, the pad of her thumb moving softly around her mound, keeping her at the height of ecstasy but not allowing her over the edge to orgasm. For endless minutes, the delicious, tantalising sensations continued, until Claudine began to raise the pace again. She pushed her fingers faster and deeper into Jemima, taking her mouth back to her clitoris, licking, sucking and tickling more and more forcefully until, suddenly, the full force of a huge climax burst over Jemima. She cried out, her limbs shuddering and her back arched, the intensity unlike anything she had known, until, at last, it subsided, leaving her breathless.

Claudine slid upwards to lie next to Jemima, her eyes triumphant. Jemima could smell her own scent on the other woman's lips. Still panting, she reached over and pressed her forefinger to Claudine's mouth.

Claudine smiled and whispered, 'And that is my favourite perfume of all.'

35

The following week, the women of Trevellyan managed to achieve some significant targets.

Loxton was on the market at last and there seemed to be a steady stream of wealthy and enthusiastic viewers. Even though the property market had been in trouble recently, it appeared that at the high end, it was still ticking over nicely. The contents had been assessed and removed by the auctioneers and they were preparing a catalogue of sale. They seemed confident of a high return. Some of the furniture was first class, and causing some excitement in certain circles. It seemed that Yolanda's taste for ornate French pieces was shared by quite a few other people equally willing to pay an extortionate sum for it.

Poppy brought in her colour samples and everybody agreed at once that her favourite nude pink was exactly the colour they wanted.

'Feminine but not sickly. Sophisticated,' said Donna happily. 'Excellent. We'll call it Trevellyan pink and I'll alert the designers at once.'

'Now it's a question of how we use it,' agreed Poppy. The bottle would be based on the classic flacon from the Trevellyan archives, except it would be curved, not spherical but more egg-shaped. Its clear glass would be slightly pleated and at the top, a heavy silver round cap would cover the spray head.

'Should we tint the juice?' Donna asked, frowning. 'We could turn it pink.'

'I think it should be a light gold colour,' Poppy declared. 'And round the top, under the silver cap, a small ribbon in our nude pink.' She brought out a sketch she had made. 'The label will be on the front, also in nude pink. The name of the perfume in clean, plain black letters: *Tea Rose*.'

'Will we use pink for all our scents?' Tara queried. 'We'd have to redesign them and we don't have much time. Should *Antique Lily* have the same pink ribbon and label?'

'Hmm.' Poppy thought. 'No, I think each will have to have its own colour. But overall, the signature colour will be this pink, and we'll use the same bottle design, box design and font.'

'Won't it be a little confusing?' asked Jemima.

'I think it will work,' Donna said. 'The bottle itself will be the link between the fragrances. Which is good,' she looked at some figures on her laptop screen, 'as Poppy appears to have settled on the most expensive bottle design possible. It's going to cost us thousands to have this made up as a model. Make that *tens* of thousands.'

'It'll be worth it,' Poppy said stubbornly. She wasn't

prepared to compromise. She had realised the vision of the Trevellyan bottle and now she would fight for it.

'The positive side is that we'll use it for all the women's fragrances. That will actually make them cheaper, as *Tea Rose* will carry all the origination costs,' put in Tara. 'And our larger orders will bring the unit cost down.'

'OK, OK, you've convinced me! I think it looks great.' Donna smiled at Poppy. 'Congratulations, you've done a top job.'

Now the reality of what it would cost them to relaunch Trevellyan began to hit home. They would not be able to calculate the exact cost until the final version of *Tea Rose* was decided on and Claudine could give them the price of the compound. Once that was done, they could begin to set production in motion.

But with the signature colour decided upon, they pushed forward on refitting the shop. Designs were submitted by various companies and the girls carefully evaluated each one, arguing, discussing, putting forward ideas and visions, until at last they had hammered out one coherent look for the shop.

The old dark wood panelling would be gone for ever, to be replaced with a fresh, white interior, with touches of the nude pink colour. On glass shelves, the products would be displayed in neat rows, enticing and beautiful, and on glass tables, displays of one particular scent in all its forms, whether perfume, eau de toilette, soap, body lotion or fragranced candle, would be set up. In one area would be the personal consultation booths, where it would be possible for customers to mix scents and customise them to their own satisfaction. At the back of the shop would be the treatment rooms, also clean, light and white.

'This is great,' exclaimed Donna. 'It's going to look gorgeous. My only worry is that we're not going to be able to create all our ancillary products in time for the opening. We've got a huge mountain to climb.'

'If we're launching in November, we've got six months, haven't we?' asked Jemima.

'Six months to create face creams, moisturisers, treatments . . . ? To commission room sprays, candles, incense sticks . . . We haven't even got the final *Tea Rose* scent yet. Incidentally, does anyone know when Claudine will be back?'

Jemima shook her head, feeling herself unexpectedly flush.

'She emailed me this morning to say she's on her way back this afternoon. We'll have her samples first thing tomorrow,' said Tara.

'We've got lots of products already,' pointed out Poppy. 'There are bath oils already in production, and hand lotions. Surely we're halfway there.'

Donna sighed. 'I wish it were that easy. But until we've decided on the final *Tea Rose* juice, we won't know how stable it is, how easily it can be transformed into other products. I guess tomorrow is crunch time.'

George and Poppy were spending more and more time together. She knew she was falling in love and it seemed that George felt the same. He wanted to spend every minute he could with her and was always waiting for her when she got back from Trevellyan.

'You don't seem to have to go to work very much,' she said, as they finished their supper.

'I was there today,' George said indignantly. 'I sold four copies of the new Julian Barnes, if you must know, single-handed.'

'Now that *is* impressive.' Poppy smiled.

'My hours aren't that demanding,' conceded George. 'Sylvester basically lets me do whatever I like. If it's a quiet afternoon, I just let my assistant get on with it and sneak off.' He leaned over and held her hand.

'I'm very glad your employer is so obliging.'

'Me too. He's a very kind uncle.'

Poppy blinked. 'Oh – is he your uncle? I thought he was a friend of your aunt's.'

'Yes, yes, he is. You know, like an honorary uncle. Because we've known him for years. So tomorrow is a big day, is it?'

Poppy nodded. 'Our perfumer is coming back with her samples. We're going to choose the new scent. It's very exciting.'

'And they loved the new colour?'

'Yes, I'm thrilled. Nude pink is now the colour of Trevellyan!'

'Mmm. Sounds rather sexy . . .' George looked at her, desire in his eyes. 'Shall we go to bed?'

'It's only nine-thirty!'

'I wasn't planning on sleeping for a little while yet.'

She laughed. 'George, you're incorrigible.' But she could not resist him.

They gathered in the boardroom the next day, waiting nervously for Claudine to arrive. When she did come marching into the boardroom, she gave absolutely nothing away. There was no sign of nerves or apprehension on her face, not a clue as to whether she was happy with her creations or not.

'*Bon*,' she said, sitting down opposite the sisters and Donna. 'Let's get started.'

Jemima tried to remain as impassive as Claudine but it was hard not to feel something. After all, the last time they had seen each other, Claudine had driven her to a peak of ecstasy. But the agreement had been that there would be no repercussions from their encounter and it appeared Claudine was keeping to it. She didn't so much as flick a glance in Jemima's direction. Instead, she put a neat black case on the table, opened it and brought out three small phials. Each had a tiny white label on it with a letter and a number inked on it. Claudine then pulled out a handful of paper strips.

'Now,' she said importantly. 'Please prepare yourselves.'

She opened the lid of one of the phials, picked up five paper strips and dipped them into the clear, hay-coloured liquid in the phial. Then she passed them over the table, keeping one for herself. Each woman took one, held it beneath her nose and inhaled. There was silence as they tried to evaluate what they were smelling.

'It's rose, obviously,' said Tara at last, 'but very fresh and light.'

'Very floral . . . quite sweet,' said Poppy.

Claudine nodded.

'It smells cool to me, a little bit . . . fresh. Outdoorsy,' declared Donna. 'I'm getting a grassy, green smell. Mmm, this is great. I like this.'

'I don't know if I do,' Jemima said slowly. Then she glanced up at Claudine quickly. 'Sorry, Claudine, I mean it's very good but . . . it's just not what I imagined *Tea Rose* to be. And it doesn't seem to be related to the original scent at all.'

Claudine met Jemima's gaze for a moment but said nothing. She simply dipped four more testers in the second bottle and passed them over.

This scent was quite different from the first. It was warm, rich and exotic, still unmistakeably rose, but this time with an oriental flavour.

Jemima sniffed happily. 'Oh, I can smell incense. This reminds me of evenings out on holiday . . . it makes me think of summer nights, souks, lanterns over bubbling hookahs . . .'

'So poetic,' said Poppy, giggling. 'But I know what you mean. I'm getting Turkish Delight crossed with old wax candles.'

'This is heavy,' Tara said thoughtfully. 'Jemima's right, it's got a definite flavour of incense. It makes me think of joss sticks at a bazaar. Very different to the first one. Sophisticated, though.'

Donna put her tester on the table, frowning. 'My worry is, will it be commercial enough? The first one is much more appealing to younger women, I think.'

Claudine patiently dipped the testers into the last bottle and passed them round.

They all inhaled again, waiting a few seconds for the scent to register in its entirety.

'I like this *very* much,' Jemima said quietly. 'Yes . . . this is the one I like best. Actually, it's amazing . . .' She sniffed again.

Claudine spoke at last. 'It is accepted that a perfume has three lives. When you first smell it or put it on your skin, you will get the top notes, the first blast of perfume. As it settles on your flesh, responding to the warmth of your body and the flavours of your own skin, it will take on a second life and you will discover its heart, the middle notes. Then these too will fade, leaving you with the base notes, the long echoing scent that is the real fragrance.'

'What is this one?' Tara said, sniffing her tester again. 'It's quite different again. The rose is rich and intense but there's something else, something smoky, woody . . .'

'Yes.' Jemima inhaled again. 'Oh God, it's gorgeous, so . . . *adult.*'

Claudine looked at her, gave a tiny nod and a small smile. 'I'm glad you like this one,' she said quietly.

'I like it,' Poppy said doubtfully. 'But is it *Tea Rose*? I think I prefer the Turkish Delight one.'

'Tell us about them, Claudine,' Donna said.

'Very well. But first you must each take the bottles and put them on your skin, in three distinct places, so that you can try them there.'

Obediently, they took the phials and passed them to each other, pressing them to their wrists and fore-arms to create a small circle of each scent.

'So,' said Claudine. 'The first you tried is T1. It is a green floral, made with rose essence rather than rose absolute – I have used the same rose in each juice, incidentally; the *rose de mai*. I created this scent to be fresh, light and zesty. It is more commercial, Donna is right. The second, T2, is an oriental scent. You were correct about that, Jemima. It has a Moroccan theme, spicy and dramatic. The earliest rose perfumes were Turkish and I have tried to bring that out. The rose I used here is rose absolute, which holds the heav-iest scent molecules and provides a richer, darker scent. Under that we have incense and dark honey. The third, T3 . . . well, I want you all to smell it now that it has had a couple of minutes to develop on your skin.'

They sniffed.

'How strange!' exclaimed Poppy. 'It's different on skin. Warmer. Less smoky – although you can still smell the smoke.'

'I'm getting a woody smell,' said Donna thought-fully. 'But I love the rose, it's so rich.'

'No, no,' said Jemima, excited. 'I know what it is, I know.' She looked over at Claudine, her eyes shining. 'It's tea. Isn't it?'

Claudine smiled and nodded. '*Oui*. You can smell tea. Lapsang Souchong, to be exact.'

'That's it,' said Jemima to the others. 'It's so smooth and sophisticated. I love it. That tea smell is so clever.

The rose is feminine and sweet, the tea is smoky and elegant and . . . there's something else.'

'The base is ambergris,' explained Claudine. 'That is what makes it so grown up, so womanly, rather than girlish. Aldehydes link it all together, making it smooth and orchestral.'

'I love the way it develops,' Tara exclaimed. 'It's so complex but not overpowering at all.'

'And I think there is a definite link to the old scent. It continues the story of *Tea Rose*, you can tell. This is perfect, it's just what we wanted.' Jemima had flushed with her enthusiasm.

Donna shifted uncomfortably. 'I agree with everything you've said, but I'm worried about whether it will appeal to the mass market. I think it needs a little work. But' – she saw Jemima's face – 'I'm prepared to agree that this is the idea we want to go with. Let's all wear this one for a couple of days while Claudine maybe gives it a little tweak. Claudine, can we get something a little fresher in there? Just for the top notes, perhaps? I love the smoky development, but I want women to get something fresh at the start.'

Claudine nodded. 'Yes. I'll go back to the lab and then FedEx you the results. You can have them by Friday.'

'But don't change this too much,' Jemima said hastily. 'This is it. This is what we asked for. It's *Tea Rose*, I know it.'

'Don't worry. From here, I can only make it better.'

*   *   *

417

Claudine was as good as her word. Three days later, a phial arrived marked T4. This one contained a fragrance of complex structure, rich scent and great elegance. It was fresh and yet smoky, soaked in the essence of precious roses but with a light touch. It was built on the warm, dark, night-time smell of ambergris, yet remained delicate and romantic, seductive and comforting.

'We've got our baby,' Donna said. 'Claudine's a bloody miracle worker. This is everything we wanted. Now we'll have to get her to start experimenting with creams, lotions, body milks . . . everything we want to be part of the *Tea Rose* range.'

The sisters grinned at each other.

'What on earth would Mother say?' Tara mused, sniffing her wrist.

'Who cares?' cried Jemima. 'It looks like we can succeed without her after all.'

36

With the formula for *Tea Rose* finally agreed, they could at last begin to make advances. With the cost of the compound and the time needed to create the perfume, Tara could start working out the practicalities of the launch.

'Talk about bloody regulations!' she cried, stalking round the office, rubbing her hands through her hair in frustration. 'Who ever guessed there were so many European directives on bloody perfume!'

The strain of what they were undertaking was taking its toll on her. Not only was she still trying to make sense of the hugely complex affairs of Trevellyan but she was also trying to keep the current sales operation on track while planning the complete overhaul of the company and organising the forthcoming launch. Even with delegating as much as she could to junior staff and to the others, she still had a vast job on her hands. She was finding it hard to sleep. Her bedroom at home had ceased feeling like her sanctuary. It still had too much of Gerald in it – the suits, shirts and ties that he'd left behind, and all the litter of their life together.

She had seen him only once. She had taken the children to the flat for them to say goodbye to him. He was going to return to South Africa and turn himself over to the authorities. He would live in their Cape Town home for the foreseeable future, while further details of his arrest and trial were finalised.

'No doubt I will be bailed,' he said. 'And I've got my lawyers on the case already. I'm sure I can get out of this. But it will take time.'

'How much time?' Tara asked. Seeing him was like seeing someone she had once known and liked many years ago, but now felt nothing for. He left her feeling completely cold and she found it hard to have any interest in his predicament, save for where it affected her or the children.

'Years, probably. The wheels of justice turn slowly as I'm sure you know.' Gerald smiled at her. 'Tara, Harold tells me you're filing for divorce.'

'That's right.'

'Please, if there's any way you could think again . . . do we really need to take this terrible, serious step?'

'I think we do.'

'Do you know how bad this will look for me? Without your support, I will be presumed guilty.'

Tara snorted scornfully. 'You're really going to have to think of a better reason than that. Is that all you want me for? To save your miserable skin? So much for love, for our life together, for a marriage!'

'I *do* love you,' insisted Gerald plaintively.

'It's over, Gerald. We both know that.' She looked at him sadly. 'I guess we'll have to agree how often the children will come to see you. I assume you won't be doing much travelling once you get there.'

'Unlikely,' Gerald agreed. He seemed beaten.

'We'll discuss all that when we need to. I'll tell Robina to bring the children in. We'll stay for an hour.'

'Only an hour?' Gerald stared at her beseechingly. 'Tara, I may not see them again in months.'

'An hour,' she said stubbornly. But when she saw Edward and Imo run into their father's arms, delight all over their faces, and the way Gerald lit up as he hugged and kissed them, she was filled with remorse. She left them together, and went out to walk through the City on her own, crying softly as she realised the enormity of what was happening to them all.

'So you're saying that the marketing campaign is going to come in at one point six million pounds.' Tara stared at the figures in front of her. 'Plus the costs of creating the perfume, the bottle, the box, distribution, the refit of the shop, new staff . . .'

'The press samples, the launch . . .' added Jemima.

'Yes, thanks.' Tara looked desperate. 'The money we're making at present just about covers the current operation and staffing levels. The three of us are on minimum salary. We don't have enough to cover all this.'

'We should be able to get a lot of press for free,' Donna said, 'if Jemima puts her mind to it.'

'What do you mean by that?' Jemima asked frostily.

Donna shrugged. 'I mean, you're news. The public are interested in you. You're going to have to sell yourself. Magazine interviews, newspapers, press . . . you've got to start making calls, pulling strings, talking to contacts. You must have tons of them.'

'Yes, of course I do and I'm willing to use them when the time is right.'

'Well, the time is right now, honey.'

Jemima looked sulky, evidently feeling that she was being criticised, but Donna ignored her and turned to Tara. 'What money do we have coming in?'

'Once the auctioneers have done their work, we should have a sizeable sum from Loxton's contents. Up to six million. Maybe even more. There'll be tax and various costs to come out of that, though, and the sale is not for another two months. We're going to have to try and get some credit to tide us over until then.'

'Well, that's a start,' Donna said. 'Except I do have some bad news.'

'Oh God, now what?' Tara looked strained.

'The figures I've given you don't include the States.'

'What?'

'Distribution, marketing, advertising . . . whatever it costs in America will be extra.'

Poppy gasped. 'But we'll never afford it. That will be millions more, won't it?'

Donna nodded slowly. 'It sure will.'

'Fuck!' Tara threw down her pen and stood up. She marched to the window and stared stonily out. 'Fuck, fuck. It's all over then. We might as well forget it.' She turned back, her face angry. 'If we don't have the

States, we have nothing. We can never achieve our goals without it.'

There was silence as they all absorbed this.

'It can't really be that important, can it?' asked Poppy quietly. 'Can't we still be a success here without launching in the States?'

Tara sighed. 'Oh, yes, we can do our best. But we'll have shot our bolt. Our one chance at relaunching Trevellyan, creating a new, global craze for *Tea Rose* . . . it'll be gone.'

'While we're completely depressed and miserable, I may as well add to the bad news. I had a fabulous idea for the face for the marketing campaign.' Jemima pulled out a magazine picture and laid it on the table. 'It's Neave, the new Irish supermodel.'

They all stared at the picture.

'Of course. Brilliant. She's great,' said Donna. She smiled but still looked worried. 'And she's the ultimate now face. But would she do it?'

'In a word, no.' Jemima made a disgruntled expression. 'I rang her agency. They're not interested. She's being inundated with offers and they say she's far too busy. Besides, they don't consider Trevellyan well known enough and they're bound to want to align her with a genuinely famous brand.'

'We couldn't have afforded her anyway,' Tara said bleakly. 'Oh, Christ. What are we going to do?' She went back to her chair and slumped down in it.

Poppy looked over at her, worried. She had never seen Tara so defeated before and now it seemed she was completely beaten.

'If it's really that bad,' Jemima said quietly, 'then maybe we should consider selling. Remember I told you that I bumped into Richard Ferrera in Paris? Well, he's still interested in buying Trevellyan. He said that we could all stay on as directors and run the company, but that he'd own us.' She looked at her sisters in turn. 'I mean, we need someone with a vast amount of money, don't we? Someone who can afford to fund our big plans. He's American too, so he'll know how to run things Stateside.'

There was a pause while they considered this. Once, not that long ago, they would have all protested that selling was the last thing they would ever do. Now it seemed as though it might be the only way out.

Tara spoke at last. 'I'll look into it. I'll see what our position is in terms of the will – how we could go about selling the company . . . *if* we need to.'

'I can do that,' Jemima said. 'You've got so much on your plate already. I'll make an appointment at Goldblatt Mindenhall and get them to talk me through it.'

'Thanks, Mimi.' Tara smiled over at her. 'That would be a great help.'

'Oh, and Ferrera's invited us to a huge party as well,' added Jemima. 'It must be quite soon.'

'I know what that is,' Donna said. 'He and Erin are doing a big glitzy bash to celebrate their partnership. I think you should definitely go. See what being in business with Ferrera looks like. From what I've heard, no expense is spared when it comes to his parties. It should be worth seeing.'

'Then I'll email his office in the morning,' said Jemima. 'And we'd better start thinking about what we're going to wear.'

There was an email waiting for Jemima when she got home. It was from Harry.

Jemima.

I think this stand-off has gone on long enough. I would like you to come down to Herne. We need to talk. Can you make it this weekend?

Harry.

She stared at it, feeling faintly sick. So this would be the moment of truth. No doubt he was going to ask for a divorce. What else could he do? The two of them had a laughable marriage. They barely spoke, almost never saw each other. It was all over, they both had to face that.

So why did it make her so miserable to think about it?

I suppose I don't like failing, she admitted to herself. *That's what this will look like.*

She got up and wandered into the kitchen to make herself a cup of tea. Perhaps divorce was for the best. Harry could marry Letty. She was young and pretty and no doubt would give him the parcel of children he wanted . . .

She clasped the bench suddenly, bending over it,

surprised by the sudden jolt of pain that shot through her stomach. Breathing slowly, she tried to overcome it, and then it was gone. She hadn't realised that just thinking of what had happened could still affect her like this.

When she had recovered and drunk her tea, she went back to the computer.

Hi, Harry.

Yes, I'll come down this weekend. I'll arrive on Saturday morning before lunch.
See you then.

Jemima.

37

George ran his nose along Poppy's neck, sniffing her appreciatively.

'So this is the new scent, is it?' he asked.

'Yes, this is it. Do you like it?'

'I'm not much of a fan of perfume generally. Can't bear women who are drenched in the stuff. They make me sneeze. But I like this . . .' He sniffed again. 'It's not too strong. And not too floral. I hate perfumes that smell like a giant bouquet. What's that shop where they make all those natural soaps and bath things? The ones that look like giant cakes of fudge? Can't bear the smell of that place. Just walking past it makes my stomach turn.'

Poppy laughed. 'So you're obviously very discerning! At least it gets past your stringent quality test.' She lifted her wrist to her nose and sniffed it. 'I'm getting fonder and fonder of this scent. It's like the original *Trevellyan's Tea Rose,* and yet different. It has its own character and identity. The other one smelt old-fashioned, you couldn't get away from that, even when it was properly made. But this is just what women today want to wear.'

'Then it looks as though everything's going to work out, doesn't it?'

They were lying in bed, relishing the warm sunshine coming through the skylights in Poppy's bedroom ceiling. Above them the blue sky blazed and wisps of white cloud floated slowly across the windows. It was going to be a hot day.

Poppy sighed. She picked up George's hand and twisted her fingers through his. 'I love your hands, do you know that?' She kissed his knuckles in turn. 'They're so large – but not hairy or rough. Just capable and strong.'

'I'm delighted you approve.' He pulled her close to him so that she could smell the warm muskiness of his skin. 'But tell me how things are going – does it look as though everything will work out?'

'I had no idea you were so interested in the perfume business.'

'Don't be silly, I'm interested in you. And this is taking up just about every waking thought for you, isn't it? It's obviously crucial to you. I'm anxious about you, that's all.' He stroked her hair softly.

'There's just so much to cope with.' Poppy was quiet for a moment and then said, 'Once, I went walking in Snowdonia with some friends. We were going to climb Snowdon – it's the highest peak in Wales. When we got there, I looked up and thought,

"It's really surprisingly small. This shouldn't be much trouble at all." So we started to walk up this mountain and as we went, I realised that what we were climbing wasn't the mountain itself – it was just one of the foothills. The higher we got, the more I could see that beyond our little hill was a great mountain, going up and up. That was really where we were heading. It's like that now. When we started, it seemed quite simple and straightforward. Launch a new perfume, give the company look a shake-up, job's done. But of course, it's not that simple at all, and the further we go along, the harder the climb appears.' She sighed. 'Tara's just been in touch to tell me that we've been refused planning permission for our refit, because the wood panelling in the shop is protected. I'm sure we'll get round it somehow – our designers are terrific – but it's just another problem to cope with. Nothing seems to run smoothly no matter how well we plan. Then there's Tara herself. I'm worried about her.'

'Why?' George stroked her arm tenderly. 'From everything you say about her, she seems like a tremendous coper.'

'She is – but imagine how hard all this is, especially with what's happening to Gerald. I never much liked him, but I don't wish all this on him, even if he is a crook. The press are ripping him to pieces and they're trying to take Tara with him. It makes me so furious – as if she knew anything about it! There's no one in the world as straight and honest as Tara!'

'It's OK,' George soothed her softly. 'I'm on your side, remember? And Tara's come to that.'

Poppy smiled. 'Sorry, darling. I just worry about my big sister and how much she can take before she breaks. Donna told me that Tara left early the other night to meet an agent who was seeking properties for her. She's only planning to sell her house and buy another at the same time as all this is going on.'

'Maybe she needs something to take her mind off the business.'

'Maybe.' Poppy sighed. 'I just can't see a way out of our main problem and I don't think Tara can either. We need money – big money – to make this work, and we haven't got it.'

'Can you borrow some? Surely there are venture capitalists out there who'd like to invest?'

'Tara says it would be difficult. There's a much less benign financial climate these days. It's getting harder to borrow and our results are so poor and we're so inexperienced that people are going to be wary of investing in us. That's why any money left over after the sale of Loxton's contents has to go to the business – it's our only way of getting some cash.'

'All your inheritance?' George said. 'Are you sure that's wise?'

'Why do you say that?' Poppy said, a flicker of anxiety in her voice. She had never been so happy as she was since she had met George. There was something about him that made her feel utterly relaxed and comfortable, totally accepted for herself. He had never seemed interested in knowing how much money she had, or who her glamorous friends were. All he wanted to do was spend time with her, just the two of them, talking. He never wanted to go to fancy restaurants or glitzy parties. He was happiest eating toast with her and reading the papers together, talking and laughing about the silly things they'd noticed that day. And he was completely supportive of her Trevellyan work, never bored or uninterested by it. He was always ready to listen when she moaned about what was happening in the office, or came home too shattered even to smile. But was he really interested in her money after all?

George picked up on the note in her voice and grinned. 'Oh, darling, please don't think I'm worried in case you end up poor and I have to dump you! You couldn't ever be much poorer than I am, and I'm perfectly happy. I don't care how much money you have.' He looked in her face, staring deeply into her eyes. 'I know it hasn't been long. We've only been together a few weeks . . .'

'Six weeks, four days,' whispered Poppy.

'. . . I'm glad you're keeping track. But it's long enough for me to know that I love you.'

She'd been longing to hear it and hoped it was true. Now she knew it was. A huge smile broke across her face and she hugged him impulsively. 'Do you? Do you? I'm so happy! I love you too!'

He laughed. 'You do?'

'Yes, oh yes. I've never been so happy.'

He kissed her softly, lingering on her lips for a long time. Then he said gently, 'I don't care if you're Poppy

Trevellyan or Poppy Put-the-kettle-on or whoever. You're you. The girl I love.'

While Poppy was making the most of her morning before heading to the office, Jemima had already been up for hours, keen to make her appointment at Gold-blatt Mindenhall.

'Lovely to see you again, Lady Calthorpe,' said Ali Tendulka as Jemima was shown into his office by the secretary. He gestured to the leather armchair in front of his desk. 'Please sit down.'

'Do call me Jemima. I think we're on . . . *intimate* enough terms for that, aren't we?' She sat down, crossing her legs elegantly and seductively.

Ali Tendulka sat opposite her in his chair and leaned back, pressing his fingertips together, smiling at her. 'Very well. To what do I owe the pleasure of this visit, Jemima?'

Jemima glanced about the office, with bookshelves crammed with legal reference books and files, the desk and its mountainous in-tray and computer. 'I need to ask a favour.'

'You do surprise me. Of course I'm happy to help you in any way I can – provided it's within the law, of course.'

'Of course.' Jemima smiled at him, lowering her lashes flirtatiously. 'The favour is entirely legal, I promise you that. It's the small matter of my mother's will.'

Ali raised his eyebrows and laughed. 'The *small* matter? I got the impression it created quite a stir.'

'Yes, you're right. It did. But we need to be absolutely sure about the conditions of the will. I'd like you to look at the small print for me and find out what provisions there are for selling the company, if that becomes a necessity.'

'You're planning to sell . . . ?'

'Not necessarily,' Jemima said quickly. 'But we need to know exactly what constraints we're acting under. The terms of my mother's will are hardly predictable, I'm sure you'll agree.'

'Absolutely. In fact, it's the oddest will I've ever had dealings with.'

Jemima leaned forward, giving Ali a clear view of her plunging cleavage in the tight, low-cut white shirt-dress she was wearing. 'There are a couple of other things. I want you to double check when the will was signed and dated. And if there are specific mentions of my mother's jewellery. We thought the jewellery was included in the contents of Loxton, but it's not there and no one has been able to locate it. Obviously it's worth quite a lot. We want to find out where it's gone.'

'I don't think that should be a problem.'

'Good. Perhaps we can meet for a drink when you have the answers. Always so much nicer to mix business and pleasure, don't you think?' Shooting him one last dazzling smile, Jemima stood up. 'I look forward to hearing from you soon.'

The photographs lay in neat rows on the desk. Most of them showed Tara Pearson, usually with a large pair of dark glasses on and a grimace of distaste twisting her mouth, heading from her home to her car, or from her office to her car. One showed Jemima Calthorpe, an insouciant smile on her face, striding proudly away from the photographer, self-confidence almost rippling in her wake. Another was of Poppy Trevellyan, her green eyes startled, her chin pressed down towards her chest as she tried to avoid the prying lens.

Flick Johnson made a noise of irritation. She fidgeted and rubbed her hands together. She was desperate for a cigarette but never had time to make the trip from the newsroom downstairs to the outside world for a puff. The result was that she was giving up smoking against her will and fighting constantly against her craving. She scanned the pictures of the Trevellyan sisters again.

'Why the fuck are you bringing me these, Ben?' she snapped.

Ben, a tall, gangly young reporter who'd been at the paper only six months, came over to have a look. 'It's those Trevellyan girls, innit?'

Flick grimaced. 'I'm perfectly aware of that, I've run enough pictures of 'em in my time. I've had it up to here with the bloody Heiresses. Everyone banging on about how much money they were going to get when their parents popped their clogs.' Flick picked up the photograph of Jemima and scowled at it. 'Look at this one. Pure arrogance. I hate this kind of pampered princess. She's got no idea how the world really works or how much misery ordinary people have to deal with. I bet she doesn't so much as have to pull her own knickers up after she's taken a piss.' She sniggered. 'Though I've heard she's very good at getting them down.' She pushed herself away from the desk and said, 'The point is, why the fuck are these pictures on my desk?'

'One of our regular paps sent them in, in case we want to run them.' Ben pointed at the pictures of Tara. 'This is the one in the news, innit?'

'She *was* in the news, several fucking weeks ago. She's no use to me now, unless something happens. Her husband's not even in the country much longer. When he comes to court, it might be worth trying to get some pics but until then – the story's dead, mate.'

'Oh right.' Ben nodded. He was an adolescent mixture of confidence and self-doubt, obviously terrified of Flick, who was an old hand in papers and had no fear of speaking her mind and administering a good tongue lashing when she felt like it. 'I'll tell the picture desk. Fuckin' morons,' he added, to pass off responsibility for wasting Flick's time.

Flick leaned forward again. She put one hand to her dark blonde ponytail and started whirling the hair round her fingers in the habit she had when she was thinking. She stared at the pictures. 'The old one. Tara. She's not looking happy, is she? I suppose that's what it's like when it turns out your old man's up for grand theft and facing a stretch inside.' Flick examined the pictures a little more closely. 'But the funny thing is, she's not doing the usual rich wife thing of standing by him. I mean, he's only stolen some money, he hasn't buggered any farmyard animals or anything – not as far as I know, anyway. Most wives would do their best to keep their bloke out of prison, wouldn't they?' She became thoughtful. 'And now these girls have actually got their hands on the family millions, they're not looking too happy about it, are they? Pretty damn miserable, if you think about it.' She turned to the young reporter. 'What do you notice about most of these pictures, Ben?'

'Errr . . .' Ben gazed at them all intently as if thinking hard but his mind was obviously blank. 'Errr . . . dunno.'

'Wanna be an investigative journalist, do you, kiddo? Try turning on your fucking brain. Nearly all these pictures have the girls entering and leaving the same place. Their family company.'

'Yeah. So?'

'So these rich bitches have never had to do a day's work in their lives! OK, apart from the oldest,' Flick conceded, 'she's a banker or something. But the other two . . . wafting through life like a couple of pretty butterflies sucking the nectar. And here they are, going to work every day almost like normal people.'

Ben frowned. 'So what?'

'So what? So I get the feeling there might be a story there, you great bloody numbskull!' Flick sat back in her chair. 'Remember when the blonde one went out with that rock star? No one could get enough of her. Then she went and married some lord, their wedding pictures were all over the place, supposedly they lived happy ever after. You don't see 'em together much, though, do you? Well, I think it's time we all found out what happened next to the Heiresses, don't you?'

Ben nodded, smirking.

38

'Lord Harry's been called away this morning,' the housekeeper said frostily. 'Something to do with estate business. The new manager.'

'OK, Teri. Thanks.'

The housekeeper turned and stalked away, leaving no doubt as to her lack of pleasure at seeing Jemima back at Herne. As for mentioning the new manager . . . well, Jemima knew exactly what kind of point Teri was trying to ram home. She could forget it. There was no way Jemima was going to let any sly little digs get to her.

She left her bag in the hall, a long stone-flagged room with high mullioned windows and a large fireplace, big enough for a man to stand up in, at either end. Over each fireplace hung a vast portrait of one of Harry's ancestors. One was a florid, Regency buck, in a tight scarlet jacket, buff breeches and high buckled shoes. From his white stock rose a plump red face, the dark hair on top brushed forward in the neo-classical fashion of the day. He was painted against a torrid background of grey clouds and distant fields and villages, no doubt supposed to represent his large estates. The other painting portrayed a Cavalier and his wife, the lord in a suit of blue satin with a high lace collar of intricate work and long boots, his lady with similar rich lacework at the bosom and sleeves of her flowing silk gown, her fair hair falling in short, pretty ringlets round her forehead and over her ears. Her hand rested on the jewelled collar worn round the neck of an elegant greyhound.

For how many centuries had Harry's ancestors enjoyed wealth and influence? How many Lord Calthorpes had strode across this hall, warmed themselves in front of these fireplaces, and talked about the political issues of the day? Jemima smiled wryly to herself. How many had made their poor wives miserable?

She had been dreading this trip to Herne. It felt as though she were about to get some bad news, a negative prognosis. Something that would change her life yet again. She didn't want to face it.

As she'd driven down the long drive towards the house, she'd been struck again by the beauty of Herne. How different it was to London, with its hot pavements and dusty roads and millions of people. Here, it was peaceful and cool. Early summer, she felt, must be the most beautiful time of the year in England. The park was clad in fresh lime greens, the trees dressed in new leaves, the grass young and juicy. The countryside was alive with activity and mad with life:

birds darted in the hedgerows, chirruping madly, bees buzzed lazily in the warm air, eddies of tiny summer flies whirled about after their own strange devices. Amongst all this, the house sat, ancient, benign and almost heartstoppingly beautiful.

She had filled with sorrow as she took all this in. It could have been her home, the place where she belonged. But that would never happen now. It was becoming clearer and clearer that Harry couldn't forgive her for what had happened. She wasn't even sure she could forgive herself.

Harry had never understood how unalike they were, what different lives they led. He'd been worshipped all his life. His parents adored him, he'd been cherished from the day he was born. He didn't know what it was to crave approval, to need love, to find it anywhere you knew how.

My problem, Jemima reflected, *is that I never learned how to say no. Not to other people and not to myself.*

She didn't want to stay in the castle on a day like this. It was always dark and gloomy inside and when the summer came, it felt emptier and lonelier than ever. Perhaps it could have been different if he'd allowed her to make it the home she'd longed for with him. Jemima had envisaged the most glorious parties at Herne. She'd wanted to invite all her friends for weekend after weekend. She'd yearned to throw open the doors, clean out all the rooms and have people to stay. What was this huge house designed for, if not people? Those lords in the Great Hall did not live in this place alone, or just with their wives and children. The place would have been crammed full of friends, relations, servants, staff, animals and all manner of passers-through. That was the nature of these homes. They were never intended to be private houses, they were built to be great and extraordinary public places, where a noble family could be observed going about its life, where dozens of people were fed and housed each day. They were not supposed to be shut up and closed off, with no one to admire the brilliance of the stonework, the ornate plaster, the rich tapestries and fine damask curtains; the paintings of long-dead people were staring out in their galleries at nothing.

Harry did not agree. He was desperate to preserve the house and that, for him, meant closing it away, mothballing it. No one would be allowed in save the honoured few, his friends from school and university, his close-knit little circle.

That was his way of saving Herne: cutting back, shutting down. The house was hardly heated in winter. The interior, save for Jemima's own room, had not been touched in nearly twenty years. Money went on immediate and urgent repairs and just getting through another year. Harry would not hear of opening the house to the paying public.

'They'd destroy it,' he'd say stubbornly. 'Besides, who'd want to see it in this state? It would be more trouble than it's worth.'

Jemima had always felt that was a shame. There were so many treasures that no one ever saw. It was like Karl Lagerfeld designing his latest collection and then shutting it away for no one to see, enjoy and applaud. To her, beautiful things were made to be looked at. What else were they for?

She wandered through the deserted house. At the door to the estate office, she stopped, remembering the day almost two years ago when she'd gone in that fateful afternoon. She pressed her ear close to the door and listened. There was no sound from inside. Once, the door had stood open most of the time, Guy's merry voice coming loudly from within as he chatted on the phone or to his assistant. Harry would bound in and out all day to chase up bits of estate business or just for a bit of time to relax and banter with Guy. Guy always made him smile. He was a ray of light in the house. Everyone gravitated towards him. Even Teri, whose favourite had always been Harry, couldn't resist taking him cups of tea and plates of biscuits.

Now the office was closed up and deserted. The new estate manager must work off site, Jemima realised. Harry didn't trust anyone any more, it seemed.

She let herself out of an external door and into the gardens. On this side of the house were the kitchen gardens, still faithfully tended by the gardener of twenty years, and they produced mounds of delicious fresh fruit and vegetables. It was too early in the year for the harvest to have really begun, but the signs were there: soon there would be strawberries, raspberries, blackcurrants and redcurrants. The vegetable gardens would be teeming with lettuces, tomatoes, courgettes, peas, beans, corn and more. The greenhouses would provide yet more: grapes, cucumbers, peppers, Italian bell tomatoes, basil . . . There was far too much for the household to use. Harry sent most of it to local farm shops. Every little scrap of profit helped.

She walked up and down the pathways between the beds, savouring the fresh, green scent of the gardens, the earthy, peaty smell of plants soaking up sunshine and feeding their fruit with it. The red-brick walls were reflecting the morning heat. She pulled off her pink cashmere jumper and found it was plenty warm enough to wear only her little white Comme des Garçons T-shirt. From the gardens, she walked towards the old stable block, now empty. Harry kept two hunters but he no longer stabled them here. He didn't have the time or staff to manage their upkeep, so they were at stables a couple of miles away where they could be cared for and exercised properly.

The stables were cool and dark, scented with hay and the faint tangy aroma of manure. Old tack hung on the walls and bits of ancient farm machinery had been dumped here too.

'Another waste,' muttered Jemima to herself. 'It's all falling further into rack and ruin.'

She looked at her watch. Surely Harry would be back by now. She wandered slowly to the house, reluctant to leave the peace and quiet of the old stable block and carriage houses. They were so picturesque, with their quaint arched doorways, battered wooden gates and flagged floors. But she knew she couldn't put off seeing Harry much longer.

She was coming back to the side door when she heard the roar of an engine and the crunch of gravel in front of the house. Harry had returned. Inside the house, it seemed gloomier than ever in contrast to the bright day outside. She walked along the corridor towards the hall. Suddenly, a dark shape appeared in front of her. She blinked.

'Hello, Jemima,' said Harry quietly. 'Good to see you.'

He came towards her, his outline resolving in the full, flesh and blood Harry she remembered so well.

'Hi, Harry.' She tilted one cheek up for him to kiss.

'Have you had lunch?'

'No.'

'Then let's go and do that. Teri's laid something out for us on the terrace.'

They went out to the terrace. It was beautifully warm, sheltered from the breeze, the old grey stones already toasty from the absorbed rays of sunshine. Teri had put on a spread of cold ham, chicken, cheese, salads and fresh brown bread. A Pouilly-Fumé was chilling in a bucket beside two crystal wine glasses.

'This is very nice,' Jemima said, sitting down.

'It feels like summer's really here, doesn't it?' Harry joined her. 'God, I love this time of year.'

'Even though you can't shoot anything.'

'Plenty of other things to keep me occupied.' He passed her a plate.

'How is everything at Herne?'

As they ate, Harry told her how the estate was progressing: the farm was doing well, the yields were

444

high. The price of wheat was helping, of course, and he was glad he'd stuck to arable when people were urging him to turn more land over to dairy production. Rents were good and steady. But the house was still sucking away most of his income. The bequest from Jemima's mother was earmarked for the roof, and just that one job would use almost all of it.

'So there's still a lot to do here. As soon as one problem gets cleared up, another raises its ugly head,' Harry said. He sipped at the cold white wine. 'And you? How's the Trevellyan project going?'

'Things are certainly quite different to how they used to be,' Jemima said almost wistfully. 'We're progressing well but I'm afraid I will have to sell my flat.'

'What, Eaton Square?' Harry looked concerned. 'Really?'

Jemima nodded. 'It's worth a lot. I've got to free up the cash. We desperately need it.' She told him briefly about the situation they'd found themselves in, about the way that the French department store managers had been so dismissive of her, and how their English counterparts had been much the same when she had tried to approach them, if a little more friendly in the way they did it. She explained about the cost of launching a new perfume and of her struggle to come up with a famous face for the brand. And the fact that unless they could break into the American market, they were doomed to remain just a small-time niche perfume house for ever.

By the time she finished, Harry was smiling at her.

'What?' she said, slightly cross. 'It's not funny, you know.'

'I know, I know. It's just so strange to hear all these things coming out of your mouth. Not so long ago, it was all about your society friends. I mean, what's Tiggy up to? And Martha? And Gigi de Monte Carlo, or whatever that ridiculous princess's name was?'

'They're all fine.' Jemima shrugged. 'I haven't seen anyone for ages. Just my closest friends, really. And my sisters. We seem to spend all our time together these days. I'm too exhausted after a day in the office to go out much.'

'You look different too.'

'Oh, don't . . .' Jemima rolled her eyes and blushed slightly. 'I'm hideous, I know. I haven't had my eyebrows threaded for weeks. My hair hasn't been touched for a fortnight. I've had to give up my usual treatments. There's just no time. It doesn't matter all that much, though, as I'm not seeing anyone or going anywhere. Still, there's a big party next week so I'll be able to justify a bit of spit and polish for once.'

'Whose party? Anyone I know?'

'Oh no. It's business.'

Harry laughed out loud, rocking back in his chair.

'What?' pouted Jemima. 'What's so funny?'

'It's business! You should see your face – all wide-eyed, as if you've never gone to any other kind of party in your life. Honestly, Jemima, usually you'd be rabbiting on about who's shagging whom, and how much money Toto Boringville is spending on his

446

birthday bash, and where you're going to spend your next holiday – where are you going this year, incidentally?'

Jemima blinked at him. 'Are you mad? I can't go anywhere. We're launching in November. It's so close and there's so much to do.'

Harry leaned towards her, his blue eyes serious. 'Well, well, I do believe you've found a purpose in life. At last. And do you know what? It suits you.'

Jemima felt affronted. She had always had a purpose in life. Perhaps it wasn't so obvious as Harry's – he had this house to maintain. But hers had been to live happily and well and to enjoy herself. She had to admit, though, that these last months had been absorbing and interesting. She had learned so much . . . 'Perhaps you're right,' she conceded.

'I am right. You know what? You look younger, without all that gunk on your face and that perfectly glossy hair. You look natural, pretty . . . and you've got a spark about you that says you actually do something with your brain.'

Jemima stared at him. She couldn't pretend it wasn't very nice to be complimented by Harry. But really – what was the point? It was ironic that he was starting to respect her now, wasn't it? When it was all too late.

'Is my spark as interesting as Letty Stewart's?' she asked quietly.

Harry said nothing but stared out towards the lawns that stretched away to the dark woods beyond. Only his knee twitching gave away his inner turmoil. She watched and waited, the silence between them stretching out until she was desperate to break it herself. At last he spoke.

'It's true that Letty has visited me here a couple of times. She came with Rollo and Emma. She's a very sweet girl. Lots of fun.'

'I'm *sure* she's simply masses of fun,' Jemima said tartly. 'But I can't say I found her terrifically amusing.'

Harry shot her an agonised look. 'Please, Jemima. Let's talk about this sensibly without getting snide or nasty or upset or rude.' He took a gulp from his wine glass. 'I asked you here because we need to talk about where we stand, about what's happening between us. We need to talk about the future of our marriage.'

'*Is* there any future for our marriage?'

'That's what we have to find out.'

'Are you in love with Letty Stewart?' she demanded. She realised that the question had been drumming away inside her head for weeks now and that she was desperate to know the answer. She had come prepared for Harry to make a great declaration of his new passion, of his desire to divorce her at once. The fact that he'd been so friendly, that he'd talked to her about the estate and about Trevellyan had wrong-footed her. Now she remembered how badly she needed to know.

He stared at her, his gaze skimming her face and body. He looked down at her white T-shirt, straining tightly across her chest, the slim jeans, the striped canvas and cork sandals on her feet. He looked at her soft blonde hair, longer now, falling in loose waves over her shoulders. For a moment, she thought he was going to reach out to her, but he didn't.

'You sent me to her,' he said at last. 'Remember? You told me to go to her bed.'

'So I suppose you went and screwed her, did you? How you must have hated that! Don't pretend it was my fault; you were slavering over her all bloody evening! You didn't need much encouragement.'

Harry took a deep breath. 'Look, I promised myself I wouldn't let this degenerate the way it usually does. We always get furious with each other and then call each other names, then someone storms out and that's the end of rational discussion for another six months. Not this time. We have to get past that.'

'How can we?' whispered Jemima. A soft breeze blew her hair across her face and she brushed it away. 'You're sleeping with someone else.'

There was a long pause. Harry seemed to be struggling with himself. Then he said slowly, 'But, Jemima, look at what you've done . . .'

Her temper flared up again. 'Oh, I knew it wouldn't be long before we got on to that!'

'We have to talk about it!' exclaimed Harry. 'We have to talk about the fact that you'll shag anything that moves. Do you know how that feels for me? When I walk into a room and know that you've had half the men in it and will probably have the other half before too long? I know you cheat on me, and I know you get pleasure from it, from knowing I know. You want to punish me, and I don't even know why. Christ!' He buried his head in his hands. When he spoke his voice was muffled. 'I even had to see it with my own eyes.'

'I only do it because you don't love me!' she cried.

Then she stopped suddenly, abruptly. *What did I just say? What the* hell *did I just say?*

He looked up at her, and rubbed his hand through his fair hair, leaving it spiky and dishevelled. 'How can you say that, Jemima?' he said in a small voice. Then, loudly, 'I fucking adored you! You said you loved me too. We got married, we promised to be faithful to each other, and I believed we meant it. And then you slept with Guy!'

She stood up, her voice trembling. 'You didn't understand about that, you've never tried to understand. I tried to explain –'

'What was there to understand?' he demanded. His eyes were angry now. 'I walked in on my wife and my best friend, and he had you up against the wall, fucking you. I could see his bare arse moving while he pumped into you, and your face . . . you were in fucking ecstasy. It was only when you realised I was there that you stopped looking like a pig in shit. Don't try and tell me that you didn't enjoy it, that he made you do it.'

'He didn't *make* me do it!' she protested. 'But he gave me no choice! He set out to seduce me, he knew exactly my weak points, he made it his mission to charm me, to get me . . .'

'But Jemima, you did have a choice. You could have said no. You could have said "I'm married and I love my husband, I belong to someone else", but you didn't. You said yes! You let it happen.'

'I know, I know . . .' Her hands were trembling now, her legs felt weak underneath her. *I'm usually so strong, so capable. Why do I feel like a child?* She knew why it

450

was: she had been in the wrong. She needed forgive-
ness. She longed for his pardon, but she didn't know
how to ask for it and she was terrified that the answer
would be no. She was afraid that Harry would turn
his back on her and banish her, just as her father had
turned his back on her all those years ago. So she had
decided to show him that she didn't care, that she
wasn't sorry, that she didn't love him. But the truth?

She couldn't face the truth, even now. She knew
that. It was too painful, too dreadful. She turned
towards the house and started to stumble away.

'That's right, Jemima! Run away, just like you always
do,' cried Harry.

Her eyes filled with hot tears. She heard up him
stand and come after her. She began to hurry towards
the terrace doors but he caught up with her and
grabbed her hand, turning her round.

'Please,' he said in a desperate voice. 'All I've ever
wanted to know is *why*. We were in love, I know we
were. I would never, ever have cheated on you. Why
did you sleep with Guy?'

She couldn't meet his gaze. She stared down at the
grey-green stone of the terrace. It was blurred by tears.
They spilled over and ran down her cheeks. 'I don't
know,' she said, her voice cracking. 'I'm so sorry.' The
words seemed so feeble, so incapable of expressing
the bitter regret she felt over a moment's weakness.
'He flattered me. He paid attention to me. When you
were out, hunting or fishing or working, he was always
there, ready to talk and laugh. He sympathised with
me because you left me alone so much, and I was

451

bored in the house all day with nothing to do. It was such a change from my life in London. But Guy was there.' She sniffed and tried to wipe away the tears that were falling faster and faster. 'I can't really explain how powerful he was, he knew exactly how to charm me. He was jealous of you, I realise that now. He wanted to win me from you, even if only for a moment. I think he just wanted to know that he'd had your wife. He couldn't have your title or your money or your house, but he could get you where it would hurt you most.'

'But you *let* him,' whispered Harry. 'How could you know all that and still let him?'

'I know it now. I didn't know it then. I didn't realise how stupid I was being, how easily I was falling into his trap.' She stared at him, straight in the eye. 'You know that all my life I've yearned for affection. I've always expressed it physically. I realise you're not the same as me, that you don't treat sex the way I do. For me, it was always fine to sleep with partners, friends, strangers . . . as long as you're both happy it's OK. I was young, I didn't really understand what a marriage meant. I didn't anticipate how seriously you took it. I didn't appreciate how deeply what happened with me and Guy would wound you. But now, when I think about you and that . . . that Letty . . .' She began to sob. 'I'm so jealous! It hurts so much. Now I realise how you must have felt. I don't know how to tell you how sorry I am. I was stupid and selfish, and I wish, wish, *wish* it had never happened.'

He put his arms round her and hugged her closely. She pressed her head against his chest, remembering how warm and sweet it had always felt.

'Can you forgive me?' she whispered between sobs.

'Jemmie, Jemmie,' he murmured.

Her sobbing eased off and she felt calm. She pulled back to look at him.

He gazed down at her. His own eyes were wet. 'It's so hard. I want to forgive you. But I can't, not after ... If it had just been that, then perhaps we might have got over it. But the baby ...'

She cried out, pulled away from him and dashed inside, half blinded by her tears and the sudden indoor darkness. She ran through the drawing room, down the hall and found herself in the library. Inside, she looked wildly from wall to wall as though expecting to see a getaway route. When there was none, she ran to the library steps, a polished mahogany ladder on a rail that could be moved smoothly across the high shelves. Crawling behind it, she curled herself up and buried her head in her arms, crying softly to herself.

A few minutes later, she heard Harry come into the room and walk slowly over to her. He crouched down beside her and put his hand lightly on her head.

'Don't cry, old girl,' he said gently. 'I'm sorry, I really am. It must have been so terrible to lose it like that. I feel for you, even if it was Guy's baby.'

She lifted her head and looked up at him, her blue-grey eyes still filled with tears. 'But Harry,' she whispered. 'It wasn't Guy's baby. It was yours.'

39

The atrium was too hot in this weather, Tara decided. In the winter it was deliciously warm, but on a day like today, it was like lunching in a greenhouse. Still, this was her first lunch out with girlfriends in an age, so she ought to try and enjoy it.

She, Susannah and Olivia had met at the Chelsea restaurant for a lovely, relaxing girly lunch. It had been supposed to be a way to forget about all the stresses and strains of the week but of course, the rogue photographers hanging around outside her house had reminded her that life was far from back to normal. And then they had spent most of the time talking about the situation with Gerald over their chicken liver salads.

'It's just so awful, darling,' Olivia said sympathetically. 'I don't know what I'd do if Jeremy put me in the same situation. I'd probably throw him out too.'

'It's not quite as straightforward as that,' Tara said, but she didn't want to go into detail even with her closest friends. It was too private and painful to talk about.

'So what are you going to do now?' Susannah asked.

'The house has got five viewings today.' Tara shrugged. 'It's in a very desirable location. You can't fault Gerald on that. Perhaps he should have gone into property, he's always had an eye for a good house.'

'Where are you going to go?' Olivia asked, picking up a morsel of lettuce on the end of her fork and looking at it appraisingly.

'I don't know. I'd like something with some charm, some character. But to get the space we need for the value of half the Holland Park house – well, I don't know. We might have to go south.'

'Richmond?' asked Olivia, raising her eyebrows.

'Or Wimbledon?' enquired Susannah, pouring out some more fizzy mineral water.

'I was thinking about Clapham.'

'Oh, poor darling,' cooed Olivia. 'Are you sure that's necessary?'

Tara laughed. 'You don't know it at all, do you? There are lots of lovely houses round there, and very reasonably priced too. You can get a large house in a great location with a big garden for around two to three million. And these days, there are some real bargains to be had.'

'Really?' Olivia looked astonished. 'Only three million?'

'Yes. So I'll easily be able to afford something decent with the half of the money I get from Holland Park, and still have something to tide me over until I get Trevellyan back on the road or have to go back to my old job.'

'Will Eric take you back?'

'I hope so,' Tara said thoughtfully. 'He knows I was damn good at my job.'

'Yes, but Curzons are thinking of cutbacks, or so I gather.' Susannah gave her a concerned look. 'You know how things are so much tougher in that market at the moment.'

'Yes, we've all heard that. But there's still a hell of a lot of business to be done and money to be made. The world doesn't stop turning just because a few banks have cocked up. Confidence will win the day, I'm sure of that.' Tara smiled at her friends. 'Anyway, if Eric doesn't want me, I'll find someone who will. Or I'll set up on my own.' She lifted a glass. 'Now, I'd like to make a toast. This morning my husband flew out of Heathrow on his way back to South Africa. God knows I don't wish him ill but I'm glad to see him go. I've been under his thumb for most of my adult life and it's time for me to take control and start living the way *I* want to live. No more ridiculous, beige-coloured mansion done up like a country club. I'm going to find out who I am and how I want to live.'

'Hear, hear!' cried Susannah, clinking her glass against Tara's.

'To you, Tara,' said Olivia, tapping her own glass to the other two.

'And . . . I'm going to spend more time with my children too. I've got to get to know them before they grow up without me. And now their father's gone, they're going to need me more than ever.'

They all sipped their champagne. Then Olivia said, 'But Clapham, darling . . . honestly, are you sure you can't afford to stay in Notting Hill with us?'

Tara laughed. 'You'll be surprised by what I find. You'll see.'

Tara sat at the desk in the study, making notes on her laptop of what needed to be achieved the following week. The study looked quite different now. She'd had all of Gerald's possessions boxed up, having thrown out whatever was beyond repair after he'd run amok, and the boxes were piled up against the wall, waiting to be dispatched to South Africa. The shelves were bare and the room curiously featureless, except for the vast plasma screen and the desk, where Tara had set up her computer. The phone rang as she was filling in a spreadsheet to calculate production expenses.

'Tara Trevellyan,' she said into the earpiece. It was strange but pleasant to use her maiden name again. She hadn't been Tara Trevellyan since she'd been at Oxford.

'Tara, it's me. Jemima.'

'Hi, Mimi. Are you OK?' Jemima's voice sounded peculiar, almost tinny.

'I wondered if I could come round.'

'Of course. I'm not doing anything much. The babies are in bed. It's a shame they won't see you, they miss their Aunt Mimi.'

'I'll take them out soon for a lovely day. But tonight, I really need to talk to you.'

'Come over. I'll get Viv to make something delicious.'

An hour later, the doorbell rang.

'I'll get it!' Tara shouted, heading for the door. She opened it to Jemima who was wearing a large pair of dark glasses, despite the evening's gloom outside. 'Hi, darling.' She kissed her sister's cheek. 'I hope you didn't drive in those things – very dangerous.'

'No I didn't. But when I parked the car, I noticed someone sitting in a grey Citroën opposite the house. They're watching it. I didn't like the look of them.'

'Press, I suppose.' Tara shut the door behind her. 'I thought they would lose interest once Gerald had left the country but maybe it will take a day or two more.'

Jemima took off her glasses. Tara gasped. 'Holy shit, Jemima! What's happened?' Jemima's eyes were swollen red, the lids purple and translucent and twice their normal size. 'I've been to see Harry.' Her face began to crumple.

'Oh God. OK. Look, come to the sitting room. I'm going to get you a brandy or something and you can tell me all about it.'

Sitting on the sofa, a cashmere blanket wrapped around her to stop her shivering, Jemima sipped at the cognac and told Tara what had happened that day.

'You mean he didn't know that the baby you lost was his?' Tara said, incredulous.

'That's what I could never understand. That's what hurt me so much. When I had the miscarriage, he was so cold, so horrible to me. I knew that what had happened with Guy had hurt him, but I hoped that

458

the baby would make everything all right between us. We'd wanted a child so much. We'd spent hours talking about how we'd bring him or her up. We wanted lots and lots, if we could have them. When I told him I was pregnant, he was so happy. He knew it couldn't be Guy's, I was sure of that, because . . . well . . . Guy and I had only had sex that one time and for obvious reasons it wasn't brought to a conclusion.'

'Oh, Jemima.' Tara reached for her hand, her eyes sad.

'I know, I know . . . it was the stupidest mistake I'd ever made. I wish it had never happened. But it did. And I thought that we could get over it, that it was something we could put behind us. At first it seemed as though we could. Then, suddenly, Harry changed. He turned cold but he wouldn't say why. He started to treat me as though he hated me, and then, when I lost the baby . . .' Jemima closed her eyes at the memory '. . . he didn't seem to care. He didn't even seem concerned about me. When the doctor told us that the baby was dead, he just shrugged and walked out of the room. He left me alone.'

'So that explains it. I never could understand it, it didn't seem like Harry at all. But why on earth did he suddenly decide that the baby was Guy's?'

'Because Guy told him.'

Tara was shocked. 'Told him? How? Harry would have refused to see him, wouldn't he?'

'Guy heard about the pregnancy, I suppose, and for reasons I can't begin to understand, he wrote to Harry. He told him that the affair had been going on for a long time and that the baby was definitely his, I'd told him so.'

Tara leaned forward and rubbed Jemima's hands. They were icy cold despite the warm evening. 'Oh, honey. Harry was an idiot for believing him. Why on earth would he take Guy's version over yours?'

Jemima laughed bitterly. 'Oh, you don't know Guy. He's so clever with words, he's such an expert manipulator. He would have used things I told him innocently. He'd have constructed very plausible scenarios. I can hardly blame Harry for being taken in by him. I was.'

'But still,' Tara said softly, 'he should have spoken to you about it. Mimi, what a frightful mess.'

'I've cried and cried all day,' Jemima said. 'It's all so awful – all the misunderstandings and hurt. When I think back to how I felt when he left me after our baby had died . . .'

'So how did you leave things today?'

'Once we'd brought it all out in the open and realised what had happened – well, it was very strange. We were both sitting on the floor in the library, squeezed behind the stepladder. Honestly,' Jemima laughed, 'a bloody great castle to roam around in and the only place we can find is crammed behind a ladder. We talked for a long time. At the end of it, Harry went very quiet. Then he just kissed me on the cheek and told me he had to be alone for a while. Then he vanished.'

'What did you do?'

'I don't know. I waited. I lost hope, all over again.

I needed him, but he didn't come back. In the end, I picked up my bag from the hall, got in my car and drove back.'

'So you didn't say goodbye?'

Jemima shook her head. 'He was nowhere to be seen. He didn't answer his phone or my texts. I couldn't bear to stay in that place on my own. I really needed to be with someone. I hope you don't mind that it was you.'

'Of course I don't. I'm glad you thought of me.' She sat down on the sofa next to Jemima and put her arms round her sister. She hadn't ever seen her as dejected as this. 'Mimi, you still love Harry, don't you?'

Jemima drooped her head on her sister's arm and nodded silently.

Poppy noticed that Jemima was not her usual ebullient self at work on Monday morning, but she decided not to press her about it. It seemed that someone's fortunes were always on the wane when someone else's were rising. Not so long ago, Jemima had been blissfully married while Poppy was trying to deal with the heartbreak of splitting up from Tom. Now Jemima's relationship was on the skids while Poppy's was going from strength to strength.

She'd forgotten how much being in love could envelop the whole world in a rosy glow. Everything felt beautiful and positive and she was certain she could achieve anything with George by her side. He was the sort of man she had longed for: sensitive, artistic, funny and kind. She'd always known that money wasn't important to her and that she needed a man who felt the same. She just wasn't sure how she would ever meet him. And then fate came along and put him in her path. How very, very lucky . . .

'Poppy, are you concentrating?' Tara said severely.

'Yes, yes,' Poppy said quickly, banishing thoughts of George from her mind, and sitting up straight. 'You were just talking about the refit.'

'That's right. We've had a couple of men from the planning office round. We've shown them our revised plans. The designers have come up with ingenious false walls that will fit over the panelling, leaving it completely untouched, and also seal it off from moisture and help preserve it. That seems like an adequate compromise and we're hoping the planners will go for it. We should hear later. If so, we can press ahead.'

'We've got people coming in later with samples for fixtures and fittings, so please be free at three for a meeting here in the boardroom,' said Donna. 'But the main thing is that we need to turn our attention to the marketing campaign. We have to get started. Most importantly, we have to begin generating as much press interest as we can. I want to get them hungry for information on what's happening here, and start sending out the message that something big, exciting and newsworthy is on the way. Now. I want to talk to you about this party you're going to on Wednesday.' Donna pulled a piece of stiff card from her folder and pushed it out on to the table so they could all see it that it was a large invitation with flowing dark engraved lettering, embossed with the FFB logo and Erin de Cristo's company cipher.

'The Ferrera party,' Jemima said, perking up. 'It's a pretty invitation, isn't it?'

Donna raised her eyebrows. 'As plush as I expected. And this bash is at Spencer House, I see. How grand. They don't let just anyone in there, you know. I'm jealous.'

'Do you want to come too?' Tara said quickly. 'I'm sure I could arrange it.'

'No. Might be a little awkward, with my ex-boss there. You can tell me all about it afterwards and from what I've heard, it's going to be quite the event of the season. I've had a little chat with a friend of mine in the de Cristo camp and she's filled me in on a few of the names who are going to be there. It's A-list, people, it's very, very glam.' Donna reeled off the names of several Hollywood actresses, high-profile models, businessmen and influential media types.

Tara raised her eyebrows. 'That is impressive. This guy has a good operation.'

'So you three really have to pull out all the stops for this party. I want you to get noticed! And you must network as much as you can. Schmooze all the journalists you can. Look fabulous and for Christ's sake, wear *Tea Rose*!' Donna glanced over at Jemima. 'By the way, Neave is going to be there.'

'Is she?' Jemima looked eager for a moment and then her face fell. 'It's no good, her people just aren't interested. Besides, she's being auditioned for some big movie role, apparently. There's no way she's going to be tempted to promote our fragrance when her future seems to lie in films. She's probably got her eye on being the face of Chanel one day, not Trevellyan.'

'You never know. See if you can charm her, anyway. Now, I've lined up everything for Wednesday already, we're going all out to make you three newsworthy. I've booked a suite at Duke's Hotel on Saint James's. It's a few minutes from Spencer House. That's where you'll be getting ready and I want you there no later than lunchtime on Wednesday afternoon.'

'What on earth are you going to do to us?' Poppy asked, a little fearfully.

'You'll see.' Donna smiled. 'I promise you'll like it.'

'What've you got?' Flick said. She pressed the phone close to her ear, and spun her chair round so that she was facing out over the river. It was the way she always liked to sit while she took her calls. It also meant that no one in the newsroom could lip read her conversations or note her expressions.

'Not much,' said Ben. 'Adrian tailed the older sister today. She did fuck all.'

'What about the middle one?'

'I went round to her flat but there was no sign of her. She was gone all day and then bowled up at the older one's place in Holland Park.'

'Mmm. Maybe I'm barking up the wrong tree here. Maybe there's really nothing to this story. But something tells me I'm right. Don't ask me why. Have we tried tailing the younger one?'

'No one's interested in her, are they?'

'No, you're right. We'll keep on the other two for a few more days. Listen, I've got an idea. I want you to go to that castle in Dorset, the one that belongs to Jemima's husband. Sniff around there and see if anyone's got any juicy gossip or some good leads.'

'Dorset?' Ben groaned. 'Fuck off!'

'Do as you're told, matey, or it'll be the worse for you. And you'd better come back with something worth bending my ear about, all right?'

'Ah, shit. All right.'

Jemima was finding it almost impossible to concentrate. Why hadn't Harry contacted her? It had been two days, and she'd heard nothing. Surely he would let her know what he felt now that he knew the truth. It was all she could do not to phone Herne and beg to speak to him, but she knew him well enough to be certain that she had to wait. All she could do was be ready to take his call or his email. But the suspense was appalling.

Her laptop chimed to tell her a new message had arrived. Quickly, she clicked on her screen, hoping it was from Harry. Disappointed, she saw it was from ali@goldblatt-mindenhall.com:

Hi, Jemima

Give me a call, I've got some results for you.

Ali

465

She phoned him at once.

'Yeah, I've had a look through the details of your mother's will. The question of whether you can sell or not is quite a complex one and the answer is contained in an appendix to the bequest clause, laying out the terms and conditions, if you like.'

'Right. So what's the upshot?'

Ali paused for a moment. 'You can't sell. Or at least, you can, but you have to offer the company to Jecca Trevellyan or Jecca Farnese, depending on which name she is currently known by, and give her the chance to match the price. If she can match or exceed the price, you're obliged to sell it to her.'

'What? This is absolutely crazy! What was Mother thinking of?'

'She certainly wanted to bind you into this family business of yours, didn't she? This will is pretty water-tight, I'm afraid.'

'I suppose the comfort is that Jecca couldn't possibly afford it – at least, I assume she couldn't.' Jemima thought quickly. 'Ali, could you start trying to locate Jecca? We've all been closing our minds to her and hoping we'll never have to bother with her, but from the looks of things, it's going to be much better to be prepared.'

'Is this still a favour?' said Ali in a low, intimate voice. 'If it is, we're going to have to have favours you can do to repay me.'

To Jemima's surprise, she felt a churning of nausea in her stomach. *Ali's a sexy, attractive man*, she reminded herself. *We've already had very pleasant sex together. Why would I feel sick at the thought of sleeping with him?* 'Um . . . this is company work, actually. We do need to locate Jecca Farnese.' She had never been able to bring herself to call Jecca by her adopted surname. 'I'll send over a file with everything in it you'll need to help you get started.'

Ali laughed softly 'OK. No problem. I'm on it. Oh, and by the way – the latest version of your mother's will was dated two weeks before her death.'

Jemima blinked. '*Two weeks?* What changes were made from previous versions?'

'I don't know that. I'll have to look out what we have on file.'

'OK, Ali. Thanks.'

'You're most welcome.'

Jemima put the phone down and stared at it thoughtfully. Two weeks? That seemed a little too recent for comfort.

40

The suite looked like a very opulent dressing room for three gorgeous princesses, although right now the princesses themselves were in varying stages of preparation for the big night.

Poppy's hair was stretched over enormous rollers and she was sitting in her underwear in front of the dressing-table mirror, her head back so that a make-up artist could work on her face.

Jemima had squeezed herself into the tightest corset she could get into and was now prancing round the room in her panties, nylons and a pair of satin high heels, singing Madonna songs while the hairdresser tried to persuade her to sit down and have her heated rollers put in.

Tara, a little more decent in one of the hotel's bathrobes and her hair in tin-foil strips, was standing with Donna by a rack of beautiful evening gowns, each one more exquisite than the last.

'They're all John Galliano?' Tara asked.

Donna nodded. 'They're thematically linked, look. Obviously you can't all turn up in the same dress, and the same colour would look perhaps a little gauche. But these are very similar, each just a touch different. We've got cool ivory, satin pink and mint green. I think Poppy should be in the green. We've had her hair tinted auburn which will look fabulous with it. As for you and Jemima, you can fight it out as to who wears ivory and who wears pink.'

'I think I know who's won that battle,' Tara said wearily, nodding at Jemima's feet as her sister skipped by. The satin high heels were in a delicate shell pink.

'OK. But cream is very becoming, especially with your hair tinted a little darker. You'll look stunning . . .' Donna smiled at her encouragingly. 'While your dresses are subtly different, you'll wear the same make-up, that's vital. You must all have the exact same shade of red on your lips. And I've got these matching diamond necklaces as well.'

Donna produced a black velvet jeweller's case and opened it to reveal a simple but exquisite necklace of tiny, overlapping leaves, each one encrusted with white diamonds.

Tara whistled. 'Shit, Donna! Three of these? They must have cost a fortune!'

'They are indeed worth a small fortune. Luckily for us, they are on loan for the evening. That's why Bert is sitting outside.'

'I wondered who the bouncer was.'

'Very necessary for insurance. Believe me, you three are going to make quite a splash tonight. There'll be

469

lots of beautiful women, most in standard black, a few showing far too much tit and arse to be pretty. But no one will come close to you, I promise. It's the power of three.'

'Very clever,' said Tara admiringly. She could see exactly the effect Donna was after.

'It's what you pay me for.' Donna smiled.

Five hours later, the girls were at last ready to go. Donna had made them eat a small meal before putting on their dresses: protein rich to fill them up but nothing that would swell their stomachs. Then, after their make-up was retouched, they got into their dresses and stood side by side.

'Stunning,' breathed Donna. 'Don't you agree?'

The make-up artists and hairdressers gazed proudly at their handiwork.

'You look like something from a fairytale,' said one. 'Three beautiful sisters.'

'Or the Oscars night. Like Grace Kelly, Rita Hayworth and Ava Gardner,' added another.

'Oh, we like you,' purred Jemima. 'You say just the right things.'

But they all knew they were knock-outs.

Poppy's auburn tint made her hair a rich chestnut red and the make-up artist had given her all-over body make-up to make her skin even more alabaster. Her mint-green silk gown had a thick pleat of material that skimmed her shoulders, criss-crossing over the bodice to a tiny waist. The skirt was long, to mid calf, cut close to the body and slightly flared at the back, and she wore matching mint-green satin heels, five inches high.

Next to her, Jemima was all pink and blonde, her silk dress embroidered down one side with silver flowers. The fabric followed the same pattern as Poppy's dress, wrapping about the shoulders and criss-crossing over to the waist, but her dress had a small pink belt with a diamond clasp nipping her in at the waist and her skirt, which fell two inches below the knee, was fuller, with net skirts underneath.

Tara pivoted on one cream satin heel, admiring her dress. It was, she thought, sexier than the other two. It was low-cut with a sweetheart neckline and cap sleeves. Just below the waist, the skirt was gathered up to one hip, where a large, silver embroidered flower, the mirror of the ones climbing down Jemima's dress, held pleats of ivory satin material in place before they fell sexily downwards to her knees. The darker hair suited her, she thought. Her skin seemed finer and her eyes bluer.

Three mouths were painted with the same rich, pink-red, 1950s Hollywood shade. Three matching necklaces glittered round their throats. The peep-toe satin slippers had been perfectly dyed to match each dress, but they were identical in style.

Donna was right, the effect was mesmerising.

'The power of three,' said Donna again, unable to hide her pleasure at the effect she had created. 'Three Charlie's Angels. Three Trevellyan sisters. One last thing.'

She opened her handbag and took from it a small

471

atomiser. Stepping forward she sprayed it hard, wafting the scent across all three sisters.

'Remember . . . *Tea Rose*. I want you to mention it to every single person you talk to tonight. Now, it's nearly nine o'clock. The car is waiting for you downstairs – I know, you'll be in it for all of three minutes, but you can hardly walk down Saint James's, especially not in those rocks. So, come on, girls. Let's go get 'em.'

Spencer House was lit up, its windows blazing. Leading up to the front door was a red carpet, edged on either side by ropes. Behind the ropes, the press were massed. Hundreds of photographers, the ones at the back mounted on stools or stepladders, went crazy each time a limousine arrived to unload another famous face.

'Over here!' they shouted, bellowing the star's name, hoping to get them to stare, just for an instant, down their lens so they could snare the perfect shot. When people they didn't recognise emerged – heads of banks, businessmen, minor actors and models, women who were less than dazzling – there was a noticeable diminishment of excitement. The bulbs stopped flashing, the cameras were lowered, the ruder paps even told the poor things to get a fucking move-on and shift inside, to make room for the real stars.

Inside the Trevellyan limousine, the girls were nervous. Donna had allowed them one glass of champagne each to calm their nerves. 'Any more and you'll topple over on those bloody heels on your way in. That's not the reason I want you to be noticed tonight.'

'I've never wanted the press to notice me before,' breathed Jemima. 'It's strange how vulnerable it makes you feel.'

'I just hope we're not opening Pandora's box,' muttered Tara. 'You know, once you've let it out, you can't put it back. Poppy, are you really that white or is it your make-up?'

'It's make-up and sheer terror,' said Poppy, her eyes wide. 'This must be worse than going up the aisle. I'm sure I'm going to fall over getting out of the car.'

'It is worse in some ways,' said Jemima, already a little high on her champagne, having sneaked another glass when Donna wasn't paying attention. 'But look on the bright side; no matter what happens tonight, it won't be a life sentence.' She giggled.

The car drew to a halt. It was their turn. The door was opened by the uniformed footman waiting at the edge of the red carpet.

'We look gorgeous,' said Jemima. 'Come on. Let's do it.'

They emerged to a flurry of flashbulbs. Three beautiful women in stunning gowns, looking like glamorous stars? Of course they would have their picture taken . . . Then, briefly, the energy lessened. Who were they? Did anyone know? Did anyone care? Then the murmur started. The paps recognised Jemima first, from her Billy days, then Tara, then they guessed. *Trevellyan.* The muttered word flew round the press ranks as the cameras were lifted again and the bulbs popped.

'This way, Jemima!' they bellowed.

'Tara, over here!'

'Oi, Popsy, or whoever you are, look this way!'

'They're facking gorgeous,' said one photographer to another. 'Are they really English? They look too facking good.'

'They're the real thing,' his friend answered. 'But no one guessed they could look like this.'

The girls turned one side and then the other, giving the photographers what they wanted. Then, when they all felt instinctively that the press had had just enough, they turned and walked gracefully up the red carpet and through the front door, into the dazzling rooms beyond.

The house was a superb small palace built by the Spencer family in the eighteenth century as a showcase for their wealth and taste, and it was one of the finest examples of neo-classical architecture. Its interior had been restored to its original dazzling richness, and tonight it looked its very best. Uniformed footmen distributed champagne. The elaborate gilding, ornate plasterwork and fine family portraits were gently lit by candelabra. Vast displays of flowers exploded between tables offering every type of delicacy: a bowl carved from ice was lavishly full of Sevruga caviar; trays displayed rows and rows of intricate canapés, full of colour and delicacy. Bars in each beautiful, classical room, offered the finest wine, liqueurs and cocktails. Everywhere they looked, the interlinked letters of FFB were in harmony with the Erin de Cristo logo. This was a great tribute to the partnership of two successful companies, and famous faces moved easily through every room, enjoying the splendid hospitality. Gorgeous gowns were displayed alongside the most expensive suits in the world: Armani, Prada and Savile Row with its unmistakeable elegance and superb cut.

'Let's stick together,' whispered Poppy, holding her sisters' hands. 'I'm really nervous!'

'You'll be fine,' said Jemima sternly. 'You look fabulous and we have to split up to mingle. I should find Ferrera – I ought to thank him for inviting us.'

'Perhaps you'd better break the bad news,' said Tara. 'That we can't sell to him after all – at least not without offering the company elsewhere for the same price.'

'For all that matters,' said Poppy. 'We don't even know if Jecca would be interested in getting her hands on the business. She probably couldn't give a shit about us and our company.'

'You look too beautiful to have words like "shit" coming out of your mouth,' Jemima said solemnly.

Poppy laughed. Her auburn hair shimmered in the candlelight. It fell in long dark waves, glittering richly over her white shoulders. 'I wish George was here,' she said longingly.

'Forget lover boy for tonight,' counselled Tara. 'And by the looks of it, there are plenty of loaded guys here if you're feeling in the least like straying.'

'I don't think so,' Poppy said, tossing her head. 'But thanks for the suggestion.'

They each helped themselves to glass of Krug from the tray of a passing waiter, and began to wander through lavish rooms.

'There's Angelina Jolie!' hissed Jemima as they

walked past a small brunette talking earnestly to a man in a dark suit.

'I just saw Madonna gossiping with her besties, Gwyneth and Trudie. And I spotted George Clooney.' Tara giggled. 'I haven't been to a party this grand for a long time. Ferrera must have spent a fortune.'

'There's Rosie Scott-Evans, I must go and say hello. She's PR and very fertile ground for *Tea Rose*.' With that, Jemima glided away and before long was surrounded by friends and acquaintances, chattering animatedly, and making them all smell the new scent, basking in the nods of approval and admiration she received.

'She's good,' said Poppy, as she and Tara saw how well Jemima was networking.

'It's her forte, sweetie. I'm much better in the board-room.'

'I'm not quite sure where I'm best but I don't much like being looked at.'

Nevertheless, Poppy was getting a huge amount of attention: she stood out from the other glossy, perma-tanned blondes and brunettes with her paper-white skin and red hair. People were muttering as she walked past, asking who on earth she was. Then, to her immense relief, she saw someone she knew well.

'Tara, it's Archie Arundel, look.'

'For God's sake, go and say hello. It will break the ice.' Tara shooed her sister away and then continued on her own. This was certainly a triumph: the guest list was glittering and it felt the height of luxury. *I suppose this is what we're aiming at*, Tara thought. *It seems so far away from what we can achieve. If only we could sell out to Ferrera. We'd have all this too. We'd be made.* In the state dining room she passed Erin de Cristo holding court, obviously enjoying her night.

'Darling, it's vulgar, I know, but I just don't know what to spend my money on!' she hooted. 'I was going to get a villa in Capri and then I remembered – I've already got one!'

Her coterie laughed loudly.

Tara walked on, and a few moments later, she was greeted enthusiastically by some of her girlfriends and was soon absorbed into their group. When they wanted to hear about Gerald, she told them instead about *Tea Rose*, that they must spread the word with all the ladies they lunched with: a new scent was coming, the biggest new launch since Chanel's *Allure*.

The party continued, the guests relaxing as the champagne and vodka cocktails soaked into their bloodstreams. Official photographers and diarists circulated among the guests, taking photographs and looking for spicy stories for their columns. Jemima, for the first time in her life, sought them out and told them about the Trevellyan plans. She gave it a glamorous spin: Trevellyan was not a failing company with one last chance of revival, oh no. It was a grand old company business, vast and successful but a bit of a dinosaur, being pulled into the present day by three vibrant sisters with dreams of creating one of the great, classic scents.

'Trevellyan will no longer be a company of yester-year, it will be current and exciting, it will meet the needs of the twenty-first-century woman,' Jemima explained. 'We've developed a whole new image for the company and plan to expand into beauty treatments and a range of delicious fragrances for the body and the home.'

'Thank you, Lady Calthorpe,' said the journalist, busily writing everything down. 'That's so interesting. Is there any chance we could have some photographs of you and your sisters? We've all noticed how charming you look this evening.'

'You're very sweet. I'm organising a photo call for everyone who wants to take pictures a little bit later. We'll be in the Music Room at eleven o'clock.'

'Excellent.'

A footman came up to them. 'Excuse me. Mr Ferrera and Miss de Cristo request that guests go to the terrace. Thank you.'

Everyone was moving through the house towards the terrace. Some made their way out into the garden itself where a golden dais had been erected, surrounded by flaming candles. The night was velvety dark blue and it was warm enough to stand outside, even in thin silks and satins. When the guests were massed so that they could see the stage in the garden, Richard Ferrera and Erin de Cristo appeared from the darkness and mounted the platform. There was a round of applause. Ferrera, dashingly elegant in a dark Kilgour suit and mustard-coloured shirt, smiled, obviously enjoying the moment. De Cristo looked tiny beside him, stick thin in a dress from her latest range: a Grecian-style tunic of sparkling silver.

'Thank you,' he said as the applause faded. 'You are all very welcome. Thank you so much for coming. It's an honour to have you here to celebrate a very special moment. We at FFB are so happy that Erin de Cristo has decided to join us. Together we have amazing plans to take her signature style, glamour and unmatchable elegance to even greater heights of success. We want you all to be a part of that story.'

There was another ripple of applause from the appreciative crowd.

Erin de Cristo spoke in her high voice. 'I'm so thrilled to be Richard's partner. I know he shares my vision and my values. Above all, I know he appreciates creativity and artistry and would move mountains to promote and protect that. That's why FFB is the perfect home for my company. Thank you all so much – I love you.'

Ferrera continued quickly, 'Now, please continue to enjoy the party. But first – a little moment of celebration. Please indulge us.' He made a signal and all the lights on the terrace went out, those in the rooms looking over the gardens were dimmed, and the candles round the dais were snuffed.

An instant later, a firework display began, first with quiet showers of golden rain and ripples of incandescent stars exploding gently upwards from the garden. Then the colours and sounds gathered pace, as stunning firework flowers appeared, blossoming in the sky in reds, blues, oranges, greens and golds. Their beauty made even the jaded crowd sigh and aah. Finally, great golden starbursts flared magnificently into the darkness and in the grand finale, the inter-twined initials of FFB and Erin de Cristo appeared, glittering against the night sky. It was the signal for wild applause from the guests and then, as the lights came on again, a movement back inside, to the limit-less champagne and delicious food.

'Money literally up in smoke,' Jemima murmured, coming up to Poppy.

'Yes, but so pretty!' replied Poppy. 'I loved it. I haven't seen fireworks in ages.'

'We're having a photo call in twenty minutes in the Music Room. It's got lovely blue chalky walls and our dresses will look wonderful against it.'

'All right, I'm going to fix my make-up, then.'

'OK. Don't be late. I've put a lot of work in and I think we're going to get some good press tomorrow.'

Poppy went off to find the ladies' cloakroom. It was almost deserted, just one pretty girl fixing her lipstick. She and Poppy smiled at one another and the next moment, Poppy had the place to herself. She took her compact and lipstick out of her silk evening purse. Donna had made sure they all had a stick of their new shade for repairs, but really the make-up had stood up very well. Those artists knew their job: her face looked almost as perfect as it had the moment they had finished. She leaned forward to the mirror to inspect it a little more closely. Then she heard a sob come from the stall behind her.

'Oh God,' said a small, lilting, tear-soaked voice, 'what the hell am I gonna do?'

Another sob could be heard.

'Are you all right in there?' Poppy asked, going over to the cubicle door.

'No, I'm bloody not!' declared the voice. The door was kicked open from the inside to reveal a gorgeous dark-haired girl sitting on the loo seat. She was wearing half a long black taffeta gown – the bottom half. The top was hanging off her at the waist, leaving her clad in only a strapless bra. 'Look, my dress! It's ruined!'

'What happened?'

'I caught it on something on my way in here. The whole thing split down the side. So much for haute bloody couture. Now look at it! I can't wear it out there. What'll I do?' The girl blinked her green eyes at Poppy.

'Don't panic,' Poppy said brightly. 'I've got a needle and thread. I'll sew you back up.'

'You *have?*' The girl looked disbelieving. 'No one carries a sewing kit with them.'

'I do,' Poppy said. 'I'm a notorious buyer of second-hand clothes and they have a habit of falling to pieces or losing buttons at the worst possible moment. So I started carrying a needle and thread with me. You wouldn't believe how many times it's come to my rescue.'

'And now it's come to mine,' said the girl, sniffing. 'This is so kind. Thank you so much.'

'Don't worry. Now, if you turn round a bit, I'll be able to locate the seam. I don't think you should take that dress off – it looks very complicated – so I'll just do a basic running stitch that will hold the seam

481

together until you get home. Luckily I have a dark thread that shouldn't be too conspicuous.'

'You're an angel,' smiled the girl, turning round so that Poppy could start repairing the damage. 'I really owe you one.'

Tara walked through the sumptuous rooms, moving as though with a purpose but actually just drifting, watching the knots of people in conversation, the men in their black tie and the women at the peak of their beauty, as polished and preened as they could possibly be. The free booze was already beginning to tell on some of the faces which were growing increasingly flushed and animated. She passed a room that had been turned into a discotheque, the floor glittering with tiny stars and coloured lights flashing on the ceiling. A fashionable pop song was booming round the little room but only one couple was dancing, a girl in a long white dress waving her hands in the air while her partner shuffled round her, shifting his shoulders and bobbing his head. *They probably had a few drinks before they got here*, Tara thought, amused. *It will take everyone else a while before the dancing urge kicks in.*

She lifted another flute of champagne from the tray of a passing waiter and sipped it. She was nervous tonight, uncharacteristically so. After all, she went to these things all the time, on her own behalf and as Gerald's wife. Only a few months before they'd been to a State Banquet at Buckingham Palace and she couldn't have been less worried. She giggled to herself.

I have a feeling that invitations to the palace are going to be rather thin on the ground for Gerald these days.

She shrugged mentally. *I suppose I'm anxious because so much rides on this evening. I've never had to go out and sell myself quite so blatantly. I've never had so much invested in it.* Passing a great gilt-framed mirror, she saw her reflection and was startled. Was that beauty really her? Her eyes were smoky and feline, her brows elegant arches on creamy skin. The newly darkened hair was sultry, falling over her shoulders in glossy waves, and her perfectly painted mouth was nothing short of seductive. And it had to be admitted, her dress was stunning.

I suppose I'm a single woman now, as well, she thought. *How strange.*

Feeling suddenly vulnerable despite her knock-out appearance, she took a gulp of champagne and turned on her heel, determined to make her way back to the main reception room and find Poppy or Jemima for a bit of support.

'Tara, is that you? Blimey!' It was a friendly voice, one she recognised at once. She blinked and realised that she had almost walked into Vince Fowler, a banking wizard she'd known in the early days of her career. She'd always liked Vince – he was a decent man with his feet on the ground, an East End boy who'd made good but never let it change him. He was still happily married to his childhood sweetheart and still lived in the same Essex house he'd bought ten years before, when he'd made his first ten million. Vince grinned at her, balder and fatter than he used to be, but still Vince. 'You look fantastic, love. I hardly recognised you.'

'Hi, Vince.' She leaned in to kiss his cheek. 'How lovely to see you. Thanks for the compliment. I'm out to impress tonight. How's Cheryl?'

'She's good, thanks. Not here tonight, though; our youngest is a bit poorly. So who are you trying to impress?' Vince frowned. 'Not this Richard Ferrera bloke, I hope.'

'Not specifically him. Just everyone really. Why?'

'Well, that's a relief. You don't want to be having anything to do with him.'

'Oh? Why not?'

Vince eyed her glass. 'Still on the bubbly, are you? Listen, come with me. There's a rather fancy little chilling-out area where they're serving some terrific vodka cocktails. Let's go and get one, and I'll tell you all about it. It'll be nice to catch up a bit.'

When they were settled in the calm, candlelit room, soothed by soft classical music and armed with their cocktails, Vince told Tara what he knew about Ferrera. 'This is second-hand, you understand,' he explained. 'It's through my dealings with one of his subsidiary companies in the States. I took the MD and his wife out for dinner with me and Cheryl and after a bottle or two, the gossip started to flow. They told us a lot about the big boss off the record and I'm telling you, he doesn't sound like a nice guy at all. His divorce was pretty dirty, apparently. He's got a lot of power and he uses it to crush any opposition. His wife got nothing; he left her as good as destitute just because he could.'

'He's been flirting with my sister,' Tara said, worried. 'According to her.'

'You want her out of that one, as quick as poss,' advised Vince. 'He's terrible to women. And he's got some girlfriend anyway.'

'Thanks. I'll tell Jemima.'

'But the way he treats his women is nothing to what he does to the businesses he takes over . . .'

'Yes?' Tara said, leaning forward so she wouldn't miss a word. As Vince went on, she listened intently, her eyes widening with interest.

Jemima walked elegantly into the Palm Room, chatting happily to a friend. Then she spotted Ferrera, deep in conversation with a short, dark, rich-looking businessman.

'Excuse me, Sara, I've seen someone I must speak to. I'll see you later, OK?' Parting from her friend, she approached Ferrera. He glanced upwards and when he saw her smiling at him, he quickly excused himself from the businessman and came towards her.

'Jemima.' He kissed each of her cheeks. 'You look dazzling tonight. Dazzling.'

'Thank you. This is a wonderful party.'

'I've been meaning to contact you,' he said softly. 'I enjoyed our time in Paris together.'

'So did I,' purred Jemima. His nearness reminded her of how badly she'd wanted to sleep with him that night. He was wearing his cologne, that woody spicy citrus scent, and she had a flashback to their dancing together. She remembered how lust had swept through her. It was weird but she didn't feel that now. Nevertheless, she felt it was important to pretend that she did. 'It was quite an evening.'

'It certainly was. I've been told you and your sisters have been making a stir here this evening. I would love to meet them.'

'I can arrange that,' Jemima said. 'We're all going to be in the Music Room very shortly at eleven o'clock. You can meet them there. But look, here's my sister Tara. Tara!' Jemima beckoned her over. 'This is Richard Ferrera, the head of FFB.'

Tara held out her hand but her eyes were cold. 'So you're the man who wants to buy our company,' she said.

'Well . . .' Ferrera looked momentarily discomforted but quickly regained his suave self-possession. He shook her hand. 'I don't think this is quite the place to discuss business, do you?'

Tara's voice sounded precise and clipped after Ferrera's smooth American accent. 'Surely this is an excellent place. We're here to celebrate your business success, aren't we? So I ought to let you know that Trevellyan is most definitely not for sale.'

Ferrera raised his eyebrows. 'I've already got that impression from your sister,' he said calmly, a small smile playing about his lips. 'But it's good to know for sure. Well, I wish you as much success with your venture as I've had with mine.'

Tara looked a little disconcerted by the businessman's politeness. Then she frowned and said pointedly, 'I suppose it all depends whether we're keen to use the same *methods* to get the results you achieve. Not everyone is as ruthless as you are, you know.'

'Tara,' said Jemima quickly. What was wrong with her sister? Did she have any idea of how rude she sounded? For God's sake, this man might end up being their only hope, after all. Jemima laughed. 'Oh, Richard won't know you're teasing him!'

'I don't know if I'll ever understand the British sense of humour,' Richard said. He stared straight into Tara's eyes. 'You're very like your sister, though. She's always disarming me with her approach to life.'

'Is she now? Let's just hope that's all she disarms!' exclaimed Tara, and then stopped, looking confused. She swayed slightly. 'I mean . . . she is a married woman, you know!'

Oh Christ, she's drunk, thought Jemima. Smiling at Ferrera, she said swiftly, 'You must excuse Tara, she's been through a very stressful time lately. I'll just take her to have a quick sit down.' She grabbed Tara by the arm and started to steer her away. 'And we have an appointment elsewhere, so we have to go, don't we, Tara? This is a gorgeous party, Richard, thank you so much for asking us . . .'

'Jemima, wait, I have something I must tell you,' began Ferrera, frowning. 'I need to have a private word with you –'

'Sorry, Richard, we have to go to the Music Room. I'll find you afterwards.' She continued out of the room, pulling Tara with her. 'Why the hell were you so rude?' she hissed as they went. 'Do you know how bad that looked?'

Tara hiccupped slightly. 'I've just had it up to here with fucking businessmen who spend their lives lying and cheating and helping themselves and destroying what others have created. They're all fucking crooks!'

'You're drunk, aren't you? How much have you had?' demanded Jemima.

'I'm not drunk. I've had champagne and then I met Vince Fowler and we had cocktails together. Two or three, I think.'

'Tara, you get pissed after one glass of wine. What are you doing drinking cocktails on top of champagne?'

Tara leaned in to her sister and said confidentially, her voice slurring slightly, 'Vince gave me the low-down on Ferrera. He's got inside knowledge. Mimi, Ferrera's going to destroy Erin de Cristo! She's going to be voted off the board, lose creative control, everything! It'll be a disaster for her. It's the way he works.'

'How does Vince know this?' Jemima frowned.

'He heard it from a man who works for one of the FFB subsidiaries.'

'So it's rumour.' Jemima looked round swiftly to make sure no one had heard Tara. 'Look, just because Gerald turned out to be a crook it doesn't mean Ferrera is too . . .' she caught a glimpse of her sister's face. 'That's what all this is about, isn't it?'

Tara looked stricken. 'I don't know . . .'

'Look, you must pull yourself together. We're going to have our photo taken. We have to look radiantly happy, without a care in the world. Please, Tara, please try . . .'

488

Tara sighed. 'All right. I'll do my best.'

'Good. Now let's go and get you some iced water and coffee.'

'You have skin just like mine,' said the girl as Poppy sewed up the seam of her dress. 'It's hell, isn't it, being so fair? Everyone else can go out in the sun and get a lovely tan. Not us. It's factor seventy for me, baggy T-shirts, hats and sarongs all the way.'

She was really ravishing, Poppy thought, and that soft Irish voice was gorgeous. 'Yes. But it has its compensations, I suppose. Sometimes I like being pale and interesting beside everyone else with their bronzed skin.'

'Yeah, me too. Is it nearly finished?'

'Almost. Just a stitch or two more and you'll be done.'

A woman came bursting into the cloakroom. 'Neave? Neave? Are you in here?'

'Here I am,' said the girl calmly. 'I had a dress emergency.'

'What happened?' demanded the woman anxiously, pressing into the cubicle and ignoring Poppy completely.

'The damn thing tore. This kind angel of mercy is helping me.'

'Oh. Look, Neave, we have to get out and mingle. I've got this huge producer lined up to talk to you. He can't wait.'

Oh! thought Poppy, realising who the girl was. *This is the model Jemima was so keen on. No wonder, she's stunningly beautiful.*

'This is my agent, Caroline,' explained Neave with a smile, refusing to be rushed by the other woman. 'Caroline, this is Poppy.'

'Great to meet you, Poppy, and thanks for your help but we've really got to get a move on ...'

'You're finished,' Poppy said, biting off the thread. 'That should hold.'

'Listen, thanks so much. I really owe you one.' Neave smiled at her. 'Caroline, do you have any of my cards on you?'

'Sure, sure.' The agent scrabbled in her purse for a card and held one out to Poppy.

'No,' said Neave. 'One of my personal cards.' She turned to Poppy. 'Those are my business ones, with Caro's details on them.'

Caroline handed Poppy a pale grape-coloured card engraved with the word 'Neave' in curling letters. Underneath were various telephone numbers and email addresses.

'We'd better go,' Neave said, as her agent fussed around her. 'I've got to charm all these very important people, apparently. Lovely to meet you.'

'Lovely to meet you too,' said Poppy. 'Bye.'

She watched as the model and her agent left the cloakroom, staring after them thoughtfully for a while. Then she suddenly remembered her own appointment and hurried out to join the others in the Music Room.

Photographers and journalists, alerted by Jemima, were waiting in the Music Room. Jemima and Tara were already there, looking anxiously for Poppy.

Jemima's relief when she saw her sister come into the room was evident.

'Hello, darling!' she called smoothly. 'We're all ready for you.'

Poppy went over and the three sisters stood together, Jemima in the middle and Poppy and Tara on either side of her, the delicate ice-cream tones of their dresses contrasting beautifully with each other.

The photographers began to click away, pleased with the harmonious group, the blonde, the brunette and the redhead, matching but not identical. People began to gravitate into the Music Room to see what was happening and who was being photographed. Their name began to be muttered.

This is working! thought Jemima happily. *Despite Tara's attempts to fuck it up by getting pissed and being so rude. What the hell was she thinking? We may need that man . . .*

She turned this way and that for the photographers, enjoying the attention and the admiring eyes and envious glances of the other women in the room.

We're going to get good press tomorrow, she thought, pleased with her efforts. *Tea Rose and Trevellyan will be everywhere.*

She became aware suddenly of someone walking to the front of the press pack, stalking in front of the lenses. It was a woman in a rich, scarlet gown that fell to the floor. Her dark hair was piled high on top of her head and her mouth was a red slash of scarlet. A ruby necklace glittered at her throat. She stood in front of the three sisters, her arms folded and a smirk on her face.

Oh my God! Jemima gasped with shock. 'Jecca!' she said, astonished.

She felt the other two stiffen with surprise, too shocked to say a word. Before them was the girl, now a woman, on whom they had not laid eyes for years. At sixteen she had left the family home. At eighteen she had vanished without trace. Now she stood before them, unutterably glamorous with her dark, Italian colouring and flashing brown eyes.

'Hello,' she said, a sardonic smile twisting her mouth.

Tara had turned dead white. 'What are you doing here?' she managed to say.

'That's a lovely way to greet the sister you haven't seen in seven years,' Jecca declared loudly. She obviously wanted everyone in the room to hear. A silence obligingly fell, as journalists scribbled furiously on their notepads and everyone waited to hear what would happen next. *Sister?* You could almost hear the word reverberating through everyone's minds. *Another Trevellyan sister?*

Jemima felt sick and her legs almost buckled beneath her. She clung on to Poppy for strength. Poppy was staring at Jecca as though she were seeing a ghost.

'If you must know, I came here to see you.' Jecca moved slowly along the row of photographers and journalists, staring at each sister in turn. 'It's been so long, hasn't it, *darling* sisters? You've all quite grown up. Tara, you really should try and put some weight on, darling. You're all skin and bone. Is it still the bulimia?

492

Or is that villain you're married to treating you badly? Poppy, you've blossomed into a lovely young woman. You had such promise. But no doubt the other two are doing their best to turn you into a boring, money-loving princess, just like them. As for you, Jemima . . .' Jecca sniggered, '. . . from what I've heard, you're still the biggest whore in town. No wonder your husband has thrown you out.'

There was an audible murmur of interest around the room. The journalists could not get Jecca's words down fast enough.

Jemima felt a cold chill of horror in her stomach. This was her worst nightmare. Everything was unravelling. She realised that Ferrera was standing in the doorway, watching everything, his face like thunder. He must be appalled, having his party ruined by the Trevellyan sisters like this. How had Jecca managed to arrange this revenge?

She wasn't finished yet.

'I wanted to see the three of you because I have to let you know that I'm not about to let you cheat me out of my inheritance.' Jecca whirled round to face the journalists. She held out her arm, indicating the Trevellyan women. 'I grew up with these people. I am their adopted sister. But they have tried to deny me my legal right to share their inheritance. I'm here to tell you all now that I refuse to let that happen. I am entitled to my share and I intend to sue you for a quarter of the percentage you own between you.' Jecca paused to let this bombshell sink in, then she smiled the most charming, seductive smile she could produce.

'It will be a hard battle. I've no doubt you bitches will do all you can to stop me. I'm sure you'll use your money to put up the best fight you can. But I don't care, because I can count on the support and help of my darling partner.' Jecca spun to face the door and blew a kiss in Ferrera's direction. Everyone turned to look at him as Jecca cooed, 'My adorable Richard will be with me every step of the way.'

41

Ferrera was furious. Jecca had never seen him so enraged. It was almost dawn but neither of them felt in the least tired, they were too keyed up by the dramas of the evening. Ferrera had managed to keep a lid on his anger until they reached the privacy of the master bedroom in his opulent Kensington apartment. Then he had turned on Jecca, asking her what the hell she thought she was doing. His fury was all the more chilling for the way he remained outwardly calm and in control: only the ice in his eyes, the set of his mouth and the muscle twitching in one cheek betrayed how deeply angry he was.

'You knew I intended to confront them,' Jecca said haughtily, tossing her head. She wasn't about to let Richard see how his rage was making her frightened.

'You were going to speak to them privately – not in front of the fucking press! Do you know what's going to be all over the papers tomorrow? Huh? Not the great success of my ravishing and unbelievably expensive party! Not the superb partnership with de Cristo! No – some bitch fight between rich girls who can't agree who gets the biggest diamond! Jecca, you've gone too far.'

'I don't see why.' Jecca was stubborn. 'I did what I had to do. It won't damage you in the long run. It means you might get your hands on Trevellyan sooner rather than later.'

Ferrera snorted in frustration. 'You don't get it, do you? I don't like your methods, Jecca, I don't like them at all. You hijacked the evening, even though you knew how much it meant to me.'

'You can talk.' Jecca's eyes flashed with passion. 'Your methods can be pretty questionable at times. Besides, I couldn't bear it any more. I hated the way you've been flirting with Jemima! I wanted it finished. Now it is.'

'You know perfectly well there was nothing in that,' Ferrera said, exasperated. 'You know exactly why I had to do it.'

'Perhaps – but I'd had enough!' She rustled her skirts like a flamenco dancer preparing to strike the opening pose.

'Jecca, let's get something straight. We do this my way, or not at all, do you understand? You are not to blunder in like this again. You might have spoiled everything – we'll just have to see what the fall-out is tomorrow.' Ferrera walked over to a small Louis XVI sofa, put his hands on the delicate carved back and sighed. He was a master of control and he wasn't about to let Jecca see how disgusted he was with her stupid, little-girl tricks. Did this mean his association with the Trevellyan sisters was at an end? Goddamn it, that wasn't supposed to happen. Not only could it damage his business ambitions but it meant no more intimate business dinners, and while he never intended to take his flirtation with Jemima anywhere, couldn't he at least enjoy the company of an intelligent, witty woman from time to time – one who didn't start screaming at him at the smallest provocation? And that older sister, Tara . . . He almost smiled remembering her indignant tipsiness. What on earth had she been talking about? It didn't really matter, he'd been too struck by her looks and the curious mixture of strength and vulnerability he could sense in her to pay too much attention.

Jecca came up behind him. She always knew when it was time to calm down and defer to him. She thought she could read him like a book and bend him to her will with her ripe body and beautiful face. Ferrera turned to look at her, staring into those rich dark eyes. *Jecca, you don't know the first thing about the way I work.*

She smiled, pressing against him seductively, displaying her soft breasts in the low-cut gown to their best advantage. She gazed up at him. 'Come on, Richard. Forgive me. I got carried away, yes. But you know how passionately I feel about this. You know what that family did to me.'

'Yes . . .'

'All I want is what's rightfully mine, that's all. I just don't want to be cheated. You know how that feels, darling, don't you?' She smoothed one hand down his thigh and across his crotch, smiling when she felt a stirring response. 'Tonight has made me feel very sexy,' she breathed. 'I felt so powerful, so in control . . .' She unbuttoned his trousers and slipped her hand inside, pulling out his already semi-erect cock. 'I want you to fuck me now,' she said and then went down gracefully to her knees and took his cock into her mouth. She sucked for a moment, feeling it swell and harden in her mouth. Sliding her tongue round the tip, she ran her hand down the shaft to the base, smoothing her fingers across the skin and moving it gently.

Ferrera looked down: the sight of her pulling his cock into her mouth between her scarlet lips and playing softly with his balls was unbearably exciting. He felt himself engorge inside the delicious warmth and grow bigger with the butterfly-wing tickle of her tongue across the top of his penis. No matter how angry Jecca made him, he couldn't deny her physical attraction. She knew how to arouse him, how to make it impossible for him to resist her.

She pulled back. 'You know what I want,' she said.

He pulled her up, took her to the bed and bent her over it so that she was lying on her stomach. He gathered her long red skirts and pushed them up to her waist, revealing her soft brown bottom. She was wearing no panties, just a lace suspender belt that held up her stockings. She knew how he liked such things and he breathed in appreciatively at the sight of her long slim legs encased in black nylon, her feet in scarlet heels, and the contrast of her bare skin. His penis reared up even more forcefully.

Parting her legs, he revealed her inner lips, already damp, swollen and eager to engulf him. Pressing the head of his penis to her, he pushed his way in quickly, relishing the hot tightness within. Jecca gasped.

'Harder,' she ordered, turning her face on the bed cover, clutching the material in her fist. 'You know how I want it – as hard as you can.'

He was eager to oblige. The fierce anger he had felt needed release and now it mutated to a sexual ferocity as he pounded into her, raising her hips and pulling them to him with both hands. Jecca sighed and panted, moaning with each deep inward thrust. He pushed harder and harder, not caring about anything but reaching the powerful climax he could feel stirring in his depths. He could hear Jecca crying out more loudly now. He knew she loved this. She was grinding her pubic mound on the edge of the bed, getting her pleasure from that as much as from his thrusting.

He wanted her, he couldn't help that. He loved her Latin passion. It spoke to him, teased him, seduced him. He was furious with her, though, and he would have to think later about how to deal with her. But first . . .

He pumped into her with all his strength, keen for the great release. Then it came, boiling up inside him and bursting out with exquisite pleasure.

Jemima stared at the papers spread out on the desk in front of her. The sight of them and their screaming headlines made her feel sick. 'SOCIETY SCANDAL,' yelled one. 'THE HEIRESSES HAMMERED,' cried another. Even the broadsheets covered the story, although in slightly more restrained language. The photographs were all of the girls. One or two showed them in their full glamour on the red carpet. Most had them white-faced and shocked as Jecca confronted them.

This was it. All their efforts, all that expense, for nothing. They may as well consider the whole enterprise over right now. And if Jecca was going to sue them, they'd have a costly legal battle to fight as well. What kind of a case did she have, for God's sake?

The telephone rang and she picked it up. 'Yes?'

'Jemima, it's Ali. I wanted to let you know I've located Jecca Farnese.'

'Oh really?' snapped Jemima. 'It's a bit fucking late for that, darling! Haven't you seen the papers? We managed to find her ourselves.' She slammed the phone down and went back to staring at the damage.

'This isn't all bad,' declared Donna, striding about the boardroom. The sisters were sitting, slumped and defeated and she was determined to put the fight back into them. 'I know it feels like it at the moment, but it's really not. We wanted publicity and we got it, in spades.'

'Yes, but we wanted positive publicity.'

'Ever heard the adage about no such thing as bad publicity? This story is going to fascinate people. They'll want to find out what this Jecca wants to get her hands on so badly. It makes Trevellyan look good and desirable and glamorous. And you're in every paper and gossip mag, looking fabulous. Even that cow couldn't spoil that.'

'But Jecca's going to sue us,' Tara said dully.

'So let her. What kind of case has she got anyway?'

'What I don't understand is *why*,' said Poppy. She pulled at her hair, still auburn from the party, twirling it nervously round her finger. 'Why does she want to hurt us like this? The whole family only tried to help her, to look after her. Even if she felt excluded by the will, all she had to do was talk to us.'

'When was that ever Jecca's way?' demanded Jemima. 'When did she ever take the route of peaceful negotiation when there was an alternative of naked aggression? No. I have a theory about why she's doing this, why she thinks she's entitled to so much.' She paused, and the others waited, staring at her. She took a deep breath. 'I've always suspected ... I've always thought ...' Her expression changed to one of pain and she stared at the table. 'I never wanted to say it out loud. It's too dreadful. But I suspect that Jecca may have been Daddy's mistress.'

Poppy gasped with horror.

Tara clasped her hands together tightly. 'What makes you think that?'

'Just look at what happened,' Jemima said. 'Daddy was always fixated by her. He adored her, we all knew that. He never punished her, never rebuked her. She could do what she wanted with him. Then when she left home at sixteen, he set her up in that flat in London, not far from this very building. I always felt his love for her was too strong. He wanted to be too close to her, and I think she knew it. I've always suspected that she seduced him knowingly, very calculatedly, to make him her creature.'

Poppy shuddered. 'Could she really do it? He was her father!'

'Her adopted father,' Jemima pointed out. 'And you know Jecca. She was capable of anything. And I expect she thought that she'd be able to get a huge juicy inheritance out of Daddy – she probably thought she could get it all. But something must have gone wrong and she ran off before Daddy died. Mother must have suspected, at least.'

Tara frowned. 'I don't know, Mimi. I find that hard to believe. My theory is different.'

The other two looked at her questioningly.

She continued, 'I've been trying to locate Mother's jewellery, you know that. Victor Goldblatt called me yesterday to say that nearly all of it has been located in a bank safe, put there in Mother's name. No one knows who deposited it there. He's sent me an inventory and it includes the most personal of Mother's pieces. But something vital is missing. Do you remember that locket Daddy gave Mother one Christmas? The silver one with the swan engraved on the front?'

The other two nodded.

'Do you remember what was inside it? Daddy took a lock of each of our hair and had it twisted into a small plait that was curled inside the locket and sealed under the glass, remember?'

'Yes – I always found it rather creepy,' Jemima said. 'It gave me goosebumps.'

'But the point is, it had our hair in it. Both of yours, mine – and Jecca's. And it's vanished.'

The other two looked at Tara apprehensively.

'So?' said Poppy.

'That hair has a sample of Jecca's DNA. It could prove whether or not she is Daddy's natural daughter.'

'His *natural* daughter?' Jemima was shocked. 'What are you talking about?'

'She's the child of Luca Farnese, we all know that,' exclaimed Poppy. 'And she doesn't look anything like us. How could she be Daddy's daughter?'

'I know, it seems crazy. But what if Daddy had an affair with Isabella Farnese and Jecca was the result? It would explain why he loved her so much – because she reminded him of his dead lover and because she was his natural daughter. I think Jecca's got her hands on that locket so she can use it in whatever legal case she's planning to show that she's Cecil's real daughter and so entitled twice over to a share of the company. If our DNA and hers were close enough, it would prove we had the same father.'

There was a silence as this sank in. Donna watched them, baffled by the sudden revelation of family secrets.

'So the question is,' Poppy said slowly, 'was Jecca Daddy's daughter – or his mistress?'

Tara nodded. 'That's what we have to find out.'

Flick Johnson tossed the rival newspaper angrily across the room.

'Where the fuck were you when this happened?' she demanded.

'Sorry, boss.' Ben looked shamefaced. 'No one thought it was going to be anything more than a standard do.'

'Yeah, well . . . you look like an idiot. Now I want to try and get hold of this sister, see if she'll give us her side of the story.'

'Yeah, but boss, I did get somewhere. I've got a couple of spicy little titbits I think you'll be very interested in.' Ben smiled and prepared to tell Flick what he knew.

42

The only spark of hope that could be saved from the nightmare of the Ferrera party was Poppy's meeting with Neave in the loos. She explained to the other two how she had come to the rescue of the supermodel.

'All thanks to my trusty needle and thread. She said she owed me one.'

'That's great,' said Donna. 'This is exactly what we need. Something positive. I want you to call her, Poppy. Meet up for a girly lunch or something, draw her in, get to know her. And maybe ask her if she'll consider being our face. OK?'

Poppy nodded. 'I don't know how I'll do it, I'm dreadful at that kind of thing. I'm always too embarrassed to ask for favours. But I'll really try, I promise.'

'Good. Jemima, you have to get on the phone to people today, and start sorting out this mess. I think that a spread in a glossy magazine will help and for

God's sake, talk to those friends of yours at *Vogue* about a feature for the November issue. That will be put to bed any day now, so please get on to it.'

Jemima nodded. Was there really any point? Was the company even going to be theirs in November?

'And Tara, let's talk about production and press samples. I've got some samples of lotions and milk that Claudine's sent over . . .'

Thank God for Donna, Jemima thought. *At least she's still positive, and determined to carry on. Without her, we'd really be sunk.*

Jemima was waiting for Iris, her contact at *Vogue*, to get back to her. She had sounded interested and said she would put it past the editor but she was sure they'd run with it.

The phone rang and she picked it up, expecting to hear Iris's drawling tones. 'Iris?'

'No. It's Harry.'

Her stomach swooped over and she sat back in her chair, feeling breathless. 'Hello.'

'I've just been in the village and seen the papers. Christ, Jemima, I'm sorry. That must have been so awful.'

'It was.' Jemima had told Harry all about Jecca when they'd first married. It had seemed important that he know.

'I can't believe she's back like this. As though she's not had enough of making you suffer. I'm really sorry. But if it's any consolation, you looked completely beautiful.'

She smiled. 'Thanks. I've been waiting for you to call me.'

'I had to sort some things out in my head. I just had to be sure about everything, do you understand? But I think I am now. I want to see you.'

'Do you? When?'

'As soon as I can. Shall I drive to you?'

Harry hardly ever offered to visit her in London. Surely this was a good sign. Her skin tingled. 'Yes, yes. Come to Eaton Square. It's going on the market next week, it might be the last time you see it.'

'Where are you going to live?'

'I haven't decided. I'll work something out. Can you come?'

'Yes. I'll be there tomorrow night.'

'OK. That's great. That's wonderful.'

They said goodbye and Jemima put the phone down. Something good might be salvaged from this mess. She prayed it would.

Tara let the agent lead her through the property, pointing out all its advantages. She kept impassive, refusing to look impressed by what was on offer. But in her heart, she was rejoicing. This was exactly what she wanted.

Located not far from the enormous green common in the middle of Clapham, the house was on an exclusive street, but unlike the terraces of Victorian villas that surrounded it, it was detached, standing on its own large plot. Once it had been a private school and now it had been beautifully converted into a spacious, seven-bedroomed family home, with enormous, high-ceilinged light rooms. It was decorated in a contemporary style with polished wooden floors, white walls and superb lighting. The kitchen was in hand-made, duck-egg blue wood, dominated by a huge range cooker. There was a vast playroom, perfect for the children to mess up any way they liked. Best of all at the end of the garden was a small cottage where the headmaster had once lived and which would make two staff flats.

What charmed her was that she simply could not imagine Gerald in this environment. His stuffy suits and club ties would look completely out of place in this fresh, modern home, even if there was a huge wine cellar under the house. His stupid trophies and stag's head and antique oars would look even sillier. And as for beige carpets . . . *forget it!* thought Tara with satisfaction. She liked the aura of normality in the area. It felt as though real families lived nearby, following normal lives. Children would ride their bikes round here, fly kites on the common and play foot-ball and cricket. Holland Park was far too rarefied for all that, far too soaked in money, far too afraid of having its children kidnapped for a vast ransom. Tara had never realised how stifling she found it until now.

'And as you can see, it has every amenity the modern family is looking for,' concluded the estate agent. 'So . . .' he looked anxiously at Tara for a reaction. 'What's your initial feeling?'

'Hmm.' Tara thought a for a moment and then decided to put him out of his misery. 'I'll take it.'

Not bad for a lunch hour, she thought, getting back into the car.

Ali Tendulka tapped his pen on his paper and raised his eyebrows at the sisters sitting opposite him.

'Jecca Farnese's lawyers have been in touch with us. They're going to mount a legal claim to their client being owed a quarter of your percentage share.'

'Shit.' Tara bowed her head. 'How does this affect business?'

'Your day-to-day business can go on as normal. It's in Miss Farnese's interests for the business to be as successful as possible so she doesn't want to scupper it –'

'Except, if we're successful, she won't get the business when the year is up,' pointed out Jemima.

'We don't know if she's aware of the terms of the will,' remarked Tara. 'And perhaps she'd rather have a quarter of a successful company than the whole of a shit one.'

'But all she needs to do is wait out the year, watch us fail, get her hands on the company and sell it to Ferrera,' said Poppy.

'Maybe, with their special arrangement –' Jemima spat out the words; it had stung badly that Ferrera was obviously sleeping with Jecca. As usual, Jecca had managed to hurt her where she was most sensitive '– Jecca is worried she won't get top dollar from the man she's sleeping with.'

'Who knows what her motives are,' sighed Tara. 'She's a complete mystery. She's got something up her sleeve though, we can be sure of that. I think we should press on with *Tea Rose* and all our plans, and expect to win if she takes it to court. Let her fret about it. We'll get on with what we know we can do – revitalising Trevellyan. After all, we've come so far. The shop is almost finished and Claudine is coming back next week with more samples. She's also reworking *Antique Lily* and creating a possible new scent. So all that's going very well.'

'Iris wants to run the *Vogue* feature,' put in Jemima. Iris had called just after Jemima had spoken to Harry. 'We'll have an interview with her next week.'

'You ladies are very impressive.' Ali smiled at them. 'A couple of months ago I sat here while those old guys tried to bluff their way out of the mess they were in and you clearly knew nothing about this game. Now, you're on top of it.'

They looked pleased at the praise. 'Maybe not on top,' Tara said, 'but we're on our way.'

Jemima left the office thinking hard. Seeing Jecca again had been a shock, but realising that the evil cow was serious about trying to get her hands on Trevellyan any way she possibly could was much worse. How would they stop her? It was obvious that the awful confrontation at the Ferrera party was just the first step in a public relations war, to get popular opinion on her side. Was Richard in on this from the start? He must have been. They were an item, that much was plain. It was all so horrible, it left such a bitter taste in the mouth to know that all along he'd been playing with her, that his friendship had been a front and nothing more.

Thank Christ I didn't sleep with him!

'Lady Jemima?'

Jemima turned round to see who was speaking to her. 'It's Lady Calthorpe, actually, but yes?'

A scruffy-looking young man in jeans and a jumper emerged from a shop doorway. He flashed a press pass at her. 'Ben Davies. *Daily Chronicle.* I wondered if I could have a quick word with you?'

'What about?' Jemima said warily.

'I'd like to talk in private if we can. I know a pub round the corner if you don't mind.' The man grinned at her. 'I promise you'll find it interesting.'

Jemima stared at him. Usually nothing would induce her to have anything to do with the gutter press. She knew all too well from her friends' experiences how words could be twisted and quotes made up. But something about this man bothered her. He looked triumphant, as though he held some kind of power over her and was relishing the moment.

'I don't give interviews,' she said coldly.

'It's not an interview I want,' retorted the journalist. 'I've got some information for *you,* as it happens. And if you want to find out what it is, you'd better follow me.'

He turned and sauntered off. Jemima watched him for a moment, then quickly marched after him, pulling her sunglasses down over her eyes as she went.

'Hi, Neave, it's Poppy here. We met in the loos at the Spencer House party last night?'

'Yeah, hi Poppy.' The Irish voice was smooth and friendly. 'How're you doin'?'

'I'm fine, thanks. Look, it was so nice to meet you the other night and actually, I know it's a bit cheeky, but I've got a favour to ask. I wondered if we could go for a drink or something . . .'

'Yeah, that would be lovely but I'm flying to New York in a day or two, so I'm not going to be around for a while, so –'

'Are you free tonight?'

'Tonight? Hold on . . .' There was a pause while Neave consulted her diary. 'You know what? I am. A meeting's been cancelled. But I have to warn you, it isn't easy going out for a drink with me. I don't want to sound bigheaded, but I'm hounded by press at the moment. It's just the way it is.'

'Don't worry, I understand,' Poppy said. 'Look, I'm a member of a small arts club in Notting Hill. Why don't we go there? It's very quiet and discreet. Plenty of famous people hang out there and no one will bother you, I promise.'

'Sounds great. It'll be such a novelty to be out somewhere without being hassled. It's a date.'

After they'd made their arrangement, Poppy put the phone down, and looked at her diary. For that evening she had scrawled 'Dinner, George'. She'd have to cancel. He'd understand, it was work after all and he was always so supportive when it came to Trevellyan.

She stared at her diary for a while. She'd missed him lately. All the office stuff and the parties had kept them apart.

Sod it, she thought. *If I'm busy schmoozing Neave tonight, I deserve the rest of the afternoon off. George is working in the bookshop. I'll go and surprise him.*

She shut her diary with a snap, picked up her bag and headed out of the office.

Jemima came out of the pub, white-faced. Her hands were shaking. She walked across the road, almost getting run down by a taxi.

'Oi, you dozy bint! Watch where you're going!' yelled the driver, accelerating past her.

Jemima barely noticed. Instead she walked in a daze back to Trevellyan. She met Donna on her way out. The other woman stopped, concerned when she saw the state Jemima was in.

'What's wrong, honey? You look awful,' she said, reaching for Jemima's hand.

'Donna . . .' Jemima stared at her, frightened. 'I didn't think it could get any worse. But it just has.'

'Come inside,' Donna said, taking control at once. 'You'd better tell me what's happened.'

In her office, Donna got Jemima into a chair and made her a cup of hot, sweet tea. Jemima clutched the mug gratefully, and told her how the journalist had sprung out of nowhere.

'He took me to a pub. He told me his paper had a scoop on me, that they're going to run it on Saturday. They've found out all about my affair with Guy, all about the baby . . .' Jemima looked too frozen with shock to cry. 'Donna, my husband is coming to see me tomorrow night. We've only just begun to get through this. If it's splashed all over the newspapers, I think it will destroy us. It will be the end of any hope we have of getting back together. Harry's very proud. He hates publicity, he hates people knowing about him and his private life. It's taken so much for him to get to this point, I know it has. It will destroy him. It will be the end of us.'

'Your family is nothing if not complicated,' muttered Donna. 'OK, look. I don't have any idea who Guy is or about the baby but I can see it's important to you. I don't need to know. But we do need to think about damage limitation right now. Why did they tell you this? Why didn't they just run it?'

'He said he wanted to give me the chance to put my side of the story across.'

'Mmm. OK. Then maybe that's what we'll have to do.'

'What? Talk to the press?' Jemima shook her head. 'Harry would never approve.'

'Then we'll think of another way. Which paper was this bloke from?'

'The *Chronicle*.'

'I have a contact there. Let me get on to it, and I'll see what I can find out.'

Jemima sat drinking her tea in a daze, while Donna made some calls. Twenty minutes later she put the phone down.

'There's some good news. The story's come from a source in Dorset, close to your husband. It's a hot story – about how you had an affair with your husband's friend, got pregnant, lost the baby, your husband kicked you out.' Donna held up her hand to stop Jemima from saying anything. 'You don't have to explain anything to me. That's the story they've got, that's all. The thing is, they're worried about running it. They've not got any other evidence apart from this one source who isn't one of the parties . . .'

'It's not Guy, then,' muttered Jemima.

'No. They're trying to track him down apparently. But if the story is wrong, you could sue, they know that. They wanted to frighten you into confirming it. Did you say anything at all?'

Jemima shook her head. 'Not a word. I just listened and then walked out.'

'Good. So here's what we do. We tell the *Chronicle* that the story's not true and that if they print, we'll sue their ass. But we'll say how much it could damage you if it's hinted at, so we'll trade with them. They spike their story and you'll give an interview to the paper about your glamorous life, the truth about your romance with Billy or whoever, the way you've discovered that hard work is more fulfilling than a jet-set lifestyle. They should love that. To be honest, they should be bloody grateful to get such a good story from you, one that's watertight and exclusive.'

'Do you think they'll go for it?' asked Jemima, hopeful.

'I think they might. I'm not going to talk to this kid Ben. He's too junior. I'm going over his head to his boss Flick Johnson. There's just one thing.' Donna fixed her with a fierce look. 'Your husband Harry has to be prepared to back you up on this. And if they find this bloke, Guy or whatever his name is, and he decides to sing, you're up shit creek.'

Jemima nodded. 'Please, Donna. Just do whatever you have to do.'

43

Poppy walked towards Bloomsbury, her spirits high. She was surprised and happy that Neave had agreed to meet her. A supermodel like her must have a diary packed with commitments. It was lucky that she'd had that cancellation.

Summer was well and truly here. Tourists were out in their dozens, loaded down with cameras and knapsacks. Office girls dawdled on extended lunchtimes, soaking up the rays of the afternoon sunshine. The trees in Bloomsbury were green and shady, looking fresh and wholesome against the white stone of the buildings. Poppy sauntered past the antiquarian print shops and little stores devoted to stamps or coins or other artefacts, glancing in the windows as she went. In a small street opposite the British Museum, she found what she was looking for: a bookshop, its windows displaying the latest volumes of literature. She went inside.

The interior was cool and light, with bare wooden

floorboards and the shelves painted in a soft blue-grey. Poppy walked past tables loaded with glossy volumes to the counter at the back. A man was standing there, flicking through a book. He looked up as Poppy approached.

'Hello, can I help you?' he asked.

'Yes. I'm here to see George.'

'George?' The man frowned.

'Yes. Is he on a tea break or something?'

'There's no one here called George. Just me and Andy and Gideon. And Charlene on Saturdays.'

Poppy was puzzled. 'Are you sure?'

The man laughed. 'Er, yeah. I am pretty sure, yes. Seeing as I'm the manager. There really isn't anyone working here without my knowledge.'

Poppy stared at him, her mouth hanging open.

'Perhaps you've got mixed up with another book-shop. Have you tried Waterstone's up the road?' the man said kindly, obviously feeling sorry for her.

'No, no, it was definitely this one. Yes, the Earle Street Bookshop. This is the one. It's owned by his uncle, Sylvester.'

'I don't think so, love,' the man said. 'Who's Sylvester? This is owned by Annie Vaughn. She owns the Earle Street Poetry Press as well.'

'Oh,' said Poppy. 'Well, thank you very much for your help.' She turned slowly and walked out of the shop.

Once she was past the British Museum, she began to run. Flying along the streets, dodging startled pedestrians, skipping past prams, she hurried home, only thinking of finding George as quickly as she could. She arrived in the square red-faced and panting. With a last burst of energy, she dashed into her building and up the stairs to the Fellowes flat. She pounded at the door.

'George, George, are you in there?' she demanded. She paused and waited. There was only silence within. 'George!' she yelled. 'Where the hell are you?'

She saw the white corner of a piece of paper sticking out from under the door. She bent down and pulled it out. It was an envelope. It had a name written on it in black ink: G Marlow.

She looked at it, feeling sick. Then she turned and ran upstairs.

Donna saw Jemima into a taxi home and then rang Tara and explained what had happened.

'I think she's OK,' Donna said. 'She seemed a lot calmer when I left, but maybe she shouldn't be on her own tonight.'

'OK,' said Tara. 'Christ, what next? I'll call her and ask her over here for supper. I'll keep the children up a little later so she can play with them. That always cheers her up and helps her see the bigger picture. Thanks, Donna. It looks like you've got us out of a crisis once again.'

'You're welcome. But I have to say, the Trevellyans are one dramatic family. I never know what the hell will happen next.'

'Nor do we,' said Tara with a laugh. 'Nor do we.'

* * *

Be normal, Poppy told herself as she sat in the bar of the basement club in Notting Hill. *Don't let anyone see that anything's wrong. Especially not Neave.*

She'd got ready in a daze, hardly able to register how her world had changed in such a short time. One moment, she'd been full of the joys of young love. Now it was all dust and ashes and her mind was whirling with questions. Why on earth had George lied to her about his job in the bookshop? Not only had they never heard of him, but none of the story was true. Why make up such things? What could he gain? And then there was the letter. Why would anyone be sending post for G. Marlow to the Fellowes flat? She felt a terrible sense of foreboding about the whole thing. There was no time to think about it now, though. She had an appointment to keep.

She'd dressed automatically, putting on a light summer dress, pulling in the waist with a vintage Pucci scarf and slipping on some flat turquoise sandals she'd bought on a beach holiday the previous year. Then she'd set out west, catching a bus that trundled down Oxford Street and along Hyde Park, towards Notting Hill Gate. They passed Tara's road as they went through Holland Park and Poppy was half tempted to jump off the bus and run to her big sister's house. She'd love to see Edward and Imo, and maybe confide in Tara what had happened, get some comfort and advice. But no. She resolved to stay on the bus, meet Neave and do her best to convince her to join them.

A sudden buzz of interest in the room made Poppy look up. Neave had walked in through the door and, in a place where no one was impressed by fame or wealth, her appearance had still created quite a stir. She sauntered in with the unselfconscious grace of a panther, wearing a cool white cotton shirt and a tiny, ruffled, A-line mini skirt in pale green. Her legs stretched endlessly away to a pair of black wedge Rupert Sanderson sandals. Her hair fell in a long glossy dark ponytail down her back and she wore a chic pair of Marni glasses.

Wow, thought Poppy in awe. *What must it be like to walk around provoking that kind of response in people? What's it like to be so gorgeous that everyone stares, even when you're just out in normal clothes and no make-up, being yourself?*

She stood up. 'Hi, Neave!'

'Oh, hi there!' The gentle Irish accent was unmistakeable. 'It's my guardian angel!' She went up and gave Poppy a kiss. They sat down at a small table and Poppy ordered them drinks of lime and soda.

'Great place,' Neave said, taking off her sunglasses and revealing her extraordinary eyes. 'It's so chilled out and unpretentious. Do you want to know a secret? I hate glossy parties! If I have to go to one more stately home dressed up in taffeta, drink one more glass of champagne or eat another spoonful of caviar, I think I'll go mad. This is my kind of place: simple, friendly, artistic.'

'All the paintings on the walls are by members,' said Poppy, nodding towards the canvases.

'How cool!' Neave peered at them. 'People here are really talented.'

'I'm not much of a fan of that high-society world myself,' Poppy said.

'Really?'

'Uh uh. I hate snooty restaurants and launch parties and all that stuff. That's much more my sister Jemima's scene. I prefer to stay at home and eat cheese on toast and watch television or read.'

'We're so the same,' said Neave, laughing. 'How on earth did we end up in the worlds we're in, huh? Tell me what you do.'

Poppy told her all about Trevellyan and the work they were doing there. Neave was fascinated.

'You're learning as you go along, are you?' She smiled. 'Like me. I got discovered in a Dublin department store when a woman came to buy a jacket and asked me to model one for her. Turned out she was a scout from an agency. Before I knew what had happened, she'd signed me up and whisked me away and suddenly I was living half my life on aeroplanes and the other half in strange cities.' Neave shrugged. 'But I can't complain, I guess. It's made me money and opened doors to worlds I once only dreamed about. Then I got signed up by Caroline and she's convinced she's going to get me into the movies.'

'Do you want to act?'

'I guess so.' Neave smiled her dazzling smile. 'They say I come across well on the screen.'

'Really? I can't imagine why.' Poppy laughed. 'You're absolutely made for it!'

'I'd like to give it a try anyway. I've always fancied having a go at acting since I was Mary in the Nativity play.' Neave assumed a holy look and turned her eyes to heaven. She said in a babyish voice, 'Oh, Joseph, the angel says I'm gonna have a baby and he shall be called a Manual.' She glanced at Poppy. 'I'm not kidding. That's what I said! I got a bit confused when the angel said Emmanuel.'

Poppy laughed again. Neave was funny and charming. She would be the most wonderful ambassador for *Tea Rose*. Poppy's mind was already designing a poster and photograph campaign, even sketching out a television advertisement.

'I was wondering . . .' she began.

Neave cocked her head and look questioning. 'Yeah?'

'Neave, I'll come straight to the point. We need a face for Trevellyan. A fabulous, fascinating face like yours. My sister Jemima has already approached your people but they said no, so when we met in the loos that night, it seemed like destiny. Maybe you were meant to come and join us and be the face of *Tea Rose*. We're going to have the most stunning campaign, it's going to be a huge launch. It would be so worth your while and I know you haven't signed with anyone yet. So . . . would you consider it?'

Neave blinked her green eyes and looked regretful. 'Oh, Poppy, I'd like to help you out, I really would. But Caroline doesn't want me to sign up to anything like that yet. We've had offers, of course, but she's turned them all down. We've got a major movie in the pipeline and if it comes off, Caro reckons it will double or triple my price, and then I'll get a huge cosmetics or fragrance deal, a long-term contract.'

'Oh.' Poppy's face fell.

'I'm sorry. I just can't commit to anything right now.'

'Don't worry,' Poppy said, trying to be stoical. 'We couldn't afford to pay you that kind of money and obviously someone of your stature is going to be able to command a giant fee. So I suppose it just wasn't meant to be.'

Neave smiled kindly. 'I guess not. But I'll do anything I can, you can be sure of that. If you're having a launch or anything, I'd be happy to come and lend a hand. Have you got a sample of the scent?'

'Right here.' Poppy took a small glass atomiser from her bag. The samples had arrived in boxes that day, ready to be sent out to the press. She passed it to Neave who sprayed it on her wrist and smelt it.

'Hey, I like that.' She frowned and sniffed again. 'Yeah, that's really nice. Much better than some of the stuff I've been asked to represent. Shame.'

'Never mind. Keep the sample,' said Poppy. 'Are you hungry? Shall we get something to eat?'

They went through to the dining room, which opened out on to a courtyard garden, and sat down to eat. They chatted about their lives and likes and discovered that they had a lot of things in common, from their love of cooking Italian food to the fact that they had both had giant crushes on Justin Timberlake.

'I liked him even when his hair was curly,' declared Neave, laughing. 'Hey, are you OK?' she said, noticing Poppy's smile fade.

'It's nothing . . . well . . . actually, it's my boyfriend,' Poppy said slowly.

'Having troubles? Has he cheated on you?'

'Not exactly.' She explained what had happened that day. 'I just can't understand it,' she finished. 'Why would he lie to me about where he works, or what his name is? I can't see a reason for it.'

'There must be one,' Neave said, putting down her fork. 'But you're right, it's very strange. Is he a stalker?'

'No, I don't think so. He's just so incredibly normal and I really thought we were in love . . .' Poppy's eyes filled with tears as she thought back to the blissful times they'd spent together. 'I can't think what it all means.'

'Hey, love.' Neave put her hand on Poppy's arm. 'Just don't leap to conclusions. There might be a perfectly innocent explanation for all this.'

'I'd love to know what it is. Because no matter how I look at it, the last thing it seems is innocent.'

44

Jemima was too nervous about seeing Harry again to go to work. She stayed at home instead, using the time to help Sri clear up the flat for the estate agent's photographs. She had already had to take the painful step of giving Sri her notice but had also been able to recommend her to a friend who was desperately in need of a good housekeeper. Sri would be going to her at the end of the month.

'Thanks so much, Sri, the sitting room looks lovely,' she said. 'The agents will love it.'

They were indeed very impressed with the property. 'Flats like this are gold dust,' said one appreciatively. 'I don't think we'll have any trouble moving it at all. I've got a couple of Russian girls on my books desperate for a flat like this. And it's very nicely done up. So be prepared for a quick sale.'

'Thanks,' Jemima said, unable to hide the regret in her voice. Now that the moment she had dreaded was finally here, she was sad but it was almost a relief. The flat was going and that was that. She would have several million from its sale and a big chunk of that would go into Trevellyan. She might never see it again but so what – she had to take a risk for once.

By the time Harry was due to arrive she was almost shaking with nerves.

How strange to be so terrified of seeing my own husband! She tried to laugh but she couldn't avoid how serious this evening was. It would determine her future with Harry.

The doorbell rang promptly at seven and she buzzed him up, taking one last glance in the mirror before she let him in. As he leaned in to kiss her on the cheek, she realised with surprise that he seemed as nervous as she was.

'Can I get you a drink?' she said.

'Yes, please.'

'Gin and tonic?' She mixed him a Tanqueray and tonic, with a good measure of the Tanqueray, and made one for herself.

'So you're really selling the flat,' Harry said, seeing the estate agent brochures on her table. 'I never thought you'd be able to let it go.'

'It's time to let a lot of things go,' she said quietly. 'I've realised I can't live in the past for ever. I have to move on and make something of myself. I've been thinking about what you said to me, about how I'd found a purpose in life. I think that's true, and now I've found it, I don't want to let it go. It's worth losing the flat if I can keep Trevellyan alive. And we're so close now. Really, so close. We have a fabulous scent and the whole look is coming together much better than I ever imagined.'

'Where will you live?' Harry said, sitting on the arm of a sofa.

'Tara's said I can have a room in her house whenever I need it and I think I'd like that. Perhaps I've been alone a bit too much over the last few years. It's not good for me. I'd like to be part of her family and see the children more. I think it could be a good solution.' Jemima sat down herself. A big gulp of gin and tonic had begun to relax her a little.

'And when you're not in London?' Harry asked, raising his eyebrows.

'Well . . . that rather depends on you,' she answered quietly.

'Shall we talk about this now? I was going to wait until dinner.'

'No, let's talk now,' Jemima said hastily. 'I really can't wait. It's going to be too awkward if we don't.'

'All right.' Harry got up and walked over to the window, looking out over Eaton Square. 'I suppose you wondered why you didn't hear from me after what we talked about in the library that day. The truth was, I had to think over what you'd said. And I had to be sure I believed you and trusted you again. I'm sure you appreciate that.'

'Yes,' she whispered.

'So I went to find Guy. I had to talk to him. He was so convincing, you see. He made me believe him even though I knew what a snake he was. So I drove up to

Aberdeen, where he's been working. We talked, man to man. I explained what you'd said and he eventually backed up your story.'

'Eventually?'

'Oh, he tried to brazen it out for a while, tried to maintain the story that you'd had a long affair together, but suddenly I knew he was lying. I could see the falseness in his eyes. I realised he's been taking me in most of my life. I trusted him like a brother, but he was no friend to me.'

'I'm so sorry, Harry. I'm so sorry I hurt you.'

He went over to her and sat on the sofa beside her. 'Listen, you've asked for pardon. I've forgiven you. Now, we have to let it go. I've had a chance to realise that I lost a child, and to mourn for that child. But I also have the chance to get you back, with everything that promises: a life together, a happy home, perhaps children. So let's never talk about Guy again, either of us. All right?'

'Yes.' She smiled. 'Does this mean you want us to make another go of it?'

'I really do. Do you?' He searched her face, his gaze vulnerable in a way she'd never seen before.

'Yes.'

He leaned towards her and very gently kissed her on the lips, then pulled away. 'The last time I did that, you didn't like it much.'

'No – but you were very drunk,' she reminded him. 'I don't mind it now but first, I need to ask you something.'

'Yes?'

She looked down, smoothing her hand across a cushion. At last she said slowly, 'Letty Stewart . . .'

'Ah. Letty. There's nothing going on. Whatever there was is over. Letty knows that.'

'That night I sent you to her – did you . . . did you sleep with her?'

'I don't think we should rake over the past. Let's just accept that both of us have made mistakes and make a fresh start.'

Jemima smiled. 'OK.'

'Now, where were we?'

'I think you were kissing me.'

'Oh yes . . .' He grinned at her, a sweet lopsided grin she hadn't seen for so long, and then leaned in again to kiss her. This time it didn't stop with a touch of his lips to hers. This time, he put his arms around her and they kissed properly and passionately.

He pulled away just long enough to say hoarsely, 'My God, I want to sleep with my wife.' Then he returned to her mouth, kissing her with such intensity, it felt as though he couldn't get enough of her.

'Let's go to the bedroom,' whispered Jemima. 'I want to do this properly.'

The passion between them was like nothing she had experienced before. On the one hand it had the familiarity of old lovers who knew each other's body intimately and how to please the other, and what each of them loved best. He knew how she adored being kissed slowly and intently round her shoulders and neck, how she loved him to penetrate her and then come out, so that she could hold his penis wet with her juices, while he explored her with his fingers. He knew when to turn her over and take her from behind, how to touch her exactly right as he fucked her hard. He knew when to bring her back beneath him so that she could wrap her legs over his broad back, urging him into her.

But along with that knowledge of each other, there was a completely unexpected deep excitement of the new: this was her lover, reinvigorated with passion for her. His kiss was like a new kiss and his touch thrilled her just as it had when they first fell in love. Everything about him filled her with ecstasy. When they finally collapsed, spent and satisfied, she touched his face softly and said, 'I'm so happy. I thought I'd lost you. It's like you've come back from the dead.'

He wrapped her in his arms and said, 'I'll never let you go again. I promise. Jemmie, I want you to come home.'

They dozed in each other's arms and then got up and dressed again and went out for dinner.

Harry was more alive than she'd seen him for years.

They walked through the summer evening up the King's Road and found a little restaurant that Jemima liked and took a table outside to enjoy the last of the sunshine.

'There's something I need to tell you,' Jemima said hesitantly. 'I don't want it to spoil our wonderful evening but we have to talk about it.'

Harry looked apprehensive. 'Yes?'

Jemima explained about the newspaper splash planned for that weekend. 'I'm sorry,' she said hastily. 'I know how you loathe this kind of thing.'

'I do. But the point is, how did they get hold of the story?'

'It's someone in Dorset, apparently. Someone close to you. I don't know who.'

'I'll find out.' Harry looked grim. 'I have an idea. So, what's the plan?'

'Donna, our marketing advisor, knows someone at the paper. She thinks that they won't risk publishing if they can't get hold of Guy to corroborate the story.'

'They won't find him. And if they do, he won't talk, I'm sure of it.'

Jemima wondered exactly what had gone on in Aberdeen to make Harry so sure that Guy would keep his mouth shut but she decided it was wiser not to ask.

'To take the heat out of the story, I'm going to give them an exclusive interview, about our life and what I'm doing at Trevellyan and perhaps some stuff about Jecca – how we feel about her threat and so on. But I need to know you're all right with that.' She looked at him anxiously.

'I hate the press,' he said frankly. 'And I think that once you let them in, you've got no excuse to keep them out. But I know you need to do this. Whatever you want me to do, I'll do it.'

'Even pose in your underwear?' she teased.

'If you feel the all-too-human desire to show me off, what can I do?' Harry joked. 'But I'd prefer it if we don't make too much of a habit of it. I'm a lover of the quiet life, you know.'

'I'm rapidly coming round to your way of thinking,' Jemima answered with a smile.

Poppy lay on the sofa in her flat, staring at the ceiling. She had heard nothing from George last night although she had sent him a text: *Where are you?*

Then at work today she had had to break the disappointing news about Neave.

'Don't worry about it too much,' Donna had said encouragingly, although her disappointment had been clear to read. 'It would be great to get her on board for the launch. And in the meantime, I'm going to approach Kate Beckinsale's people. There's a chance she might be interested.'

Then, this afternoon, after Poppy had inspected the model of the bottle she had designed for *Tea Rose* and signed it off, her phone had beeped at last.

Sorry darling, read the text. *Called home on urgent family stuff. Back tonight. See you later? G xx*

Yes. See you later. Come to mine when you are back, she had replied.

Now it was just a matter of waiting.

At seven-thirty, there was a knock on the door. Poppy got up off the sofa and went to answer it. As she opened it, George bounded in like an excitable puppy.

'Hello, hello!' He seized her and kissed her quickly, smiling. 'Did you miss me? I had to go back and see my family. Summoned by my papa. God, it's miserable going back to our town. I never liked it. Witney must be the dullest place on earth.'

'I thought your family lived in the West Country,' Poppy said.

'Oh – yes, well, some of them do. And my parents lived there till quite recently. Then they moved to Witney.'

'I see. So the Fellowes family lives in Witney, does it?' Poppy pulled away from him and scanned his face. It looked so open and honest, his clear brown eyes wide and trustworthy. 'So if I went to Witney, I'd be able to look them up, would I? The very nice, very decent Fellowes clan. Is that right?'

George tensed a little. 'Yes,' he said slowly. 'Why do you ask?'

'I just wondered.' She put a hand on her hip and stared at him, unsmiling. 'I just wondered if perhaps I might find there was no one there by the name of Fellowes. No one you're related to, anyway. In fact, I'm a bit confused about where I might find any of your relations. Where do the Marlow family live?'

George froze and his mouth fell open. After a second, he stuttered, 'I . . . I . . .'

'You're surprised by that, aren't you? But that's not my only question. I wondered what you do with yourself all day, seeing as you're not in the Earle Street Bookshop. They've never heard of you there. So much for your uncle Sylvester, he doesn't seem to exist either.'

George's gaze became agonised. 'Poppy, please, let me explain –'

'I don't want to hear any more of your lies!' she shouted. 'Did you really think I wouldn't find out? How stupid to tell me you worked somewhere I could easily go and ask about you!'

'I *do* work there,' he protested.

She laughed in bewilderment, hardly able to believe his affront. 'The manager had never heard of you.'

'That's because my name isn't George Fellowes,' he said quietly. 'You're right about that.'

'Who are you then?'

'My name is Gideon. Gideon Marlow.'

She stared him disbelievingly.

'I'm telling the truth,' he said. 'How did you find out my surname?'

She held out the envelope she'd taken from his flat. 'This.'

He looked at it and then glanced up at her. 'Oh. I see. A bit clumsy. The whole reason for calling myself George is that Mrs Fellowes really does have a nephew called that. It seemed to back the story up.'

'But why?' whispered Poppy. She sank down on a pine dining chair. 'Why did you have to pretend to be Mrs Fellowes's nephew? What could it possibly gain you?'

He ran his hand through his soft brown hair. 'I can't tell you that, Poppy, I'm really sorry.'

'Get out,' she said harshly.

'What?'

'You heard me! Get out! Get out!' She stood up and started to shriek. 'I never want to see you again. You've lied to me, I can never trust you. Get out of my flat! Go away!'

'No, Poppy, please, just let me explain –'

'You've just said you can't tell me the truth. I don't even want to know. I just want you to leave and never come back.'

'But I love you,' he protested. 'I can't go like this.'

Her eyes flashed fury at him. 'How can you love me? You've lied to me since the first day I met you.'

'I didn't want to!' he shouted. 'I . . . had to!'

'*Why?*' she demanded. A small quiet moment followed her question and for a second, she thought she had reached him and that he was about to tell her. Then he screwed up his face in frustration.

'I can't tell you! Not yet!'

'Please, please, just go . . .' She could feel herself losing control and she desperately didn't want him to be there when she cried. 'George . . . Gideon . . . whoever you are. Get out. I mean it.'

He heard the desperation in her voice and reluctantly he turned to the door. 'Poppy, please can I come back later when we're both a little calmer and I've had a chance to sort this out?'

'No.' Her voice was like ice. 'I never want to see you again.'

45

The boardroom table was littered with samples again and the women were having a wonderful time trying out all the treats Claudine had brought back with her from France. She looked as chic as ever, her dark bob freshly cut and dressed in her favourite Chanel, this time a light summer dress sprinkled with tiny stars.

'These are fabulous, Claudine. How did you manage to come up with so many products so fast?' Donna said, smoothing a soft milk into the skin on her forearm.

Claudine gave a little smile. 'I have some very good friends who create these skin products in their laboratory. They develop ranges for many of the top names in skin care. I explained what we needed and they gave me access to their newest ranges. They are top class and all plant based.'

'Fantastic,' breathed Tara, sniffing a small tub of rich cream. 'This is *Tea Rose*, isn't it?'

Claudine nodded. 'We have a rich moisturiser, a light moisturiser, a night cream, hand cream, face and body wash, and soaps. There is scope for more in time.'

'I love these candles,' declared Jemima, holding one of them up. 'They smell divine. Can I take one home?'

'Of course,' Claudine said, smiling at her.

Only Poppy seemed unable to work up the enthusiasm of the others. She tried all the lotions and murmured her praise, but she was distinctly low key.

'This is so inspiring,' Donna said, clearly delighted with Claudine's work. 'Now we can recruit staff and start designing treatments. Claudine, come and see what we've done downstairs. You'll love it.'

They all went down to the newly refitted shop. It was almost finished, just waiting for the final decorative touches and the new products. Claudine admired the fresh, white interior and the feeling of space and light that had been created. She was charmed by the booths where customers would be able to mix scents and experiment with creating a fragrance, and she thought the treatment rooms had just the right feel of luxurious spa meets healthy living.

'There is only one thing,' she said, frowning and pointing outside. 'What colour are those men painting the shop front?'

'Pink,' said Donna. 'Our signature nude pink, the one we chose for *Tea Rose*.'

'It is all wrong.' Claudine waved a dismissive hand.

'What?' Poppy said dismayed. 'But why?'

'Come outside and look.' They all trooped outside and stood on the pavement, watching the men in their overalls slapping pink paint on the old navy blue woodwork.

'You see?' Claudine pointed upwards. 'What looks charming on a bottle of perfume or on its box does not look so good all over the shop! This is far too pink. Your shop looks like a place for little girls. Or like one of those cheap high-street sex shops where women buy nasty feather boas and dirty little toys.'

They all looked up, dismayed.

'She's right, I'm afraid,' Jemima said softly. 'Not about the sex shop bit, of course. But it's just too pink. We'll have to think again.'

'And fast,' said Tara grimly.

Poppy couldn't tell the others what had happened with George. Or Gideon, or whoever he was. It was simply too humiliating. They had seen her tired eyes and miserable expression, so she had told them that she and George had broken up but that she didn't want to discuss it further. Instead she sat silently flicking through colour charts, trying to find the right shade for the Trevellyan shop front.

Her phone rang and she picked it up. 'Hello?'

'Hi, darlin', it's Neave. How are you?'

'Oh, hi. I'm fine. Where are you?'

'In New York. I've got a shoot here. I'm having my hair done as we speak. I'm gonna be here for hours, it's so boring. So – did you find out what happened with that boyfriend of yours? I've been worryin' about you.'

'We've split up.' Just saying the words brought a hammer blow of depression down on her.

'So what was his explanation for his fake job and his fake name?'

'His job's real, his name is not.' Poppy took a deep breath. 'He says he's called Gideon Marlow and that he's not Mrs Fellowes's nephew, so he's nothing to do with the lady who owns his flat. But I couldn't get anything else out of him. He refused to say a word. I couldn't believe that he would rather let me send him away than give me a word of explanation.'

'That's bizarre. Run him through Google,' Neave said, 'or even better, get a private detective on to him.'

'That seems a bit extreme . . .' Poppy frowned. 'Do you really think it's that serious?'

'You have to admit, it's very odd behaviour, darlin'. It's not right. You need to get to the bottom of it.'

'Maybe.' Poppy turned over another page of her colour chart. 'I just don't feel like I can face it right now. I can't believe I've lost George. I loved him and now I've found out he doesn't even exist.'

'Ah, poor lamb,' said Neave sympathetically. 'Course you can't face it. Don't you worry – you just take care of yourself, OK? I'm comin' back in a few days. We're flying to LA tonight and then after a few meetings we're catching a flight back to London. As soon as I've had a chance to catch my breath, I'll take you out for a drink. We'll have some fun; we'll be single girls together, all right?'

Poppy smiled. That did sound fun. She had a feeling that while Neave might not enjoy glossy parties, she would certainly know how to enjoy herself when she felt like it. 'OK.'

'Good. Now cheer up, darlin'. I'll see you soon.'

Jecca put the phone down, looking satisfied.

'Who was that?' Ferrera said from behind his newspaper. He had listened to Jecca's side of the conversation but she had kept it brief and had done most of the listening.

'My lawyers. They seem to think I've got a strong case. They're confident it will be in court in just a few months. In other words, before *Tea Rose* is launched in November, which is exactly what I wanted. I want to be in there for that. I want to be a part of it.' She walked over to him and sat down. 'You know, that company should rightly be mine. All of it. It was my Italian ancestors who made it what it was. The Trevellyans have always been parasites, making their money out of my family's talent and skill.'

'They weren't too bad at the business side of things,' Ferrera said carelessly.

'Yes, and I'm a Trevellyan too, don't forget that. I have a right to everything those girls have got and I intend to get it.'

'This is becoming an obsession for you,' observed Ferrera.

'So?' demanded Jecca, quick to rise to the bait as usual. 'You're obsessed with your business. Why is it wrong for me to be the same?'

'You take it further than I would.'

'Perhaps.' Jecca smiled to herself. 'It's only natural to feel passionate about something that is my family's heritage. But yes, I do persist where most people would stop.' She fingered the locket that hung on a chain round her neck. 'But my challenges are more extreme than most.' She looked thoughtful. 'Particularly as one of my best sources of information has just dried up.'

'How so?' Ferrera asked.

'Oh, nothing . . . just someone who kept me abreast of things.' Jecca smiled at him. Her charm was extraordinary when she chose to use it but Ferrera was beginning to learn not to let that sensuous smile and the melting dark eyes override his sense of danger where Jecca was concerned. 'What's your plan for the day, my darling?'

'I'm going to New York this evening. I told you that.'

Jecca pouted. 'Of course. Have you changed your mind about taking me with you?'

Ferrera shook his head. 'I'm afraid not. This is business. I won't have time for partying and socialising and you'd just get bored in the penthouse with nothing to do.'

'No, I wouldn't!'

'Yes, you would. You're staying here. The matter is closed.' He folded up his paper with the barest hint of irritation, to show Jecca she should stop pushing him. 'Surely you'd rather stay where you can keep a close eye on things at Trevellyan.'

'There is that, I suppose,' Jecca said thoughtfully.

542

'And I may make a rather startling move very soon. Surprise everyone.'

'Beware of surprises,' Ferrera remarked, getting up. 'The harder you concentrate on planning them, the more likely you are to be surprised yourself. At least, that's what I've always found.' He walked towards the door. 'By the way, I want you to keep me informed about anything you do. Do you understand? I will not be compromised by your actions, Jecca. Do I make myself clear?'

'Crystal, darling, crystal!' Jecca blinked big eyes at him, looking as innocent as she could.

He could see all too clearly that she had no intention of obeying him. She truly believed she could outwit him, and that he and his company were just a useful stepping stone towards her greater ambitions. 'Good,' he said calmly. 'I'm glad we understand each other. You know how to reach me.'

46

To everyone's surprise, it was Claudine who enthusiastically brought together the last elements of the relaunch. She provided the wonderful products for the new Trevellyan range, and managed to persuade her friends to sell them at very reasonable prices, considering their properties. It was Claudine who spotted that the nude pink was quite wrong for the shop front, and Claudine who picked out the delicate blue that would replace it. Poppy had brought several suggestions to the table but Claudine, with her unerring good taste, knew which it should be immediately.

'This one,' she declared. 'Chic. Modern. Still linked to your original navy blue but with a lavender, almost pinky base. This is the one.'

They had all agreed at once. The nude pink would be reserved only for *Tea Rose*. The subtle blue would become the company colour.

It was Claudine who went with Tara to the factory

near Birmingham to oversee setting up the production of *Tea Rose* according to her new formula, and spent an afternoon training the lab workers there in her own, very special ways.

'You're brilliant, Claudine,' Tara told her, and Claudine only shrugged as if slightly surprised that it had taken everyone so long to realise what she had known all along.

'I'm glad to be of help,' was all she said.

Then, back in the office, she provided the answer to what had seemed their biggest dilemma.

'How did the *Vogue* interview go?' Donna asked.

'Very well,' Tara said. 'It was quite fun to get all dressed up again to be photographed, even if it did remind me of that awful night at Spencer House.' She shuddered slightly. 'But the interviewer was very polite. She didn't even mention Jecca once. It was all about our glamorous lives and based around our successes and our talents. They loved *Tea Rose*. I had to promise to send over some bottles as soon as we have them.'

'We can't give away too much product,' said Donna sternly.

'No, but *Vogue* . . .'

'OK, point taken. Yes, *Vogue* can have whatever they want. What about you, Jemima? How did the interview with the *Chronicle* go?'

'Funnily enough, they wanted to know all about Jecca,' Jemima said drily. 'Unlike the ladies at *Vogue*, they couldn't get enough of it. But thankfully they had no interest in anything to do with my home life aside from how much money I spent on clothes, where I get my hair done, and how much Herne Castle is worth. I have to go down there tomorrow for pictures. They want the lord and lady at home.'

'When's it out?' Donna asked.

'Saturday.'

'I still don't understand why you've done an interview with them,' Poppy said, frowning. 'Aren't they a little bit downmarket for us?'

'Good publicity,' Donna said quickly. 'I used a contact. Who cares if it's upmarket or downmarket. It all helps.' She swiftly changed the subject. 'So that leaves us with two big questions. Who's our face? And what's going to happen with the States?'

'Any news on Kate Beckinsale?' asked Tara.

Donna shook her head. 'Doesn't look good, I'm afraid. We'll have to think of someone else to approach.'

'The sale of the Loxton contents is going through soon,' said Poppy. She felt uncomfortable talking about the *Tea Rose* face, as though it was her fault that Neave had said no. 'So we'll have more cash to put into our budget for the US campaign.'

'And I've got three viewings of Eaton Square this afternoon, from the kind of girls whose daddies pay in cash,' announced Jemima. 'I'm sure that will mean another couple of mill for the US campaign.'

Donna sighed and shook her head. 'It isn't going to be enough, ladies. It just isn't. We've spent so much already. I know we should be able to afford it, with the millions you're pouring in from your own money, but we won't.'

They were all silent and morose as Donna's words sank in.

Claudine frowned. 'But I don't understand. If we can't afford it, why should we pay for it?'

'Because we need to launch in America,' Tara said wearily. 'If we don't, we may as well not bother launching at all.'

'So get someone else to pay for it,' Claudine said with a shrug.

They all looked at her, bewildered, having forgotten she was even in the room.

'No one will lend us that kind of money,' said Tara. 'Not without the kind of securities that we just can't offer.'

'You don't need to borrow the money,' Claudine said impatiently. 'Do you think you are the only small perfume house with this problem? Of course not. Plenty of small European houses, with a great success here and in America, do not have the kind of power and presence needed to manage their business in the States. So, they go into partnership with someone who can. They go to a big company, creator of hundreds of bestselling fragrances – not just luxury perfumes but the smells that go into our laundry, our cleaners, our shampoos, our mouthwashes, our medicines, everything – and license them to do that work for them. A company that has the money and the network to distribute their perfume. *Et voilà* – money and success for everyone.'

There was another silence as everyone considered her words, but this time with a seed of hope within it.

'I can't believe I didn't think of that. It's the perfect solution,' breathed Donna.

'Oh my God, you're a genius!' exclaimed Jemima, throwing her arms around Claudine.

Tara smiled. 'I'd better get on a plane to New York right away.'

Jemima popped into Claudine's temporary office before she went home.

'Hi,' she said shyly. 'I just wanted to thank you for your great suggestions today. I think you've cracked it for us.'

'It is what you pay me for.' Claudine smiled at her a little mischievously. 'How are you, *chérie?*'

'Fine, fine – really, fine.' Jemima sat down a little awkwardly. 'I just wanted to say . . . about Paris. Well, we haven't spoken about it since you got back.'

'Please.' Claudine waved Jemima's words away. 'Don't think of it. I have heard that you and your husband have reconciled. That is very good. I knew that our little liaison was no more than a spontaneous bright moment, to exist only then, like a dream. I did not expect or want more. I shall treasure the memory of it because it was rather beautiful. But that is all.'

'I suppose I shouldn't flatter myself that you wanted more.'

Claudine shrugged. 'You are fascinating, of course.' She smiled her mysterious smile. 'But so am I.'

'You certainly are.' Jemima laughed.

'I am happy for you. Go home to your husband, I can see you want to be on your way.'

Jemima jumped up. 'Good night, you fascinating thing!' She blew her a kiss and then hurried out into the corridor, hearing Claudine laughing lightly behind her.

Jecca looked with disgust at the newspaper on the table in front of her. Ferrera had left two nights ago and she had no one she could share her feelings with. She jumped up, feeling thwarted, and started to march about the apartment.

The pictures made her sick: the golden couple smiling lovingly at each other as they relaxed on their country estate. *Yuk!* Seeing Jemima playing happy families with her tedious husband was nauseating. Jecca couldn't believe that the papers had swallowed that crap. Everyone knew that Jemima had been cheating on him virtually since the day they were married! But something had happened to bring them back together. Well, there was nothing she could do about that.

But it was what Jemima had said in her interview that stung most of all: 'We don't know why Jecca has turned against the family in the way she has. She vanished without a word years ago, so it was no wonder my mother didn't include her in the will. She rejected us long before we rejected her. If she wanted to work with us in our very exciting project here at Trevellyan, she could have approached us rather than going through the courts. Surely we could have resolved this amicably, without the vast expense of lawyers and a court case. Our fondest wish is that we can all be reconciled again.'

'Lying bitch!' hissed Jecca. 'You hate my guts. And I hate yours.' She stalked over to the window and looked out over the leafy borough of Kensington. 'Well, well. We might just have to take this up a notch a little sooner than I expected.'

She went over to the phone, picked it up and dialled a number. 'Hi. Yes, I want you to get me Poppy Trevellyan's private number. I don't know, just do it. Now.'

She put the receiver down and crossed her arms thoughtfully. At the party she had relished taking on the Trevellyan sisters *en masse*. Now she was prepared for single combat.

47

Tara had wanted to sleep on the plane, but she was far too keyed up. Only the day before her offer on the Clapham house had been accepted. That morning, she received the news she had hoped for: there was a buyer for the Holland Park house, a wealthy Arab prince who was delighted with the place because it was only doors away from members of his extended family. He would pay cash and he wanted to exchange quickly. The documents would have to be couriered to Gerald in South Africa for his signature but Tara didn't see a problem with that. Her husband knew that he wouldn't be living in England again in the near future, if ever.

But if things turned out the way she hoped, it meant she might be able to move into the Clapham house within two months, before the launch of *Tea Rose*. Then they could start to live their new life. And maybe after Christmas, she would take the children to South Africa for a trip to see their father. It was easy to recognise that calls via video phone and laptop were not going to be enough. And Edward and Imo mustn't lose touch with Gerald, no matter what he'd done.

The plane began its descent into New York. Tara loved the city and was secretly delighted that her work allowed her to visit it, even if it meant leaving the children for a few days. Thank God for Robina, whom they loved and trusted. They were safe with her, Tara knew that.

She had decided not to stay in the New York house, even though it was still available to her. It was too marked by Gerald's presence but, more than that, there was no one there to prepare it for her. It would be cold, dark and dirty, and altogether less than welcoming. No, she would stay at one of her favourite hotels, the Soho Grand in downtown New York. It might not be as convenient as something in the midtown district, but she valued its calm, elegant rooms and the vibrant, artistic neighbourhood.

There was so much to think about. Besides the plan of uprooting her family and moving to a new house, dealing with a divorce and her husband's situation, she also felt that they were at crunch time as far as Trevellyan was concerned. If this distribution partnership idea came off, then they might just save the day. If not, then she may as well call Jecca and ask her to come and collect the keys to Trevellyan House there and then.

Now there was a spanner in the works she hadn't anticipated. She had always feared that one day that angry little girl who had fractured their lives, their childhoods and their family might reappear and cause more havoc. But she had not foreseen this dramatic return.

So all along, Jecca had been with Ferrera. That was so odd. She couldn't understand how that had come about. Jecca must have somehow got herself to the States after she vanished, and at some point her path must have crossed with that of the charismatic businessman . . .

But who was Jecca? Was she really Cecil's daughter? Was she Tara's own half-sister? Tara frowned, watching the Manhattan skyline grow ever closer as they came in to land at JFK. It was so hard to believe because there didn't seem to be an ounce of Trevellyan blood in her. She looked so different to them, her Italian heritage dominating her personality and features, that it was hard to see how she could be Daddy's daughter. But something had to explain his attachment to her. It had been too strong to be normal. Was it, as Jemima suggested, sexual? Tara tried to imagine it for a moment, and then banished the picture from her mind, sickened.

If only they could find out once and for all, perhaps this strange situation could somehow be resolved. Then a thought suddenly occurred to her. She pulled out her BlackBerry and quickly fired off an email to Jemima, pushing send just as the flight attendant came by and asked her to switch it off.

Jemima took advantage of her visit to Herne for the photo shoot to stay on for a couple of days with Harry.

It was like being on honeymoon again. They spent long mornings lying in bed together, chatting, making love, dozing and then starting all over again. Harry abandoned his old bedroom at the front of the house and joined her in her cosy boudoir.

'You've really made this nice, you know,' he commented as they lay in bed.

'Do you think so? You know, that's the first time you've ever said that.' She grinned. 'Maybe you should let me get my hands on the rest of the house . . .'

'Oh, I'm not sure,' Harry said doubtfully.

'I'm teasing. I know nothing is allowed to change. Not for a while, anyway. But, I've been thinking. There is something we could do here.'

'What?' Harry sounded tentative. He didn't want the loving calm that existed between them to come to an end just yet.

'Well, we've just had all this publicity, through that silly newspaper thing. And the *Vogue* article will come out when we launch and they were so interested in this place and what we were doing with it . . .'

'Yes?'

'What about if we left the house strictly alone – but did something with the old stables?'

Harry frowned. 'The stables?'

'Yes. We could turn them into something really interesting. I was thinking about a day spa, using the Trevellyan treatments and products. Then we could open a restaurant as well.' Jemima became full of enthusiasm as she talked about it. 'Think about it. We've got more fresh produce than we know what to do with. We've got meat, vegetables, herbs, fruit. We could run the most fantastic organic restaurant, and even open a farm shop if we started making our own jams and all that sort of thing. But best of all, we could offer Trevellyan treatments and have a Trevellyan shop here. It would be a neat little enterprise. What do you think?'

'Oh my God,' Harry said. 'That's quite a lot to absorb straight off.'

'OK, so think about it. But I could use some of the flat money to set it up. And it would bring in an income without you having to open up the house to the public. I know you've never wanted that.'

'Jemima . . .' Harry turned over to face her. 'Just us for a while first, OK? I'm not saying no. I actually think it sounds really interesting and anything that interests you and keeps you at Herne is something I'm keen to consider. Plus, if it makes money to help preserve the house, all the better. But first, let's just concentrate on us.'

'All right, all right.' Jemima put her head on his chest. 'It's just so hard, when I've got so many ideas, when everything at Trevellyan is approaching its big moment.'

'I know, darling. I know.' He kissed the top of her fair head and stroked her back.

Poppy could hardly believe what she was hearing.

'What the hell do you think you're doing calling me?' she said furiously.

'Poppy, please.' Jecca sounded amiable, friendly.

'You're the only one I can talk to, you know that. Jemima and I have always hated each other and Tara has always resented me. You're the only one who didn't have that kind of relationship with me.'

'Maybe. But my loyalty is to Tara and Jemima, you know that. I'm not about to strike any secret deals with you, so don't think for a moment that you can use me. Anything you say to me will go straight back to the other two.'

'I understand that,' said Jecca evenly. 'But at least you'll listen to me. The others wouldn't even do that.'

Poppy thought for a moment. That was true. And perhaps it would be to their advantage to hear what Jecca had to say. 'All right, then. Talk.'

'I want to meet in person.'

Poppy gasped with horror. 'No. No way.'

'Please, Poppy. I'm begging you. Give me twenty minutes, that's all. I just need to explain myself to you.'

'I thought you did a pretty good job of that at your boyfriend's party.'

'We were all a bit carried away. I'd appreciate the chance to talk to you in a calmer way, without all that noise and attention.'

'I really don't want to meet you, Jecca.'

'But this is a chance for us to get this all sorted out. Why should we have to face each other in court, with all our dirty linen being washed in public, when a short meeting and a few words could solve everything? But I can't do it over the phone, Poppy, you must see that.'

Poppy stood up and walked to the window, staring out across the square without seeing it. At last she said, 'All right. If you honestly think we can get this sorted out as easily as that, then I'm prepared to meet you. Where will you be and when?'

Jecca was waiting for her when she walked through the restaurant and out into the garden at the back. Poppy saw her at once, sitting neatly on a garden bench in the courtyard, a glass of water and lemon and a bottle of Badoit on the table beside her. She was wearing red again, this time a button-through dress, and ballet pumps. Her sunglasses were perched high on her dark hair as she flicked through a magazine. As Poppy approached, she looked up and smiled.

'Hi, thanks so much for coming.' She stood up and went to kiss Poppy but the other woman held out her hand coolly, so they shook hands instead. 'You've changed so much.'

'So have you,' Poppy said coldly as she sat down. Jecca had always had striking dark looks but now they had matured into a real beauty. It wasn't just her looks, though; Jecca's voice had also changed. She had a slight American intonation now. So that answered the mystery of where she had disappeared to all those years ago.

'Tell me about yourself,' persisted Jecca, pouring a glass of water for Poppy. 'We must have so much news to catch up on. I've heard you're an artist now. I always knew you'd be the one to really make something of

557

yourself. You had a special aura, you know? Not like the other two. They were very ordinary.'

'Jecca, I'm not here to make small talk or to have a joyful reunion with you. As long as you are pursuing my sisters and me through the courts, I can't do idle chit-chat and mutual admiration.'

Jecca's smile faded for a moment, but she quickly cheered up again. 'All right. Fine. If that's how you want it.'

'I do. Do we still have anything to say to each other?'

'I think we do. I need to tell you the truth about me, so you can understand why I'm doing what I'm doing. Perhaps you and the others have speculated about this before now, maybe you've even guessed.' Jecca's hand went to her locket and she started twisting it. 'The truth is that I'm Cecil Trevellyan's daughter, his natural daughter. I'm your half-sister.'

'Can you prove it?' Poppy asked at once, watching Jecca twist the necklace round and round.

'Of course.' Jecca shrugged. 'If I need to. But I think we all know in our hearts that I am who I say I am. Your father ravished my mother not long after she arrived in your home. I was the result.'

'How do you know that?'

'Because darling Daddy told me, of course! He couldn't hide anything from me. You know how he was with me.'

'Yes,' said Poppy huskily, suddenly choked. 'That's why it killed him when you vanished.'

'He always knew where I was,' said Jecca carelessly.

'I don't believe you. He was heartbroken, we could all see that. There's no way that was put on.'

'Have it your own way. It's my word against yours. Like I said, I have proof and I'm not afraid to use it.'

'Why are you telling me this?'

'Because I want to make you an offer. If you and the others bring me in now, give me my quarter, recognise me as your real sister, I'll drop my case.'

'That's your offer?' Poppy exclaimed, astonished.

Jecca nodded, blinking innocently, her dark red lips curving into a sweet smile. 'I still think back fondly to the years we spent growing up together. Remember how we played in the nursery? How we ran round the garden and went swimming? I miss those days. I miss Tara and Jemima too, believe it or not. I want us all to be a family again.'

I don't think I do believe it, thought Poppy. Surely the last person in the world that Jecca missed was Jemima. She looked quizzical. 'Let me make sure I've got this straight. We accept you back, and accept your claim that Daddy was your father, give you a quarter of the company –'

'Maybe a quarter of everything is more realistic,' Jecca put in quickly.

'– and you drop your case. Why didn't you suggest this sooner? Why the big scene at the party?'

Jecca smiled slyly. 'I suppose I had to get your attention somehow. It was a little over the top, perhaps, but I'm not one to do things by halves.'

'You certainly succeeded in grabbing our attention,' Poppy said grimly. 'Didn't it occur to you that it would be much harder to start pulling the loving sister act afterwards?'

Jecca said nothing. She lifted her glass of water to her lips and took a sip.

Poppy continued. 'I think that awful scene at Spencer House was all part of your attempt to black-mail us into giving you what you want, wasn't it? You got us precisely the kind of attention we didn't want, revealing family secrets and dragging us into the tabloids. My theory is that you're actually telling me that if we don't agree to your demands, you're going to start spilling more beans. Your claim that you're Daddy's daughter, for example. You could get some juicy coverage out of that one. Enough to put the launch of *Tea Rose* in the shade.'

Jecca raised her eyebrows and shrugged lightly. 'If I were a part of the business, I'd have no interest in doing anything that could threaten *Tea Rose*'s success. And you know, there's lots I could do to help you.'

'Really?'

'Uh huh. After all, I am fucking one of the most influential men in the luxury industry. Doesn't that count for something?'

Poppy winced with distaste. 'Not in my book.'

Jecca looked disconcerted for a moment, then her face darkened. 'Still the same, aren't you? Judging me. You Trevellyans always tried to make me feel second best. You waltzed round, oh so superior, treating me like dirt because I was some nothing little orphan. Do you think I've forgotten any of that? How you made me suffer all those years?'

'That's not true,' Poppy whispered. 'We were children. We would have welcomed you into our family if that was what you wanted. There was room for us all. But you never did want that, not from the very start. Nothing was enough for you. What you really wanted was everything for yourself. And you still do.'

'Shut up!' cried Jecca. Her fists clenched on the table and her eyes flashed. 'Your family would be nowhere if it weren't for mine. It was our talent that made you! Do you know how it killed me to see your mother dripping in her furs and jewels, revelling in her huge house, while mine lay dead in the ground? How do you think it felt to know my father had lost everything while yours sat on his stupid ass doing nothing, raking in the money the Farnese family had made for him? Everything *should* be mine, if there were any fucking justice in the world.'

There was a long pause and then Poppy said quietly, 'You've made yourself quite clear, Jecca. I think I understand now.'

Jecca closed her eyes, taking a second to control herself. When she opened them, there was no trace of the rage that had just gripped her. Instead she smiled sunnily. 'So will you consider my proposition? I think we could be a strong team, the four of us.'

Poppy stared at her, amazed. Did she seriously think that they would want her anywhere near them, especially now that she had revealed the vein of bitterness and hatred that lay within her? She didn't appear to notice anything inconsistent in her behaviour at all. Poppy grabbed her bag and stood up. The emotions

561

coursed through her and she didn't think she could keep her composure much longer. She had to get out of there. 'I'll tell the others. We'll think about it and let you know.'

'Good.' Jecca smiled up at her. 'Going already? Do stay and chat. I'd love to reminisce about old times.'

'No, thanks. Bye, Jecca. I'll be in touch.'

48

Tara lay down on the bed in her hotel room, exhausted. The heat in New York was intense: she'd forgotten what summers here could be like. No wonder people abandoned hot, sticky, smelly Manhattan and went to the cooler seaside, if they could. But at least her room had air-conditioning – *bliss.*

She tried not to feel too depressed about the meetings she had had that day. People had been polite but brutal in their assessment of Trevellyan. No one in America really cared that much about the brand. It sold OK, on the back of its history and prestige. The new scent was nice enough. Was it a winner? No one really liked to say, the mind of the average perfume buyer was impossible to read. They all maintained similar expressions of bland uninterest and they all asked the same question that ended in an abrupt halt to the meeting. Who did they have to be the face of the scent? *No one? Oh. OK. Thanks very much, we'll think*

*about it and let you know but to be honest, it's unlikely.
Sorry. Goodbye.*

Tara tried to stay positive. *There's still tomorrow*, she thought. *I've got two more meetings and I only need one bite on the line . . .*

She'd been thinking of trying to catch up with some friends this evening but after her long day, she didn't feel much like socialising. Maybe she would just order room service and eat here in her room, watching some old movie. That sounded nice.

But first, she decided, she'd go downstairs to the bar and treat to herself to a big, expensive cocktail, something to knock the edge off the day. Then she'd come back here and order herself a Caesar salad and eat it in her underwear.

She changed from her business suit to a Matthew Williamson mini tunic dress in bright bold colours and slipped on a pair of high sandals – perfect for a drink in the hotel bar. Then she checked her reflection, reapplied her lipstick, brushed her hair and went downstairs.

She made her way out to the Yard at the back, a bright, cheerful outside space where people were sharing pitchers of mojitos, margaritas and sangria while they munched on burgers and chicken skewers. The daytime heat had abated and now the evening was pleasantly warm and relaxed, as people began to revive in the cooler air.

This is what I love about New York, she thought, looking about. *It always seems so on the pulse, so intelligent. Hard working but hard playing too. You have to be special to make it here.*

She ordered a mojito and when it came, she savoured its sweet mintiness, exactly right for the summer evening, and watched New York's cool urban youth talking, drinking, laughing and eating. How long ago was she a young woman with only herself to think about? How long since she'd whiled away an evening like that, looking so relaxed and so in control?

Never, she realised with surprise. At Oxford, she'd spent her life working hard, encouraged by the intense academic atmosphere of her college. She hadn't been able to understand how other students had time for partying, sport, acting or journalism; she was far too busy in the library, applying herself to her books. Desperately worried she wouldn't achieve her potential, she developed an eating disorder and grew thinner and thinner even as her results got better and better. By the time she left university, she was neurotic, obsessed with her skinny, boney body, and in possession of a double first class degree. She was snapped up at once by a major bank and started her journey towards professional success, working hard as she always had. But there was no pretending she was happy. She never had the kind of easy confidence the people round her seemed to have. She began to think she'd never learn how to live. Then she met Gerald.

She could see now that she just replaced one form of control with another. Gerald seemed to set her free with his love and devotion, but the reality was that he just erected a new kind of prison for her, one that looked deceptively like freedom. He found her a clinic to help her with her eating disorder, and encouraged her in her job and as a woman. He began to dictate how she should look and dress and how their houses should be decorated. He decided when they would have children, which in reality was before Tara herself felt she was ready, although she would never wish Edward and Imogen away in a million years; but by then, the habit of obedience was so ingrained in her that it was impossible to break it.

Only Trevellyan had been able to set her free. Only when the challenge presented itself was she able to do something for herself, and that one act of rebellion had set off a whole chain of events that released her. It hadn't even been a gradual process. One day she had been in Gerald's thrall, still terrified of him and awed by his power. She'd let him physically humiliate her, for Christ's sake! Then, the next, with the combination of her own success and his appalling failure as a businessman and husband, she was liberated.

Now there was a new life to look forward to, she realised. A fresh start. She couldn't wait to move to the new house, to an area where no one knew her, where she and the children could start being a normal family – well, as normal as they could be with Gerald's trial hanging over them. And she would start to learn to please herself. After all, there was no one to crave approval from now: her parents were dead. Gerald was gone. Her sisters had begun to look up to her and respect her for the first time in their lives. Above all, she knew her children needed her to be a strong, capable, protective mother, and she finally realised she could be that.

She felt a surge of strength and optimism. *I can do it. I know I can. I have to make sure I find the balance, that's all. I have to work, but not at the expense of my entire life. I need to care for the children, but not at the expense of my own sense of self. I need to discover what I love about being alive, besides work, success and all the trappings.*

She finished her drink and sighed happily. Then she turned to go back inside and up to her room.

She saw him in the lobby, talking to a suited man, and stopped short. Could she pass him without his seeing her? He was deep in conversation. Perhaps if she just sidled past . . . or perhaps she should turn smartly on her heel and go back to the courtyard, order another mojito and wait until the coast was clear.

She dithered too long. He glanced up and saw her. He recognised her instantly and was similarly confused. How should he greet her? The last time they'd met, she'd been three-quarters cut and had been less than polite. Then his innate sense of decorum took over and he smiled at her, excused himself and walked over.

'Mrs Pearson,' Ferrera said. 'What an unexpected pleasure. What are you doing in New York?'

'Good evening, Mr Ferrera. I'm here on business.

And I'm Tara Trevellyan now.' She tried to hit just the right note between cool and courteous. She was embarrassed to remember the party. She couldn't recall exactly what she'd said now, but she had the feeling she'd implied Ferrera was a less than upright businessman or something similarly rude. Whatever she'd said, she'd certainly embarrassed herself by being drunk. Well, she would have been a hell of a lot ruder if she'd known what she knew now – that he was in partnership with Jecca and very probably funding her lawsuit against the Trevellyan sisters.

'Tara Trevellyan. It has a nice ring to it – I can see why your parents gave you the name.' Ferrera smiled. He looked very handsome, his cool Ralph Lauren linen suit setting off his dark skin, brown eyes and slightly spiky hair. *Don't let him charm you*, Tara told herself sternly. She should walk away right now, turn her back on him and leave. She despised him after all: he was a man who had treated his ex-wife appallingly, destroyed the integrity of the businesses he had acquired and, worst of all, was literally in bed with the woman who was trying to bring Trevellyan to its knees. But her good manners were so ingrained in her, she couldn't bring herself to do it. Instead she said coolly, 'What are you doing here in the Grand?'

'Business, of course. What else is there?'

'Don't you ever take any time off?'

'Sometimes I do.' Despite his healthy appearance, Ferrera suddenly looked tired. 'Actually, I'm due a break round about now. I've been working non-stop for months, overseeing our European expansion. It's worth it, of course. And I care so damn much about this company, I couldn't bear to think of it not being the success it should be just because I fancied going surfing.'

Tara felt sympathetic despite herself. She knew that feeling of bone-crunching exhaustion, when rest was not an option. 'But everyone needs to recharge now and then or they risk breaking down completely. And then what good are they?'

'That's more of a British mindset than an American one. We like to press on, keep going, never stop.'

'No wonder you all have cardiac arrests and nervous breakdowns at fifty,' Tara said tartly.

Ferrera laughed. 'You remind me of your sister. And I mean that as a compliment.'

Tara stared at him and then said slowly, 'Which one? My sister Jemima, or the woman you're sleeping with?'

Ferrera's smile faded slightly. A spark of anger filled his eyes.

I've gone too far, Tara thought. *What is it about this man that makes me so antagonistic?* Then, to her surprise, he laughed again.

'You don't have any compunction about being rude to me, do you? It makes a refreshing change. Do you have plans for dinner?'

'As it happens – yes.'

'What a shame. I was hoping to talk to you. Are they too important to be changed?'

'I don't know about that. My television may be disappointed if I don't go back and eat my salad with it,'

Tara said wryly. Then she remembered herself and became cool again. 'But I don't think it would be right to have dinner with you.'

'Well, naturally, I wouldn't want to get in the way of an arrangement as special as that. But I'd really like you to consider my offer. I realise there are difficulties between us but I think it would be to both our advantages if we were able to have a sober, civilised talk.'

Tara flushed slightly at the word sober, hoping it wasn't a dig at her tipsiness the night they had met. There was no denying that Ferrera was charming, and she liked the fact that he wasn't trying to flirt with her. Should she turn down this chance to find out more about him and his methods? After all, if he was in league with Jecca to take over Trevellyan, it might be useful to understand a bit more about how he worked.

Ferrera sensed her weakening. 'Come on. Salad is salad. I know somewhere very good we can go.' He saw that she was still hesitating. 'I can guess what you're thinking. I'm your rival, as far as you're concerned. How about we declare tonight off the record?'

Tara looked sceptical. 'Mmm. I'll believe that when I see it.'

Ferrera laughed again. 'All right, let's just do our best, OK? We're both too obsessed by business to avoid discussing it completely. But please – I really think it would be a good thing for us to talk.'

Tara thought for a second. Her empty room and the television suddenly seemed a lot less appealing, and she knew she should seize the opportunity to learn a little more about Ferrera. 'OK. I accept. Where did you have in mind?'

Poppy's mobile beeped and she picked it up. 'Neave? Are you back?'

'You'd better believe it! I'm back and I've got some exciting news. Wanna go out and celebrate?'

'Now?'

'Yes, now! Strike while the iron's hot. Besides, there's something else I want to talk to you about.'

I need something to cheer me up, Poppy thought. Neave had been doing a good job of making her feel better. The loss of George – or whoever he was – was beginning to hurt her badly. It wasn't just the pain of betrayal and the questions that ran endlessly through her head day and night, it was that she missed him, plain and simple. In the months they'd been together, she had come to love his company and to rely on it. He had assuaged the loneliness that had gripped her after she'd lost Tom and then her mother. Now it was back with a vengeance and the worst of it was that no one understood how she felt: her sisters hadn't even met George and she couldn't bring herself to tell them what he'd done to her.

The scene with Jecca had only added to her depression. Tomorrow she'd have to pass on the so-called offer to Jemima and Tara but she could guess what they'd have to say to it.

She put on a vintage white sundress, a Panama hat and Ray-Bans. Then she headed for Soho to meet Neave.

They met in a private club. This one was not like Poppy's arts club: dingy, a bit grubby and full of poets, artists and literary types. Neave's club thronged with the beautiful people – actors, actresses, models – and their supporting cast: the agents, stylists, publicists, hairdressers, make-up artists and nutritionists, plus various best friends and hangers-on. Film producers were hunched over tables, making deals with financiers. Directors were schmoozing journalists, trying to interest them in their latest releases. Ad-men were looking for inspiration in bottles of fine wine and plates of nachos. Editors of newspapers were cutting deals for tell-all stories with ex-wives of popstars, while grungy bands were hanging out, making constant trips to the smoking terrace, drinking too much and eating too little.

'Oh my God, what a place,' said Poppy, blinking. 'I think I've led a very quiet life. This is much more the kind of club my sister Jemima goes to. In fact, I think I can see a couple of her exes over there.'

Neave looked unimpressed by the well-known faces everywhere. 'I much preferred your joint. This is way too showy and pretentious for my tastes. I mean, there are three different bars, two restaurants and a private cinema. My agent put me up for membership and they let me in right away, so here I am. At least it's somewhere I can hang out and not get bothered.'

Poppy was unconvinced. Even the bored, spaced-out boy band in the corner perked up when they saw Neave, nudging each other and whispering loudly. The model looked heartstoppingly gorgeous as usual in tiny cut-off denim shorts, a plain white T-shirt and flat Prada sandals.

'I don't usually do this 'cos frankly, I've had enough of the stuff to last me a lifetime but I'm going to order champagne. When you're celebrating, it's obligatory. But let's have the pink stuff to liven it up a bit,' Neave said, clapping her hands with glee. Poppy was touched by the innocent enthusiasm that was written all over her face. She was so beautiful and sophisticated-looking it was hard to remember that only a couple of years ago she had been a shop girl in Dublin living with her parents.

'What are we celebrating?'

'Let's get our drinks and then I'll tell you.'

When the flutes of Dom Pérignon Rosé were sparkling in front of them, Neave picked hers up and said in a dramatic, but hushed voice, 'You are lookin' at the new Bond girl!'

'No!' exclaimed Poppy. She gasped and stared at Neave, astonished.

'Yes!' cried Neave, and she burst into merry giggles. 'But you have to keep it a secret. No one knows officially yet. It's going to be announced at a big press conference next week. They're going to dress me in the most stunning green frock I've ever seen!'

'Oh, Neave, that's amazing. Congratulations, I'm so pleased for you.' Poppy leaned forward and gave her a hug. They'd only known each other a short time but somehow they'd really bonded. *Perhaps it's because our hearts aren't really in this world of money and material success,* Poppy thought. *We'll never forget what's truly important.*

'I wanted to tell you,' Neave said, 'because I knew you'd be happy for me. Your first thought wasn't "hmm, what can I get out of it?". That's what I see in the faces of most of the people I know, even my oldest friends. Even some of my family. You wouldn't believe who comes crawling out of the woodwork to sell stories about you when you get a bit famous. It's so depressing. My agent is over the moon, of course. She thinks that this is just the beginning. She's picturing me collecting an Oscar!' Neave laughed. 'I told her, "Caroline, there isn't an Oscar for wearing the most revealing swimsuit." She said that she didn't mean for this film, but maybe further down the line one day.'

'You're going to be a movie star!' Poppy grinned.

'So they say. And listen, I owe it to you.'

'You do? How?' said Poppy, bemused.

'Your handy little needle and thread. After you came to my rescue in the toilets, I went out, met the big-guy producer, and he liked me and started the whole ball rolling.' Neave sipped at her champagne.

'I think you're giving me a bit too much credit. I'm sure it would have happened anyway –'

'Maybe, maybe not, but I know I couldn't have gone out there that night without your help, and that's the night that counted.' Neave fixed her with a deep, emerald-green gaze. 'So I want to do something for you. I want to be the face of your perfume.'

Poppy stared at her, stunned, as the reality of what

574

Neave had just said sank in. 'What?' she whispered, hardly able to believe it.

'I want to do your campaign. Not for top-dollar either. For whatever you've budgeted. I mean it, Poppy, I owe you, darlin'. I love the fragrance, I think it could be a hit, and how would that hurt me? So I want to do it.'

'But what about your agent?'

'When I can peel Caro off the ceiling I'll tell her that I'm doin' the campaign and if she doesn't like it' – Neave snapped her fingers – 'she can lump it! But she's so excited about the Bond movie, I don't think she'll care. She might have one or two things to say once we've got a contract but we'll deal with that when we have to.'

'This is so exciting!' Poppy cried joyfully, throwing her arms round her friend and hugging her, much to the envy of the rockers in the corner. 'Thank you so much, Neave, it's just the nicest, nicest thing you could possibly have done. I'm so grateful. It means so much to us all.'

'You know why else I decided to do it? 'Cos you didn't press me. You accepted my decision when I said I couldn't do it, and you took me at my word. You respected me. I liked that.' Neave grinned. 'So you see, it really does pay to be a good person. That's why I did something else for you.' She looked suddenly solemn.

'What's that?'

'Your story bothered me. It doesn't sound right. And I can see how much it's upset you. You've lost your sparkle, darlin', anyone can see that. So I phoned somebody I know – someone who helped me out when I was being hassled by a strange man last year. I gave him the details you told me about your boyfriend.' Neave took a paper file out of her bag. 'He's done a bit of investigation and this is what he's turned up. I haven't looked at it, so it's up to you what you do with it. Good luck, sweetheart. I hope it tells you what you want to know.'

49

Jemima's car crunched along the driveway towards the grand Edwardian mansion at the bottom. Then, halfway down, she made a left turn, pulled round the corner of a hedge and came to a stop in front of a modest red-brick, two-storey cottage.

She clambered out of the car with the large bouquet of flowers she'd picked up on the way, and looked appraisingly at the cosy little house. The front door opened and a middle-aged woman in an apron came out, wiping her hands on a tea towel.

Jemima broke into a broad smile and waved. 'Hi, Alice. I made it.' She walked towards the cottage. 'It was a quick journey too, not bad at all.' She handed the flowers over with a kiss on the other woman's cheek. 'These are for you. A house-warming pressie.'

'Oh, you shouldn't have, miss. It's present enough just having you visit us. Come along in and I'll make you some tea. I've just baked one of my lemon sponges.'

'You are wicked, Alice. You know how much I love those sponges but they're so full of butter and sugar, I really shouldn't.'

'Once in a while won't hurt,' Alice said mildly, just as she always had when they were children, before spoiling them rotten.

She led Jemima inside and showed her round the cottage, pointing out with pleasure the good-sized rooms and the clean, modern decor.

'It's a lovely place, you must be so pleased,' Jemima said as they went back to the kitchen for their tea and cake. 'Are the family nice?'

'They seem very decent people,' Alice replied. 'They've got four children but none of them babies any more, so there's lots of coming and going. And they have a couple of other places where they spend time. That's where they all are at the moment, at their villa in France. When they are here, I have the usual duties: managing the house, doing some light cooking – they get chefs in for their dinner parties – and so on. Tony does the maintenance. It's working nicely and we've got a couple more weeks to settle in before the family gets back.'

'I'm so happy for you. I hoped that you and Tony would find somewhere else you liked.'

'It's true I was worried. We'd spent most of our lives at Loxton and we were very happy there, even up to the end when everything changed so much. Your mother was on her own a great deal at the last,' Alice said sadly. 'I was glad we were there for her.'

Jemima stared down at her cup. 'I know we weren't always the best of daughters. We could have been

578

more attentive to Mother. I don't think any of us knew how close to the end she was.'

'Don't be blaming yourself,' Alice chided, patting her hand. 'Don't forget, I was there for the early days too. I know what happened and how she treated you when you were girls. She wasn't the best mother in the world by any stretch – in fact, she could be downright cruel. If her daughters didn't love her in the way she wanted, she had only herself to blame. I didn't think badly of any of you, if that's what you're worried about. You all had your own lives to lead.'

'I know. But still.' Jemima looked up. 'I wish she hadn't been alone quite so much. She didn't see anyone in those last days.'

Alice looked away and fiddled with the cake knife, then brushed some stray crumbs carefully into the palm of her hand.

'Did she, Alice?'

Alice frowned and made a non-committal noise.

'I have to ask you something very important,' Jemima said, her voice grave. 'I think you know what it is and I can see already that you're reluctant to tell me. Is that because someone has made you promise to keep your silence?'

Alice couldn't meet her gaze and her expression was troubled.

'I don't want you to break your word, not unless you think it's the right thing to do. But please, Alice, think carefully before you answer my next question.' Jemima paused and then said slowly, 'Was it Jecca who asked you to keep this secret?'

'Oh no,' Alice said quickly, and then stopped short, as though she'd already said too much.

'What I want to ask you is whether Jecca came to see my mother immediately before she died . . . Can you answer that question?'

'Yes, yes, I can,' Alice said. 'She did come. Only a few days before. She asked me not to say anything about her coming to see Madam and gave me fifty pounds.' Alice snorted. 'She thought she could buy my silence, but I didn't say I would keep the secret. I just let her assume it and then I gave the money to the church fund, so I don't consider myself under any obligation to *her*. But what she didn't know was that I heard every word she said to your poor mother.' Alice looked suddenly grieved. 'Madam got me to hide in the bathroom, she asked me to listen. She said she needed a witness, just in case. I don't know what she was expecting but I don't think it was anything like what she heard. Your mother didn't deserve what she got from that woman. Always a nasty piece of work, that girl was. And as for what she did to you when you were growing up . . .' Alice shook her head. 'Wicked, that's what it was. Nasty, spiteful and deceitful she was. Your father should have stopped it but he never did.'

'What did Jecca say to Mother?' Jemima said, urgently.

'Terrible things.' Alice shook her head.

'What were they?'

Alice looked at her sadly. 'I can't say. It was your mother who made me promise, you see. She told me

580

I couldn't tell any of you girls, that I had to take the secret to my grave.'

'You must tell me, Alice, you really must. Mother would want you to – the whole future of the company could depend on it. You know how she loved Trevellyan. Jecca wants to get her hands on it and take it away from Tara and Poppy and me. She's taking us to court. You know what Mother would ask you to do in these circumstances. She would release you from your promise.' Jemima clasped the older woman's hand. 'Please, Alice, I beg you.'

Alice looked agonised. 'It's so dreadful, Miss Jemima, I don't know if I could bring myself to say the words. Your mother didn't want you to know. She said it would break your hearts. It almost broke mine to hear it.'

'What did she say?' Jemima said, trying to keep the strain out of her voice. She was tense all over, waiting to hear what Alice had heard.

'It's filthy, miss, and I'm sorry you have to hear it from my lips. But if it's as you say, I can see that your mother would have wanted you to know.' Alice took a deep breath. Jemima leaned forward to make sure she would catch every word. 'That Jecca told your mother that she was your father's natural daughter, that he . . . forced . . . the Italian lady, Isabella, to have relations with him and that she, Jecca, was the result. She said that Mr Farnese killed himself with shame when he found out that his wife had been had by another man and was expecting his child.'

Jemima bit her lip. She'd been expecting something

like this but it was horrible to hear it out loud, especially from Alice, who was so comforting and so familiar. 'Poor Mummy,' she whispered. 'What an awful thing to discover about your husband, when he's not even there to defend himself, to tell her whether it was true or not. But I can't believe Daddy raped anyone, if that's what Jecca was trying to say.'

'Oh, he didn't,' Alice said. 'Your mother knew that. We both did. There was no rape involved.'

Jemima was bewildered. 'What do you mean?'

'That silly little girl forgot that we'd been there at the time, when her parents had arrived out of nowhere on our doorstep and persuaded your poor father to let them in. We saw exactly what happened.' She looked sorrowfully at Jemima. 'Your father fell in love with the Italian woman the moment he saw her, there was no denying that. We could all see it, plain as day. But she did nothing to discourage him – in fact, she led him on, flirting and laughing and sneaking off with him. That's what killed her husband. It was obvious to me that she'd had enough of him and all his problems, and fancied getting her hands on a rich man. She drove her husband mad, ignoring him, insulting him, being positively spiteful to him. She made it clear it was finished with him and that if your father wanted her, that was fine as far as she was concerned. When the poor man drove his car into the river, she didn't even shed a tear. Cold as ice, she was. Like her daughter.'

'Do you mean that, as far as you know, Jecca really was Daddy's daughter?' Jemima said wonderingly. It was so hard to believe, so difficult to imagine.

'She very likely was,' Alice agreed. 'Leastways, he fell in love with Isabella, she made her mind up to see what she could get out of it and the baby arrived nine months later.'

'And Mother never knew. Not for sure, anyway, not till Jecca told her.'

'She had a good idea it might be the case, right from the start. It was what made her so powerless over the girl. But she never spoke about it with Mr Trevellyan, I'm sure of that. I'm certain they never discussed it.'

'Why not?'

'They didn't have to.' Alice's face became grave again. 'You see, the following year Isabella died from complications with a pregnancy. The baby grew in the wrong place, in a tube instead of in the womb. Something ruptured and she died almost on the spot. There was no chance of saving her. Terrible, it was. But there was no question whose baby that was as Mr Farnese was long buried and by that time we all knew how crazy your father was for Isabella. He just doted on her. The only thing he wouldn't do for her was cast away your mother. Anything else though ... It was terrible to watch him let her stay on after her husband's death, humiliating your poor mother for her sake. And he went mad with grief when she died. After that, he poured out all that love on to her daughter instead, on to Jecca. She couldn't put a foot wrong as far as he was concerned, and she knew it.' Alice shook her head. 'Surest way to spoil a child in my opinion. But there we are.'

'But . . .' Jemima was baffled. 'I don't understand. If Mother already had an idea that Jecca could be Daddy's daughter, why was she so shocked when Jecca confronted her with it?'

Alice's face turned grey. 'Yes – when the girl said she was a natural Trevellyan it was no great surprise, even if it was harsh to hear, 'specially the way she said it. Your mother was composed. She said that if Jecca was Cecil's daughter, she had to be prepared to prove it in a court of law. Jecca said she'd be happy to, that she intended to get her share of everything. But . . .' Alice faltered. 'What she said next was that your father . . . she and your father . . .' Alice closed her eyes and grimaced. Then she opened them, stared straight at Jemima and said quickly, 'I'm sorry, miss, but she said she and your father were lovers for years, from the time she turned twelve years old until she ran away. And that's what killed your mother.'

50

Ferrera had been as good as his word. He took Tara to a quiet, quirky little restaurant in the Village and they ate lobster, fries and salad. To her surprise, they didn't talk about business at all. Ferrera was relaxed and open with her, charming but without any hint that he was flirting with her. He told her how New York had changed since he had grown up there.

'There was always money in New York,' he said, dipping a French fry in some ketchup. 'But there were many more people who had almost nothing. These days there seems to be money everywhere. Some of the poorest places are now the most exclusive.' He grinned. 'It makes me laugh sometimes, all these rich kids desperate to live in the kind of warehouses once reserved exclusively for pan-handlers, addicts and rats.'

'You sound like you know the rough side pretty well,' said Tara, interested despite her resolution to stay on her guard.

His face darkened. 'Yes. My background was very

tough. Very poor. My parents were immigrants from Mexico, working hard to raise five kids in a rough part of New York. Even though they worked all hours to support us, we had almost nothing. The hardest day of my life was when I was thirteen years old. I saw my father crossing the road to join us and get knocked down and killed by a car. That day changed everything. We had no compensation, no help. My mother had to raise us all on her own, and I had to become a man, just like that. The man of the family. So that's what I did.' He shrugged. 'It's amazing what you can do when you've got no choice. I went out to work from the age of fourteen, fitting in odd jobs whenever I could. My mother insisted I study hard in school, there was no debate about that, but I also wanted to help her, so that she didn't have to slave all the time.' Ferrera looked thoughtful, an almost wistful expression on his face. 'You know what I remember? Once a year, she bought herself a present. It was just a cheap, stupid thing – a bottle of drugstore perfume that couldn't have cost more than just a few dollars. But she treasured it and loved it, and used it incredibly sparingly, to make it last the whole year. I knew that when she wore it, it made her feel special. For a moment, it lifted her out of her trouble-filled day-to-day existence, and gave her a sense of there being something better beyond the hardships she endured. It made her feel like a woman, not just like a worker or a mother or a cook or a housekeeper. It was her very own luxury and it meant everything to her. I was fascinated by that. I still am.'

'It must have been hard,' Tara said, unable to hide her admiration for what Ferrera had achieved, and touched by his story. She'd always been proud of her own accomplishments but she could see that they had been made a lot easier to achieve with a first-class education and the safety net of wealth and privilege. 'I understand now why the world of luxury lured you in. Where is your mother now?'

His eyes brightened and he grinned at her. 'My mother is enjoying a *very* pampered life, in her New York duplex which I bought her last year. She can have as many bottles of perfume as she wants.'

Tara picked up her wine glass, smiling back. 'So it had a happy ending. Her story, I mean. She worked hard, she brought you up well and now she has the reward of a successful son who'll look after her.'

'Yes – that's true. But there are plenty of other moms out there, doing what mine did and not getting the happy ending because their kids stay in the same kind of life – maybe get into drugs, flunk school, can't get a job. Rich kids do that too, but their money buys them out of trouble. Poor kids sink to the bottom of the heap and are never seen again, except maybe in prison or in welfare lines.'

Tara was surprised at his sudden passion. 'I suppose that's the way of the world.'

'It doesn't have to be. We can do something about it. I try and help where I can but the challenge is enormous . . .' Ferrera trailed off, lost in thought for a moment. Then he changed the subject suddenly. 'Have I told you about Santa Anita?'

Tara shook her head. *Who is this man?* she wondered. His honesty and openness were startling and affecting. She couldn't help warming to him – perhaps it was his drive and ambition, or perhaps it was his obvious determination to help other kids who'd started out like him, even though he was reluctant to talk about it. But how did that square with the man she thought she knew?

'It's my estate on the Mexican coast. It's so beautiful there. It's where I go when I need an escape, somewhere to retreat to and gather myself together.' He told her about the golden sands and dazzling blue sea of the Pacific coast, the lush greenery and tropical blooms of pink and yellow. 'There are four villas. The main one is for my use and the others are guest villas. Most of the time they're unoccupied but occasionally I'll take a party of friends out there and we'll chill down by the ocean, having cook-outs on the beach, playing football on the sand and winding down with some cold beers and the most beautiful view you've ever seen in your life.'

Tara smiled. 'I don't know. The Bahamas have their charm – we have a cottage there.'

'Uh uh.' Ferrera shook his head. 'They have nothing on the Mexican coast. It's the most stunning place in the world. But maybe I'm biased. My family comes from that area originally. I always feel like somehow I'm coming home when I go there.'

'Home,' Tara said quietly. 'It's such an emotive word, isn't it? We place so much on it. It means more than you can ever explain.'

'Where's your home?' he asked. 'Your real home?'

Tara thought for a moment. 'I suppose it's wherever my children are. They are home for me. I've got plenty of dwelling places – too many, really, I'll be glad to get rid of some of them and all the expense and hassle. I could leave them without a backward glance tomorrow as long as I had my children with me.'

Ferrera gazed at her, searching her face. Then he said softly, 'Maybe you should come out to Santa Anita some time. Your kids would love it. You look like you could do with some time off. The sand, the sun, the sea . . . it would do you good.'

'I bet you say that to all the girls,' rejoined Tara playfully.

He looked a little sheepish. 'Well . . . I guess I do invite quite a lot of people, but you know, most of the time it doesn't really mean anything. But this is different. I mean it.'

Tara was surprised. She gazed down at her plate, feeling suddenly vulnerable.

'Hey, let's go somewhere for coffee.' Ferrera signalled for the bill. 'It's great walking round here on a summer's evening.'

They wandered through the Village, watching all the different New Yorkers, going about their business. They passed the basketball courts alive with athletic young men vying for the ball, chess games being played in the streets, lovers sitting on benches, kids dancing on the pavements, old men shuffling about in shabby jackets and battered hats. Beautiful girls strolled about in packs, their bare midriffs and long slim legs on show. Couples queued outside the movie houses for the next picture.

They stopped for coffee in a small café, sitting out on the street and watching the world go by.

'You know, you're not what I thought you would be,' Tara said as they sipped their espressos.

'What did you think I'd be?'

Tara didn't say anything, feeling suddenly embarrassed. How could she say that he was supposed to be rotten through and through? It just didn't fit with the man sitting opposite her – unless he was a very skilled actor indeed. 'Just different, I suppose,' she said at last. 'I've read things in the papers, about your divorce . . . things like that.'

'You, more than most, should know not to believe that stuff. I understand that it's reported my ex-wife gave an interview in which she claimed I'd divorced her without a cent of alimony. Well, let's just say my accountant would beg to differ.' Ferrera smiled at her. 'I've read quite a few things about your marriage as well, if we're being honest here. You've separated, is that right?'

Tara nodded. 'Yes. But I can't really talk about it. It's all very recent.' She felt awkward to have brought up the subject of his ex-wife but relieved that he denied her account of their divorce.

'I wouldn't ask you to.' Ferrera watched her intently for a moment and then said, 'Listen, I think we should meet again. When do you go back to England?'

Did she want to meet him again? Yes . . . yes, she did.

She was surprised to realise that she'd enjoyed their evening together. Besides, they hadn't even touched on the subject of Jecca, or on his business intentions. 'Well, I'm due on a flight the day after tomorrow. I've got a couple of meetings in the morning. Then I'm seeing some girlfriends and going shopping. I want to get some gifts for the kids. Then home.'

'Meet me for lunch the day after tomorrow. Come to the FFB headquarters. We're on Park Avenue – I'll email you the details. Will you do that?'

'I won't be able to stay long,' Tara said doubtfully. 'My flight's at six.'

'Don't worry, you'll make your flight. I promise.'

Poppy closed the file and shut her eyes. It was too much to absorb all at once. The scale of the betrayal shocked her. The planning involved was so cynical. It made her feel sick and used and utterly stupid.

But it also made her strong. She felt a cold, powerful fury like nothing she had felt before and that made her able to face things she hadn't thought she could face.

After a few minutes' thought, she knew what she would do, and exactly what she wanted to achieve. She found her mobile and called George's phone.

Two hours later there was a knock at the door. Poppy opened it. He was standing in the doorway, red-faced and out of breath, his bicycle helmet dangling from one hand.

'I came as fast as I could,' he panted. 'I cycled all the way from Nunhead.'

'Come in.' Poppy stood aside to let him pass.

Once inside, he turned back to look at her, his face alight with happiness. 'I'm so glad you called me! I've been so completely miserable since we parted. All I could do was sit there and hope that you'd have a change of heart and give me a second chance. You've got to believe that I love you, I really do. I know I told you some lies, but that part was true, I promise. I love you, I truly do.'

Poppy stared at him, all the hurt and anger flooding back. She had spent a long time pacing round the flat, trying to calm herself before he got there so that she could talk to him rationally. Now she wanted to scream at him again, pound on his chest and demand to know how he could love her and lie to her so appallingly. She closed her eyes and breathed deeply. When she opened them, she said as calmly as she could, 'I'm prepared to believe that you think you love me.'

'I do, oh, sweetheart, I do!' George protested, obviously desperate to convince her that now he was telling the truth. 'I've missed you so much.'

'All right. But you'd better sit down because I want to talk to you about everything else. The things you claim you can't tell me.'

George looked agonised. 'Please, Poppy, can't we just forget all that?'

'Do you really think I could possibly just conveniently *forget* that you've been conning me since the moment we met?' she spat, her anger boiling up. 'Don't you think I want some answers? Credit me with a little intelligence, please.'

He sat down and hung his head. 'All right, all right,' he said. 'I can see it's got beyond that point now.'

She held up the dossier that Neave had sent her. 'I've done a little investigation, and I've found quite a lot of interesting things about you. For instance, I know that you're an actor. Not a very successful one, by the looks of things. Gideon *Wright* doesn't seem to have made the big time exactly. What have we got here?' Poppy pulled a print-out from the file as George looked on, astonished. 'A few provincial theatre tours in minor plays. Some television appearances – *Casualty. Midsomer Murders. Hollyoaks. Lewis.* All one-off roles. Nothing you can build on.'

'I've acted at the National!' George protested.

'Yes, but only in minor parts and in the chorus. You haven't exactly played Romeo, have you?' She glared at him. 'Not on the stage, anyway. So tell me, how did this ridiculous scheme come about?'

George looked sullen for a moment and then his sulkiness evaporated. He looked sad and tired. 'It's not something I've ever even thought of doing before. No one I know has ever done anything like this. I don't even know why I was picked, but my agent was approached and asked if I'd be interested in a private acting commission. Perhaps my photo in *Spotlight* was the reason – I've no idea. But the money was good – Christ knows I need it – and I didn't really see what harm it could do.'

'So what was the point of it all? I mean, I can guess, but I'd like to hear you say it,' Poppy pleaded as she sat down.

'They said it was nothing that could hurt you personally. They told me that all I had to do was let you tell me anything you wanted about your business and your plans for the new perfume, and pass it on. Simple as that.'

'How on earth did you think I wouldn't find out? What about your job at the bookshop? Didn't it occur to you that I might go in and ask for George?' she demanded.

He looked shamefaced. 'I didn't think it through. I never thought you'd come in unexpectedly. You were mostly at the office. I just had an idea that if you ever said you were coming, I would make sure I was there.'

She half laughed, though she felt like crying. It was so like George not to think it through quite well enough. She caught herself. *I mean, Gideon.* Sadness rushed through her. 'Did you honestly think that none of this could hurt me personally?' she whispered.

'Look, they told me you were a rich bitch, a spoiled, over-indulged It girl who deserved a dose of reality. They said it was just business. I didn't expect all this to happen. I didn't plan to fall in love with you. And I saw very quickly how much this all meant to you.'

'But that didn't stop you, did it?' Poppy said quietly. 'You went on, pumping me for information about our plans, and passing it on.'

'I had to tell them something!' he protested. 'If I stopped, they would have suspected something and taken it all away: the flat, the money, my relationship with you.'

'So it was the trappings you really wanted, was it? Was it fun playing the privileged rich boy?'

'It wasn't that!' George said angrily. 'But if I lost it all, I'd have had to explain myself to you and I wasn't ready to do that.' He looked at her pleadingly. 'I told them only the bare minimum, I promise. I pretended that you didn't like to talk about your work, that I had to persuade you to tell me anything. I even gave them some false leads – I just couldn't go too far in case they suspected.'

'When were you ever going to stop? Surely you knew that some day you'd have to tell me the truth.'

'Yes. I just hoped that I'd be able to sort it out somehow before then. I was hoping that *Tea Rose* would still be launched and it would be a huge success and they would just lose interest. Then, somehow, I'd be able to make you fall in love with the real me. Not George Fellowes. Gideon Wright.' He looked mortified. 'I mean, Gideon *Marlow*. That's my real name. I took on the Wright for my stage name.'

'Yes. That did make you a little harder to trace, apparently. You're a man of many identities.' Poppy got up and began to walk about the room. Then she spoke quickly, as though needing to get her thoughts out before she lost track of them. 'All right, Gideon – I suppose I should call you that now – here's the deal. I don't know what lies ahead for us. Probably nothing. But you've done a very bad thing and if you want me even to consider forgiving you, then you'll have to make it up to me. Do you understand?'

'Yes, of course. I'll do anything. I want us to have another chance.'

'I can't promise that. If you do what I ask though, I can promise that I'll try to *think* about a fresh start.'

Gideon looked apprehensive. 'What is it you want me to do?'

'I can't pretend it's easy. In fact, you probably won't be able to do it. But I want something very important returned to me. Listen and I'll explain.'

51

The news that Neave had agreed to be the face of *Tea Rose* created a welcome moment of joy and celebration for everyone at Trevellyan. Donna danced round the office, whooping with delight. If she were honest, she had begun to doubt that they would ever see the results they wanted from the hard work and money they'd put into the relaunch. Without a face to generate attention and excite the press, *Tea Rose* would be a damp squib, no matter how much they tried to whip up enthusiasm. Sex was such a vital angle. A fragrance like *Tea Rose* didn't have the inherent glamour of a scent by a house like Chanel or Gucci. It had no designer name to give it an identity. It needed a personality people could understand, an image of beauty, style and femininity they could aspire to, and Neave was that person. She was the sexiest, most womanly supermodel in years. She had enchanted the public like no other, and her appeal seemed universal.

The fact that she was going to be a Bond girl was

the icing on the cake. With movie stardust sprinkled on her, Neave was all the more exciting and glamorous.

Jemima returned to London in high spirits, thrilled at the news that Neave was on board and keen to get on with the campaign. They were perilously near their deadlines. They had to have images ready for the print advertising, and prepare film for the cinema and television campaign. Poppy, Donna and Jemima would work together to style the adverts. They had hired the most expensive fashion photographer in town to take the pictures, a canny referral from Iris, their friend at *Vogue*. Poppy's art school contacts had put her in touch with an up-and-coming young ad director who would shoot the twenty seconds of film for the television campaign Donna had hurriedly booked. Just having these people involved would be enough to get the media even more interested in the story of *Tea Rose*.

There was so much to be done, and they had to fit all of it into Neave's incredibly hectic diary. She only had three windows when she could be available, before she went off to Mauritius on another shoot, and from there to Italy before heading off to the States.

Jemima had wanted to wait until Tara returned from New York before she told her sisters the terrible revelation about Jecca and their father but it was too much to deal with alone. On the evening before Tara was due to return, she and Poppy stayed late in the Trevellyan office, long after everyone else had left, and Jemima told her sister everything Alice had said.

Poppy looked as shaken and sickened as Jemima had. 'It's frightful,' she whispered. 'Horrendous.'

'If it's true, and Daddy did sleep with Jecca from the time she was twelve, that makes her a victim. It's abuse, Poppy. Clear and simple. It means we have to completely rethink our position.' Jemima sat perched on the desk, her arms crossed. She was trying to stay as calm and rational as she could but it was hard, given what they were discussing.

'But . . .' Poppy shook her head. 'Could it be true? She's lied about so much. Why not this as well?'

'There's no one to contradict her. Daddy's not here to defend himself.' Jemima paused and then said quietly, 'Did you ever get the faintest hint that this was happening at the time? Did he ever . . . did you ever think that he might . . .'

'Be interested in me like that?' Poppy looked indignant and appalled at the same time. '*God, no.* No! Never! Did you?'

'No.'

'That's what I can't understand. If Daddy was in love with Jecca's mother and, presumably before that, with our mother, well – his tastes were obviously for adult women, not girls. Not children.'

Jemima nodded. 'But perhaps his passion for Jecca overcame that. She was very well-developed for her age – physically and emotionally. Perhaps as soon as she began to look like a woman, like her mother, he couldn't stop himself.'

Poppy shuddered. 'It's too awful. I can't believe it, I just can't. And I wouldn't put it past Jecca to lie,

599

either. She'd stoop as low as she had to, to get what she wants.' She buried her face in her hands.

'She's evil,' Jemima agreed solemnly. 'She's always been the same.'

'Yes. But you don't know what she's capable of. I didn't want to tell you. It's so humiliating, so awful . . .' Poppy's eyes instantly welled with tears.

'What is it, sweetheart?'

The story came bursting out: how Jecca had hired an out-of-work actor to befriend Poppy, persuaded the downstairs neighbour to vacate her flat for a handsome fee, and put Gideon into it, posing as George Fellowes, pleasant, floppy-haired bookseller, as far removed from the world of perfume as he could get. While Jecca may not have been able to force a love affair between the two of them, she obviously hoped that some kind of closeness would result, something that she could capitalise on.

'It was Neave who found out,' Poppy finished, her hands clasped tightly together with the strain of telling her story. 'She thought something wasn't right. She has to deal with weirdos all the time, she says, and she's learned to notice the signs.'

Jemima was furious. She strode about the office, looking for things to slam and cushions to punch. 'God, the things I could do to her! That utter, utter . . . I can't think of a word bad enough. The lowest, shittiest, vilest behaviour – it's unbelievable. This is personal, Poppy, it's so personal. She'll stop at nothing.' Jemima came to a sudden halt on another circuit of the office. 'We have to tell Tara. We have to tell her all of it as soon as we can. She has to know, so she can be on her guard.'

'We can probably reach her now. It's morning in New York,' Poppy said.

'Does she know about Neave?'

'We emailed her first thing.'

'Good. At least there's something to brighten her day. Shame we have to spoil it with this.'

'Yes.' Poppy wondered whether to tell Jemima about her own, private scheme and then decided not to. If it didn't come off, it would be just another disappointment that they didn't need.

Tara was glad to escape the midday heat for the air-conditioned cool of the FFB offices, but it didn't raise her mood.

Just hours ago she had been perfectly happy. One of the meetings the previous day had shown promise. She'd had fun catching up with her girlfriends last night. Then the wonderful news about Neave had come through and she'd danced about her hotel room with joy. After that, she had spent a blissful morning browsing through the gorgeous shops and boutiques on Fifth Avenue, looking for presents for the children and some little pieces to take home for herself and Jemima and Poppy. She had also been looking forward to lunch with Ferrera. To her surprise, she had enjoyed their dinner together immensely. He had been so easy to talk to, full of charm and dry wit, and there was no denying he was very attractive. He had almost made her forget that he was linked to her adopted sister.

She resolved to stay on her guard for their lunch, and do her best to find out what she could.

Then the call from England had changed all that. Now she had been cast into depression. Instead of feeling light and happy, as she had earlier, she felt weighted down with sorrow. Everything had become black and miserable.

She was shown into Ferrera's office, a huge room with walls of glass, each one displaying an incredible vista of Manhattan with a view that stretched north towards Harlem and south to Wall Street and the Village, with Central Park far below, a rich oasis of greenery among the hot streets and high-rises of the city.

Richard Ferrera got up from behind his desk and came over to meet her. He smiled openly, holding out his hand in greeting. She took it but returned only a faint smile. His face darkened as he realised that their previous accord was gone.

'Tara, is there a problem?'

'Yes, yes there is.' She faced him square on, her shoulders tense. 'We can't have lunch together. I'm sorry, but I don't think we have anything to say to each other.'

He looked puzzled and surprised. 'Why on earth not? What's changed? I thought we had plenty to say the other night, and we didn't even begin to discuss our mutual business interests.'

'I'm sure you were looking forward to getting on to that. God knows what you had in mind. Whatever it was, I'm sure it wasn't nice. Probably unethical. Maybe even illegal.'

Ferrera pulled back, his face grave. 'That's a very serious thing to suggest.'

'It's a serious thing to do,' retorted Tara.

'Where has all this come from?'

Tara stared at him, her eyes glittering with fury. Then she said quietly, 'Sometimes you have to judge a man from the company he keeps.'

'Oh.' Ferrera nodded slowly. 'I see. You're talking about Jecca.'

'Yes, I'm talking about bloody Jecca!' Tara threw down her handbag and put her hands on her hips. She was angry and here was someone she could direct all that anger towards. 'You were very clever at dinner – you almost made me forget that you're in cahoots with her. But I've just had a very, very rude reminder of what she's capable of, and if she is, there's no reason why you shouldn't be too. You're in a relationship with her, for Christ's sake! I'm a fool if I forget that even for a second.'

'Actually, Jecca was part of what I was wanting to talk to you about today. It seems that we'll have to deal with that a little sooner than I was expecting. Please, will you stay and let me explain? We don't have to go out for lunch if you'd rather not.'

'You can't charm me again,' Tara said rebelliously.

'That's not my intention. But I can see that you've got the wrong idea about Jecca and me. You think we're a team and that we're up to our necks in some joint scheme to cheat you out of your inheritance. You're wrong about that.'

She stared at him. That was exactly what she thought.

How could she be wrong? Everything pointed to that conclusion.

Ferrera pressed on. 'Please. What harm can it do to listen to what I've got to say?'

She thought for a moment. She wanted to turn on her heel and march right out. Just being near someone who was involved with Jecca made her feel sick. And yet . . . could she be wrong? 'All right,' she said at last. 'I'll hear you out. I'll give you twenty minutes. Then I'm leaving.' She sat down on the chair opposite his desk.

'My relationship with Jecca is a strange one. It may not be quite what you think –' Ferrera began.

'You're sleeping together, aren't you?' Tara snapped.

He held up his hand. 'Please. Just let me say what I've got to say. Yes, it's true that our relationship has been sexual on occasion. But we're not partners. We aren't together.'

'She said you were.'

'Jecca says a lot of things that aren't strictly true. And people see what they want to see. They jump to conclusions. Jecca came into my life a few years ago. She targeted me very carefully and bided her time before she made her move. By then, I have to admit, I was fascinated by her. She crossed my path in all sorts of ways, each occasion taking care to spark my interest but not to fulfil it. Eventually, she came up to me at a very exclusive event at the Met, the kind where everyone is influential. She explained to me that she was one of the Trevellyan sisters, that she had broken away from the family firm and wanted to make herself

604

successful in her own right and perhaps take control of the family business, revitalise it. She had big plans, she said, but she needed a mentor and partner. She wanted me to be that person.' Ferrera straightened his cuffs and coughed. 'I can't pretend I wasn't flattered on several levels. I also knew of Trevellyan and was well aware of its potential. It was on my own private list of targets ripe for taking over. And I had no reason to doubt her story – she had the identification, the cut-glass accent, an answer for every question I had. I saw a good opportunity and took it.'

'She has a habit of convincing people to trust her. They always regret it,' Tara said.

'I think you're right.'

Tara looked puzzled, wrong-footed by his honesty. 'So you're not a couple?'

'At first we were. I fell for her, I'll admit it. But it wasn't long before that feeling died. I told her at once that no matter what happened, we would never be together. She didn't seem to mind much. And by then, we were working together, which seemed to be much more important to her.' Ferrera smiled thinly. 'I think she had bigger ambitions and decided she'd come back and snare me at some future date.'

Tara frowned, trying to make sense of this complicated relationship. 'So she works for you?'

'She did. In fact, she still thinks she does. But I am not a fool, you know. It soon became apparent to me that Jecca was not normal – that's why I fell out of love with her as rapidly as I fell in. I've taken care to make sure that her role within my company is almost in name only. She thinks she has great influence over me but that is something she chooses to believe, and I have allowed her to continue to do so because it has suited my purpose. I saw that she had talent and charisma but I learned early on that she had no links with Trevellyan that were any real use to me, until she told me that she would inherit the company exactly one year after her mother died.'

'Then you saw your chance.'

'We both saw it. Jecca said that she would sell me the company as soon as it was legally hers. That was our understanding. She would profit and I would get what I wanted. But I began to catch Jecca out in her deceptions. She lied to me. Not just once or twice but continually. I don't think she even knew she was doing it sometimes, it was second nature for her. She has no distinction between truth and illusion. Whatever she tells herself, she believes. It makes her powerful and very credible because she honestly believes what she's saying at any one moment, even if it contradicts what she's just told you.' Ferrera sighed. 'I could not tolerate that kind of behaviour in someone I was in business with – it's simply not tenable to have a proper relationship with a fantasist. But I also sensed that Jecca was dangerous – better to have her on side than make an enemy of her. I was intrigued to see what she would do next. Once she learned she was going to inherit the company if you and your sisters failed to improve it, she was jubilant. She didn't believe any of you could achieve such a thing. But as the weeks went by, it became clear that you all intended to do your utmost to save Trevellyan. She learned of your plans for *Tea Rose*, that you had recruited Claudine Deroulier to redesign the scent. She realised each of you had the talents you needed to revive the company and create a hit perfume. That panicked her. She decided to start a second scheme, in case you were successful in turning the company round. She would wait and then sue for a share of the company and thus cover her back. She would win either way.'

Tara nodded. 'That sounds like her.'

'My default setting with Jecca is not to believe her. It's become clear that my chances of acquiring Trevellyan through her are slim. Even if she were to inherit it, I would not be in the least surprised if she then betrayed me and sold it elsewhere, thinking she could get a higher price. She's not to be trusted.' Ferrera smiled darkly. 'The moment I understood that, I took steps to begin isolating her and cutting her out.'

'Why don't you just sack her?' demanded Tara.

'That's a fair question,' he said, sitting back in his chair. 'The brief answer is that the time isn't right. She's had access to confidential FFB information for a while – though nothing recently, of course. If she wanted to damage me, she could, and she won't hesitate if I piss her off. But she is not as clever as she thinks she is. That's why I'm not afraid of her, why I keep her close where I can observe what she's up to. She hasn't been aware of the real state of affairs for some time now. Soon, I'll be able to get rid of her completely. That's always been my plan.' He shrugged.

'Whether you believe me is up to you.'

Tara stared at him open-mouthed. Games within games, deceptions within deceptions . . . if Ferrera was telling her the truth, Jecca was nowhere near as strong as she appeared. In fact, she was living on borrowed time. 'And does all this stop you sleeping with her?' she asked quietly.

Ferrera looked shamefaced. 'To keep me on ice, she tries her seduction routine from time to time. Sometimes it has worked, I admit it. I'm not proud of it but she's a beautiful woman, full of fire and passion, and I'm only human – sometimes a lonely, tired, stressed human who needs to be comforted for a while.' He stared down at his desk and then looked up again, staring her full in the face, his expression set and determined. 'But nothing has happened between us for a while now. It never will again.'

Tara was filled with fury. Why were men so stupid, letting Jecca's beauty turn their heads so that they couldn't see what she was really like? First their father – poor Daddy, viciously accused of wicked acts by that vile bitch – and now Ferrera. She spat out, 'So you were willing to sleep with her, despite thinking she's a pathological liar and a nutcase? Just trying to help douse all that fire and passion she has to struggle with, were you?'

Ferrera's eyes glittered dangerously for a moment and she caught a glimpse of a ruthless side of him that frightened her. Then he laughed. 'No one speaks to me like this! I've been honest with you. I can't do anything more. I'm sorry if the truth upsets you.'

'It's all very well to laugh!' The emotion built up

in Tara. Here they were, talking about Jecca as though she were just some interesting case study in neurosis. 'Jecca is dangerous and destructive. You don't know what she's done to my family! She's had my sister duped by a con man, she's trying to take our company away from us ... but worse than that, she's accused my father of terrible things – rape, abuse, seducing her when she was just a child. You don't know how this hurt us, how awful it is. I loved my father, I can't believe he was capable of what she says!' She drew her breath in sharply with a shudder, and realised that she was fighting tears. *I can't cry in front of this man*, she thought and then suddenly knew that it wasn't simply tears that were threatening to overwhelm her: a great tidal wave of violent emotion seemed to rear up over her and she started to shake.

'Tara ... Tara ...'

Ferrera's voice seemed to be coming from far away. She dropped her head into her hands, possessed only by confusion, grief and limitless, impotent anger. She couldn't cope with it any more, she knew that. It was too much, too much ...

52

The shoot took place at a warehouse in East London and was shrouded in complete secrecy. It was vital that no one found out Neave was the face of *Tea Rose* before the time was right to announce it.

Neave took the whole thing in her stride. She had become used to the world of modelling in the few short years it had taken her to rise to the stratosphere of fame. While the camera crew and director set up their shot on one side of the warehouse, the still set was being prepared at the other end. In the midst of the noise and chaos, Neave sat calmly as the make-up artist painted her face and the hairdresser fussed around her head, taking locks of long dark hair and pressing them round curlers. Poppy sat on a chair next to her and they chatted as she was made ready.

'Did you ever make use of that stuff I gave you on yer man?' Neave asked tentatively.

Poppy nodded and gave a rueful smile. They said no more about it.

When Neave was finally ready and looking utterly gorgeous, she moved through to the dressing room. There the extraordinary dress that Poppy had designed for her was waiting. It was strapless and made of sheerest pink veil, petal after petal of it layered until it achieved the soft density of a real rose. Neave put it on as Poppy fussed about her, pulling the dress about, pinning it and making last minute adjustments. The end effect was stunning, with Neave's hair in a dark cloud of soft curls, and her breasts rising, voluptuous and inviting, from the dress of dreamy tea-rose pink, that clever, sensuous nude that managed to avoid any hint of childishness or sickly sweetness.

Neave used all the arts she was so skilled in as she posed for the photographer on the set, a background of dark grey like stormy clouds that faded to pink. She lay on a bed of soft cushions and looked as dreamy and sensuous as a woman waiting for her lover. The photographer murmured praise and encouragement as she took pictures from every angle, sometimes calling for more light, sometimes for less. At her direction, Neave turned, moving her arms, letting her hair fall over a bare shoulder or across her face. Her eyes closed, her mouth opened as her hands twisted together delicately, like a butterfly closing its wings.

What is she thinking of? Poppy wondered. It looked as though Neave was lost in a dream of eroticism.

'Gorgeous, oh yes, beautiful,' coaxed the photographer. 'Yes, more of that, lovely, stunning, superb . . .'

I would never be able to be so unselfconscious. She's so fluid, so graceful.

It was hard to tell how the pictures would turn out: obviously Neave looked incredible, but would these photographs stand out from the millions of others used to advertise perfumes, handbags, sunglasses and other luxuries?

We've got the most exclusive supermodel in the world, Poppy told herself. *And one of the best fashion photographers in the business. It's got to succeed.*

When the stills were finished, they stopped for a light lunch and then Neave was retouched before going to the film set to record the television segment. It would be short and to the point: a shot of nude pink, then the camera pulling back to reveal that the pink was Neave's skin, as a rush of music – a deep dark chord with a throbbing drum and a high beautiful voice sailing above it in an exotic, eastern wail – rose upwards. Neave's face was revealed and she turned her extraordinary eyes to the camera, showing their strange feline quality and intense emerald green. Then, moving with extraordinarily raw sexuality, she breathed, 'The essence of everything I love . . .'

The closing shot would reveal the bottle of *Tea Rose,* elegant and desirable against its signature nude pink.

'It's going to look amazing,' Jemima said to Poppy. 'I can't believe we pulled it off. Thanks to you.'

Poppy smiled. 'We've all played our part. I'm just glad I had something to contribute.'

'Something? Only the thing that's going to save the day – our face. As soon as we reveal the campaign, Trevellyan will be everywhere, I'm sure of it.'

'I just wish Tara was here to share it,' Poppy said, a little wistfully.

'She said she's staying a little longer in New York. I'm not sure why – perhaps it's something to do with Gerald's house. She'll be back soon, anyway.' Jemima smiled. 'And then we'll unveil our plans for *Tea Rose* to the world.'

Tara opened the door of the bedroom and emerged into the bright white opulence of the Park Avenue penthouse. Sunshine poured through the glass walls, illuminating the simple modern Swedish furniture, huge abstract rugs and glass tables. The room was expansive and airy, the kitchen area a glossy white at the far end, then a large eating space that grew into the entertaining area, where the windows looked out to the same aspect as could be seen from Ferrera's office twenty floors below.

Above the kitchen space was a mezzanine floor, a kind of library and office area. As Tara stood, lost and bewildered, looking into the empty apartment, she heard footsteps and then Richard Ferrera emerged from the bottom of a spiral staircase. For the first time since she had met him, he was not wearing a suit; instead, he was dressed in a white T-shirt and jeans, a simple outfit that made him look absurdly young and very American.

'Oh hi,' he said. 'You're awake. Did you sleep OK? Would you like some coffee? I'll put some on for us.'

He walked over to the kitchen. Tara noticed that his feet were bare.

'There's something to be said for living over the office.' He grinned, looking back at her. 'Very handy for having people to stay suddenly.'

'What happened?' Tara said tentatively. 'I remember our meeting and our talk and then . . .'

'You weren't well,' Ferrera said simply, as he filled a coffee pot and set it on the stove. 'I think it's all been too much for you. It's no surprise. You've been under enormous stress lately. The last few months have been way too much for anyone to cope with on their own. You've lost your mother, inherited a company, left a job, sold at least one house and bought another, and split up with your husband, who's been arrested for fraud. That's before we get to Trevellyan, *Tea Rose* and our friend, Jecca.'

Just listening to him made Tara feel exhausted. 'So what happened?' she asked weakly.

'You sort of collapsed – but it's nothing to worry about now. My doctor came and examined you, and gave you a shot to help you sleep. You've slept for about sixteen hours. I guess you needed some rest.'

Tara tried to absorb this. She had only a faint, dreamy recollection of what he was saying but enough to know he was telling the truth. 'I suppose my plane's left then,' she said ruefully.

'Been, gone, and probably come back again by now.' Ferrera smiled. 'Don't worry, we can get you on a plane whenever you like. You can even use my plane if needs be. I took the liberty of calling your office in London and telling them that you'll be a little delayed and that you'll be in touch. I hope that was OK.'

'Yes, yes, but my children . . . they're expecting me back.'

'I'm sure your sisters will be taking care of that. And I'll make sure you get home as soon as possible, OK? In the meantime, use my phone and make any calls you like.'

'Thank you,' Tara said weakly, grateful that for once there was someone to organise everything efficiently.

'Excellent. Sit down, you still look a bit weak. I'll bring you your coffee and then fix you something to eat.'

Tara slumped onto a sofa, beginning to feel a little more like her old self. She looked about the clean, bright room, admiring some of the vintage pieces. She spotted some original Arne Jacobsen chairs and some Timo Sarpaneva glassware. The lightness of Scandinavian design had always appealed to her, and she loved the bright fruit colours of Ferrera's furniture, particularly one of the curvy, organically shaped sofas in mandarin orange.

Ferrera came over and handed her a cup of coffee. 'I remember how you like it from dinner.'

'Thanks.' She smiled gratefully and took it. 'You know, this is embarrassing. I'm really not sure why I'm here.'

'Like I said, it all got a little much. The doctor thinks you'll be fine after some rest but I'll ask him to come back and check you over if you like.' Ferrera sat down opposite her.

'No, no, really, that's not necessary.'

'You know what I think you need? A holiday. Some

time to get away from it all for a bit, unwind. Be with your kids.'

Tara laughed. 'I can't do that. Not till November at least.'

'Really, why not?'

'Because that's when *Tea Rose* is launching.'

'But that means that most of the hard work will already be done.'

'Not the publicity and the marketing, or the organising of the launch,' Tara pointed out. 'That will keep going until the day itself.'

'All right, but can't someone else do that? Why else did you hire Donna Asuquo? And I thought Jemima was handling a lot of the publicity – after all, she must have one of the best contact books in London.'

'Yes,' Tara said slowly. 'I suppose that's true.'

'Of course you'll want to be there when it goes live, but you've got a few weeks until then, haven't you? Why not take a break? Let some other people shoulder the burden for a few weeks.'

Tara narrowed her eyes suspiciously. 'But *you* would never take a holiday at such a vital time.'

Ferrera held up his hands. 'Please, Tara, I'm not trying to twist you to my own ends. I don't need a vacation because I'm not on the edge of a nervous breakdown.'

Tara sipped at her coffee and then said, 'I can't take a holiday. I haven't sorted out our distributor yet.'

'Ah yes, well, that's what I was going to discuss with you yesterday, actually. I've got a proposition for you.' Richard sat back in his chair and smiled at her. 'I'd like to suggest that Ferrera Fine Brands becomes your US licensee and distributor.'

Tara blinked with surprise. It was almost too much to take in. One moment he was telling her to take a holiday and the next he was discussing high-level business propositions.

He looked concerned. 'I'm sorry . . . I'm rushing you. I should have waited until you were more yourself. It's just that I'm so excited about the potential for both of us . . .'

Tara frowned as his words sank in. 'No, no, I can handle it. But . . . why?'

'I can see what you're thinking. You think I'm trying to buy the company sneakily. Believe me, I'm not. I realise you're not going to sell. Ideally, I want to own all the brands I possibly can, but if I can't, then it still makes good business sense to consider other opportunities. I know a lot about what you're doing with *Tea Rose* and I think it sounds fantastic. I believe you're going to have a hit on your hands and I want to be a part of it, if I can. Money is money, Tara.'

Tara hardly knew what to say. Could this really be the answer to their problems? It couldn't be that simple, could it? Then she remembered exactly why it was impossible. 'We can't work with you –' she began.

'I know what you're going to say. Jecca.' Ferrera stood up. 'You think that's a reason we can't work together. I'm going to convince you that it's a reason why we can. All you have to do is listen.'

'I don't know . . .' Tara wanted to be convinced. She wanted to believe that Richard Ferrera was the man he seemed to be: upright, honest, truthful. She'd enjoyed her evening with him and been touched by his passion and the story of his childhood. He'd looked after her over this last strange day, when everything had crumbled down on top of her. But was she being played for a fool? Was he leading her on, just as, by his own admission, he was leading Jecca on? How could she trust him?

'I can guess what you're thinking,' he said. 'I want you to come for a walk with me, OK? Will you do that? I promise you'll know what to think at the end of it.'

They walked through Central Park together. It felt like a day off. Richard was still in his T-shirt and jeans, and he loaned Tara a Calvin Klein sweatshirt and a pair of Armani linen trousers. When she'd belted in the waist and turned up the legs, they looked like sloppy boyfriend wear, a fashion she hadn't tried before but which she rather liked. Thank goodness she'd worn ballet pumps the day before, they fitted well with her new casual style.

'Hey, you look great!' Richard had exclaimed appreciatively when he saw her. 'I've seen you as the belle of the ball and as the smart businesswoman but you know what? I think I like this Tara best.'

'Thank you!' she said, doing a twirl for him.

They grinned at each other for a moment, then the moment turned infinitesimally awkward and they dropped their gaze. In the cool fresh air of the park, their harmony was restored and they talked and laughed as they walked.

618

'Tell me about your kids,' Richard said. Tara had phoned home as soon as Robina and the children were up, to make sure everyone was fine, to send them her love and tell them she would see them later.

Tara had been missing them horribly and didn't need any excuse to start chattering away about how sweet and clever Edward and Imogen were, how full of fun and how endlessly fascinating. 'Well, they're fascinating to me, I suppose!' she said at last, a little embarrassed at how she'd gone on.

'You sound like you're a really great mom,' Richard said, smiling. 'Is there anything you can't do?'

'Well . . .' Tara tried to shrug away the compliment.

'I mean it. Look at you – you're a wildly successful businesswoman. You may have come from a privileged background but you can't buy the smarts and the dedication that you've got. You've got two beautiful kids you clearly adore and who sound like they're being raised brilliantly. And now you've turned your hand to the perfume industry, and it looks like you're going to make a success of that too.'

'Don't speak too soon, for God's sake!' Tara said hastily, terrified of being jinxed. Perhaps Richard was right – perhaps she ought to focus in on the things she did right for once, instead of her failures. The thought seemed to light a tiny flame inside her, one that started to banish the darkness that had engulfed her the day before. No matter how bad things got, she still had her children. They needed her and she had to be strong for them. And she still had herself: her experience, her nous and her will to succeed.

'And you're very beautiful too,' Richard added softly. Tara felt her face flame.

'Hey, I don't mean to embarrass you!' he said quickly. 'And I don't mean it in a creepy way. I just wanted to say it, because you are and sometimes it looks like you have no idea that you are and you need someone to tell you. That's all.' He stared at the ground as they walked, then looked up with a grin. 'Do you want some ice cream?'

They bought huge Italian ice creams and ate them wandering along the park's winding, green-lined paths, chatting about anything that came to mind except for business and the woman whose shadow seemed to come between them.

Tara had just begun to wonder where they were heading, when Richard took one of the routes out of the park and led her down a few blocks to a smart apartment building. He rang the bell to one of the apartments and they were buzzed up immediately. They took the lift to the sixty-eighth floor and then walked along to the corridor to Apartment 6820. Ferrera knocked on the door and it was opened almost at once by a petite Latina-looking woman with perfect, tanned skin, long glossy dark hair and enormous brown doe eyes. She was wearing tight blue jeans and a tiny T-shirt that showed off her impossibly perky breasts.

'Hi, hi,' she said brightly. 'Come in. You must be Tara. Hi, Richard, honey' – she leaned forward to kiss Ferrera on the cheek – 'great to see you.'

'Hey, Mia.' Richard sauntered in to the apartment

after the beautiful woman. Tara followed on behind, wondering what on earth was happening.

'How are things?' Mia asked as they walked into a sumptuous sitting room with a breathtaking view of Central Park. 'Everything OK?'

'Yeah, fine,' Richard replied.

'How's your mom?' Mia asked.

'She's doing great.'

'Good. Give her my love, will you? And tell her I'm gonna see her real soon.'

'Tara.' Richard turned to her. 'Mia is my ex-wife. I wanted you to meet her, so you could maybe put some of your doubts to rest. Mia, if it's OK with you, I'm going to leave Tara here with you for a while, just to have a chat.'

'Yeah, great!' Mia said brightly. 'Can I get you some ice water, Tara?'

Tara sat down on the sofa, feeling bewildered, as Mia rushed about getting her a drink and making sure she was comfortable. This wasn't the scenario she had got from Vince Fowler at all – where was the down-trodden, cheated ex-wife, surviving on little more than a few measly dollars? This apartment and those breasts didn't come cheap, that was for sure.

'Richard tells me you guys are thinking of going into business together,' Mia said, returning from her kitchen with some water for Tara and then sitting opposite her on the sofa, one slim leg tucked up under her tiny bottom. 'But apparently you've heard some stories about his shady dealings.' Mia rolled her eyes to heaven. 'I just don't know why people want to say this stuff about him. He's the most honest guy I know and yet they're always trying to bring him down, you know? The latest rumours are all about me, apparently. Richard said you've heard some of them.'

Tara nodded. She couldn't help warming to this pretty woman who seemed so open and welcoming.

Mia laughed. 'Man, the things they say! We're supposed to have had one of the bitterest divorces in history, with plenty of dirty tricks on both sides. I don't even know the half of the rumours, but I do know that apparently Richard squashed me like a fly and left me broken and ruined for daring to cross him.' She shook her head, incredulous. 'They just don't know this guy. The worst you can say about him is that he is intensely private. That's why he won't hit back about these things, and he could if he wanted. I'm very comfortable. I've got no complaints about the way I was treated – we worked it out between the two of us as far as we could before the lawyers were brought in.' Mia held up a hand. 'Now, I'm not saying he's perfect, no way. He's dedicated to success and he's not above playing a tough game when he has to. But show me the self-made multi-millionaire businessman who isn't!'

Tara's head was in a whirl. Could she trust this woman's word? Her gut feeling told her that Mia Ferrera was genuine. After all, how on earth could Richard have set this one up? And she knew enough divorced couples to know how rare an amicable divorce really was. Could she say these kind and generous things about Gerald? She absolutely could not. 'So . . . why did you break up?'

Mia's eyes saddened for a moment. 'I guess we just weren't right for each other in the end. There were no hard feelings. But it turned out that we shouldn't have got married. I'm just glad we realised that before kids were involved, you know?' Then the woman leaned forward again, her expression serious. 'All I'm saying is, if you want a business partner, you could do a lot worse than Richard.' She stared at Tara for a few moments and then smiled, revealing expensive white veneers. 'And I guess you guys are an item too, huh?'

'No, no, no . . .' stuttered Tara, embarrassed. 'We're not.'

'Oh, OK.' Mia nodded. 'Well, honey, you're the first woman he's ever brought to meet me. My guess is, he wants you to like him. Your opinion must really matter to him.' She smiled again. 'And you should go for it. He's a great guy.'

53

Poppy opened the door of her flat. Gideon, as she was beginning to learn to call him, was standing on the step outside. He had dropped his old-English-gent dressing now that he no longer had to assume the identity of George Fellowes, and he was wearing jeans and a white linen shirt. It still made her heart turn over to see him, though.

'So?' she said frostily.

He smiled at her shyly. 'Can I come in?'

She hesitated for a moment, and then stood back to allow him into her flat. He went in and stood by the fireplace, too unsure of his welcome to sit down.

'So how did it go?' she asked.

He fished into his pocket and withdrew an envelope. 'Success,' he said proudly, and held it out to her.

She took it, holding it carefully and feeling the small, hard bump inside. 'And you managed the swap?'

Gideon nodded, grinning. 'Yep. It wasn't easy. You

can thank the two seasons I spent working as a conjurer's assistant in Blackpool.'

Poppy looked back at him, her eyes bright, smiling at him for the first time since she'd learned the truth about him. 'At least it was good for something.'

They stared at each other for a moment, then Gideon said slowly, 'Poppy, I've done what you wanted. Does this mean . . .'

She looked away at once, reddening. 'Don't say it. It's too soon. Far too soon.'

He walked over to her and took one of her hands, his eyes imploring. 'Please, please . . . I've tried to explain to you. There's nothing more I can say about that. I'm horribly ashamed of the way we met and the lies I told and so desperately sorry. But it doesn't change the fact that I love you. And I thought you loved me too. Did you?'

Poppy wanted to snatch her hand away and yet, she couldn't resist the feeling of his large warm hand holding hers. It made her yearn for him to take her in his arms and bring his mouth to her mouth. She almost quivered with the desire that suddenly shot through her, burning a hot trail through her stomach and into her groin. But how could she? After the terrible things he had done?

But he's tried to put it right, she thought, remembering the little package in her other hand. *And I do believe him, I really do. I know he loves me for myself.*

'I did love you,' she said at last. 'But I don't know if I can again.'

'Can you . . . try?' His soft brown eyes pleaded with

625

her. He rubbed his thumb gently across the top of her hand. 'Please, just give us another chance. Will you do that? I promise I'll never lie to you again.'

It was almost too hard to resist the impulse to pull him to her. She closed her eyes. *Oh God, I hope I don't regret this.* 'I can't make any promises,' she said at last in a small voice. 'If we do this, we have to start again.'

Pure joy beamed from his face. He wrapped his arms round her and lifted her off the ground, laughing. 'That's great, oh my God, that's so great! I promise I won't let you down again.'

'I've enjoyed some corporate hospitality in my time,' Tara said with a smile. 'But this really is something special.'

They were sitting in Ferrera's private jet. They had taken off half an hour earlier and were now flying through the night sky, the cabin windows revealing a velvet dark blue horizon sparkling with distant stars. The crew were preparing dinner in the galley while Richard and Tara sat in white leather chairs at a walnut table. An unobtrusive screen at the window end of the table showed the progress of the plane as it soared over the Atlantic.

'I'm glad you're here,' said Ferrera. 'It's pretty boring on my own.'

'Really?' Tara looked out at the starry sky. 'That's hard to imagine.'

He lifted his glass of champagne. 'I want to toast our new partnership.'

Tara smiled and lifted her glass to his. 'To our new partnership,' she echoed.

'I'm sure it will be very successful for both of us.'

'That is the idea.'

Ferrera grinned. 'Do you think your sisters will accept the new arrangement?'

'I'm sure they will.'

'Good.'

The dinner came, laid before them by discreet staff who vanished back to the galley as soon as they had finished. Cold Scottish salmon, brown bread, lemon juice and black pepper was followed by a *poulet des Landes* roasted with a stuffing of foie gras and served with thyme-scented roast vegetables. Pudding was the lightest, freshest lemon sorbet Tara had ever tasted.

'You know, I really liked your ex-wife,' Tara said, as they ate.

'Yeah, she's a good woman. It didn't work out for us but that doesn't mean we can't be friends.' Richard smiled at her. They'd left Mia's flat together after that short visit, but he didn't ask her what the women had discussed. Instead, as they walked back, he told her everything she needed to know about his relationship with Jecca, and why he thought that Trevellyan and FFB were perfect business partners. All the way to his apartment, she'd listened, trying to absorb what he was telling her, while not being distracted by his dark brown eyes, expressive hands and strong shoulders.

'There was something I wanted to ask you today in the park,' Tara said, fiddling with the stem of her wine glass. 'About Erin de Cristo. It's the last little niggle. My source – OK, not the most reliable source, it turns out – told me that you were planning to strip control from Erin as soon as the ink was dry on your contract, and impose your own vision for her company.'

Ferrera frowned. 'Where exactly did this rumour come from?'

'I really can't say. I'm sure you understand that.'

'OK. Whoever said it had their reasons for wanting to undermine me, but I can assure you that none of it is true. I'm not so stupid as to want to kill the goose that lays the golden eggs. Erin's artistic vision and creative ability have made her millions. Now I want them to make me millions too.' He shrugged. 'If it ain't broke . . .'

She smiled back at him. 'And I'm sure that any minute now, you'll have Erin on the line to tell me so herself.'

He laughed. 'If that's what it takes.'

When the meal was over, she leaned back, happy. The fine wine they'd been drinking had relaxed and warmed her, so that she was deliciously fuzzy at the edges. It was so peaceful up here, so far from all the troubles and difficulties down on the ground. 'Wouldn't it be lovely to just stay up for ever, sailing through the sky?' she sighed.

'I think you'd soon grow tired of it,' remarked Ferrera. 'You like to be kept busy, I can see that.'

'I'd miss my babies.' As she thought of Edward and Imogen, she was seized with longing to see them, to hold them and smell them. She imagined them asleep in their little beds at home, their fair heads on the pillows, tiny bodies curled up as they slumbered. How desperately she loved and missed them. 'Do you want to see a picture?' she asked.

'Of course.'

She pulled her purse out of her bag and reached for the snapshots she always carried with her. 'Here.' She passed them over, beaming proudly. 'I've got some video of them on my laptop but luckily for you, it's packed in the locker.'

'Oh, they're gorgeous,' Ferrera said admiringly. 'They look like you.'

'Do you think so?'

'Yes – see, your daughter has pretty blue eyes, just like yours.' He glanced up at her, smiling. 'I mean it. You have stunning eyes. You are a truly beautiful woman.'

She was suddenly self-conscious and felt herself pink slightly, just as she had in the park earlier that day.

'I've embarrassed you again,' he said, looking uncomfortable. 'I always forget that British women aren't very good at accepting compliments. But I can't help speaking my mind. I'd like to do business with you because I respect everything you've achieved. But more than that, I enjoy your company. You make me laugh and you also make me want to reach out and look after you, even though I know you are a strong, capable and independent woman. You've been through so much. Most ordinary people would have buckled under the strain long before now.' He smiled at her.

Tara felt breathless. This evening was so bizarre already – like something out of a movie . . . it was all too perfect, too luxurious. She hadn't expected it. She ought to be wearing a fabulous evening gown and jewels but instead she was in a business suit. She wished she looked beautiful and seductive. *I want to be as passionate as Jecca*, she realised. *But he's seen me at my worst – hysterical, crying, almost comatose. And then this morning when I came out of the guest bedroom in that robe – my hair everywhere, my face a mess . . .*

But why should she care? What did it matter?

Oh God, I fancy him, she realised with horror. *No. No. I can't! He's probably slept with Jemima. She hinted as much when she said they'd met in Paris. He's definitely slept with Jecca. I just can't even think about it, it's too distasteful.* She looked back at him as he sat across the table from her. Could he possibly want to seduce her? She thought back over everything that had happened between them, from her tipsy harangue to their quiet, intimate dinner and the sweet, friendly walk they'd shared today in Central Park. *He took me to meet his ex-wife. He cares what I think.* Mia had thought they were an item. Could they be?

Three days ago I hated him! I thought he planned to destroy me. Now he wants to save my business, he thinks I'm beautiful, capable, funny . . . Can everything really change so quickly?

Ferrera seemed aware of some discomfort between them. He looked concerned. 'Are you tired? Would you like to rest?'

She blinked at him. She'd been lost in thought and hadn't realised she was staring at him. 'I . . . I . . . I suppose I should try and sleep. It's going to be a busy day tomorrow.' She didn't feel in the least tired but the atmosphere was becoming distinctly strange: she had the feeling that anything might happen up here in their little capsule, locked away from the world. A surge of power rushed through her. *If I want it, I can make it happen*, she told herself. *I just have to be sure that I want it.*

'Let me show you where you can rest.' He got up and led the way down through the cabin to a door. He stepped aside, allowing her to see what lay beyond. It was a bedroom, like that of a luxurious hotel, with a large double bed swathed in pearl-grey satin, black polished tables on either side, and chrome lamps with pale grey shades. A smaller door led to a tiny shower room and lavatory.

'Is this for me?' she said, stepping inside. 'But where will you sleep?'

'I'm happy enough out in the cabin,' he replied. 'I'll do some work. Perhaps watch a movie to help me unwind. There's a stretch-out divan if I need it.'

'Oh,' she said. She glanced back at the bedroom. She knew that Ferrera meant what he said – he was perfectly willing to sleep in the cabin. He expected nothing more. She felt the pivotal strength of the moment. In another instant, she could accept his generosity and he would leave her alone. Or . . . Turning back to look him full in the eye, she said huskily, 'I don't like to deprive you of your bed.'

Ferrera showed a tiny start of surprise but he quickly mastered it. He smiled at her a little quizzically.

'You're very welcome to my bed,' he said in a low voice.

She took a step towards him so that they were

standing very close together. 'It looks lonely there, for just one person,' she breathed, her eyes full of meaning.

'Tara,' he said, and reached for her hand. His grasp was smooth and warm. 'You've been under a lot of strain. I don't want to take advantage of that.'

'No, of course not,' she said, only able to think of the heat coming from his hand and the overwhelming desire she had to kiss his full lips and run her hand along his jaw, where a dark shadow of evening stubble was just appearing. 'That's OK.'

There was a pause. 'You're not supposed to agree with me,' he said softly.

'What?'

'You're supposed to protest that you're fine, that you can't think of anything nicer than allowing me to take advantage of you.' He laughed lightly. 'That's what I was hoping, anyway.'

'Oh, oh. Oh, yes, you're right, you're completely right!' She felt flummoxed, like a gauche schoolgirl in the presence of a worldly wise *roué*. 'I mean, I do want you to take advantage of me.'

'Are you sure?'

'Um . . .' She wished she could concentrate on what they were saying but his nearness was too intoxicating. He was the first man she'd been this close to since she'd married Gerald, and the effect was overwhelming her. All she could think was how it would feel to kiss him.

'We can't stand here talking all day,' he murmured, putting his mouth close to her ear and almost making her shiver with pleasure. 'But I'm beginning to suspect that you're not able to finish a sentence.'

'I'm not,' she said. 'You'd better start without me.'

He moved his mouth slowly to her lips. With infinite patience, he kissed her, putting one hand behind her head and wrapping his fingers gently in her hair. She clutched his other arm. Her legs felt weak and his strength immediately held her as everything became focused on their mouths meeting, and the kiss that was growing in sweetness. He was an excellent kisser, and it felt utterly natural. All her fears that she wouldn't know how to kiss a man who wasn't Gerald vanished. In fact, she'd never had a kiss like this, so soft and floating at the same time as firm and confident. He was embracing her now, running his hand up her back and round her waist, relishing the feel of her body beneath the soft cool material of her silk shirt.

'Are you sure about this?' he asked breathlessly, breaking their kiss for a moment.

'I want to make love with you,' she murmured.

He kissed her again, pushing them both into the small bedroom and kicking the door shut behind them.

Should I stop this now? she wondered. *Is it wise?* It crossed her mind for an instant to say 'we'd better not' – but then she tried to imagine making this delightful feeling stop. That was impossible. She was on the ride now. She wouldn't get off until it was finished.

He returned to her mouth, pressing his tongue inside it, exploring her, while one hand began stroking her leg, pushing her skirt upwards until he reached the top of her thigh. She slipped her jacket off, letting it fall to the floor and revealing the gossamer soft silk shirt. His hand left her thigh and moved to her breasts, undoing the buttons on her shirt to display her bra and the small mounds of flesh inside. For a moment she hoped he wasn't disappointed – she was so flat-chested compared to other women – but she didn't have long to dwell on that as he ran his hand over her tits, murmuring appreciatively. She pulled away from him long enough to slip off her shirt and deftly unhook her bra, before he couldn't bear it any longer and pulled her to him. He dropped his mouth to her nipples, sucking deeply on each one until they sprang out, pink and stiff.

She breathed in hard as the tingles of pleasure rippled outwards. She surrendered to the waves of arousal that were engulfing her. When had she last felt like this? With Gerald, towards the end, she had had to use every ounce of imagination to become excited. With this man, the touch of his thumb on her collarbone was burningly arousing. She could already feel an ache growing in her groin, and the hot swell that told her she was ready to receive him.

He pushed her back on to the smooth grey satin bedcover until she was lying on her back, her chest bare, her skirt rumpled round her middle. He undressed himself swiftly, dropping his clothes to the floor until he was wearing only his boxer shorts, then he eased her skirt downwards so that she was wearing only her lace briefs.

'You're beautiful,' he breathed, looking at her, his gaze raking her body.

'Can we turn down the lights?' she asked shyly, trying not to catch his eager eyes. His face was impossibly handsome and his body was the same: a golden honey-brown, with dark hair covering his chest. She couldn't help but look at his long, thick penis that was pressing outwards from his boxer shorts, embarrassed despite her arousal and the lust coursing through her. She had not yet lost all her inhibitions.

'You should have more confidence,' he said, smiling. 'I mean it, you're gorgeous. I want to see you.'

They lay together on the bed and kissed again, taking their time, allowing their blood to come slowly back to the boil, exciting each other with the stroking and nibbling of their exploratory kisses. He returned to her breasts, kissing each one in turn, circling the nipples with his thumb and making her sigh with pleasure at the sensations he was creating. Then he trailed his fingers lightly down over her stomach to her panties, rubbing his fingertips along their edge until he suddenly slipped them inside and into the short bush of her pubic hair. She shivered uncontrollably as his fingers touched her clitoris, and then slid down to explore the wetness below.

Her muscles tensed and she kissed him harder, rubbing her hands over his chest, touching his small hard nipples and grasping the firmness of his biceps. He left her for a moment to take her hand and guide it to his cock, which was now fully engorged, pressed flat against his stomach. She wrapped her fingers round it, moving the soft skin gently up and down, then pulling her hand over the velvety head. He moaned softly. For long, appreciative minutes, they played with each other until Tara thought she could not stand it much longer. The sexual passion he was igniting in her flared up, taking control of her. She rolled over and moved downwards to kiss his cock and take its head in her mouth, sliding her tongue over the top of it and tickling the tiny slit. Then she straddled his legs, pressing her chest down on the stiff rod of his penis, moving up and down on top of it. He moaned and his breaths sharpened until he could obviously take no more and pulled her upwards until her own hot sex met his and she instinctively felt him urge her to move her hips, rubbing against him with short, fast strokes.

He watched her, his tongue flicking out to lick his lips, breathing hard.

'Do you have a condom?' she asked breathlessly.

He nodded quickly, rolled to one side and collected a small packet from the bedside table. She moved off him to allow him to slide it quickly on, then returned. She put a leg on either side of him and raised herself up. Then she grasped his penis, pulling it away from his stomach until it pointed upwards, and lowered herself down on to it, moving as slowly as she could, savouring every sensation as the tip pushed against her and then found its way into her depths. She felt herself stretch around his thick girth, and the exquisite sense of being filled up as she sank down until their pelvises were pressed together. Then she began to thrust up and down, slowly at first, and then faster and faster. His hips moved more powerfully as they found their rhythm and his face contorted with the pleasure she was giving him. The more they fucked, the more she could take and she urged him on, to push into her harder and harder. She sensed his climax approaching and began to grind down, so that his pubic bone pressed against her clitoris, sending her towards the orgasm she could feel building inside. As she rode him, he slipped his hand to her mound, finding her clit with his thumb and rubbing it with sure, swift strokes that matched his own thrusts into her. They saw the peak approaching in each other's eyes and that sent them both whirling towards their climaxes, both crying out with the extraordinary ferocity of pleasure that possessed them.

She fell forward on to his chest and he wrapped his arms around her until they had both recovered sufficiently to speak.

'Oh my God,' she said breathlessly. 'That was amazing.' She looked at him, her eyes astonished. '*You* were amazing.'

'It might not all be to my credit,' he said modestly. 'They say the high altitude increases the intensity of physical sensation.'

'Really?' Tara kissed his chest. 'Well, there's only one thing for it, then. As soon as we land, we'll just have to do it all over again.'

54

The phones in the Trevellyan offices were ringing off the hook. The news had broken that Neave was the face of *Tea Rose*. At her Bond girl press conference, she had obligingly announced it, guaranteeing maximum exposure.

'This year is so excitin' for me,' she told the roomful of eager journalists. 'I'm gonna be a Bond girl, *and* the face of the sexy new scent from Trevellyan, *Tea Rose*. My agent once said that she wished she could take whatever it is I have and put it in a bottle. Now someone has. It's the most wonderful fragrance: fresh, romantic and incredibly feminine.'

The press duly wrote it all down and printed it. The newspapers and magazines started calling the next day, with beauty editors begging for samples and promising wonderful puff pieces if they could get an exclusive with Neave or the Trevellyan sisters, or even better, with all of them.

Jemima released some pictures of the photo shoot

as teasers, to get anticipation building for the launch of *Tea Rose*. They were published everywhere. It seemed that the public really couldn't get enough of Neave – any shot of her was gold dust. Little phials of *Tea Rose* in nude-pink boxes, accompanied by a stylish booklet of portraits of Neave, the Trevellyan sisters and the whole extraordinary, glamorous story of a perfume loved for generations, forgotten, and then born anew for modern women. The press lapped it up.

The brand new *Tea Rose* mini-site was being designed, while the tired old Trevellyan website, not much more than information for trade customers, was being completely overhauled in the beautiful new company colours and fonts. A virtual tour of the reno-vated shop and treatment rooms was designed to showcase the fresh, modern look and entice the high-end customers in to try for themselves everything on offer. Gift packages and hampers were available to order online, stuffed with Trevellyan goodies, for friends, family or corporate clients.

The shop itself was almost ready to open, its new staff trained in using the gorgeous French skin prod-ucts scented with Trevellyan fragrances.

'I'll never have to go anywhere else,' Jemima declared. 'How frightfully convenient – my beautician right below the office.'

'And if your plans come to fruition, you'll have your personal spa at home in the country as well,' Poppy pointed out.

'Mmm, yes, won't that be nice!' Jemima smiled. 'It all depends how the finances work out. We'll see, as

Mother used to say. I want to discuss it with Tara. She's back in the office this afternoon, isn't she?'

Poppy nodded. 'I think she's going to be so impressed with what we've achieved in such a short time. The whole campaign is virtually ready.'

'Let's hope she has good news for us as well,' Jemima said. 'If she hasn't managed to pull off a distribution deal, it could still all go wrong.'

'But we've got Neave now. She's so big in the States, it's bound to work in our favour.'

'I hope so, Pops. I really do.'

They were assembled in the boardroom when Tara arrived: Jemima, Poppy and Donna, all looking serious and businesslike. It seemed like an age since the sisters had sat there, bewildered by the industry they had been unwillingly thrust into. Now they appeared thoroughly at home in the boardroom, in charge of the tasks they had been entrusted with and confident of their product's imminent success.

Tara walked in, smiling, looking smart but decidedly feminine in a dark blue Vivienne Westwood skirt and white, short-sleeved blouse with a dark blue ribbon belt tied round her waist in a bow. 'Hi, everyone. Great to see you all.'

'You too.' Jemima raised her eyebrows. 'You look perky.'

'Yes. I feel perky. For the first time in a long time, I feel bloody fantastic, if you must know. My trip to New York was very interesting and very productive.' She sat down and put her laptop case on the table.

'I've got some good news.' She looked at each of them in turn, building the anticipation. 'We have a US partner.'

Donna clapped her hands, smiling broadly. 'Yeah!' she exclaimed. 'That's fantastic news, well done, Tara! What's the deal?'

'We're going to sell a five-year licence for a very, very healthy sum of money indeed, and we're going to work in partnership with our new licensee to expand the brand all over the world, not just in the States. We'll retain complete control over the formula, marketing concepts and creative direction, though we will work together with our new partner to fine-tune our ideas for particular markets. At the end of five years, we can reassess the partnership, and relicense, if that's what we want to do.'

'Wow!' breathed Jemima. 'That's wonderful. Well done, Tara.'

'It lets you two off the hook a little. Poppy . . .' Tara turned to her. 'You don't have to go through with the sale of Loxton's contents, if you don't want to. I know the house is gone, but we can still keep what was inside.'

Poppy smiled. 'I'm glad we've solved the problem but I don't think I want to keep all that stuff. I've really said my goodbyes to most of it all ready. And what would we do with it? I think I'd prefer to let it go and then decide what's to be done with the money. It can't hurt to have a little financial security, can it?'

'No. You're right. It's good to feel free of it all, isn't it? And Jemima, it looks like you can keep Eaton

Square after all. I'm planning to look afresh at our financial structure and salary arrangements in the new year. Then you should be in a position to maintain it.'

Jemima smiled. 'You know what? I feel like Poppy. I've said my goodbyes. It's time to move on with my life. My future lies with Harry now, and I think I should finally give up my bachelorette pad. Besides, I've earmarked the money for other things. Harry and I will probably buy a little flat in London some time, but I want to develop a Trevellyan spa and restaurant at Herne. And Harry still needs money for the Great Hall and a dozen other things, so –'

'You're selling your flat and putting the money into Herne?' Tara said disbelievingly. 'Have I come back to the same planet I left last week? And what's all this about a Trevellyan spa – I mean, it sounds fantastic. What's it all about?'

'I'll tell you later. I've got some wonderful plans, you'll love them.'

Donna interrupted, too impatient to wait. 'But Tara, you haven't told us – who is the new partner?'

'Oh, yes, I was just coming to that.' Tara stood up gracefully and went to the boardroom door. She opened it, stood aside and announced, 'Ladies, may I introduce our new licensee and partner – Richard Ferrera.'

On cue, Richard walked into the room, looking suave in a Jermyn Street suit, red silk tie and hand-made Church's brogues, a broad smile on his face. 'Good afternoon, ladies. It is my total pleasure to be here.'

The others gaped at him, unable to say anything until the shock of seeing Richard Ferrera in the Trevellyan boardroom had been absorbed.

'What's he doing here?' demanded Jemima, finding her tongue at last.

Tara held up her hand for calm. 'I told you, he's our new partner.'

'How can he be?' asked Poppy, horrified. 'He's Jecca's partner! We all saw them together at Spencer House. That means Jecca has won after all. Tara, how could you?'

'Wait, wait, you don't understand.' Tara turned to Ferrera. 'Richard, you'd better explain.'

'Of course.' He sat down and faced the suspicious faces opposite him. 'First, I'd better tell you that Jecca Farnese and I have no further relationship, business or otherwise. In fact, in about twenty minutes, she'll be escorted from my apartment in Kensington by two large security guards. She'll be allowed to take her personal possessions but nothing more. Her access to FFB and any information she has stored on company hardware ceases immediately.'

There was a pause as they imagined how Jecca would react to this scenario, and the atmosphere in the room lightened considerably.

'Isn't that just going to enrage her further?' Poppy asked. 'And make her even more determined to take us to court and fight for her share of the company?'

Ferrera nodded. 'As I understand it, Jecca has tried to cover every eventuality with her case. She claims that, as well as being an adopted Trevellyan, she is also your father's natural daughter. Tara has told me that she's even made allegations of a sexual relationship, as though that will reinforce her claim to a kind of compensation in the form of a share of the company. It's distasteful to talk about, of course, but we have to face the reality of it. Jecca is certainly not afraid to stand up in court and lie. But I think she's made a classic mistake. She's put too many ingredients into her wicked spell.'

'In England, we might say she's overegged the pudding,' added Jemima.

Ferrera smiled. 'A good expression. Of course, the best-laid plans can go awry, we all know that. And the first rule of deception must be that you never commit your plans to paper.' Ferrera pulled a piece of paper out of his pocket. 'So I guess Jecca is about to feel very, very sorry that she wrote me this letter.' He unfolded the paper and smoothed it. 'Allow me to read you the relevant part.' He scanned the bold, dark handwriting and then began. '"The silly old man always did whatever I asked, he was my slave. Everyone knew it. He felt so guilty over what he'd done to my parents that nothing was enough to make it up to me, he did anything I wanted. I can use this to my advantage when it comes to the crunch. There's no one to contradict whatever I choose to say happened between us."'

They waited for more and when there was none, Jemima said in a disappointed voice, 'So she doesn't actually say that she's going to lie about a sexual relationship.'

'No. That would be a little too neat.' Ferrera looked

over at her seriously. 'But it throws a serious doubt on her claims. And what victim ever called her abuser her slave and a silly old man? It's got to undermine her case.'

'Do you think there's the slightest chance it could be true?' Poppy asked fearfully. 'If she really were abused by Daddy . . . well, I couldn't live with myself if we dismissed it as lies.'

Ferrera leaned forward and stared her straight in the eye. 'I honestly believe she made it up. She told me a great deal of her sexual history, with much relish. She told me that she lost her virginity at sixteen to a boy who was not much older. At no point did she ever mention a sexual relationship with your father. I know Jecca. She has no inhibitions. She would most certainly have told me if it were true.' He sat back and took a deep breath. 'My own theory is that she's come up with this story to divert attention from something else: the fact that she was never legally adopted as a Trevellyan.'

'She wasn't?' Jemima said, wide-eyed with surprise. The three sisters glanced at each other, astonishment on their faces. They had grown up believing that Jecca was their adopted sister.

Ferrera shook his head. 'Now, that's one thing she did tell me. She tried to make the old man do it but his wife, your mother, wouldn't sign the papers. She wanted my advice about how easy it was to forge official papers. I told her it was difficult and not the kind of thing I could help her with.'

'So that's why she's suddenly claimed she's Daddy's

natural daughter,' breathed Jemima. 'Her case for a share of the company is much weaker if she was never legally adopted as a Trevellyan.' She whistled lightly. 'Good old Mother. I never thought I'd say *that*.'

'But when we talked about your visit to Alice, you said that she thinks it very likely Jecca *is* Daddy's daughter,' Tara said gravely.

'That's what Jecca must be banking on,' answered Jemima. 'She must think that she's got witnesses to back up her claim.'

'But surely a DNA test would solve it easily,' Tara commented. 'It would say definitively one way or the other, wouldn't it?'

'If she has any doubts, she could refuse to have one, I suppose, although it would weaken her case.'

Tara clenched her fist. 'That must be why she stole the locket from Mummy's dressing table. She must have done it when she visited that last time. It's got her hair inside, which we could have tested ourselves to find out whether she was related to us or not.'

'So she stole the locket to stop us doing that. But more to the point,' added Jemima, 'she can use *our* hair to fake a DNA result if she isn't Daddy's daughter. She could use our sample instead of hers.'

Tara went pale. 'Oh my God, you're right. I hadn't thought of that. Christ! I can't believe she managed to steal that locket.'

Poppy reached her hand inside her handbag and drew out an envelope. From it she removed a slim silver chain, at the end of it a smooth oval pendant with a swan engraved on the front. She placed it on the table and pushed it into the middle so that they could all see it.

'Do you mean this locket?' she asked innocently.

'Yes?' Jecca said tersely as she opened the door. She was feeling bothered, and the last thing she wanted was unexpected visitors.

Richard had got back from New York yesterday and yet he still hadn't been home to the apartment. His assistant had said he'd decided to stay at a hotel in town for business reasons but wouldn't say which hotel it was. Jecca was beginning to sense that things were slipping out of her control. She'd been so obsessed with her Trevellyan battle that she hadn't paid much attention to Richard lately but now she thought about it, he hadn't spent one night in the same place as her for weeks. She hadn't cared, so long as he was still playing his part in her plans. She had been confident that any time she chose, he would come running back. How could he resist her, after all?

Now she suddenly wasn't so sure. And the more she thought about it, the more signs she saw that all was not right. Her access to the FFB intranet had been denied that morning – a glitch, she'd thought. She'd had no company emails for weeks. And Richard had not been in touch for some time. In fact, for months now she had been the one doing all the chasing, so . . .

Just as these thoughts were running round her head, there had been the knock at the door. She opened it to see two burly security guards standing there. 'Yes? What do you want?' she demanded.

'We're here to help you leave, miss,' said one. 'Could you gather any personal possessions – clothing and toiletries only, I'm afraid – and be ready to go in five minutes.'

'What the hell are you talking about?' Jecca was stunned.

'You heard him, miss,' said the other one in a deep growl rich with testosterone. 'Five minutes and you're out of here.'

Jecca folded her arms and smiled sarcastically. 'I don't think so.'

The guards looked at each other, clearly relishing her refusal. That was the way they liked it.

Five minutes later, Jecca was screaming and swearing, her cries echoing down the stairwell as the two guards herded her out of the building as gently as they could, considering her efforts to pummel them both.

'You shits, you fucking meatheaded fuckheads! You can't do this to me! Don't you know who I am? I'm calling Richard right now and he's going to have you fired! But before he fires you, he's going to have you fucking skinned alive, you idiots! Give me back my phone and I'll call him.'

'Sorry, miss,' said the bigger muscle mountain in his deep voice. 'The phone is company property.'

'Arrgh,' screamed Jecca with frustration. 'Just give me back my phone and my computer, please! Come on, guys! At least let me back in to get my clothes!'

'You had five minutes, miss. You chose not to collect your things as we advised you,' replied the first one, pushing her into the lobby. Jecca had used her time to try and call Richard or his assistant but with no success. She simply could not believe this was happening.

She changed tack suddenly, and stopped her ranting. Instead she cocked her head seductively and purred, 'I'll make it worth your while . . .'

The guards exchanged amused looks. 'Nice offer, miss, but it's more than our jobs are worth. I'm sure you understand.'

Jecca's face transformed again, back to looking like a furious little demon with eyes spitting rage. 'Fuck you, then, motherfuckers!' She stormed out ahead of them, down the stairs and into the lobby.

That bastard Ferrera has totally fucked me over! she thought, fury coursing through her. *What a shit. I can't believe it. Those bitches must have got to him in the end. I wonder which one it was. Jemima, I expect, arrogant whore. I don't care. I still have my secret weapon.* She smiled to herself and put her hand to the locket at her throat. She lifted up the smooth case and looked at it. She frowned. It was the same size, shape and colour as her locket but it seemed different. Her locket had the delicate engraving of a swan on its surface. This had none. Panic rushed through her as she snapped it open. She gasped. The twist of hair, with its four different coloured strands plaited together, was nowhere to be seen. There was only a small slip of folded paper. She picked it up with shaking fingers and opened it. Two words were written in bold black letters on the tiny scrap: HA HA.

The residents of Flat 4, a retired banker and his wife who devoted herself to charity work, were coming back in after a quiet afternoon drink at the Dog and Duck across the square, and were astonished to see, in their usually tranquil lobby, a striking young woman with olive skin, dark eyes and long black hair throw herself to the floor, kicking, screaming and shouting incoherently, for all the world like a spoiled five-year-old denied her favourite toy.

'Oh dear, she doesn't look too chipper,' remarked the banker to his wife.

'No, she doesn't. I wonder what's wrong?' answered his wife, worriedly observing the young woman's tantrum. 'Do we think we ought to ask her?'

'I wouldn't, dear,' muttered her husband. 'She looks like she might bite.'

They walked calmly on together.

55

The shop was thronging with beautiful people. Jemima had raided her address book and brought along the cream of high society. Stunning young girls clutched champagne flutes and posed nonchalantly in their designer dresses as they talked to shabby chic young fops and slightly paunchy businessmen. Actors, writers, musicians, hedge fund managers, designers, chief executives, glamorous housewives – they were all there, celebrating the launch of *Tea Rose*. On the pavement outside, paparazzi photographers snapped away as famous guests drifted in and out.

Even Harry was there, smartly turned out in a jacket and tie, looking on proudly as his beautiful wife, stunning in a Marchesa beaded chiffon gown, welcomed everyone into the party. The shop looked fabulous, with giant glass vases holding great bunches of cool white hydrangea. The Trevellyan products, in their smart new livery, looked hugely tempting on their glass shelves, and people were happily sniffing at the tester bottles and trying on all the different fragrances. On the main table in the middle of the room was the display of *Tea Rose*, an angular pyramid of nude-pink boxes, surrounded by chunky *Tea Rose* candles and topped with an over-sized bottle of the brand new scent. It looked gorgeous and utterly desirable.

On a television screen at the back, the film advertisement played on a loop, in between documentary footage of its creation. Every few minutes the camera would focus on Neave's lovely face as she held a bottle of *Tea Rose* and sighed, 'The essence of everything I love . . .'

There were so many people at the party that it had spilled upstairs, where the offices and boardroom had been prepared, with another bar, tables loaded with sushi and more *Tea Rose* displays, and the door to the roof terrace had been opened for smokers.

Harry went to find his wife. He wrapped his arms round her. 'This is a triumph,' he murmured into her ear.

She turned round, beaming, and kissed him. 'We couldn't have wished for better. I'm glad we did it here and not somewhere anonymous. It feels like we've brought everyone home.'

'I'm so proud of you.'

'I'm so proud of *you*. You've been socialising more than I've ever seen you do before.'

Harry grinned. 'Have to oil the wheels for you, darling. I've been talking to a very charming Russian girl, Dashya, and her nice friends.'

'Yes, she bought my flat in Eaton Square. Her

girlfriends all want to live in the same building.' Jemima shook her head. 'And they used to call *us* the heiresses. We had nothing on these girls. They are seriously rich.'

'By the way,' Harry nodded towards the door. 'Someone wants to talk to you. A lawyer.'

'Oh?' Jemima looked around fearfully.

'One of yours,' Harry said, gesturing behind him. 'He says he wants a quick word.'

Jemima saw Ali Tendulka hovering in the doorway, scanning the room.

'OK, darling. I'll be right back.' She went over to Ali, weaving her way through the crowd. 'Hello, Ali.'

'Hi, Jemima. What a fantastic party. You must be delighted.' Ali smiled at her.

'I am. The television campaign is launching tonight and we're going to be in stores around the world tomorrow morning. Advance orders are amazing. Ever since the campaign with Neave became known, it's been a whirlwind. Macy's in New York have reordered three times.'

'I'm very happy for you. And there's some icing for your cake as well. I've just had a notice from Jecca Farnese's solicitors that their client will no longer be pursuing her claim.'

Jemima's face lit up. 'Really?' She clapped her hands. 'Oh, that's fantastic. Thanks, Ali.'

'You're welcome. Whatever I can do to help.' He grinned at her again. 'I'm really happy at the way it's all turned out. I mean that – about everything.'

'Thanks,' she said sincerely. 'Me too.'

'Are you happy?' Tara asked Poppy, as they stood for a moment at the edge of the crowd, taking a breather from their hostess duties.

'Oh yes! This is just amazing. It's turned out even better than I could have dreamed.' Poppy's eyes were shining and she was high with enthusiasm. She looked beautiful in a vintage Valentino dress, sexy and black with silver edging.

'We have you to thank for Neave,' Tara said, putting her arm round her sister. 'That's what's made all the difference.'

'She's such a nice girl. I really think we're going to be friends. She's done me a couple of big favours. Getting the low-down on Gideon was inspired.'

'Oh yes.' Tara raised her eyebrows. 'I wondered what was going on with him. Are you two back together? Did he manage to win you over with his locket trick?'

Poppy laughed. 'It was impressive, wasn't it? I wish you could have seen your faces when I pulled the locket out of the envelope. He was pretty desperate to win my trust back. He had to tail Jecca for days and then call in some big favours in order to get near enough to her to switch the lockets. Just be thankful that there are out-of-work actors slaving away in restaurants, hairdressing salons and department stores all over town. Gideon got to her when she was at her beauty spa, enjoying a facial and massage.'

'But how did he swap the things without her noticing?'

'He used to work with a magician in Blackpool. One

of his jobs was removing watches, wallets and jewellery from the audience without them noticing so that they could be used later in the tricks.' Poppy grinned. 'He's a real little pickpocket, as it turns out.'

'Well, well.' Tara laughed. 'I'd like to have seen Jecca's face when she realised she had the wrong locket.'

'She's gone very quiet, hasn't she?'

Tara nodded. She looked fantastically chic in a Ben de Lisi cocktail dress in black jersey, the straps broken by silver hoops just below the shoulder. Her dark hair was pulled back into a glossy bun and thick silver hoops dangled from her ears. 'Richard tells me she's out of his life and his company. When he heard the horrible claims she was making about Daddy, he felt he couldn't have her around for a moment longer. He'd been about to cut her loose anyway. This just hurried it along.'

'I want to hear more about *Richard*,' Poppy said meaningfully but just then, Gideon came into the shop, looking extremely smart in a Paul Smith purple velvet jacket, shirt and jeans. 'I'd better go say hi, but don't think I'm going to forget that I want to find out exactly what's happening!'

She went up to Gideon and kissed his cheek. He looked adorably boyish and very British, his hair freshly trimmed and his shoes polished. 'Hello.'

'This looks fantastic, Poppy. Have you seen the scrum out there?' Gideon gestured towards the shop front, where there was a large crowd of press and onlookers.

'Neave's coming soon. It's for her really,' Poppy said.

'It wouldn't have happened without you.' He reached down, took her hand and squeezed it. 'You look fabulous, too. Positively edible, in fact.'

'You don't look so bad yourself. But I'd better watch my jewellery, hadn't I?' She grinned at him.

He laughed and wrapped her in a hug. 'Am I really forgiven?' he murmured in her ear.

'Let's just say, you're on probation. But one more strike and you're out.' She kissed him, happy to the core to have him back.

At eight-thirty, there was a ripple of excitement in the room and a whisper of 'Neave ... Neave's here' seemed to pass from mouth to mouth. Outside the shop, a barrage of camera bulbs exploded like fireworks as Neave turned to face the press with professional ease, posing this way and that for the cameras. She was wearing a shiny silk Versace dress in the same colour as her eyes, its thigh-skimming sexiness offset by the demure high neck with a little pointed collar and the wide black belt cinching her in at the waist.

After the photo call, she came in accompanied by her agent and publicist. Tara, Jemima and Poppy were waiting for her with broad smiles, kisses and her favourite Dom Pérignon Rosé.

'Thanks so much for coming, Neave,' Tara said. 'We really appreciate it. I know it clashed with your filming schedule.'

Neave smiled. 'It was no problem. I just did my prima donna routine, y'know. Only kidding. Hey, girls, this looks great.'

They showed her round the shop while the other guests did their best to pretend that they hadn't noticed the gorgeous supermodel in their midst.

'Now it's time,' Jemima said. 'Come on.'

The four of them went to the middle of the room and stood together in front of the *Tea Rose* display. The television screen darkened and a hush descended as all eyes turned to the women in the centre.

'Thank you all so much for coming,' Tara began. 'Tonight is a very special evening for us and we're so grateful that you're here to share this pivotal moment in the history of Trevellyan and the story of *Tea Rose*. Tonight, a new scent is launched that we believe will bring this house into the twenty-first century and beyond. The name Trevellyan is reborn and revitalised. It's going to be the house of choice for scent and cosmetics for the modern woman, and the new *Tea Rose* embodies everything we hold dear: style, beauty, sophistication and femininity. And, of course, it's very sexy and very special. I want to thank the amazing, delectable Neave, who has all those things in spades, for bringing her extraordinary star power to this fragrance. Without her, our task would have been so much more difficult. She's our fairy godmother. We love her and we thank her.' Tara looked gratefully at Neave, who smiled modestly as the other two applauded her. The room joined in, whooping and cheering. When the roar subsided, Tara continued.

'But of course, there are so many others we owe so much to. I want to thank Donna Asuquo, who whipped us into shape and brought all her valuable knowledge and experience to a project that was risky, to say the least. We couldn't have done any of this without her.'

Donna nodded happily as the crowd applauded her.

'And Claudine Deroulier, our amazing nose. She is a true alchemist, conjuring precious smells from her laboratory. We can't begin to understand her gifts and abilities – we're just glad she shared them with us. *Merci*, Claudine, *pour tout.*'

With typically French grace, Claudine, chic in a Balenciaga cocktail dress, bowed as they all clapped.

'Thank you too, to Richard Ferrera. He's not here tonight as he's coordinating our US launch, but we owe him a great deal. And finally, above all else, I wanted to say thank you to my dear sisters.' Tara looked at Jemima and Poppy, smiling and taking their hands. 'At the beginning of this year, we had no idea what lay in store for us. Our lives were very distant. Now, we've been together more than we have since we were children. We've argued, laughed and cried. We've rediscovered each other, and we've been on an amazing adventure. We've also worked our asses off. I'm not sure yet what the outcome is, but I do know that it's transformed our lives for the better. Jemima, Poppy – I can't imagine this without you. I love you both so much. Thank you.'

The sisters hugged as the room exploded in wild applause and delight. Champagne corks popped and *Tea Rose* was toasted.

Jemima looked at the other two, her eyes shining. 'This is what it was supposed to be,' she said. 'We did it.'

'We did it,' echoed Poppy. 'I knew we would.'

'I knew we *could*,' said Tara. 'And I'm so happy we did.'

Epilogue

The sun blazed down on the golden sands, making the surface of the sea glitter silver and blue.

Tara lay on her towel with a book, looking up every now and then to see Edward and Imogen playing happily in the sand. Their sandcastle was taking shape, as they trotted back and forth filling buckets with sand and then tipping it on the growing mound.

Looking back up the beach, she could see Jemima and Harry in the shade of their villa. Now that Jemima was four months pregnant, she didn't like to sit in the sun, saying she was afraid of cooking the baby. Instead, she reclined on a long wicker sofa, well padded with soft cushions, while Harry attended to her every need, bringing her lime juice and iced water to drink and plates of delicious Mexican food to tempt her appetite. Not that it needed tempting – Jemima was enjoying everything that pregnancy brought, in particular being able to eat whatever she wanted, except for seafood, which Harry forbade her to touch.

It was so wonderful to see their relationship blossoming once more. It had been transformed and they both looked blissful, like newlyweds, unable to keep their hands off each other, always touching and kissing and making sure the other was happy.

Jemima had bought herself a small London crash pad with some of the proceeds of the sale of Eaton Square, but she only stayed there a few nights a week, as she was overseeing the transformation of the old stable block at Herne into a luxurious beauty treatment centre and new Trevellyan shop. It would be up and running at about the same time as the baby arrived, but it didn't look as though Jemima was going to let that stop her.

'I'll just wear the little poppet in a sling,' she said brightly, 'and it can go everywhere I go. Easy.'

Tara, who already knew what babies were like, suspected that Jemima hadn't grasped quite how much a baby would transform her life – but what did that matter? That great adventure was waiting for her, as it did every woman who became a mother. The wonderful thing was that she had Harry's love and support, and the baby had an amazing place to live and grow up in. Herne was a happier home now, especially after Harry had sacked two of his employees, people who had sold their stories to the *Chronicle*. It was a sign of his total loyalty and commitment to Jemima.

She heard voices behind her and then saw Poppy running past her down to the sea, wearing her white bikini bottoms and a T-shirt. This fierce sunshine was hard on Poppy's fair skin and she had to slather on her sun lotion practically every half-hour, but the lure of the delicious warm waters of the Pacific was hard to resist. After her, Gideon was pounding down the sand, running to catch up with her.

Tara watched them run into the ocean, laughing and splashing each other before diving into the water and swimming.

She wasn't sure about that relationship. It seemed a little unequal to her, with Gideon adoring Poppy like an eager puppy. And the whole thing had been based on a strange deception – could a partnership like that succeed? Gideon obviously believed he had redeemed his earlier sin by stealing Jecca's locket for Poppy. The full story had never been cleared up entirely to Tara's satisfaction. How involved with Jecca had Gideon been? He claimed never to have met her, and that everything was done through his agent, but Tara was suspicious. She had the distinct impression that Gideon had met Jecca, but she couldn't say why.

Did Poppy think the same? she wondered. *Perhaps she didn't mind. It had got them the result they needed after all.*

Besides, if anyone had to grapple with the reality of sharing a lover with Jecca, it was her.

A shadow fell across the towel. She looked up and saw Richard standing above her, shirtless, wearing baggy old linen shorts and deck shoes.

'Hello, my darling,' he said, and bent down to kiss her. She sat up and made room for him on the towel. He knelt next to her and put his arms round her, hugging her.

'How are the children?'

'Having a marvellous time. This is the most perfect holiday. Thank you.'

Richard smiled. 'It's my pleasure, you know that.'

'Yes.' She nuzzled into his warm neck, savouring the smell of his flesh.

'I want you to be here many more times. Maybe not with your entire family every time – but you and the children, always.' He kissed her face lightly. 'Mmm, you taste of coconut.'

'It's a new Trevellyan face product for the beach. It's doing amazingly well.'

'Ah yes, Trevellyan.' Richard gazed out to sea.

'I'm sorry, darling, I promised I wouldn't talk about business.'

'No, no . . . actually I came to talk business with you.'

'Really?' She was apprehensive. 'What is it?'

'Do you remember what the date is today?'

She thought hard. 'Time just melts away here, it's so magical. Is it the twelfth?'

'It's one calendar year since you inherited Trevellyan and took over the board.' He pulled a piece of paper out of his pocket and unfolded it. 'This just arrived on the company fax.' He handed it to her.

Tara took it swiftly and scanned it. Then she looked up at Richard, her face beaming with delight. 'Oh my God!'

'What was it you had to do? Increase sales by a factor of three?'

'Yes, yes.' She looked at the paper again, as if unable to believe what she saw.

'If I'm right, that means you've done it.'

'We haven't just done it – we've gone way beyond. Sales are up four times what they were one calendar year ago.' She sighed happily and laughed. 'I knew we'd made it, but I wasn't sure by how much. This is amazing. The company is safe. It's a success. It's better than it ever was.' She threw her arms around him and laughed. 'Bloody hell, Richard, the company is safe.'

'Is life good?' he asked, looking at her proudly, brushing a wisp of her hair away from her cheek.

'Oh, yes, so good. My divorce is due through in a few weeks. My new house is wonderful and I love the neighbourhood. The company is doing well. And . . .' her voice dropped down to a husky whisper '. . . I have you.'

They kissed slowly and sweetly. Then Tara pulled back and jumped up. 'I can't wait,' she said, 'I've got to tell the others the good news.' She brushed her hair out of her eyes and ran towards the sea, waving the paper above her head triumphantly. 'We did it! We did it!' she yelled. The children turned to watch her run past and laughed as she whooped and danced on the wet sand. Poppy and Gideon emerged dripping from the sea. Jemima and Harry wandered on to the beach to see what all the fuss was about.

Richard watched as the sisters were united in the sunshine, hugging and laughing.

The heiresses had fought for their inheritance, and won. The power of three.

He got up and went to join them.

Acknowledgements

Thanks to everyone who helped me write this book, including the wonderful team at Arrow – the brilliant Emma, Kate and Nikola in editorial; Claire and Louisa in marketing; Emma for the fantastic cover; Laura in publicity; and Rob, Oli and the rest of the sales team. Thanks so much, it's been a real blast.

Immense gratitude to my splendid agent, Lizzy Kremer at David Higham and all the people there who've been so supportive.

Thanks to Chandler Burr, the man who knows most about perfume and the business of perfume. His writing was informative and inspiring.

Grateful thanks to Lydia West for checking my French and, of course, to my friends and family, who make all of this possible.